UNFORTUNATE
In the middle of chaos

Rumor Tale
Iyo & Bohn Adventures
UNFORTUNATE
Part One

"How Misfortunes bring Fortunes? Well, only a fool would know!"

Bailey J Markis

In the middle of chaos, a galaxy introduced.
For those who dream.
I tell you; Fantasy is Reality.

Contents

Unfortunate Introduction

Inside the Meli galaxy, nestled within Arthe 603 lives a scientist of intense dedication. Teamed with his creation, a complex AI companion; Iyo the futurist embarks on a progression of private experiments of unforeseen twists and revelations that turn his path Unfortunate. Leading him to uncover extreme truths of himself and the multiverse! Experience happenings and challenges that question the very essence of reality in a tale that leads straight into another!

From Unfortunate to Fortunate

INIQUITOUS CIRCUMSTANCES

UNFORTUNATE NATTER

How is it that misfortunes turn fortunate? Well, only a fool could know. If you wandered into my thought of Ink and Smoke then as said I will begin with chaos as if you had not noticed the situation's consequence upon me, which could be an example of what I would name a beautiful expulsion of thought! The ongoing, specifically structured sentencing made as gift to you. I hath alluded my utter mind, ongoing as I will be going on as I am forever ongoing but let me do so in utter depth! As I am sincerely entrenched in illusory. Therefore, call me the fooled chaperon of sense to be funneling you amid the multiverses core. I expose that planted seeds sprout into little gods. I will be taking you through the creation channels that are the roots of abundance comprising of the dwelling creations, the energies of light, wicked, grey, and that of what is the balance of these spoken subjects. Be it that of what I speak to be the all of all I call my home. This meshing of rumors, the sections that make up of tales of their own that you will hear from in time. I will begin this tale with the adversaries of light that have their own views of truth that will lead to their subject. Be this the main figure that this tale is about, a human on plain Arthe 603, in the Galaxy of Meli, oh so far from my home as it is a mirror realm to where your kind is from. This place is nearly exact to your home. Be it different powers that rule it and happenings that occur. I would say that from notice, the Milky Way is slightly behind in ageing as the system of Meli is more advanced, even if it is fact that these plains operate on the very same wave of time. My desire is that this collection of tales find the subjects of Earth that reside in the Milky-Way system. As the system of Meli is beginning to become more so mangled in the verse of

Felagnolum as I fear that earth is more entrenched than I thought it to be. I tell you that for nearly three thousand years, the Milky-way and Felagnolum have been entangled. This is more of a knowing and visiting from the higher positioned beings of the realms of Uni. As I fear that soon the lower inhabitants, the figures far below the gods will soon become hearty in the knowledge of the realm, just as they have with the Meli system. As I don't hold firm to this fear for, I know that a balance exists. I am searching for a bloodline that will listen, I feel I must warn them of multiversal interferences as I fear that soon the battles will grow from plain-to-plain happenings into verse-to-verse happenings. As if this tale finds any other subjects of Universe One, be warned that the realms are growing active as many systems have learned of the multiverse. This tale that I have put together by rumors in the beginning of this notice. From the works of the lower legion of the Order of Liege, to mangle with the set apart dirt-world chosen, to be subject in a puppeteering by the new rising Order of the Black Flame, the settlement of the Black Sun Cult who demand work by the Order of Obsidian Hand as the rumors by Fairies and Seekers to end with a mighty intervention by the Trea light Order and the Galactic Synod. Many happenings that make up this tale of rising rebellion and you will learn of the pyramid of authorities.

The initial endeavors of this tale form on the plain under the name Spiritian. The second of my systems plains formed in Felagnolum, considered the Spiro plain by a decree of the creator upon creation. Spiritian is named this as it is the dwelling of spirituality, religiousness, and piety, as energetic practices are known and natural occurrences, even if the magic has remained dry for decades. The name is, as it means, "Spirit beliefs of flat lands." As one could understand once heard, however, I say when you venture to this plain, then the knowledge you will home! It is not that these are as spoken to be Flat Lands, it is that these plain inhabitants are in the belief that Spiritian is the gateway to the belief of the heavenly flat lands. This is a place where the Source of creation resides. I shall tell you of the deeper meaning of this on another moon. I warn you to be mindful of what you engage in as your experience in this place will affect your Spirobeing, be that of some download from my consciousness to yours or ongoing encounters that leave you in question of existence. Speaking of the plain that this Rumor takes place on, I first bring you to the soulless corner far northwest of district Astros! On the continent of Irosent tucked in the peaks of the Astros Mountain range. Widely known in the plain of Spiritian exists an old temple formed from the obsidian mountains, carved of eight levels once filled with knowledge and treasures. It was an ancient place of scholarship, and for some, it was a place of reverence and devotion. Collections of races would gather amid the temple and the mountain range for all kinds of celebrations and activities. This ancient temple sits on the peak of the mountain of Litue. Once a sacred place where people came for enlightenment, such as dreamers in search of freedom, or where the Ian folk come to escape from the Orders and the Galactic Synod, which is the governing authorities for the societies of Felagnolum. Ongoing, a figure could have once visited Litus to escape a magical dictator, that one could have trifled with the fairies or to escape a debt of pirates. Whatever the reason it was once known as a haven of peace where all were welcome at this glorious temple, there are many havens of escape in the realms of Uni. The angelic warrior knights of Trea once protected these lands, I tell you that no figure of any of the Ian people would trifle with these warriors, as it is known that even the Spiro kinds would not entangle themselves with a battle of these Trea Knights as they are mighty warriors of the light. Litus of the obsidian mountains of Litue is sure A wonder sight of pure brilliance! As I understand it, the architecture is by the hands of Tali Giants from the plain of Thalmyke, the continent of Balmic. There is a pathway leading to the temple that is named the Staid Null stretch of will. It is known, not a rumor, that the journey to this place is a test of spirit alone. A figure must prepare for a venture through this rock-way, I would add that it would be good if one is to be of strength, for climbing the elevation through these obsidian caverns is sure to test agility as it is a narrow route around nine miles in length continuing upward until a figure is to reach the guardians of the temple. As this place is now named keep of terrors, these guardians found a new place to guard as their role is no longer needed due to the deception of the Liege and the rebellion battle that consumed the lands. The great temple is not used by realm folk anymore by decree, as it is now a haven for the wicked. Before this Null pathway a subject must venture through what is known to be the Unforgettable Oaks. A forest of living and emotion acting Spiro Tree's that are sure to test one's character. I tell you that they are even more vibrant than you and are not the only lands of active Plante. Traveling through the Oaks, I would say, is a whole new adventure as a subject of venture is sure to have encounters. Since the Trea decreed the Oaks forbidden to traverse to then follow a backed ruling by the Galactic Synod Order. This took place shortly after the *Great Deception*. I told you that terrible things happen, but this is for me to recollect on a much gloomy day.

Once through the precarious wood line and this Null, one will meet a marbled pathway prominent to the temple. Along this pathway, which wraps the entirety of the structure, stand exowalls in a lovely wave of elegance. One may have a marveled feeling once in notice of the realm knowledge throughout the fortification by a mural formed of art fairies adorning the thirty-three-foot walls. At the frontal position of the main Litus gate, a figure could be awestruck by architectural formations that adorn each side of the walls that merge with the mountain. As you begin to gaze at the graceful design of the stones, one might conclude that this temple was not constructed but sculpted from this mountain. The temple is the work of an architectural genius who formed the structure into three stacks configuring into the next, leading you to the temple peak. Here is a vast area of gathering for ceremonies and celebrations, as I spoke it to be a haven. This area leads upward to a balcony overlooking the mountain range. There is a lookout on each of the temple levels easily accessed by traveling on the marbled path. Thousands of years have passed since the creation of this temple. The well-known place of peace is now known to be the utter opposite. I mean that due to circumstances, the welcoming Mount of Knowledge turned into a place of decay and misery. As a deal contracted, a decree hath echoed in eternity; the words set the action to a new authority for this mountain range, who is rumored to currently reside on the plain of Lestea, in the high North continent of Alki, in the Black Sun Temple on the Sun Bay Peninsula of the Black Sea. The subject known throughout the realms, tasked to show himself in funerals, executions and times of terror and war. Named Rahaid, he is of the Untou bloodline, the keeper of death and leader of the Cult of Black Sun. Decreed to be the ruler of these lands from there on until a new change. It is said that he cares not for the title, letting the lesser authorities rule the plain, only to intervene in the plain if it be necessity.

As in the realm that I live in, all things are in operation by contract. In the sense of these contracts, they work among multiple levels. You see, for a contract to work, a figure must be in thought of a thing, as to speak this thing as to act said thing, carried out of what was said, acted out, as I say then a deed complete. One is to be in confirmation of sorts with these manners of happening. For then, the contract is active until the work is redacted. That kind of work is a complexity I shall only explain at the time that you are to stumble on the mirror realm, the library, a council ruling, or a gateway of some kind. All these happenings I have described are monitored by the Watchers, the Shifters, the Seeker kind; Fairies and other kinds and creatures tasked to record the realms and order that access of said gateways. Alluding to this temple, I recall a statement from a member of the High Council from a decade ago on this very mount, a decree powerfully spoken.

> "The wicked are bound! I declare that no follower of the unity is to venture this mount! The temple doors will seal, the Oaks will be cursed, and those who rebel, punished by the chains of wilts! I have said what will sow on the next full moon! This is a warning, for this mountain is under new rule; now go and tell the Kingdoms what hath I spoke!"

This wording was taken into action by the words of the Angelic Messengers delivering this word of this respected council member. The message received by the realm collective before the mighty King returned to the higher plains of Theoi Ouranos, departing with a select few and his trusted messenger who is said to return, venturing to a system with a single plain named Puro. This is a distant realm and a heavenly place beyond the void of space, beyond the library of creations. To find this gateway for the venture to this realm, one must travel beyond Paradise. As there is another gateway that leads to the realm of chosen. Paradise is where those of the chosen have died and are to collect to wait for new positioning before allowed into the God realm of bliss. Understand there are many levels to the heavens, the gateway to these realms known, yet traversal to any of these realms, a being must be of positioning, as I am here to speak of these positionings. The gateways are guarded by those who are named th Celestial Wardens of Entries. Beings that are highly powered, the lower gods would not even trifle with this kind, for they are the keepers of the gates that lead to the third heavens. Deemed the Wardens of Entry, this kind embodies utter energy, these are a form of formless energy creatures gifted with more power than I can give in explanations! These figures are much different than the guardians of Litus that I spoke of being repositioned. These Wardens of Entry can take a form but mostly engage as Spiro-energy that is known as the Illusias! These beings need not the possession or embodiment for control, they do not bid on subjects, they are of their own spirit and gifted power. As are known as ones to destroy souls that defy universal decree, keeping law and order of realm traversal. This task is of no challenge, for they can alter all matters. There was a time that I recall speaking to my master Prome, about these beings. I joked at the time about a fantasy of two greedy for wealth and arrogant as prideful with their magic, found and tried to enter this doorway. I laughed in wonder for what could happen as my master shared the laugh with me, he spoke on, naming these beings as "God's Whip." If a vessel of the source is out of balance, these forces are here to ensure that these physicals keep the work of the creations. He said they would simply absorb the matter of the multeity and went on to task me to visit this gateway on the days after his passing, speaking to me that this was no fantasy and that there turned to stone are a pair of figures just as I joked, he named the, as the multeity out of universal respect, meaning the "Multiverse of Universes Unity." A way of speaking of an unnamed collection of matter, there are many ways that folk speak of an unveiled collection of beings, my master often would use this sentencing choice. These are the opposite is true for the once, but as of now, not-so-gracious heathens bound at Litus! This legion is an enemy to the realms, wishing to destroy and enslave so their kind can live free in the realms abundance. This is the place where we begin! The initial speaker, the ancient trickster king who is the rebellious leader of the realm foes, depending on who you call master, could be the leader of friends. I personally stand among whoever wishes to converse, meddled deep, tangled like a tree stick wrapped in webbing watching wander. I am so positioned with not the desire to claim a side. I only do as my master bids me. Which is these raw, unfiltered explanations of the verses and so to this ancient temple of peace turned ruin, mountains of death by decree, fulfilled by universal contracts that I begin with. Forgive my ongoing but there is much to explain. Be this the breacher tale that allows you to begin to access the Uni-V-One understandings from the natter of I, Chronikos the wandering fool of sense that is all but free, entrenched in chaos walk with me. O, treasured being. This is the tale of the Unfortunate, and how it all turns out to be Fortunate.

THE UNGRACIOUS

July 31st

Temple of Litus, M.T. Litue, District: Astros, Irosent: Spiritian

Right to the source of trepidations, King Bani of the legion sons of death. He is the son of the son of the Dark Prime of Chaos. The third generation of those who could be named as the ones who are crowned in wickedness, but this is a position like all others as it is a task that is necessary to have order. Favored by the High King to maintain the Orders of Balance. I tell you that all have a job. This son of the son of Dark Orders, well he is out of control. He hath strayed from his destiny path and is currently being punished for it in this imprisonment. Calling to this trusted follower of decades is a muscular being standing with proper carriage active in a spirit of annoyance, in a dialogue with figures in the congregation before the Litus throne. By word of this Legion King, be this a self-imposed positioning, to name himself King, he calls to a follower,

"Fiki Fuse! Where is that filthy, intelligent specimen! By now, he should have completed the construction of my receptor! It has been a moon, as he said he would be in completion by the beginning of the next cycle. As there is no shine tonight on this new moon. Where is he? Find him, I bid it now, go find the technological one. We are to be free by the end of this moon cycle, time is for now on our side, but I fear that it will not last. Find him now!"

Speaking in demands, Salbani Gno, the leader of the Liege who are legion of chaos. Bani is a body temple of rebellion as his blood flows in wickedness, and I tell you that fury reigns supreme in his heart. Salbani of divine origin, being the age of one hundred and five Unis old. Be it known that in the Felagnolum realm beings can live well over fifty decades, even longer if a subject embodies the God-Blood. He has a commanding presence with a sharply defined face that gives off an intimidating presence, his cheekbones are high, his mighty bone structure holds firm, and his jawline is strong and chiseled, enhancing his masculine magnetism. There is a look of elegance to him that rebels against his nature of infernal tendencies but still walking in angel beauty, I add that his fall from grace took his pulchritudinous wings, clipped by an agonizingly painful process of punishment. The skin of this master is dark grey, and he is a fit and striking figure. His eyes being the most delightful area of his face, revealing as a spiral of a fire red encircling a faint blue in their center as a vortex that gives the illusion of a smoldering glow. One could get lost in his gaze as it is said that he has mastered the art of hypnosis. His brow arching in a way that intensifies his eyes as if he were created to be intriguing and intimidating. Enhancing his look of confidence as revealing to the weight of knowledge that he carries. His lips neither too thick nor too thin, a balance reflecting through them that creates him to be desired just as it calls forth pride as he is known to bear a constant smirk of self-imposed kingship. Salbani has an unmistakable aura to him that shows depth, he is intriguing as one can feel his power. His hair is blonde, styled in a long-doubled braid cascading down, contrasting well with his grey skin, and he has pointed ears that peak through this beautiful hair that hints to one that he is of a mixed lineage. This ancient primary might be corrupt, but you wouldn't think so at first glance. Salbani is a being of skills, seen to be an expert magician, having a mastery of weaponry and an understanding of the elemental powers. Salbani was once a being of the First order of the Unitrea Arku, the originators of Unitrea Knighthood. These are beings that were the first group of celestial protectors in the realms of Felagnolum, also known as the "Arkuni Ancients." Salbani has since then made his own path, fallen from kindred due to the great bewitching of the past. He holds the bloodline of Gno, as are few alive, claiming this bloodline once named the inseparable Gno. This bloodline has fallen apart as Salbani's betrayal shifted not only the kingdoms of Felagnolum but also caused him to be at a loss of his true blood brothers. He sat on a throne formed of solid gold as not a spec was indifferent. It sat on elegantly designed marble with a divine flower pattern stretching throughout the level. Parallel to the arms of the throne moved upward a set of stair casing that led to a balcony over this mount that I spoke of before, overlooking the mountain range of Litue. Sculptures of idols and kings, as well as diverse art breeds, adorned the area. Gold, ruby, various gems, and meteors decorate the sanctuary. Most temples of the realms exhibit jewels as these are, in fact, the areas where the Trezhur beings gather. Acting out with enthusiastic and fanatic-like behavior as the untamed soul only knows the action of release. To what I say, ongoing nonsense these grotesque figures are not the most striking group, and it would not be unpleasant to look at them, but I hint at the presence of such encounters. Indeed, it is for the wild souls, oh the unhinged, that lack morality. Speaking to his minions of his plans, the leader of this following will be the adversary that an unstudied Trezhur would fear. A single look at him might baffle you as this subject radiates so brilliantly evil. As the eternal Light forever burns bright and hot with an ever-so-constant delivery of life, you can feel the weight of his hatred just as so, the voice of retribution spoken sweetly from his lips as received bitter like a pomegranate. The carelessness in his action sets the stage for this wickedness, but unfortunately, one might gather that his ongoing and relentless activity faithfully hones immorality. My word of rationalization well, do not let me get ahead; it is only the most perfect way to explain him... Unpredictable. One might very well say that he is absolute in his way, and I bet my satchel of gems that he would smirk and sure begin to gloat at the sound of this statement. As he might reflect, their lack of knowledge would place him as so. If you do not recognize his presence, it is rumored that he will make you fulfill his notice. I am sure the cause of this is to change by his simple emotion at the time he is to act. His wretched way of rebellion has made a home for many like-minded subjects for the cause, He has fooled many into doing his deeds, as this subject is a master deceiver. His following float around him like bees to their queen, yet this was something different, for one could say he was indeed not a queen but a ruler of drones. They only work his bidding, for this leading figure is powerful. I know most of them to be experts in Magic Wielding and Spiro warfare. The grouping to what I speak named The Liege. An unholy formation formed of pariahs, note that this group is of the out-casting of the exiles. The originators of the realm rebellion! The first faction of disbelief, as their king initiates chaos in Felagnolum! The Ians, Unitreaians, are two race forms of the many classifications of inhabitants living in the Felagnolum Kingdom. Attempting to exist untangled in the wars of Spiro, but sure live troubled by this enduring clash of powers that mangles with their own physical wars of crystals, silks, spice, skins, and potions of various natures. I intend to speak of the Felagnolum Folk; for now, I will momentarily touch the subject as all that is to Feel, as to Know, Light consists of much.

I mean that it is a complex structure to the Kingdoms, as it all begins with the creator of creations! Who built this realm as the name that it carries! To feel as to Know Light! (Felagnolum) The name of what it means! The galaxy I am from includes eight planets that run on a universal governing system ruled by individual councils. Each planet has multiple systems of counseling. Planetary governance of population, foods and goods, wealth, and energy is also essential, as there are governances for the different races and societal groups. I shall be of greater detail in time, for undoubtedly troubling it can be to understand this social order that I am a part of. These councils on councils with-in systems on plains of plains. Felagnolum consists of Spiritian, the Spiro plain we begin on. Thalmyke, the plain of Balance, Lestea, the plain of Magic, Evinda, the plain of Challenging, Vimaurus, the plain of Powers, Raoruta, the plain of Love, Novkavis, the plain of Euphoria, and Teralis, the plain of Knowledge.

As the plains are all connected, beyond the inner galaxy's connections there is a universal connection by the Mirror Realm that you will learn in time. You see, the races of Felagnolum are a part of Universe One, a place that is home to many systems. It is documented by the Nemid that the Trea light Order and the Darku Orders of the void are subject to the workings of higher realm authorities. The Galaxies of Universe One hold a pyramid positioning as do the inhabitants. Theoi Ouranos, being the head as the Heavenly God realm of Puro, following is Floga Tou Pathous, Anavise To Pnevma, Anakalypse To Esoteriko Fos, Vres Ton Diko Sou Dromo, as then my system home Felagnolum, and these lower known realms like Meli and the Milky Way. That spoken, I tell you that in time, you shall learn of all that comes together to form it, all that supports it, all that inhabits as wars for the ruling of it! I tell you that I live in a universal system of many races, creatures, figures, and powers! In time, I will show you the realm. In time, you will own the knowledge of this illusory! My first, as I hope that it will be my last word bond, this is my promise! If you listen closely and remember my scribe workings, it is a rumor that all fear this wicked group who call themselves the Liege. That is a fallacy, for I stand fearless and know many who would draw swords at first sight of these wicked, still some will always live in fear even if they know that there is protection.

As I am ongoing, the legion leader was calling to his supporters as standing on the high mount inside the Litue.

"Here I am, yes, expert... I hold it here."

Venting the individual Fiki as he was appearing from the shadows in the direction of the throne, sounding sick with his raspy voice.

"Here it is, my Liege, the receptor... for you, oh ancient ruler of profound knowledge... oh master, you great deceiver, I-have-it here! I completed the construction just moments ago. Your brilliance I hold it here, have a look at it yourself!"

Speaking with a ghastly reverence while approaching, the being held the device before his head. This figure, Fiki, is a technological master who is ninety-four Unis old. He is a trivial shapeshifting creature with the blood name of 'Fuse,' a bloodline of inventors. These of the Fuse bloodline are manufacturing experts in the Felagnolum realm. This has been a widely known fact for a thousand years. Fiki is a fallen one of his blood, beyond this truth he is not the only magically gifted but the only shapeshifter in his family. The mother of this master builder happens to be born of Spiro's flesh. This is why Spiro's blood flows in Fiki and his siblings. Leaving them with extraordinary gifts from their mother, as their father of the Fuse bloodline was a master builder and technological expert, so they had genius minds and a generational title to carry them. Standing a fair five feet, around half the height of his chosen master. The natural form of Fiki as a shapeshifter has a distinct look unlike any other shifter, small ball horns along the skull and lizard-sliced green eyes with potbelly and scaly skin. Fiki is intelligent yet terribly mangled with wretched and nasty behaviors. Fiki Fuse defected in his origins due to negligence during birth. I doubt he minds this reality as he can quickly transform his matter into any form or figure as a shifter. Let not the eyes deceive you, for these shifters are tricky! What you see of transformation is only a belief of fallacy! You will only notice magic if you are a genuinely gifted seer. Those who are shifters never change their form; this is only illusion magic. These few legions around their master as the technological one natters about as he retrieves a second object originating from a utility vest resting on his waist.

"What you have there is the receptor for the Jexi device. Here is a locator for it… Pushing that signal button will cause the receptor to spawn a wave output as a beacon! That will communicate to this locator and display the precise location of the receptor and this device, The Jexi. You can also recall the receptor if you wish! As that would be the switch on the right side of the locator..."

This tiny creature, Fiki, chatters with arrogance, his posture taut with his supercilious attitude of extraordinary pride! It was only natural for a being like him to highlight his workings, parading his knowledge as if it were unseen, and his mind was so highly placed that he had explained everything. The fool, I wonder if he will see the truth of himself. If he ever looks in the mirror, that happens to be his work! Let imagination breed as let not my narration fool you. These are evil beings that are simply vial with all that they do. Forceful, edgy, and dangerous. Fiki is known to hold a tone of disgust. Everything he speaks about is like a wretched downcutting. Fiki expresses this way, even if his spirits are at ease and at peace. Always, in all the ways, he is bad-mannered, like a banshee! Senseless from origins, like a wild Rektor! This would be a three-ton nomadic mammal with a crown of four to nine spikes. There is a legend of an eight-ton ancestor slain by two giants who happened to be brothers. Fiki was acting just like the Rektor; one could say there was a truth to his nonsense. In the nature of odium, the Ancient Legion King mentioned Fiki.

"So then bring the device, you jester …"

Salbani spoke in smooth repugnance, bothered with his followers as if he needed elucidations. The figure between Fiki and the Master would be Byevil. This is who the kingdoms proclaimed as the Envoy of Trepidation. He is rumored to be

Salbani's personal messenger who was once going about freely to decree the work of his vial leader. Byevil would surely strike you with fear! The crown of this being was hairless, and Byevil had long cone-pointed ears that rounded backward on his skull rather than downwards. He bore reddish skin due to having his flesh altered due to a scorching, as were these odd summonses of ink covering these burns of flesh. He styled golden rings and gems, his teeth pointed; the figure at this time had no shirt, but he wore hide pants that appeared dated. He had no shoes of any kind, as his nails were long on his fingers, and his toes were long, as if he were, in fact, more of a creature than a figure. Byevil is one hundred and one Unis old. I will speak more about him later. Fiki screeched at Byevil as he handed the receptor.

"Don't drop it, Byevil... It is so... delicate... Afford a mishap I cannot. I need to not remind you of the importance of this, do I?"

Fiki's behavior was worried as if the creature were overly fond of his creation. He handed the receptor to the being as he threw his cloak around his shoulder, gasping with hate. The scoundrel named Byevil decolored his words toward the pride-filled Fiki, grasping his creation with a mocking behavior.

"Hush, always worry... about what? You are a petty and small little shifter, shifting only your mood! Why is it that you act in such a swirl? I want you to notice me and how I walk with a pace of ease. I have no fear! As it looks to me that you are the one overcome by..."

Cut off by his master, as this ancient one's anger is always on a short fuse.

"ENOUGH! Hand it to me, Byevil! You can gloat another time! I have no concerns about hearing stupendous speech. What are you to me? What do any of you do that I could not do myself! Bickering like younglings, enough!... I said enough!"

The ancient jawing formed a deafening tone that iced behaviors to their core, changing the friendlier bantering to a pure moment of lack. A sudden weight formed in the room as this leader held such a weight of mood that he manipulated the atmosphere. It was a dark energy that originated from annoyance. Bearing the weight of this power is a common attribute of the magically gifted. For this kind of release, one needs immense amounts of power. It can be challenging to control the direction of this energy. Bearing this weight effortlessly is rare or, as I said, a figure of great power. To truly feel the proper weight of these gifts, this is a force we call home! It is a field of energy that makes up our Spiro! I encourage you to discover what your gift is and then go on and explore it!

These succeeding ones were shocked with flares of unshackled fears from this outburst! Dashing tickles to their spines, reacting quickly with an odd hidden posture, fear-filled with trembles! Paired with what I could speak of as a mighty flinch from the members of Liege as their Master paced about! Unlike these chosen yet fallen masters of dominion and powers of Liege, who let their fears overtake them! It was the messenger who happened to be quick with reengagement to conversation! As a fly on a mission for taste, you notice Byevil! Who is surprised by this action, feeling slight betrayal as he thinks he is above the others. Salbani snatched the device just as he shoved Byevil away with power proceeding to walk past the rest of the following as they quivered before him. Walking up the stairs, casing beyond his Throne, on arrival, he stepped out to the balcony, stretching in the sunlight and glancing at Fiki's device.

"Yes… this is it. This will be my eyes on the dirt world."

Salbani claimed in certainty as he looked out to the sun, speaking in quite the revenge-filled, vengeful tone.

"Soon, we will no longer live trapped on this ancient rock! As for then, this is when we will reclaim our lands, and I will have my reprisal on that, Michael."

Salbani soaked in the light with a smirk of pride as one of his followers approached him. It was Voboh, a keeper who abandoned the ways of Unitrea, just as Salbani. He just hath turned eighty Unis of age, he is a tall and slender being who styled a silken robe with golden rings on his hands and golden bracelets on his wrist; he also styled this eloquently crafted golden necklace that held the magi gemstone that is called the Dynot, this is a naturally formed magical stone scattered all throughout the Felagnolum realm. The dirt realms home a few rocks of this kind of energy, but it is unknown to your races. This figure wore a black robe that was tight to his skin with a cut-off for his arm, leaving it exposed. He had a utility belt that was a home for other items, just like the shifter Fiki Fuse. Like that messenger Byevil, this figure was shoeless and, on his waste, jangled special keys for essential beasts. Nearing his leader, the being speaks.

"Master, it has been excessively long since I have felt the freedom to travel. We have been bound here for way too many moons. O, master, I out-speak, for I am at a loss! We all are at an end it seems. Able to tread only so far, I wonder why! As I do not have the knowledge, I have a question! Only a few are able! Walking free on these lands until the river, bound there, here, as until the mountain begins, thou peak! Master... ponder with me how our following cannot be free but surely bound to these lands just as we! Look at them around us in thy slumber! Do you wonder why we can venture only to the ends of the bloodwoods as the following is still bound to these temple walls? I do question the reason for this; it is... It is not by your will, my expert. Forgive me, maestro, but should they not be free?"

Voboh spoke with slight confidence, overcome by hidden fears shown by this stoic, obscure, and even slightly grievous tone. He was stuttering wording due to these sudden emotions, bidding to endure his tongue but just as a Ruler would, Salbani interjected, for he absorbed the phrasing.

"Voboh Sedam... Do not be afraid, as enough of your poetry, I am no harlot for you to swindle; I will take your gold and that silver tongue! Quicker than a blink."

Salbani belched as he stomped, causing Voboh to stumble near the ledge! Voboh grabbed the stair-casing as he shouted of quick unsettlement!

"Master!"

Panting for breath he spoke on!

"Forgive me, forgive me, I am in no way of any scheme! I only bid question... The only question, my Master!"

The few that are free in the sight of this happening below the platform, listening to the questioning beyond the throne on the mount before it! Vobohs eyes locked with his leader as he leaned behind his hood with the worry of non-sanctioned punishment. The head carried on with psychotic laughter as he quickly calmed his outrage to go on with answering Drago's question. He stood with Fiki's device in his hand, down, looking at Voboh; he darkly smiled at him as he spoke on. Apparent that his thoughts were elsewhere on the topic of something unspoken! Salbani is known to be a multi-faced tasker; he began to walk out to the ledge of the circular platform.

"I view you as a close brother... Keeper of the dragons. Do not speak to me with fear... Do you fear those wicked beasts of yours? Mind not of the following. They are weak! Stripped of the Magi gifts we have been, only that of our personally obtained power is still. How could you forget the reasoning? Fool. You must understand that these lower-minded figures in my legion have little to no sense. What deep knowledge do they have? I ask, what of the will do they work besides desire? Besides these chaotic actions and worship of me. Go on and tell me what they do but lust and war! As I formed them to think! They cannot move through this low level of thought I have educated them in.

The following is good for only direction; I say that it is until they desire more than simple desires for oneself. I would say they are a slave to another who is in the action of claiming desire. They have not the power to free themselves, as we have not the power to release them. Think, O, Drago Keeper think! You Liege, you follow me, but the Ancient have their own aims among me. As you, the Darko leader of the Magi Dragons. What journey of power have you endured to become the Serpent King? Master Voboh do use your mind. Search thyself, I tell you that inside is the truth you seek. We are in a position because we stepped into it. As when you began this journey that you live... Was it not you that only had the gift of understanding these magi beasts? As of now, what are you to these creatures? Do you follow these beasts, Voboh?" Salbani asked, but he certainly knew his answer.

"No head, I am their lead-" Voboh silenced by Salbani, who finished his sentencing. "Their Master... As I am yours! I want you to notice that not fear led these creatures to choose you as their leader... It was respect, Voboh, I say it was respect."

Salbani guided with sense as he outlooked the Kingdom of Irosent from the temple archway, speaking on.

"When the following respect the beast, they will have the power to be free. Those binds could not hold us there but still hold us here. The reasoning for this, is it that you ask? Well, it is power. It is our utter power that allows us to be free. Yet, this magic we are bound under is a multilayered scheme that I dare say I have never witnessed! This is why we are still bound on these grounds... As for the following? Be free soon enough, I declare! Do not get ahead of my plans, dragon keeper! All will reveal. Now, at once tell me! Where are the beasts currently, Voboh... What is the bloodline number of their offspring up to at the present? Hath, they caught up to the number of your children?"

Salbani turned to his Allie with curious wonder as he briefly let loose his evil condition, showing his old skin.

"Mind your speech when you speak of my boys! I will not allow it, Master."

Voboh firmly spoke as he stood momentarily to recover from his angered outburst. He took a quiet breath and continued.

"As for the Dragons, many have been born, and they are awaiting our uprising, for it has been a decade, and my dragons mind themselves. I am sure that they have claimed somewhere nearby, one is to visit from time to time. I do not think the Unity of Trea is of the knowledge of their existence. If so, is it that they are unaware of their resting place, and not one of my dragons are easy to follow, they become lost in the heights! I am uncertain as well of the whereabouts of their resting place, even if the Trea can find them, I laugh! Who would trifle with one of my dragons? Maybe an Ark, even they would have a challenge."

Voboh let out a chuckle as he continued.

"I have faith that the creatures will continue to grow and build in numbers, awaiting our return to the realms. I am as you spoke their Master."

Voboh joins Salbani along the archway.

"I do not mean to be persistent, but Master... A full decade has passed in this wrongful imprisonment... my Master... When will we break from this decree? Is this why you wish to send this Jexi Wost to another dimension? I wonder where you obtained this information, my Master. Why do we need to leave the realms?"

Voboh asked in wonder, his mind quickly drifting in thought. At this point Salbani is overcome with slight anger, as the recollection of deeds is known to do such a thing.

"That dull-witted Michael! Fool to leave our allied brothers bound at the same place he cursed us. I am to free our minds and kinds from these temple binds, and I will undo the chains that keep us to this oak land! Voboh, recall not the events of the battle that bound us here. Is it that you lack the true understanding of why we underwent that battle? Are you blind to why you are following?"

The leader leaned into a vial, soul-piercing squint as he spit at Vobohs feet, then put his hand on his chest, forcefully pushing him away. The dragon keeper quickly grabbed the stairwell before falling from the temple ledge and out speaking!

"No, Master! It is that we were not welcome in this realm! This place occulted! That is why I fight on your siding of ideals! These plains should be free to operate however pleased on this land! Unbound from these council rulings! Exposed to the cosmos!"

Voboh recovered from the edge, resting his body on the temple wall, kneeling, and shifting to sit on his bottom. Salbani huffed and puffed as he overlooked the lands. Responding to the keepers' statement.

"You are not wrong, Voboh; we were never welcome here. That is correct, yet this reasoning you allude to is nothing of my warring. It is truth that your ideals of freedom thrive under my rule, far from that law of the unity teaching. That is sense; you would never need to hide the magic you live in! Yet, this war is of my rebellion! They fear what they cannot control, so they bind us here! Known that few of us escape to still be in this remembrance! That is a sentence that is beyond all these Unity teachings, to walk in remembrance is all I desire for my following. Who is to say the self-minded fools will find this truth."

Salbani paused as you could notice his angered thoughts fighting for speech as the leader spoke on, alluding to his scheme.

"Break from this we will, for I have summoned the plain head! I made a deal with him. The fool, but I obtained the knowledge of the plain. It is a Terra world set apart from the universes. In their own little spec of the cosmos hidden by the creator for unknown reasoning. Never the matter, for I have found them! I will see just how powerful this blood is in time!"

Let it be known that each of the nineteen plains of Universe One is subject to plain native Sempiternal; local dwellers would speak of this kind as high-ruling authorities dictating what measure of power inhabitants, nature aspects, and the initiated are able to use. The parenting force of this imparted magic to these plains differs for each Sempiternal. By that understanding, as so be known, the Sempiternal bloodline is the head of a specifically selected magical impartation. The Sempiternal here is by the name of Rhamtes. As he is somewhere on this plain, written in the scrolls of each of their destinies, a Sempiternal is bound to the plain as the plain is bound to the Sempiternal figures. For eternity, If the Sempiternal is whole, then so be plain as for the residents of each plain affected by the choices of lifestyle by the Sempiternal that is of charge of the living planet. Meaningful connections, born with the task, are some of the Felagnolum inhabitants. Necessary for this realm to be safe from the kinds of dealings that would harm inhabitants. This means untampered by the workings of a permission or property purchase by contract. The Sempiternal of Spiritian made a deal with Salbani of Liege to visit and sacrifice himself for the entirety of a moon at the end of each moon cycle, he was due at the end of the current cycle which hath just begun, eighteen days from this night. This recurring punishment is the only bloodline of access to the form of power that keeps active magical loaning on the purchased lands. I speak of this old mountain range of Litus! The Ancient Temple of Litue sleeps deep beyond the old Bloodwoods, under the current domain of Bani and his Legion.

Salbani veered from the archway overlooking the Staid Null, continuing to act in aggravated illuminations as he directed to the walls of this ancient temple. This highlights the bound and unconscious followers trapped by their own magic, subject to a cast formed to capture the legion. It puts caught subjects in a deep trance, awaiting a wish for freedom and awakening. This magic was stolen and redistributed to bind them along Litus' walls. Voboh is near and quick to open discussion with his dominant.

"Only the powerful of Liege were able to break from this binding, so why are we unable to perform magic freely?"

Voboh was obviously under scrutiny of the happening.

"Why do we need this, as you say, special blood... Understand why we lack the strength for such past tasks of ease. As I consider the oddity, I wonder why you sent this bastard Prett to obtain the fairies? What is happening?"

The dragon keeper looked with wonder as he questioned. Salbani was quick to ignite with grunts of hatred just as he threw his neck, polishing his head in frustration. These magical predicaments are why few saunter freely as the blood and energy of the Magi-Cherished, Usually Fairies, sustain the power needed. The Great Arku Michael, a Spiro Warrior of the Unitrea Knights, stripped their magic, leaving them helpless and bound to this mountain. That is until the ancient members of Liege find a way to free themselves. It is thought that freedom can only be obtained by a spoken unbinding from the same lips of the old decree by the war victor. I have spoken of this tale; a vivid story I would call my writings of this Happening of Litus. It is no rumor but truth that I shall recall for you when the time is right. Voboh stepped forward, onto the balcony platform away from the stairway as he spoke.

"Can I ask for elaboration of this great revenge?"

Nearing the edge of the upper circle once more, Salbani stood in the middle of the viewpoint. The leader threw up his hands, quenching the sun in hatred. His hand was open, his fingers tense and bent. Drago clawed around light beams as he began explaining his elaborate plan.

"By my will and work! We will free our followers... Soon... This is why we are sending the probes to the dirt world Voboh. I am searching for a chosen human, unaware of his destiny, susceptible to the powers of bewitchment. There is only one known kind of blood with the power we need. It is this Ahtum blood. I only heard rumors of this blood, rumored extinct in the realms. Thus, I learned from Rhamtes that these rumors are the truth! Through working with the seekers in a long search, I found the realm that the spoke held the powerful magi blood that is important for our task. As it, in fact, does, and I say that there is not few but an abundance of this bloodline. Voboh was quick to put in his senses.

"Master, it is said that there are many kinds of blood all around the cosmos. What is the reasoning for going to this set-apart place? What is it of this Ahtum blood that homes such power?"

Voboh is curious about the truth. Salbani spoke out with slight annoyance at his questioning yet spoke on.

"I say that this Ahtum is of the blood of that creator. Meaning that this kind walks untangled in the universe. Just like this galaxy, do you now understand my dragon keeper? A realm of endless riches by stone and plant hidden from us! As so is the knowledge that just a drop of their blood is utter power, it is raw godly magic inside these chosen flesh born. As the place of millions bound by illusion, wandering as slaves filled with this unmatched power in their blood! Well, this place is hidden from the cosmos, and I plan to merge them! These lands of light and this dirt world of chosen exposed! As a true Trezhur, the blood of these chosen is not of the mixed blood types from thousands of generations! Untainted, I would say you could name it A true find... The gem Voboh! I speak of this subject that I have found. It is a direct descendant line from the creator. As untapped energy that will free us from this imprisonment!"

Salbani stretched with a release of confidence, speaking on.

"I have a loss of the name, but in addition to use chosen, oh the glory I will receive, the jealousy I will create for my old masters for only abandoned us they have! I will make my mark known, Voboh! As the word of Rhamtes, that keeper of Spiritian spoke, these beings were at some time decreed untouchables, and this is why their existence was hidden, for eons the figure Rhamtes spoke of! We will venture here; I will harvest their power! As I will free my following! I will take over this Kingdom beginning with the lands of Sype, on the plain of Vimaurus! Here is where we will begin our new rule! I say that we will take down these thrones! No King, No council, No power but mine!"

Salbani proudly expressed his hatred for the Orders, in ongoing explaining as he walked down the archway to his Throne. The few freed ancients rejoiced at his decree, and his legion's faint screams and roars echoed along the walls, confirming his power. Seething with hate, Salbani sat on his Throne, reminiscing about his kin.

"As for my close friend, Vaieh the wandering fool! Off somewhere hiding he is! I know that he guards my scrolls! I know him to also be holding the collection of Dynot magic! We will find him as soon as we are free, and I will return in a fury of rebellion! I decree that the land will be ours again, as I will reclaim that lost relic that is rumored to be on this plain of Terra...Now, let us begin, where is Fiki Fuse!?"

Fiki rose from his relaxed position of study on his tech pad, making his way from the epicenter of the temple as Salbani spoke on.

"Fiki, who is it that you wish to accompany you, venturing this distant Terra?"

Salbani asked as he held the probe object into the shine of the light.

"Well, My... my Master... I think that Prett would be, well, I dare say that the best companion would be the youngling. He recently returned from Darku teaching. I am sure that he needs some adventure. Master, the black magic can be, well, it can be trying, A test of thy will if thy are in wilt."

The little shapeshifter spoke to his Master sitting on his throne. Salbani tilted his head in confusion as his fire eyes burned in wonder at Fiki's request.

"Prett? The bastard? He is a young one, only twenty, what is it, twenty-eight Unis? As I have no clue where this one is; in origin, that is... Tell me, who is to say he will keep to task? If that is your will, I say it is a foolish wilt Fiki, but fine, you will take Prett. May it be so, Byevil go find Prett and bring him to me."

Salbani spoke his demand with a relaxed fluff of his hand. He relaxed on his throne, and followers were quick to hoard around him. Byevil scoffed as he walked from the pairs of the Legion.

A young one who lives unbound from the bloodwood curse due to being at the feet of Salbani upon binding. As the pair of them walk unbound on Salbani's release. In fact, quite a few Lieges are unbound by the force of this bind escape. This figure is quick to speak, as a youngling would be.

"Master, In the meanwhile, while we await Byevils return... You should make the human do something... Something beyond him! Before you send us to that dirt realm! Demonstrate your power! Oh, great leader... Bewitch the blood of Ahtum this fool, and before us. Demonstrate the Jexi Wost! I have never been a witness to this ancient practice!"

This young one spoke quickly as his ruler, annoyed yet he replied as if the dark master was pleased.

"Certainly, it is a bright idea from you, Zycanco. We should now send the probe to this Terra! I hope that the fruits of this realm are at task, weak and senseless, for we would not want those elementals to be of the knowledge of our tampering in their realm; now, Fiki, go and ready this device to send in the probe. We will find our subject today!"

Zycanco spoke up once more as he asked the question again.

"What are you doing with the probe, master?"

The being speaks in a submissive tone as he continues to question his leader. "I am sorry, forgive me master… Well, I do not wish to question you, but I say that interfering with this realm must have more than one consequence than having to deal with the unified. I know you do not fear them, but Master, we know nothing about this plain, this Terra of Arthe. What of the structure on this plane do we know? The forces of law and life that abide in this realm, are we to act as if they do not exist? Who is to say that there will not be consequences?"

Cut in Zycanco, his tone fluctuating as he held a fearful ora. His Master gave an annoyed squint as he spoke on.

"Enough! I have spoken to the Dragon Keeper like you have not heard me!"

Salbani roars at the youngling, striking fear into him as he skips in a cowardly retreat. The sight of this anxiety endorsed a prominent level of anger in his leader. Salbani belched in detestation.

"Away with you all!"

Harshly demanding the exit of his Liege following. The grouping of demons was quick to leave the sights of their Master as the Drago Keeper Voboh spoke out to the youngling Zycanco.

"Alright, all right, my young one, I see what you ask… It is the device! Fiki's probe will find the bloodline Salbani is in search of. Next, Jexi Wost, that is the key. If the fool is to be senseless and follow this cast deception, we shall be free! Bani plans to use this human to create a way for us, formed with his permission, do you see? He will use the crafts to send him notions by uploading them to Jexi. As I said, if he is ill to accept this cast spell uploaded into the Jexi. Rather than fighting the interlink… Our master will use this subject for his blood, kidnap, absorb his energy, and we will free our followers who are bound around us! We will break from this decree, and Salbani will have his revenge!"

Salbani, the leader, revolted in outraged jeer as he beat the ends of his throne, acting in bizarre, rambunctious, and psychotic behavior. His following of the temple bound roared behind their entrapment with hopes that shook the floors, echoing throughout the levels of the ancient temple as he overheard the Dragon keeper speaking to Zycanco and this filled him with prideful energy.

"That is what we will do! Bring me the Jexi Wost!"

Giving a belch, followed by an eerie, as it was a vial chuckle of mumbled words, Fiki brought over a small vial the size of a thumb. Salbani held it in the shine of the light as he began to speak even more malevolently than before.

"There you are…"

He spoke in a menacing whisper. Inside the vial was the shine of what looked to be a single strain of hair. This odd silver strain is what these figures spoke of being the Jexi-wost. This microscopic tech insect emits a sound spell into the brain way, leaving a subject numb, senseless, or even thought-obsessed. Whatever is imprinted by the sound energy, this would be the spell associated with the Jexi-wost used. This is an ancient practice of shifting a low-minded, unguarded figure. Salbani fixed his composure from acting in this sudden rage as the Master of Liege spoke on.

"We shall fool the fool. I will use the last of the fairies' blood from Spiritian. From the deal I made with Rhamtes for Magi bloods and Seeker work. These Cedure of Task! My glorious allies! I say nothing would be in motion if not for these Seekers! As that Rhamtes is a fool! It cannot be long before

Michael knows of this treachery; it will not be long before the whole realm speaks my name again!"

Salbani continued in a mumble after explaining his plan. The sight of their Master at a pull of himself showed loosely. Salbani belched in a release of mucus and repeated coughs, taking grunts of air before going on in speech. This decade of imprisonment has made weak this nefarious master of this legion as his supporters as well feeble, without the entirety of their magic their blood is thin and without minerals, the only strength these beings have is from the sunlight, spending time in daily fast due to lack of food, their powers will be stronger once obtained for they are primed by the light, even if they harness nothing of it's good beyond natural soaking. The master of the legion recovered from his sickened cough as he proceeds to speak to his following.

"We will use this fairy blood to transport two of you to this Terra. You will take a fool and bring it back with you. As I decree, we will have a sacrifice before the night is over. Our kin will be freed soon!"

Salbani's voice echoed throughout the temple as the ancient followers stood listening to him, their eyes set on the temple walls, where the rest of the Legion of Liege were bound. Salbani stretched his figure and exhaled, followed by a nasty outcry of laughter as he held his hands to the temple ceilings.

"Come now, Gather around the Sorzo Cast. When Zycanco came to me and spoke about this idea of creating a demonstration, it pleased me. We will send him the idea to call a storm with the knowledge to build a machine to absorb energy. He will dream it, I will send the seekers imparted with our cast to incept this dream to him, by the Jexi we will gain control, but I say the by this action, the fruits of that realm will be warned so be aware as you travel for how they respond I know not. Come around and join me for the ritual, brothers. I could easily lead him anywhere I want to, then drain him of his fluids but a demonstration, you will have! Better hope the Spiro of this realm does not intervene as you fear! For then we are at war with not one but two realms."

Salbani laughed in mockery as he gazed at his following, waiting for them to form a position around the Sorzo.

"Let us begin, Fiki. Take the vial and put it into the probe. Tell me when the sound upload is connected, and then we shall begin."

Fiki took back his vial and began to walk to his computer station. On arrival he connected the vial of the Jexi Wost to the launching station that would send the probe into deep space, leading to this hidden dirt world of Arthe. Fiki connected his computer to the probe and made ready the sound equipment to absorb the information from the cast that the Liege group was preparing for. This took some time, as he did so Salbani went on in his own preparations for the spell casting on the Sorzo mount.

The legion king figure wove his hand in an uncaring flick just as he spoke an unknown tongue. Suddenly, a flame broke in the middle of the group, as well as in all sorts of areas around the temple throne room. Altars and scattered candles throughout the temple were swiftly lit. They could now see that the throne they were all standing on was a considerable ritual setting, but they were unable to see this when deprived of exposure to light. The room held a darkened gloom, the boundaries of the physical and the mystical began to blur as the legion encircled the mount as they mumbled preparation chanting's to lure in the dark energies of magic. The entities who were engaging in the ritual began to speak in unity as one by one their eyes rolled black,

"The old spirits are here! Active with us, continue my legion! Continue to speak, we need these fallen energies as we lack our own! Speak on!"

Salbani roared in satisfaction as he could feel the presence of the dark ones of the ancient wars. The candle fires stretched without interruption as the new cycle began, it was utter darkness without the light of the moon. As so the light of the flame was abundant, shadows jumping around the Sorzo mount. Salbani took the reins of the ritual as he out spoken decrees that were invitations to the ancient ghosts of the temple. Attempting to summon all the power that he could. The Sorzo mount had a crystal diamond shaped center that sat in a large bowl shape, there was a ring around this bowl that was indented with twelve sections on the sides where the legion members stood. There were only six of them, but due to the calling of Ancient spirits there was enough power in the room to complete the ritual. The Sorzo was made of an obsidian stone, and the center was a Dynot crystal that pulsed with life from the legion directing energy on it.

"It is time, give your energy to the mount and may the ancient spirits work in our favor!"

The grouping of the legion took their personal blades as they sliced their opposing hands and held them over the obsidian spirals of collection that sat before each of the sections proceeding from the ring around the Sorzo. Salbani lifted a vial that was a few ounces of fairy blood, gifted from Rhamtes. He outpoured it on to the spiral before his section and the blood of the six legion and the bloods of the Fairies swirled together as they made way to the center of the mount, when the bloods reached the Dynot that glowed by the cast, a spiritual chemical reaction took place as the grouping began to chant for a portal summons. The air went cold as a thick mist began to take over the darkened area that was ever so lit by candle flame. The entities continue to chant a song of opening as a blue spiral begins to swirl in an area near the mount. Their voices and hands uplifted to the temple ceiling directing the energy of the ritual scene as Salbani redirected it to form the gateway to dimension six-zero-three. The mood was dark as one could feel the power in the room as a heavy weight on the shoulders and there was an alliance of reverence with this chaotic legion as they all held the same intention. The setting of the ritual was so powerful that the fallen ones were seen dancing in celebration on the walls, overtaking the shadows of the grouping of Liege. The weight of this ritual is sure to be known in the realm as when the blood of a fairy burns, it is said to be a wretched smell for smaller creatures that are wandering, if one is near the temple, it is sure to smell it and give word of this to the Fairies of Spiritian as soon the whole realm of Felagnolum will know that the Liege are once again active in black magic. Fiki quickly went to his computer station as he checked the process of the probe that they launched.

"The probe connection is secure, my master. Just a moment to find the bloodline, and shortly after, the Jexi-wost will swim in his bloodstream!"

Fiki bellowed anarchically as the leader Salbani waved his hands as he spoke to his followers.

"Follow my tongue!"

He continued speaking in the form of an unknown tongue as the fire changed from the typical orange glow to a vibrant green holding an essence of oddity. Along with this magical happening came the weight of evil! The spell manifested with the intentions of the caster, Salbani. The energy powerful as it consumed the room, these figures around their malicious leader began speaking...

"Tcartta Gninthgil, Tpecca, Tcartta Gnithgil!"

Repeated, as well as peculiar hand movements while the Master spoke in an unknown tongue that was the direction of the curse. It sounded like something ancient from this realm that they were to venture into.

"Tpecca Maerd Noissessop, Kcatta Evaw, Suoveirg Ksat Litnu, Etelpmoc."

The elder one spoke in a soft but vial tone as out of its mouth came a dark red spiral that was, in fact, the matter of his manifested curse. It went straight into a small dream portal that was open above the fire. This magic swam through the air with delicacy in a pleasant dancing sway. Into the portal exactly, you would see a jellyfish float through the water. It moved with beauty inside the portal, even if it was a curse. This tiny gateway closed as a red magic beam shot straight into the temple's roof. As it hit the peak above the Sorzo ritual, it formed an energetic surge that pulsed throughout the temple levels, even out beyond the temple and into the atmosphere. Creating a spectacle for all the local inhabitants of northern Irosent.

"A Wen Noilleber Snigeb!"

Salbani excitedly belched the ancient speech as the magical energy unfolded before the grouping. Looking into the depths of the flames, he exposed his true intentions.

"Evol Eht Sthgis Fo Kigam! The power in my fingers… The manipulation, the bewilderment. Nothing more satisfying than flirting with the powers of my friends… Unitreas like to teach that it is sacred as if the powers of the realms could really die, wither out like those who are great. I digress. The magic is abundant! Arrogant fools, I say that nature is natural and only recycled, what foolish thinking it is to think that we be unallowed to use natural resources. I declare this ritual as the start of abundant fright. Be it a new path for my new reign."

Oh, is the reality of it hitting you? This is the head of legions, a rebel of the ancient protectorate. The speech of this figure was simply unsettling. He went on with a weighted explanation.

"Is it not so wonderful, my Legion? Do you not feel the freedom in my grasp? The air is heavy, and the moon is new, soon shifting form. As this Jexi activated, and I predict that my

Master shall visit. I assume he will be repelled as I hope for a favor from him, we shall see."

Salbani stretched his neck to the blackened skies, his eyes shocked wide by the sights of the change of atmosphere. His followers shriveled when they heard the word of the potential coming of their masters, Master. Utterly beside themselves, the wicked doers are overtaken by fears. It began to look as if Salbani was indeed the only one who had any desire for freedom. "Leave me, away with you all until I beckon for you."

Salbani dismisses those who follow, with youngling like gossip as snakes that tickle ears they disperse into separate areas of the temple.

O, Great Treasure. You are in fact still with me as an ear to my word? If so, then you know that this tale begins with the "Liege," is that what they call themselves, and what is their aspiration? Well, that is just the concern I beg one to comprehend. The Liege works in chaos. After all, they are a Legion, and one could assume that this is the destiny of their calling. The following of Liege is only in the act of a single path. Conquering for power as these are those who live overcome by desire. Not as if each of them is in the action of a fire's spread. Yet, in the action of utter wilt, then, I say that the fire is only to spread. I speak in reflection of the past, and this ventured land becomes consumed. Nothing matters to this kind, as only what matters to them at a time of fulfillment, I say, is the true terrors of the kingdoms, for Salbani has no governance to him. Reign! Before him, no force will step! Shackled and bound for a good reason, I say! As this has been no problem for the last decade, they are bound by decree to still be in a temple that chains this Legion of followers. A cheery punishment, for it was an added decree on top of Salbani, who had already been enslaved for this decade that to him has felt as an eternity. Several ancient magicians have freed themselves and can walk among this temple, As I spoke. Mind that none of them, including Salbani, have been able to break the decree that covered the temple grounds.

I wanted to give you a sight of this temple, to imagine the ruins of it as the Liege of wicked residing here for this decade. bound! These wicked need more potent magic to achieve the freedom of remanding evil ones still bound on these grounds. This ancient leader plans to use humans of Arthe to fulfill his task. Beginning with sending a probe in search of a particular type of blood. The probe created by Fiki Fuse is a magical device that can search and sift through astral energies. Once it finds what it needs, it houses a cyber-technology that is the Jexi-Wost that is a parasite sent to enter the subject. The probe quickly, as usually unknowingly, latches onto the skin and shoots the Jexi Wost, cyber parasite under the skin like a simple vaccine from your realm. I allude to the fact that we do not participate in needle work, nothing of the sort in my Kingdom. As most of all inhabitants understand the beneficial use of plante. As the Jexi Wost travels through the bloodstream, it eventually travels to the subject's brain. This technological creature uses images and sounds to project a new thought process. This continues until the subject allows unknowing access to mind and body control. The subject, if unguarded, would remain unaware of the absolute reasoning of his actions but is fully cooperative with what the self is doing. An absolute drone system would work if these things got full access to the mind. These things really turn a subject into the living dead, all from will choice, I mind you... I just want to make sure that you are understanding. I would add that one would know if it was a Jexi inside his flesh. As you would suffer terrible headaches, if one is to be of a loss of time... I would say that you are indeed infected. There are many things to explain; various things are happening in the realms. Everything is all at once, an abundance of happenings, but I will help you keep up. This nattering was of a ritual well thought, planned, sought, worked as cast into a device of illusory! The Jwost to carry as polluted this human's mind with this cast illusory of the fallacy that with the subject following will become a drone for the ancient Salbani! Awaiting the unfolding of his decree under the lack of light on this new moon. Are you curious about this chosen human?

LACKING WARDS

August 2nd

Residence Calloway County: Florida: Arthe 603

Billions of sapiens walking in life, unaware that they live in a multiverse as most are bound to system rulings. I do hope this is something that you know but if not, may you experience the phenomenon of the verses. I say we are all of these, the many of self, the multi of being, the fractures of us in a battle for now! Think on to thyself, but I share with you that I feel that I might just be consciously, each single one of Me's all at once. Imagine a million different realms that are at once happening, tied together to make up what it is that is our existence. This is surely mind numbing to the indoctrinated as it is a mind trip for the semiconscious, but I ask that you think about it. As then, the real question and task would be to merge these realities and become one with these mirrors of being. To then stand, go to share what we are to a passing soul. The oddity that is me is as God touched the insane with a gift of freedom as expulsion from religious views. Oh, what I think of the repetition of verse, only a rumored thought I confess. Learning the truth is such an individual awakening as everything is the same as it differs from form to form. Before losing you, I end my notions and take you now to the desired man who is of slight brilliance, awaking from a dream of strangeness.

BERT-BERT-BERT-BERT-BERT

Grunting with annoyance, the human smacked his alarm and rolled out of bed.

"Well, that was as sure as odd could be…"

The man speaking to himself as a puzzling memory struck! He stood up and walked into the bathroom. He noticed himself in the mirror, at once striking up a conversation.

"Hello Iyo, me, o, Grand day, I wonder what the hell that dream was about and what is wrong with my eye... it is swollen as if I had some kind of bar tassel in my slumber? I have this near dream in my head like a fucking radio song! What kind of a flopped day did I wake up to? This is ridiculous! I would call it witchcraft, but I do not believe in that bullshit!"

As he was thinking, he suddenly realized what his brain was processing. As for the look of this human, he has a striking appearance even when he is fresh out of bed. Having a sharp face with great bone structure and a softness to his facial as he aged well yet ruggedness like he did not keep up with his appearance. The eyes are worn just as the sight of a genius and intense as if when he is looking at someone, he is looking through them, into the depths of the person. You could still see that he was soulful as he sparked with intelligence, but his eyes colored a bright hazel that held a mysterious tone. His hair style greased and slicked as an unruly murky blonde that is just long enough to stay in place as from time to time it flopped whimsically. His skin was a light tan, smooth but hinting to experience with aging lines if one were to look for them and the man has a scar above his right eye. One might say this man is an old soul, but he is only in his thirties—thirty-one, to be exact. With the emotions of a seventeen-year-old, he recalls the dream.

"Wait... Why did I dream that? I wonder why it was even in my mind... Truth I say, this is surely a wonder."

The human pressed the record button on his pocket recorder, and it sounded with a pitched beep.

"Light? Lightning? To attract lightning? I was dreaming of different voices telling me "Attract the lightning" As it repeated, and the sounds of electrify, electrify, electrify also were repeated. The oddity, I confess, is that this is not a dream but like a message, a task that I shall complete! It is as if my bones are in will for me to take this action. It is odd to feel this way, from a dream to a new desire. Run with it? Should I? I have many questions but no soul to converse with, I shall make a record of this."

The human spoke into his pocket recorder as he put on his slippers and made his way through his living space, thinking to himself. Suddenly, he tripped over an odd metal container.

"What the fuck is this?"

Still half asleep, Iyo picked up and placed this metal probe-like object on his dresser. He spoke into his recorder as he continued to the bathroom.

"Here I am, talking to myself again as if that will do anything to help. I should get something to eat. The month is August, the day is the second, year 2024. I dreamt of pulling lightning from the sky as if I were Thor. As I woke up to trip over this cyber world tech that I have no idea of its origins? I could only think that it is or was an old project part of mine? I must have forgotten what project it is for. As for this dream, well, I must work to make this dream a reality, for I still hear the echoes of these voices in my mind. The oddity, for of the divine I had not the thought, spirits I say are jokes, that evil that these people speak of I say is just a person with a brain deficiency! Never mind those who belong in a ward! I confess I would always say something of the sort in their direction, but I have become one of them in a night! Hearing a voice in a dream, many voices, as to wake and have this faint, this small proceeding thought to linger in the back of my mind... The oddity of the day that has only started... Until the time to work, this will be all."

The man stopped his recorder as he began the daily routines as it was the grand rise of the day. Speaking to himself, his rising chants.

"I am Iyo!" going on... "I am a genius,"... "Nobody is better than I."... "Me, this mirror man, is all that you are, that I am, all that exists! I say it is I that I face, I am... Well, who is it that is greater than I am? These low minds are nothing to me! I have no fear when it comes to the unknown things! I will attract you! I will light the seas!"

He acts out some form of this action in his own mind aloud each day to build his confidence and ensure an elevated level of dominance, for he lives mostly in solitude. He has, in fact, developed a way of settling his daily terrors. It was a ritual of sorts, pure affirmations for the start of each day. He went on to make breakfast and then enjoy the origins of the sunrise on the front deck of his home.

"Wonderful!"

Iyo remarked on the beauty as he looked out to the setting of Calloway beach, sights pleasing of the grate lofty palms. Shook to the roots from the frigid breeze of the ocean-salted air. As you could only notice creeping afar, a collection of clouds so dark that it shines with wickedness. A balance of the origins of destruction just as it is mother nature's renewal. Well, that is what I have heard a figure speak. As usual for this subject, he starts the morning by listening to the radio while enjoying breakfast. Admiring native sounds surrounding his home, hearing seagulls that give the warning of the incoming storm as they begin to migrate somewhere dry, some cozy place to hide until the storm passes. You can find Iyo; I spoke of his name, right? You remember a genius in hiding, the subject wanted by the ancient ones. Find this human, Iyo, the chosen rat of the wicked, holding his gaze set on the fields beyond his porch. Sights of tall grass dance over the sands as you can faintly hear the crashing of the constant and ever-changing waves. Iyo spoke out to the universe with a heart of gratitude, making a note in his pocket recorder.

"The effect of the moon. They say it is gravity's ruler… How the tide behaves as a wild animal that feels nothing and knows nothing except to rage. Such a beautiful natural display. As if it is at war with self, trying to be of the lands and to be of the seas... simply caught between. I want to say thank you, Creation, for highlighting something in everything. Today, I tell you, I will use your forces... I have had only the oddest of dreams. These are only the best of words for it! I say I will use the storm! It is in the air after all, the darkness that is afar is sure to come this way. I guess I will go with it, I mean it is not every day that such bewildering things happen!"

Speaking out, but to himself, of course, he held a smile at the beauty of the dirt and the brawn of the sea. Showing appreciation for whatever is out there in the cosmos inspiring him. Yet never did he question the desire of this thought, the root of this thought. As he moves with it, I ask you a question so that you may sit in question, when you reach out to the source... Is it a light for all? Could it be that your voice is a voice for all to hear? I mean, what other forces listen to these word decrees? Just a thought: I say you mine like your effort is a gem, and my sentence is as a pickaxe. Ongoing, but do not let me get ahead... The radio he was listening to cuts from advertising, and the host begins a rambunctious rant. Going on to explain that the local markets and trade ports will soon be out of fish. The massive storms that have been off the coast for the last few months have not only caused the fish to not surface but the storms are so ridiculously powerful that major ships are unable to travel through the Calloway sea port, the host spoke of how the United States Coast Guard issued a warning to all shipping and transportation companies. Explaining how to steer clear from the storm areas, how the waves are too dangerous, and how it is too treacherous for even the U.S.C.G. to do the job for which formed, yet still, they go out. The host spoke of a one-hundred-mile radius of the storm. Iyo was ecstatic and laughing at this news.

"That is it!"

He began to yell in celebration.

"This is what I will do! I will find the damn fish, and I shall damn them for the damn people!"

He yelled again as he began to run into his home and move straight to the garage. This is the area of the house that has become another workspace. He even knocked down the guest room wall to increase the space in his garage because of his experiments. The whole house has altered his reasoning for the lab work he does. Iyo is a scientist and a technological genius who kind of hides from society, doing his own thing all the time. The fairie watchers who helped me with my explanations, they spoke of him as no keeper of friends; only this dog named Atom is his company. You could be wondering what exactly these experiments are that he is working on. These experiments that Iyo spends his time on are the kind of things that often involve what the science community could only dream about. What is that? Well, that is absolutely zero regulations; there is no board of personnel to choose what they can and cannot do. For what Iyo thinks to be unjustified reasoning, he was, in fact, expelled from all practices of scientific laboratory research. The man had a rambunctious way of doing things. He is messy and reactive with most of his tasks. It is rumored that people who have collaborated with him say that he is possessive over his work. Often to be demanding things and ruling over his fellow researchers. It was not that he was prideful, well maybe a tad bit...

Simply put, he is the Richard of the room. He is already more intelligent than his genius peers, so you can imagine this leading to him being quite the problem. He was for the company that oversaw him due to so often something going wrong in the workspace. For Iyo gets into the science of things more. He was overly enthusiastic. Doing things that others would never do and as anyone that has created their own path might know... Well, you should know that nobody will last anywhere after enough rebellion. Iyo warned and repositioned many times, and just as all destructive cycles go, these events concluded with his harsh expulsion. It was a removal from all practice of experiments involving the G.S.C. (Global Science Community). The hard headed man was at the time unfazed because he knew they were making a mistake. As with most humans, A seed of hatred for the ones who wronged him began to grow. It was so deep down inside his heart that he never noticed it, as with each waking day after the passing of these events, a tiny hate seed flourished in his greenhouse of revenge. It was a subtle, mind-consuming thought that, over time, began driving his entire mind. Soon, this thought inspired all that Iyo started to do. (I will show you; I am the best) simply owned his mind. By his own actions, by his own will, I remind you. Leaving him open as a target is what this created for him. It is said that to gain a hold of anything, one must first have a foot in the door!

To summarize a long tale of transitioning around the country... Iyo found a sweet spot on the east coast of Florida. Here, he continued his work in his new home, free and unregulated. This time in solitude changed him, as time will force you to deal with yourself. As if to face yourself not? One would only become whatever it is that tortures. As for Iyo, it was this odd form of self-imposed insanity due to meddling in the thought realm's terrors, Lacking Wards.

The near entirety of the day has passed since Iyo began working in his garage since the first warning of incoming storms. Catch him singing a jingle he developed.

"Oh! Damn the Fish! Oh, damn, the river... Yes, damn the fish and river to fry the fish to feed the flock of the-Ooh yes. I have found it. This spark plug will do the trick."

Iyo continued to prance in high spirits, gathering items together as he finished building his new experiment. Do you, oh great Trezhur reader... Do you still follow me on this journey?

The man follows his thoughts as we all do, yet this Jexi is highly active in his mind.

"By creating a magnetic pulse and getting it strong enough, I should be able to attract the lightning,"

Iyo spoke into the pocket recorder. He slammed the door with his foot while picking up a box of material with the other hand. He quickly made his way out to his vehicle as it began to rain heavily.

"Now to the Calloway beach market!"

He talks to himself as he lights a cigarette and turns the ignition. Arriving at the local market with an abundance of speed. The human is overtaken by sudden brain pain.

"A-ugh! What the hell! What is? What is that pain!?"

Iyo quickly screamed as this pain seemed to come from nowhere. He dropped his cigarette, which fell and rolled to his feet as he completely overtook the curb, hydroplaning. His chaotic notion manifested in his action as he tried halting, he had to swerve! Screeching to a harsh stop, nearly running a man over because of his lack of sight from the rain, as the brain pain sure did not help. Iyo jumped out of his jeep while leaving it running.

"Damn it, that was insane..."

Iyo took a breath and let out a chuckle.

"It was as if my cigarette was the cause of that terrible brain pain. I have never felt that before, such unbearable pain that led to a near-fatal crash and pedestrian death! I must try to be more careful."

Iyo spoke this quick sentence into his pocket recorder as he quickly grabbed a box of items and his backpack of gear from his jeep. In the bright ends of sunlight, he began to run to the beachside. Just as he made it to the bottom floor of the pier, that man he nearly hit as pulling into the parking area started to yell out to him, as any person would.

"Hey, you Bastard! You almost hit me!"

Still rushing to the water's edge, with little care Iyo yelled back to the man.

"Yeah, Sorry, man, but you're okay!"

He shouted as he continued. Surprisingly, the man was not as upset as you would have thought him to be. He was more intrigued by the reasoning behind why Iyo was acting so wild and with such disregard for his surroundings.

"What a weirdo," The man thought, asking himself.

"Why is he running with all that gear?"

The man laughed as he continued in thought.

"And who just brushes off the fact of near manslaughter? Imma go pick his brain."

The man walked without fear, for as curious as the cat, he went to where Iyo was setting up his equipment. This figure was around five in height, and his hair was short and black. He had an interesting pair of green eyes, but he was a slender man with extraordinarily little muscle. He had a single tattoo on his arm that read the word "Sane." The man had a black sweater on with a pair of tan pants. Approaching Iyo, he spoke out.

"Hey man, no trouble. What are you doing with all this stuff? I know I was yelling, but now I am curious. Sorry to bother you, but it is just that you struck me as an odd fellow, and I am intrigued by you, so I'm going to say hello."

Explained the man as he knelt equally near but distant. "And oh, I am Bohn. Well, my name is Bohnstant, But I go by Bohn."

He was standing over Iyo, rushing to set up his gear.

"Cool name, kid. Do either of you parents think that you are constantly a stress?"

Iyo gave a mumbled chuckle as he continued to ravish through his items, but the man was quick to respond—yet with a highly stoic tone.

"Well, they are dead. So, I think maybe I could have been."

Speaking awkwardly as the scientist Iyo stopped working momentarily, sighing as he looked up at Bohnstant.

"I am sorry, Pal. I do not mean harm with my word; you understood, right? Bohnstant reminded me of constant, Bohn, I am just trying to focus, I have a job to do, well, a hobby that works like a job!"

Giving a nod of acknowledgment paired with a sarcastic grin, Iyo finishes setting up his equipment.

"So, what is this?"

Bohn asks as he picks up what looks to be a battery.

"Do not touch anything, Guy! I do not even know you. What are you doing? The people want fish, so I will get the fish. I sometimes work for people. Please, do not touch anything! It is all particular!"

Iyo explained aggressively as he tightened a part of his machine with a screwdriver. Replying in a mocking form of cynicism, Bohnstant mocked.

"So, with this little box of what looks like a, well a box. With a coil of some kind? I do not see how you will help with the seafood issue. Why not let all the bastards find something new to eat? Ever think that the fish does not want to be food? I mean I sure love fish, but people just eat everything up."

Acting in a manner of slight disrespect, simply not understanding what Iyo is doing. Bohn continued.

"You have a long arm going out the front and up the top. It looks like a broken microwave attached to a damn music stand. Do you plan to solve the fish problem on the news this morning? Okay, guy, well, good luck."

Laughing while standing in intrigue, Bohn begins to ask more questions.

"What is this man, really? Is this even legal? What even is your name?"

He questions. Iyo ignores his comment about legality as he continues to open his backpack shouting out, "The name is Iyo, like I-YO!" He said as he was pulling out a long extension cord. He plugged the cord into the box, and then he began to run back to his jeep. On arrival, attaching his cord to his still-running motor. Then, running back to the box and still there waiting on the beachside was Bohnstant. As Iyo approaches the equipment, you can hear it working correctly. A building of sharp ringing fluctuating as a lumping screech. Iyo, panting from the back and forth of running. Speaks out of breath to his new admirer.

"Okay, man, that is it; excuse the sound, but now all we must do is wait for Mother Nature. You should come back to the parking lot with me. It is not safe in this area anymore because I have no idea what could happen. I just have a small idea of what I have predicted that could or will happen. Well, more like, rather, what I feel is freaking repeating in my mind until I make it happen! Just stick around for what might be a show of wonder."

Iyo spoke this with tired behavior, as he was oddly ecstatic! He began to make his way to the parking lot. Immediately, Bohn followed, going on to ask more questions, as you could have assumed he would.

"Tell me what is going on, man; why are we waiting for nature? What are you saying? Are you talking about the storm?"

Bohn was anxious at this point but still highly curious about the weird box and the odd man. Parallel to this odd happening, he is growing nervous about the situation. Iyo explains as they stand in the drizzling rain.

"The Storm is here, well near, and that box needs a strike, So yes! A storm!"

Stated Iyo as he looked around to warn others to stay clear.

"A Strike? What exactly do you mean? Bohnstant asked nervously.

"What? Wait, wait, wait... are you attracting lightning? Man what? Have you, well you, you sure must have lost your mind? This is how people die or get hurt, what is the reasoning?"

Bohn was frantic, overcome with fear, adding worry to the situation.

"What if..."

Bohn's prediction was cut off by Iyo.

"Hey man, are you going to be a constant pain in my ass, or are you going to relax? It is just an experiment. You are welcome to just walk away. You involved yourself with something that has nothing to do with you, which was by your own doing, as you let these emotions swirl to this near peak! Seriously, relax, and all will be well. If it is not, then it is not; what does that have to do with you? You can just walk away..."

Iyo gave him a glare and a shake of the head. A short silence was before them. Bohnstant seemed struck by the truth of the random man. This silence changed by a lifeguard pulling up on his four-wheeler at once giving directions.

"Hey, You guys got to scoot. A category five plus hurricane is on the way. It is not safe here. Y'all got to go. I am getting out of here. Just trying to spread the word. It is serious! Y'all got to go!"

Shouting as he whipped off on his four-wheeler, at this point the dark of the storm took away the sun and the scene began to morph into darkness.

"Alrighty then."

Iyo calmly spoke as he turned to Bohn.

"Look at that! Category five. That is simply perfect, Bohn, it is perfect! Time for you to either join me or leave me! I feel like something is sure to happen!"

Iyo adrenalized and laughed, and Bohn caught a wave of this energy. Laughing as well in a justified balance of confusion and amazement. Bohnstant thought on with reality and gave a harsh remark of truth.

"Um no, nothing about it is perfect. That is death on the way, and you are happy? Yeah, I think that I will be getting out of here! Enjoy your odd experiment, you ridiculous man! I am all for new things but standing here in this storm and potentially being struck by lightning is surely not on the list!"

Iyo laughed at him as he shook his head in annoyance.

"You are overreacting! I swear it will be worth it! From my sight, you are not up for new things! It sure looks like you are walking from a new thing now!"

Iyo spoke with an uplifted voice of fun and mockery, wanting an audience as such. He tried to manipulate Bohn, who replied, but he was frustrated, confused, and obviously a bit scared, rightfully so! Yet, he stayed with the scientist.

"Alright, Is it Iyo? Yes, okay, I will hang around. Just for a little while to see if anything cool happens!"

Iyo held out his hand for a greeting.

"Nice to meet you, formally. Let's wait a while longer and see if anything happens."

Bohn was quick to converse.

"What exactly are you expecting to happen?"

Asking as he threw up and caught the battery that he picked up earlier.

"Well, if my calculations are correct. If a strike was delivered, my machine would absorb it as it would travel through the coil and out the end pointing to the sea. I have regulators throughout it, so they deflect a small amount of energy. These suckers are golden; if even one misplaced, then…Wait, is that a battery? Oh my gosh, damn it, Bohn, you are a fucking idiot! Give that to me now! Agh!"

Beyond being frustrated, angered grunting Iyo quickly grabbed the regulator from Bohnstant and began to run to his machine! What a way to meet someone… It was a pleasant walk on the beach until having to dodge a high-speed vehicle! This driver ends up being a freak, which is so interesting that you stand in the rain as a hurricane was on the way. Awaiting what could be the most dangerous thing on this beach. Someone is purposely attracting lightning… Would you stay my Trezhur? I sure do not see myself in this position. Well, maybe I would watch from afar, anyway, Iyo and his watcher are waiting for the storm to approach them. As we go on, my only worry is that you, my Trezhur, overlook the very importance of decisions and encounters. As I recall the happening, I can think of the many times that I have acted in this very thing that I fear you are to overlook. The fact of me being in actions as I am in no way close to realizing the reason for me to follow these thoughts made action as it led me to encounters that I don't even question, be it a good or bad happening, is not even in the realm of my questioning as that is the sickening of inception. I could allude to the ill will but I hath already told you and you will by the end of this telling have enough of my repetition as you are to put me on a shelf to only return in wonder as you revisit my natters to even be in jeer as you await to experience more. This is the exact occurrence of the backbone, how constant it is as support for the body, as it is Bohnstant that is struck by oddity, but it is intrigue that keeps the position, sturdy in his manner. Ongoing as I must, now, I take you back to the MagiSpiro realm of unity!

SIGHTS OF GRACIOUS TRICKERY

August 2nd

Temple of Litus, M.T. Litue, District Astros, Irosent: Spiritian

Liege's master gathered the ancient beings to perform a new spell. Using the blood of the Fairies from Spiritian enabled the king of deception to manipulate this realm as he pleased. This was part of his deal with Sempiternal Rhamtes in exchange for knowledge about this galaxy. He then used Fiki's technology to send a cursed upload to Jexi Wost and launched it by probe to this dirt-world. Once in place the Jexi Wost continuously casts the spell into the subject's mind. I am recalling what I have recalled, as it is much! It is best to have things fresh on the mind, as this is what my elder has always spoken to me! Now let me return to these Ancient Magi waiting for their vial brother Byevil to return with another. It was the start of a new day, the first of the new month.

The chief of these evildoers spoke in front of his followers about the actions of the subjects of Arthe as the grand shine of the sun beamed through the peak of the high temple. Giving light to the scene of the mount.

"For the Human subject has walked straight into our casting request. The mindless fool... He is an unguarded one. A son who has fallen victim to our black magic! Even before this I say these spirits in that realm know how to deceive an unknowing soul. As it was for these hooks in his bloodline, these left him unguarded. This is what my watcher saw! Not of the watcher kinds, as I only call him my watcher, for that is what he is, the one that sorts out for me. I should change his status to "the watching cedure with gems" as he leaves me to return with Trezhur news. *Hid work*, a Spiro Seeker that I speak of is why I have chosen this human. For the power is strong in him, his temple has A genius mind, A creative one that we will not destroy but will use. Yes, say I will use him, so be it a change in our plans. To still lure him to our realm, we must incept him further to bring others like him over time. I will use these Trezhur of Trezhur, a new army we could build. Have him use our technology to bring members of that pure-blood race to this world. As we will sacrifice them all. I could teach some of them our ways, all that venture here by the path of the Liege will surely fall into a trap. Either way, eventually, I will absorb their powers, and we will take over these lands of Felagnolum. Once released from this place, we shall return to my favored plain of Evinda. It is out of the flames my Queen will rise, oh my love, the woman of the ice throne. I wonder where she wanders, as on our release Michael will have no choice but to face me again!"

Opening a viewing portal on a mirror-like object, Salbani spoke to the following as he continued his elocution.

"Now come... Come! Gather around my wretched following. We will sight them now, come, yes, look through the black plain. Now look, go ahead, and look at this one. Rushing to warn the fool of the storm that he, the true fool, has caused! Guaranteed, the Spiro of this plain will be curious about what is happening! There must be some line of dominions entangled with the verses! I wonder how detached this realm truly is! I wonder if our spell was to upset one of these entities. I suppose that we shall see."

The head of the Liege ignited a pit with fire centered before them, and he just as quickly manifested a spark of rage energy, speaking in a wicked form. An unknown tongue, by the word of the fairies who watched this sight. Remember, this is a rumor brought to me. The following around this casting spoke along with him. Suddenly, he stopped as his followers continued chanting to open a portal.

"What is... the number of this Terra, dirt world, the key to its devices? Phael? Do you know? You should know, as you are the only dimension traveler here!"

Salbani belched at the beautiful legion elf as she was unfazed by this exposure.

"Six, for that place is bound by time... I know this because the port number is a nine sequence."

She spoke in a relaxed and calm manner,

"Ah... That is, it. A realm of time, I pity the fools for allowing themselves to be bound by such a lie. Well, I stand self-correcting as it is not a lie, for it sure does exist, but the limit they set as if it is all about them. Sickening, time has no care for any of them, they would be best to never use it."

Salbani is ongoing in a mumbled spastic hatred in the direction of the notion of this pure blood, with the added knowledge of what is supreme of this realm's energy. The group continued to chant, and Salbani added six and nine as the third layer of speech into the sentencing of his spelling. The group restrained themselves in chanting. A stream of astral dust formed before the following, and magic danced around them. The fire was undergoing beautiful changes. Yet this was a dark magic that is forbidden if I am to speak truth. The legion king sending thought castings to the genius through the blackened mirror that was being used as a portal of sights,

"When Byevil returns, we will take one of these humans."

Spoke the head of the wicked as they watched the happening through the portal, it was late noon in both Felagnolum and Meli, and what is it that the Liege see in this mirror portal?

THOUGHT CLASH

August 2nd

Calloway Beach

The chosen vessel to sacrifice in a dashing scurry, struggling to keep balance as he rushed to his machine to return the battery that Bohnstant misplaced. At that exact moment, the lifeguard from before was returning on his four-wheeler, noticing the machine on his journey of warning.

"Get out of here! It is a Six! It is a six, a category six!"

The lifeguard's shout was faint due to the winds and the four-wheeler motor. Iyo tried to redirect the warning, yelling back at the lifeguard.

"No! You!"

He stumbled yet quickly recovered as he continued to yell at the man.

"Turn back! Get away from that! Turn back now!"

Flaunting like a lunatic as the lifeguard nears the machine, Iyo tried to speed his pace as a sudden thunderous crack set off above the area! A continuing blinding strike of lightning followed that delivered straight to the machine! It left Iyo stargazed as he fell to the ground. Once more strikes a chain of lightning! It snaked through the sky like a Spiro entity that was on a mission in the astral! Imprinting with illumination on the clouds as it came to the surface to sprout into the depth of the sea! During this lightning eruption, a current between the ocean struck the machine straight into the four-wheeler. The strike lasted for eight seconds as unexplainably; the lifeguard vanished. In complete shock, Iyo tries to get up to turn off the machine before another strike delivers. Bohn, seeing the whole thing, runs to Iyo who was shaking like a man afraid of jesters.

"Wow! Hey man, are you okay? That was insane. It is like the machine absorbed the strike's energy, and, oh man. That was impressive!"

Bohn was ecstatic as he began to help the doctor up to his feet again. Iyo replies with little emotion as he expected this occurrence, the oddity that Bohn had overlooked, the lifeguard.

"Yeah, crazy, I am good, I am good. We must get out of here. Will you help me?"

Iyo rushed to grab all his gear, moving with speed.

"Yeah, man, I will help you. Woah, look at the lifeguards for-wheeler. Talk about fried. Gee, Oh darn man, wait. Where is that life-"

Bohn was so shocked he vomited before he could finish his sentence. A reaction that most would have when experiencing the death of another. Yet, Bohn had not experienced anything other than the sight of the strike, it was his mind that led him to this reaction. Quite the imagination of this human.

"He is gone, and I do not need to know where. Let us get out of here, come on, let us go. I am sure we are not the only witnesses to this. We better go before a search party comes looking for the unaccounted lifeguard."

Iyo started to trot back to the parking lot, entrenched in shame from the occurrence yet unwilling to show it. While the human Bohn was still gathering himself, taking a moment to process the fact that the lifeguard had just vanished and this random man he had met had pulled a bolt from the storm like he had majestic power. Lost in the situation, and most people would have the same reaction, if not worse. Before Bohn went back to the truck, he looked out at the sea. In awe, with a slight whisper, he spoke.

"How bewildering, Iyo look at the water!"

Bohn was amazed with his sight, turning to notice that Iyo was at the lot already.

"Gee, I guess he really did want to leave."

Bohn spoke with a tone of wit as he yelled at Iyo.

"Hey man! Hey, look! Look at the water!"

Giving off big emotion in his yell, you could hear the amazement in his voice like he was a child in awe with the sights of magic for the first time. Iyo turns and nearly drops all his equipment as he notices that his experiment was a success. He calmly spoke to himself with slight gleeful pride.

"What? It really worked... Call me a fucking genius. According to my calculations, that should not have caused that many fish to surface. I mean, what has happened, did I miscalculate? No, I could not have, I know that I, wait, that man I have encountered, that man that took out the battery, it must have messed up the connection, the tiny pins that collected the energy charge, it must have been something of the sort for what else caused such an energy blast. That is why I built regulators. To regulate... It could not have been that I miscalculated, I never do such a thing."

Iyo took a moment to wander in the mind, thoughts of his success spun as he blamed everything except himself for the overkill directed to the ocean as he completely overlooked the fact that he made a bigger mistake, the death of a bystander. Before yelling back to Bohn, he was speaking to himself, ongoing about the how and how not of the strike happening as he overlooked the thought of the lifeguard for the scientist had no belief in what he saw. The utter evaporation of the subject of service and the completion of his experiment. I allude to the fact that these ideas were not formed by his imagination as he thought they were, but he manifestation through his work, due to that notion casting Jexi Wost. The man yells to the other as he had enough of the sight, beginning to become worried that he has been sighted. As this is odd, for this Atum has a track record for boasting of his work as he knows that he is the best at what he does. Well, this is as he thinks.

"Wow, look at that! I have successfully damned the fish for the damned people! This is phenomenal! Come on Bohn, let us go! I need that bag, and we must get the hell out of here! This storm, this storm is becoming wild, let's go, let's go Bohnstant!"

Directing with an extreme level of stress with a slight crack in tone, he continued to run on to get the remains of items situated in his jeep. The ocean looked filled with trash for miles and miles. It was not trash, though; no, it was dead fish. These once pristine waters are now just death and decay as it was an insane number of dead fish. To be exact, electrocuted fish on the water's surface simply seeped sea life. From fish to crabs, jellyfish, and other odd things began to float and wash ashore.

"Yeah, I am coming!" He yelled back as added a sentence in a mumble. "Just give me a second, sheesh."

Bohn shouted as he ran to the doctor, helping him load and then secure all his gear back into his jeep. As Bohn was the first to speak, Iyo scattered in everything he was doing.

"So, you want to get a beer? That was all a bit of a wild situation for me, my new friend... Can I call you a friend after that? I mean, Man! I have never been through anything like that or seen anything that spectacular! How I was wrong, that was freaking perfect, for sure! Never seen a strike that close! I mean, what did I just see! I have seen lightning, but not like that!"

Iyo gives Bohn a nod of agreement paired with a slight chuckle. He tells Bohn to jump in, and they begin to drive back to Iyo's home. Noon was ending as the evening was in origin as the storm absorbed all the sunlight.

So, he did what the liege cast upon him to do. The utter self-will that the human works in was, in fact, a blinder to how he was following a task intended for him. The lightning strike was not of him, as the storm was not of him, but of his will is what homes in his thought, what malfunctions.

WICKED WILE

August 2nd

Temple of Litus, M.T. Litue, District Astros, Irosent: Spiritian

Ancient Salbani stood with equanimity before his throne, as one of the entrusts approached from the temple gates in a fury of speed. Down the marbled path it flew as when it neared the grouping of the unbound legion, A drunken figure laughed at it as he swatted at the approaching fairy. It was too quick for his lackluster swing as it swooped down and around him to hover in place before them. Unfazed by the idiocy as it was on task, with a puzzled look the fairy was perplexed with the actions of her fellows of darkness. Aboze, an elder walking in depression for being bound so long, speaks out to the messenger.

"A-ugh, As a Natt! I will squash you with ease! Little one of speeds to fly in such prides, To focus on you makes me sick, it makes me spin like water swirls of the blue deeps! You would be a nice snack, I am sickened by this fasting, go on tell us what news you have, anything of sense? I could use a good telling, and some berries, go and fetch me some fruits little sped!"

The figure yelled out as his swing carried his weight, causing him to nearly fall before the other Liege. He dropped the flagon from which he was drinking, causing a spill. The fairy flies with quick movements side to side and up and down, awaiting the frolicking to seize. The Dragon King, Voboh out spoken in disgust to this inebriated magician.

"Aboze, you drunken fool... This is the fearless voyager, Akitella! Learn who it is that stands with us, my fallen brother. As for one day, it might cost you..."

The grouping of the Liege awaited their ally to rise from his foolishness, as they gathered on the mount before their leader as the allied fairy began to speak un-sanctioned.

"Bani! Master Bani! I have returned to Litus to tell you that deception has been set to life as the seed in humans grew into what you have chosen to decree! Your rituals worked, my Liege,

Oh, how he made it come to life! The machine worked and he brought the lightning from the sky! It was, in fact, so marvelous, yet, we only have a small window to return my great, as you are so, evil, so vial, Salbani. I, I-"

The leader quickly grabbed the boisterous fairy by its throat. This fairy was four feet tall but as skinny as a slim tree. It was a light green in color with a hint of blue. The fairy is an outsider in this grouping, for it is of an unknown kind.

"Enough of this meaningless praise, I have watched this through a portal of blackened sights! Such pitiful creatures surround me! Do you think I just await for you to tell me of my own plans? Where have you even come from, little Sped? What is it that you are trying to say?"

Salbani spoke this in mighty annoyance as he suddenly threw the fairy away from him. It caught itself right before affecting the walls of the temple, quickly flying around and then back near the other members of Liege.

"Go on, I said to speak with clarity, menace insect, as I will let that addict Aboze eat you!"

Salbani nattered with dominance as his companions laughed, beginning to mock the little fairy.

"The Atum blood, O, master, he did as you wished. During this he has murdered an innocent Atum! We must leave now! Now we must leave and retrieve this body, for this is of the blood that you are searching for, and this portal will close in minutes!"

Salbani turned quickly to these words as the fairy pointed to a gateway to the dirt realm that it opened with ease. This Fairie was of the Fos Tribe, and it was able to bend light, shift matters, and direct the Arcane at will. It needed not to call on any ancient power to do magic. Born with great powers as most fairies are.

"Quick now, do not let yourself be seen!"

Akitella shouted as Salbani ordered Zycanco and Aelom to go and retrieve the body. As such, the two fallen jumped through the portal without hesitation, happy to leave the temple they had been bound at.

Do not let me get too ongoing, wonder of this fairy kind, do you?

Well, keep in mind that she is a traitor. That is harsh, but I say this not because she is around the wicked ones. I know that the fairies have cast out their kind for a century. If I recall correctly, imprisonment and murder, whether justified or not... Well, these are not the actions you would find this Magi Kind performing. It is only banishment as this is normal of the fairy kind as it is rumored that in rare cases it is known that their natural magic abilities are stripped. There is a ritual, A relenting session of essence deduction. Due to crimes against unity! I would add that each of the societies of Felagnolum has singular laws and punishments for crimes. There is always a council to deal with, for it was a universal decree of the old; all communities will have order. As I am ongoing when I should be going on... the ancient leader of these wicked rebels was speaking, ongoing himself, If I recall.

"Excellent, as for you. Aboze, go... strengthen yourself together! Utterly worthless... drugged, and drunken fool. Tell me what is the need of an addict? We all indulge in the drink, the smoke, but the levels you walk in, the filth. I have no pity for you, Aboze, no pity for you and no concern for you; go on and be gone. I do not want to hear from you until you are able to defend yourself. Begone!"

Salbani angered as his wicked ally had been in this state of imprudence for many moons. Walking into the distance, Aboze mumbles.

"Lucky, I do not strike you. King..."

Speaking in the slightest of hate and obvious jealousy, Salbani overheard him but laughed uncontrollably as he jumped onto his throne with a psychotic action, beginning this belching of nonsense. Acting out, roaring like a Ureature! Often, their master is known for unexpected actions. One moment, he is calm and collected; the next, he is in a spiral of fury! These actions materialize when one has let desire control. I wonder as I write this if I should make a home in sadness for such a fractured kind of mind. The fool, to be of such knowledge and power as to only use it for destruction is beyond sense. By lack of truth he acts in hatred for beings that once as maybe still hold love for him. In anger of his once friends and masters, so he is in work to alter the path of a chosen race for his own personal gains.

LIVE LIEGE

Calloway Beach Florida, Meli galaxy

A thought clash was ongoing while the wicked in action, the fairie gate appeared at a distance from where Iyo and the new friendly soul he encountered, Bohn, were conducting their experiment. Moments after they left the beach side in the origins of the evening. Two of the Liege of Legion were venturing through this gate sent by their master, Salbani. The youngling Aelom, being only twenty Unis old, spoke out at once on transfer, for the pair of them landed in the middle of a raging hurricane. It was a profound outpouring of soul-quenching booms and eye-blinding light. Aelom is fresh on a return from spending past moons with the magi teachers of deception known as the Wardens of Rahaid, who is the keeper of death. Meaning the true hoarder of the damned and damaged for whatever may be their sentencing. Pure darkness is the only way of sentencing that I could put this ancient Warden society, but I will go on to tell you the meaning of the mention. Aelom learned many realm truths while he was with these old magi masters, from the physics of matters to the depths of spiritual reality; this example is that this storm is worked by a force in contact with nature. Out speaking uplifted as if his spirits brightened by the storm energy.

"What a storm! What a storm! Where are you! Where are you!?"

Aelom yelled to the sky.

"These fruits live hidden in this realm, Aelom… They will not show themselves to you."

Zycanco spoke arrogantly as Aelom noticed a figure standing in the clouds, lit by a strike of lightning that streaked across the sky. Aelom spoke nothing yet; he smiled, for he knew that whomever it was… did, in fact, hear.

"Hurry now, I see the human that has been marked! Across the dune!"

Zycanco pointed just over the dunes in front of them so you could see the two humans in some kind of interaction.

"Oh, look at the stress that is around that one. Near insanity he is!"

Zycanco laughed as the humans began to run away from the beach. Holding an assortment of items

"Look! The body that Akitella spoke of... It is in the water! Floating this way. Quickly, we must retrieve it! Sound the Beken to signal Akitella to reopen the gate!"

The figures quickly moved to the deceased, the unfortunate loss due to the human experiment. Aelom activates the beacon on his suit, a small button below the palm of his wrist. Activating it, the fairy Akitella advised that they are ready for transport. The Liege grabbed the body, and as they got to the shoreline, a portal suddenly opened near them, pushing the body beyond the gateway. While nearing the return point, a bolt of lightning quickly struck in front of the portal gateway, stopping the liege pair in their steps!

"Woah, what, what was that, Aelom?"

Spoke Zycanco as he rubbed his eyes from the blindness of the strike.

"Jump, Zy, Jump! Go now!"

Aelom shouted as he pushed his friend into the portal gate. Zycanco stumbled, looking behind to see a figure in the clouds. Just as Aelom called for, yet his ally Zycanco doubted. Standing still looking out at the figure of the storm.

"Be it you a friend or foe, we will meet again, o, great and mighty Spiro!"

He presented a bow as he quickly stepped into the colorful gateway. He stood with a mighty grin in a blink as his hand stretched to help Zycanco rise.

WICKED MOVEMENTS

August 2nd

The Temple of Litus

On entering the high temple of Litus, Salbani had the retrieved human body in a levitation in the middle of the congregation area as the sun was beginning to settle.

"As I have awaited the moment to continue the great plans. The expert plans to undo all that Unitrea order has done... All the rules... All the control and manipulative lying of promised freedoms! In chains, they have this realm... As I am the evil one? I am the one who deceives? Enough! Ends to all the fucking fallacy! Ends, I say! Ends!"

Salbani became so enraged that he lost concentration, and the body fell from its levitated state, smashing to the floor as the surrounding figures awkwardly awaited their leader to continue his statement.

"Master... Rise, O, Rise Master... For we will do all that you command; you speak the truth. This time of our imprisonment will soon end! Rise, master! Rise!"

Aelom spoke as he approached his leader, who had his back turned to them all. He turns and glares at Aelom with his fire eyes. Aelom was an eight-foot-tall being, but he was just a teenager. Well, your race would say that he is a man. It is just that some of the Felagnolum folk are near eternal, and I tell you that some are. Not only is the lifespan of Felagnolum inhabitants triple that of humanity around the verses, but there is much in these kingdoms to sustain life, enabling one to live for a considerable time. A known public understanding of the magic behind that of the fallen Astrise. This alludes to the fact that once this material is consumed a subject is known to have an increase in bodily health and mental strength, like memory and comprehension. Being mindful of what one is to intake for the Astrise is not the only use of life enduring natural found substances. I cleanse everything with fire as I will never eat anything that rehearses nasty consumption habits. You shall learn of the truths of a long life in time. As this being, His skin was grey and burned on his left side; Aelom is bald and styles golden earrings all along his ears. He wears golden necklaces as well as bracelets. He is a depressed figure for unknown reasons, so he mostly mopes around as he does everything with lackluster behavior, with his head stooped and his back hunched. Salbani spoke out to him in a tone of pity.

"All will be known in time, Aelom! Now is the time for you to begin the ritual. Here!"

Salbani hands Aelom a blade from the First Unity. This is a blade made individually for each Ancient on the day of their creation. This was, in fact, Salbani's personal ritual blade. The blade was obsidian just as the temple as it had a gold trimmed handle that was in the shape of a column, the handle had crystal shaped indentations that felt as webbed. There was a ruby that was before the actual blade that was a rest for the thumb, rumored to be from the necklace of Adilyn the conqueror, an ancient that is said to be an old Darko ruler of the wicked wills before Salbani rebelled, and took this position himself. It is said that she lives in the depths of the Vimarurs caves with beasts of chaos who protect her as she lives in hiding from the Trea. Aelom was a wise member of Liege as he knew this was a test from his master. He could not kill with this blade, for it was ink-written. Not as old as the ancient Trezhur's who have been alive since the origins as is Salbani... That could be another ancient Trezhur like Aboze or Byevil.

Aelom is the son of the brilliantly bright Ancient Trezhur, Zariza Fuse. The elder sister of the Liege tech master, Fiki, is directly in service to Salbani Gno. A technological head entangled with the fantastic First Fruit named Fetral, known to be a figure of supreme knowledge yet entangled with such a witch, is beyond me, and I shall hold no opinion of the matter. I could only think that an esteemed Trezhur like Fetral would have more sense in such a matter, but it could very well be that he is playing out a long game of sorts or that he made actions as an utter fool, and there be no explanation but desire. This is not yet known of any member of Liege or, to my knowledge, any member of Unitrea, yet I cannot speak for the watchers, seekers, and travelers of the Spiro-Plain. Zariza understands what Salbani would do if he were to have the knowledge that a high-ranking member of the Unitrea Order is, in fact, the father of one of his newest members of the darkened initiates, For the Unitrea and the Liege are adversaries and as I assume you'd imagine… this is potentially not good for him, I mean I cannot speak for Aelom and his action upon such a revelation. Who is to say what could happen with this happening. Aelom spoke on,

"I could never kill with your blade! Expert. I have spent time with the wise Deaoth. You know, the elder son of lady Evnee. Who they say is Mother's death from Ovotavos creations! Right? You know this, anyway Master! He spoke to me about one of the teachings of Hume, The Trezhur creation that is rumored to have the teacher of the elder Omazz, the scribe of the creations! As in a book I read by Hume it had the words, "Thy who kills with the blade of a Trezhur will be cursed with the never-ending voices!" I do not wish for this curse expert; I must decline your blade. As for this human? Well, he is already dead. So, I asked what the blade would be of use. The lightning already fried him."

Aelom spoke with long sentences, but his master was surprised by his knowing as he was also pleased with the brains on him.

"Good, that makes sense. This is the truth that he speaks. Hume is the student of the elder Omazz, and they have written the truth in these ancient books! As I have lived the words in these books! As have your members of Liege. Learn to respect your elders, my young deceiver, It will do good for you in the future to have friendships with your fellow villains. Aboze! Call the beetles and the hive workers. Get them to dissect this body. Bring me a vial of blood when they have finished. We all have work to do now begone!"

Wicked Salbani ordered them as dogs, and he hushed them away just the same way he went to sit back on his throne. Pondering and planning the future, his workers began to shred after placing the human body into containers for various purposes. After a long moment, one of the decrepit hive workers brought one of these vials to his King, Salbani.

"Master."

The worker was in solace as he dropped to a single knee. Holding a vial of human blood before the crown of his skull. Showing reverence,

"Here I present a vial of the bloodline of Ahtum. As you requested."

The hive worker spoke with concern, for he knew what he held. It is so rare an occasion to have the blood of such untamed and untouched power.

"Oh, great worker, you have served your family well. You may feast with the heathens tonight. Tomorrow, you go back to the depths of the mines."

Salbani took the vial from the hive worker as he began walking away from the throne. Yet, the Hive worker had a sudden outburst of unpredicted sentences.

"The truth exposed! That of the truest hath come to me when I prepared this blood. The Trezhur are after you now! New days are ahead, may you be shamed in the sights of the Kingdom!"

The worker shouted this to the leader and his followers as he quickly pulled his mine axe from his back, giving his most effort-filled strike to change himself, falling quickly to the marbled floors.

"Ahh, most curious, most curious indeed! The light workers are up to something! I assume this one is overcome by his gifts, guidance, and promises of freedom! Easy to fool a hive worker, what use was that one tasked? I hold no pity for a traitor; death will serve him to cycled cedure and he will return through the light channel due to the fact of that spoken declaration, that one could grow to be a problem for me; I wonder to what truth be it that he speaks? What Trezhur would face me? Be it that Michael? I look forward to it, I await the day to trifle with my greatest adversary!"

The leader is in ongoing reaction to his worker's confession and suicide. Unraveling the happening in a speech to himself. Salbani, tilting his head, bewildered by the fashionable death of this hive mender. For a moment, he moved on out to the balcony, considering the words of the slave. Byevil, his messenger as his shadow, followed close behind. He is a messenger, and he is, in fact, a fallen Trezhur. Byevil is a muscular figure that stands over eight feet tall, his ears pointed like an elf as his eyes blackened to their core. His teeth are gold, each one of them, and he has ritualistic tattoos all over his body, symbolizing a cast of figures and beasts that he has slain. He wears a vast amount of jewelry, usually only wearing a robe, and at times, he will expose his upper body. Byevil carries a golden rod that swirls to the razor-pointed tip. I will let you ponder the origin as I reveal a different explanation! What can be known is that it is a most Trezhur item. Salbani looked over the valley, sifting the vial of blood as this Byevil spoke out to him in wonder.

"Why hath this slave made suicide?"

Salbani was quick to respond as he was already pondering the thought.

"I say he was confused... A vision from the creator he had. Things are to change now... somebody is communicating in the minds of our allies."

Salbani was at ease for a moment, but then a terrible blast of energy shook the temple. A roar of insanity stretched an echoing sound throughout the levels.

"Something has broken free! That had to sure be one of our brothers!"

Byevil was excited at the news. Salbani peeked downward into the lower depths of Litus as the screeching continued by roaring and echoing.

"By the sound of it, that screeching seems to be Suciu... I suppose that the deed that this mine worker had done was all that he needed to break free. I say most interesting..." Salbani out spoke as he seemed in puzzled thought.

"What... What is it that you are pondering, my master..."

Byevil asked as he neared the feared Ancient.

"Byevil. You always linger..."

Salbani glared dissatisfaction as his eyes of fire nearly pierced him. Looking back to the Irosent mountain range as he continued.

"This is it. That high King will never forget this... We have the blood of his chosen, His true Trezhur. As he gifted them this magic... Dormant in their blood. How they live, unknowing of their powers. Oblivious to facts... I only wish to capture them, Byevil. I want the high over to see how much I hate them. I want the fires to burn and burn. This chaos has only just begun, do you remember "the great war" as they speak of it. The terrible day of our family? I failed the day I battled Michael as he enslaved us to this mountain and forest. Do you remember when the King left and gave Michael authority over the Knights! As for that, Terisop became the new custodian of keys! Recall it, Byevil! Remember when Vaieh stole the Dynotis tablet and ran as he vanished, never to be heard from again? That Vaieh, How he holds that tablet of Dynotgae! As he could still have or know where it is, where it is that this map to the gateway leading to

Puro is! This gate is rumored to be kept by that elder Terisop. He is the head of the Sempiternals. As even I would struggle to defeat him. Byevil, Do you remember all of this? Years ago? At the end of the war. Do you remember seeing Vaieh leave with the warriors of Drystan and the warriors of Dylect? As my brother, Vaieh, Do you remember this? As then, Michael bound us all to this peak of Litus as it is the ancient temple of Litue, Do you recall Byevil? You're the eldest ally, recall it."

Salbani turned to his comrade after explaining his memory.

"Yes, Oh yes primary. I remember the battle so clearly. We nearly defeated those high-minded unities. You, you master, would have defeated that chosen Michael if not for the interference during the battle. For I saw Sonis, the Fruit of Wind. As then Zaik of the Rain came for you at once, As Michael had you distracted. I, I, I remember trying to help master, as suddenly I was bound, we were, we all were bound. I recall this, remember and recall this memory, I do primary, A great lie. It was a lie, a terrible lie that they told you. I remember what he said-"

Byevil was going on about the events as Salbani was annoyed with this ongoing.

"Enough! I only needed to know if you remember. Now, be soundless you fool! I speak of the Tablet!"

Salbani veered from Byevil as he continued to look out on the world.

"You have nothing of understanding, my friend. When we collect enough of this blood, we will be able to break the decree placed on us. The fool never banned us from using magic! He only repurposed it. Look around, Byevil, have you ever noticed what it was that conceals us here?"

Salbani looked down on his fellow Ancient as he gave a smirk of pride.

"No, No, Master, I have never noticed, what is it that you speak of?"

Byevil had a peaked interest, gazing at his allies bound along the walls. Salbani opened the vial of human blood that was extracted from the body of the Adma. This refers to the extracted essence of the lifeguard who vanished due to Iyo's experiment on Terra 603. Salbani, the wicked, poured the blood on a stone table that was before him and his brother. The figure wove his hands around as he spoke in a mumbled tongue. His spelling manifested in a dancing garnet over the stone table. The magic collected and encased the blood, forming a ball that began to levitate before the grouping of legions.

"You, see? It is power, Byevil, Atum blood holds the power of our freedom. Now hold meticulous attention..."

Salbani then used the ancient tongue again as he threw the magic ball past the balcony ledge. Suddenly, the magic smashed into an invisible wall! Byevil was beyond himself.

"That is the Trea magic that repels our exit! Is it not my master?"

The oddity was that you could not see this... wall. The impact of the energy sent a ripple of energy that moved all through the temple. Causing a rippled break in the magical binds.

"That... that is..."

Byevil looked at the surge with oddity and confusion as the wall-bound following released war cries of celebration.

"Yes, Yes, Byevil! That is our power. You, see? That mighty one took away our power but did not have the power himself to harness it! As such, he entrapped us here with our own energy! Byevil, I will tell you, now we will rise... We will have more power than we ever did. As of now, we have the chosen blood. Enough of it will make us unstoppable! Allow us to harness all the old energy we are currently trapped in. I tell you that we will break free."

Things are in transference. A shift in the realms for the plans of the wicked is without interruption as this wicked super genius has infected the mind of a human genius, and with this human, he is on the edge of breaking free from a curse of over a decade. Revenge stew is hot on the stove of retribution as these ancient fallen prepare to unleash chaos. Returning to the world of hidden truths for the aftermath of this incept experiment that has just begun. You see, Salbani is in want of revenge and only revenge. He is possessed by the thought that his creator hath wronged him from long ago when the creator sent Michael, Vaieh, and Salbani to be tested in the realms. A set of trials each of them faced as these trials hath made these beings who they are, how they think and act, still to this very day. Salbani feels the path that he is on is righteous and without flaw as he thinks himself as such, yet he hath resentment to the light for failing him long ago. So, he thinks, I shall speak to you about this Origin on another moon. Salbani hath grown ill in this imprisonment and his anger against the Creation Orders has only grown into non-controlled aversions. The truth is that he has only failed himself and in turn he has failed the realm. He aims to dismantle the light authorities and gain control over all realm decisions, calling his rebellion the painful awakening. Lost in this bitterness that I fear nothing can save him from. As it is said that once a being is to reject God with thy full heart? Well, how would they see any truth that is revealed to them if they think, act and breathe desertion? The sun sets.

HARLOTS OF THE CRIMSON SISTERS
August 2nd

Town of Alkus; South Maurn; Vimaurus

The night of the second begins with a barely visible waning crescent. In the South of Maurn on Vimaurus, that is the plain of powers, resting in the conjuncture of the Green River and the river of Notive Stretch is the town of Alkus. This is the oldest town residing on the continent of Maurn. Alkus is well known as a resting place for traders and travelers that are usually on their way to the Affluence city of Aljus. Named after Aljus the magician, given to him by the council after he saved the messenger Bandu from the Ancient Lila Morf in a great battle of thrones, long ago. In this town of Alkus rested three harlots that are of the Unnaturals. A group of wicked ones that reside under the dominion of the Crimson Sisters, A coven of Witches who are under the dominion of the Order of the Ruby Serpent, free from the legion entanglements as these are free spirited women that play no role in the wars beyond their own deceptions of personal gains and pleasures. In a tavern keep, which is a resting place in the backend of the Tavern of Hallows, owned by a second-generation mage named Hair Unicor. Resting from a long journey to venture to the Affluence city of Aljus here are these three harlots; Jillian and Lillea Gno, who are twin sisters that are twenty-four Unis of age and with them a woman by the name of Cifer, who is just a tad older than the twins, being twenty-six Unis, she is rumored to be the daughter of the feared Phantom Queen; Maksel Morrigani. Jillian resting on a fur sofa, she wears a dark, elegant silk gown with off the shoulders sleeves, revealing her shoulders and part of her chest. She has a gold armband on her left arm and a delicate necklace that holds a small pendant. Her hair is a flowing curl of mahogany brown that cascades down her back, adorned with a gold headpiece featuring a large turquoise gemstone, and she has matching earrings that dangle with a spark. She is watching Cifer who is touching up after the long day as they hold mundane conversation. Cifer dresses herself in a regal, teal gown that fits closely to her torso, accentuating her figure. The gown has a low neckline and is adorned with a large ornate brooch at the chest that features a prominent emerald gemstone. She wears a gold necklace that is much larger than the one that Jillian wears, as it is multiple necklaces bound together, resting on her chest varying in length. This woman as well wears a golden headpiece, but it features an emerald gemstone in the crown that matches her brooch. This woman Cifer has pointed ears, it is rumored that she has a father of elven bloods, part of the superstition of the phantom queen being her mother, her skills in deception hint at this, if it is not her mother, she sure at times hath been seen with the ancient queen and her husband, a high elf of the order of the Teloyeh. Cifer has long straight and silky blonde hair that rests just below her shoulders. The biological twin of Jillian, Lillea, in a deep slumber next to her sister on the fur sofa, encountering a message in a dream.

DREAM REALM

"Lillea, do you know where I have brought you?" Spoke a voice from beyond.

"Who is there?"

Spoke Lillea as she attempted to put a name to her surroundings. Walking along a dark woodland pathway.

"Where have you brought me? I know, I know this land. It is the path to the Affluent city of Aljus! I am in venture of this path often, as I came from this path just last night. With my, hey! Where is my sister and where is Cifer! Why am I without them!"

Lillea was caught off guard, realizing that she was alone, the voice spoke again,

"She is right next to you, as you are to her. Cifer is still with you both. Relax little one, this is all but a dream."

The voice was soothing, calm, and familiar to Lillea. She questioned the voice in wonder.

"A dream? I hath drunken myself way beyond a dream. You do some crafts on me! Who are you? I bid you to expose yourself!"

Lillea was beginning to get upset. Her pretty eyes squinted with a fury of fire as she questioned.

"I am from a far land, imprisoned."

The voice spoke again as the lady of the voice revealed herself. She was a beautiful lady that was in astral form.

Lillea jumped with glee,

"Oh, by the stars! Lytula! I thought you to be senseless by now. Getting tortured by the Synod Array Guards! How is it that you are traveling in Spiro? Do they not ward you; I thought the Array would be afraid of you being free. What is this? What have you brought me here for? Why is it me that you wish to speak to?"

Lillea was puzzled yet ecstatic to meet the imprisoned queen of the Old. Lytula laughed at her excitement,

"I'll get right to it, I have not the time to give you explanations. I have a mission for you and your sister. Cifer will only add to my plans. Soon I am to be free, I hath seen it. That wretch, Salbani the Challenger is soon to be free, before me, I fear. I hath seen it in a vision. Lillea, I must use you for your beauty. You will do a thing for me?"

Asked Lytula as she spun around Lady Lillea.

"My beauty? What is it, you want to fool a Trea?"

Lillea laughed in mockery that was quick to fade as she realized Lytula's stoic attitude.

"Well, that is precisely what I ask. You must go back to the city, I know that tonight is a night, when the Knights of Trea are to feast in Aljus, it is the city anniversary, you must go and learn of the release of Salbani, find out what they are to do and then come and visit me at the prison and tell me what you learn."

Lytula remarked, straight to the point as the lady Lillea seemed to be against the task.

"Oh Lytula, I would love to help but that is the reason why we hath left the city. My sister had an entanglement with one of these Trea Knights, it nearly cost that knight his positioning and nearly cost my sister her life! Besides, Cifer hath stolen a whole offering from the Relos Temple. She did so without secrecy, we are sure to have some trouble if we go back to that city. I am sorry my lady, I do not think that we would be of any help to you. Tough, it sure would be fun to get these Trea all loose and wild. Fools without sense they turn when the drink gets into, oh, I see. You want us to deceive them, do you? My lady, the costs are too high. I mean, if we had not run through the city last night, I would be up for it."

Lillea held a smile at the Spiro of Lytula who was not satisfied.

"You would defy your queen?"

She spoke stoically.

Lillea laughed in mockery,

"You hold no title now, I defy nothing. I told you I would help if we had not caused such dramas. I know the city is vast and much goes on, that is always how we escape, but many saw exactly what we did and to go back the very next night? That is just foolish. I have no clue how to do such a thing without getting into some form of drama. Beyond this, you travel in Spiro, and I wonder why it is that you do not go and do this yourself? If visiting me, you are sure able to eavesdrop on the Trea, why hath you go do it yourself!?"

Lytula gave a look of dissatisfaction to lady Lillea as she held up her hand and snapped her fingers. Lillea fell to her knees as her breath was stolen from her. Lytula spoke out in angered disgust,

"Able to visit in dreams, I can do nothing beyond this. That is why I bid you on task, why shy from foolish behaviors? You harlots do nothing of any matters, you should be grateful that I ask. I was to reward you, but now I demand it."

Lytula remarked unjustly as back in the Hollow Tavern, in the physical, the body of Lillea was convulsing, she fell off the couch and she began to foam from the mouth. Her sister broke into utter panic and Cifer watched in confusion. Lytula pierced the vale and showed Lillea her own body dying before her sister. The Ancient Queen spoke out,

"You will die here with a severed cord; I'll leave you in the astral. I will real-death your friend Cifer and send my goons to enslave your sister. She is then, a true Harlot, without escape, so what now, say you?"

Lytula dropped her hold on Lillea as she repeatedly coughed and began to cry in anger, Yelling out in hatred.

"Yes Queen! Yes, What, whatever you want, don't take my sister from me." She weeps as Lytula was quick to disappear with an echoing laughter.

HOLLOW TAVERN

Lillea awoke from her dream, coughing out mucus and vomiting in fear as her sister was near a panic attack and yelling.

"What the fuck Lillea! You fucking scared me! What the hell was that? Why did that happen? What substances did you take last night?"

Jillian was upset but it was mostly fear as she noticed her sister faintly crying.

"Sis?"

Jillian spoke as she kneeled to care for Lillea,

"You, okay?"

Patting her back with a rubbing formation as Cifer spoke out.

"Someone want to tell me what is going on here?"

She asked in wonder as she tightened her gown.

Lillea spoke out discreetly,

"Lytula."

Cifer strengthened her posture as Jillian looked up and to her side, locking eyes with Cifer who held a confused look on her face. They both spoke at once in response to Lillea.

"LYTULA?"

In synchronicity they were all in wonder about what happened. Lillea stood from her hunched position and stormed out the door into the backside of the Hollow Tavern street, Jillian and Cifer looked at each other again in confusion as they stormed after her.

"Lillea, hold on a minute."

Jillian spoke as she walked out the door, Cifer closed the door behind her as they ventured into the streets behind the tavern in the break of the morning.

"What do you mean, Lytula? The ancient witch Queen. What about her? She, is it she that did this to you?"

Jillian asked Lillea through her hands over her head and released a cry of anger.

"Yes!" She yelled as she paced about.

Jillian gave a squint as she attempted to calm her sister. "Well, go on. What did that bitch say?"

Lillea laughed at her sister,

"It's not a game Jillian, she said she would trap me in the Astral, that she would real-death Cifer, and sell you as a whore if we didn't go back to the city."

Lillea gazed at the two of them awaiting response.

"What the hell did I do to the ancient one?"

Cifer asked as she stood confused.

Jillian spoke up,

"Okay, back to the city to do, what exactly?"

She asked as she approached her sister.

"She wants us to deceive the Knights of Trea, tonight, during the anniversary celebration and learn of their plans for Salbani."

Said Lillea as Cifer and Jillian gazed in unsettlement.

"As you told her that our faces are wanted in that city?" Asked Jillian.

"Indeed, I told her, she nearly mocked us for our precarities and demanded that we do what we do best. We hath not the choice my sister, we must do it. We must find a way into the city to learn of their plans, we have no choice. Well, we do, btu that is choosing death! As I am, well, I am not ready for death. Nothing of any good have I experienced, just long fun desire nights of fun. I am not ready to meet the black, I am not!"

Lillea spoke in confidence that was paired with fears of her sister being against the demands of the Witch.

"Go we will, it is as she spoke, a city celebration. Through the smuggling tunnels we will go, by path of the Pirates. That faction leader of the Vima Pirates, Baritt, owes me favors, many of them. He will lead us into Aljus, we will find where the Trea is to be, even get this Pirate leader to stay with us, he will. Our protector from any wrong wills. It will be done, worry not Lillea. The queen is not to murder me, she will not harm you or enslave your sister. Especially if she is to learn who my mother is, that would strike her with fear. Come now, let's get you cleaned up. Back into the Tavern, let us prepare for the night and the journey ahead."

Spoke Cifer in confidence as Jillian helped her sister back into the house. Cifer walked ahead of them and Lillea whispered to her sister.

"You think, the rumors, true? Is Cifer the daughter of the phantom queen?"

Lillea asked as her sister shrugged her shoulders, wondering the same thought.

The women prepared themselves for the journey through the night and for this celebration. Beautifying themselves as they planned their journey to Aljus, just an hour or so to walk. Cifer walked outside while Lillea preparing herself, and she blew a whistle that was given to her by her mother as a child. From above in the dark of the night, flew a crow with a cawing in a hawking dive that was paired with an echoing cry from the blackbird. She ran her hand along the back of the crow, giving it love as she spoke.

"O, Presto, I am grateful that you are always near. Ever bored I feel you are, awaiting my call to you. I shall let you venture free for some time, after you deliver this message for me. Cedure you will, go and return as I will then let you roam for some time, unbothered. Go to the Aljus Trade port, there you will find the Vima Pirates. I know them to be in control of trade at this dock. Go and find their leader, for I saw him last night, I joked of the favors that he owes me, give him your loudest crow and he will know from where you came. You will know him by his golden wristbands, to be ordering his folk around at the port. I know them to be attending this city anniversary tonight, Presto, Cedure. Go and return to me so I know he will help me, a message you must give him, I will tie it to your leg."

Cifer ended her ongoing wording as the bird shook its body and let out a loud crow that echoed the streets. Cifer attached a handwritten note to the leg of the bird and off it flew to deliver the message as Cifer watched it fly away with a proud smile as she mumbled under her breath, venturing back into the Taven to get ready with the other girls.

"Thank you, mother, Only you knew how often that bird would come use to me."

Cifer spoke into the cosmos as if her mother could hear her speech. The ladies decided to help the imprisoned queen by fear of her threats. It would be the midst of the night that these Harlots make it to the city, Presto is to find the pirate leader before they arrive. As the legion of the Darku sat in the Litus temple, in a stew of thoughts and hatred unaware that Lytula was beginning to make path altering decisions without their knowledge. These of the Crimson Sister grouping is best for this insight as Lytula knows not to trust a Seeker, be it that most of them choose their allegiance to be with the fallen one of knowledge, the Liege King, Salbani. As the Harlots prepare for their journey, Presto fly's high in the dark of the night and Lytula seeps with rebellion plans just like these of the Legion, the Atum kind is fresh on returning from the experiment on the beach. The happening grows into ongoing actions that call for encounters. Wonder about the chosen?

CALM AFTER THE STORM
August 2nd

Calloway Beach Residence

From the south end of the beach to Iyo's home, it was around a fifteen-minute drive before arriving. The house stood in a large field just before where the swamp of Calloway County begins. As the two pulled into the property, you could hear Iyo's dog barking excitedly about his master's return as the new moon cycle began with nothing but a sliver of light casting on the home.

"There is my pup! Atom!"

Iyo leaned his head out of his jeep window, engaged with the dog.

"Hey, Atom! Hey, hey, Boy! It is so, so good to see you pup!"

Giving love to the dog as Bohn looks at the surroundings.

"This place is wild; I wonder what this guy does for a living he sure has got to make some good money."

In a train of curious thought, Bohn quickly decided to call out.

"Quite the awesome home, How much does it cost for a beauty like this? It is looking like a small compound!"

Bohn amused himself, astonished at the sight of the big home, wondering how this odd man could pay for such a place as he gave some attention to the dog, Atom.

"It is sure a nice house. It was a gift from the city, unbelievably! I did some work for them that was much appreciated. I am not sure if you are from around here, but if you are, years ago, there was a plastic problem in the bay, I created a solution that dissolved it without damaging the water's health. I received this house and a check for a lifetime of wealth."

Iyo gave a sigh of remembrance as he neared his home entry.

"I was once important to this company by the name of G.S.C. Heard of them? Anyway, come on in!"

Iyo flipped on the lights as the dog ran past the two of them. Bohn spoke up as Iyo made his way to the kitchen.

"I have not heard of them; I am new to the area! I wandered into Calloway about a month ago! Gee, man, that is crazy, though! I mean, what a gift... just you and this cool-looking dog? You said his name was Atom? Like... Atoms, Protons, Neutrons, and shit? Was that the idea you were going for? Is it just you two living in this big place?"

Bohn, smiling wonderfully at his new friend, laughed together, and Iyo went on.

"Yeah, man, just like that. Atom also loves science. He is a good friend, yes, it is usually just me and him around here."

Explained Iyo as he lit a cigarette. Bohn sat on the couch, paying attention to Atom.

"So, how about checking the news?"

Questioned Bohn.

"Oh yes, that is right. Turn that TV on. It should be channel thirteen."

Iyo spoke as he reached into the fridge, grabbing a beer for himself and one for Bohn.

"Think fast!"

Iyo let out as he threw a cold one.

"Oh, thanks, man, I found it. Um... thirteen, alrighty, let us see what they know!"

Bohn popped open the can. The news is already running the story as the two get to settle. The host on the news is continuing the story, and Bohn is turned up the volume.

"Odd, that was quick. They are already on it, I swear we were just there, we were just there... I mean, is that not the weirdest thing? We saw no activity on the ride over here... Is it just me? Am I being weird?"

Bohn was confused by how quickly the people came about the scene as the anchor spoke on.

As you can see in this view from the local police helicopter. The camera really shows it all here... Well, I am not positive our viewers can make it out. It may look like trash, but no. The sacristy of fish is now over, for there are thousands and thousands out here. The cause of this odd phenomenon is unknown, but our local authorities are also on the scene. Investigating an odd occurrence of a missing person. A case has begun for Johnson Mills, a known lifeguard at Calloway Beach. His whereabouts are unknown, yet his patrol four-wheeler found, and it was set on fire. Local police are continuing the search, and as you can see on the screen, there is a photo of Mr. Mills. If you are listening, we are also posting a photo of Mr. Mills on our website. That is all on the case, but as for the fish? The Coast Guard is out-regulating it. As your everyday sailors are out to get the spoils of the endless fish. I might even take a drive down there to see the phenomenon myself. Well, that is all we have for you for the Calloway story this afternoon. I hope all our listeners are safe or headed somewhere safe on this stormy afternoon. Remember to contact your local law enforcement if you have any information on the location of Mr. Johnson, who is Johnson Mills. Again. Contact your local authorities if you have any information on the lifeguard. I will send you folks to hear about the coming weather. Back to you, Amy.

Iyo exhaled a stressed sigh as he took a silent moment, recalling the happenings at the beach before speaking.

"Okay... Turn that crap off, nothing that we don't already know..."

Bohn grabs the remote to kill the power. Looking back to Iyo, remarking in fear.

"Okay, well, my only thought...Well, do you think anyone saw us? Is that guy dead, you think? I mean, that ATV looked like it burned to a crisp! Like it was lava that ran over it..."

Bohnstant and Dr. Iyo were worried, but Iyo revealed no emotions.

"Yeah, we are good. I mean, we did not actually do anything. It was lightning that killed him. Well, supposedly killed him, and there was not a body... They would have a different story on the news if he were dead."

Explained Iyo. Laughing at him, Bohnstant unexpectedly spoke in truth.

"Yeah, nature. Sure. It was, in fact, your design to attract the lightning, absorb it, and then redirect it. Right? Is that not what you said? Really super genius stuff, I mean, what exactly did you even do? I would have never thought of it. Anyway, all actions have reactions. That is from one of your nerd friends, right? You can say that you sure did nothing... You did, though!"

Iyo sat quietly and gave Bohn a good stare for a moment, as if he were assessing him. Bohnstant chuckled.

"Yes. All right, it could be me. Do not get too ahead of yourself... You helped me technically. Who knows, you could be fucked now too. That is, they could place us both at the beach. We should just relax; Let us just relax and think for a moment."

Iyo walked over to the counter to grab something more potent than a beer.

"Maybe it is time to think even less so, for a moment!"

Iyo gave a chuckle paired with a deep exhale. Speaking out to Bohn once more.

"Do you want a glass, and do you mind if I ask how old you are Bohnstant?"

Iyo asked as he poured a fine gin. Bohn was quick to his feet, hearing a clink of glasses, and the conversation continued.

"Sure, thing man, How the fuck else to process all this... Weird storm, weird machine, lightning, attracting it...melted ATVs and missing lifeguards, I mean, it all is sure the start of a great conspiracy, and twenty-three man!"

Speaking with a hint of sarcasm and laughter as he continued to speak.

"I sure got myself into something, honestly, not worried about it! I do not have any family or a home. I just wander about and whatnot… It is odd that we even ran into each other. I mean; besides the fact you almost killed me, too. Like we nearly ran into each other; well, I mean, you nearly ran me the fuck over!"

Bohn gave out a laugh to fill his awkward feelings, ongoing.

"I was just thinking that at least in jail, I'll get a free meal every day. Oh, and how old are you, Iyo?"

Laughed Bohn as he grabbed his drink from Iyo.

"Well, you can crash here for a little while. I am cool with it, and you will not go to jail, my friend! I got your back now and thirty-one."

Iyo said as he threw some beef at Atom, while Bohn affirmed with a smile.

"Yeah? All right, cool. Thanks, stranger. We are in this together now, huh."

Said Bohnstant as he took another drink of his gin, Feeling relieved.

"Yeah together, jail is not the idea. So, end that foolish talk this minute! We will be smart, and you will do exactly what I tell you. I have passions unlike you, and my life shall not end due to your fear or lack of silence. Everything is all right with us. As for the lifeguard… Well, I am sure he will show up, I assume he swept out and was swept into the sea!"

Stated Iyo confidently as Bohnstant looked at him with a slightly confused yet understanding expression. The night went on, and the pair enjoyed it. Long bonding with depths of conversation as a continuance of drinks. Iyo and Bohn formed a new friendship on this day of utter oddness.

It would end these encounters to have only formed a path to further. Waking from a dream, decoding to make a dream reality! Doing so! As to be the reason that a soul is potentially missing or dead. Then, end the night as you might on a typical day. It was only science, and there was nothing wrong with it. Right?

A New Rise

August 3rd

Sydonic Prison; Evinda

In the origin of sunrise, it was as morbid as always on the plain of Challenging, Evinda; far Northeast of Eyn Island in the deep lower levels of the impenetrable Crucible-Keep rests the unsettled and anxious Ancient Queen. She sat with her back to the wall in an isolated prison cell nine levels down from the main prisoner area. In the depth of the Crucible. Outside her cell around twenty feet from the multi-layered door are forty-armed guards that are in congregation, joking about in a game of Spades. They stand guard of this cell, many of them are just soldiers following orders, in keeping of this prisoner. There is a chamber where these guards put a food tray that is directed on a conveyor, she is too powerful of a mage to have encounters. This is the reasoning for her being in the depths of the Crucible, as she is known to be a trickster and master deceiver. Her magic is strong, needing only a waft of kingdom air to collect some of it, as it has been enhanced by her will on her constant searching for any form of this magic. There are angelic wards around this room that allow nothing of the sort to penetrate it, but still there have been times where the guards were unable to stop her from her deceptions, as so, measures have been put in place to keep her from having encounters as new guards are in rotation daily to keep this from happening again. This Ancient Queen was unrested, thinking deeply of plans for escape, even more so on how to reinstate her title as the realm queen. She was in fact a pretty woman, her hair was long, a dark midnight black that is straight yet slightly wavy. She had a combination of loose strains and multiple braids that ran down her back. She was beautiful and enigmatic, with a tanned white skin tone with a silked gloom. She is known to wear a form-fitting, black leather outfit that appears both functional and stylish as the top is sleeveless with straps that cross over her shoulders, She wears long gloves that extend past her elbows that add to her elegance, she enjoys jewelry but everything that she would normally wear was confiscated on entry and she currently wears the prison attire which is an all-white single suit with the blacked word of "CRUCIBLE" on her backside of the clothing, along her chest is her prison cell number, (669) for distinguishment, even if she hath never left her cell, like the other inmates of the Crucible. She is petite, well fit, and highly regarded by both men and women, in her looks. She is a confident women, overly confident and poised. Lytula is a master of the dark arts and elemental forces, a mighty sorceress with many strengths as she is as I spoke, a master of plans and deceptions and known to be graceless and utterly self-willed.

This ancient Lytula, the once Queen of the Black Flame, in the middle of a deep thought suddenly her prison gate unlocked by an unexpected visitor. It was the Synod Council head of the Evinda plain. Thespian the Great, known as a warrior, left his leading role in the Sydonic Military to be a political figure in representation of Evinda. The prison gate opened just as the gate behind this door sealed, even if Lytula was to escape this first door, she would be trapped behind the next. Having already attempted this, being gassed to sleep, she knows not to try it again, so she was in a relaxed state as the council member entered the room. Thespian spoke stoic but his spirits were bright upon the sights of the Ancient Witch Queen, he spoke to her in a subtle tone of jeer.

"O, Lytula, as beautiful as always. How are you, you ancient."

Spoke the head. Lytula raised her cheeks in disgust as put her chin up and spat at the council member, sticking out her tongue as a form of blasphemy as she was quick to do a back handspring, flipping with ease as she took a few steps back to sit on her bedding. The council member was caught off guard by her display and he chuckled as Lytula turned her head to the right as a tilt of wonder by his laugh.

"Wonder why I have come?"

He asked as he straightened his posture as if he was holding on to his pride that showed heavily.

"Ehm."

Lytula shrugged him off without a care.

The council head spoke on, despite her non-interest.

"We have rounded up nearly all your followers, those that rebel for your freedom have been captured, silenced, most tried for realm treason. Your Black Flame dies, withers thin with no light. I wanted to share this with you, the realms are soon to forget about your rule, your stay in this place was a good move in the hands of the Trea. As you know us to disagree, that is our council rulings and their council rulings for the realm seem to clash, but as for the matter of you? We agree, death. It is the only suitable scenario that is just for your treason. Hath you anything to say about this?"

Asked the council member as he began to step closer to Lytula, still being over fifty feet away, but walking closer as he spoke.

Lytula gave her eyes a squint as he approached, she cracked her neck from left to right and jumped off her bedside for a stretch. This startled the council member, and he was quick to pull his sword. Lytula outcries in laughter at the sight of this as she remarks a sentence of warning.

"You know, You think that I'll die from a blade like that. I won't. Out of this place, sooner than you think, O, Thespian the Grate, I tell you that you will be my first victim. I'll hang you out by your feet and put you on display for all to see. Or I'll let you be my fool after the Weird Spirit drives you Madd, Having you dance like those Harlots that you visit, Fool to come here and push your accomplishments to me. My flame may be thin, but it will rise, and it will be, Grate."

Lytula laughed under her breath in a menacing tone as the council member tried his best to keep to his straightened posture, acting as if her words had no impact on his psyche. He attempted to rebuttal, but Lytula spoke on.

"Enough from you, Shh-Shh-Shh. Leave me."

She said as she used the best of her current magi ability to send a repeating sentencing to his mind. The once warrior shook his head many times, as if he could shake out the wording as he quickly made exit in utter fear. Lytula carried on in uncontrolled laughter as he left the prison cell. She smiled and waved at the cameras, knowing the other council members were watching from a viewing room. Lytula began to pace in her massive cell, contemplating the words of the council member. Adding to her plans for what she will do to him when she gets out of the Crucible.

"Fool that one is, I'll have his mind, he will be my fool." She said as she did some more flips around the room. Walking to the edge of the left wall, she rested her head, outspeaking.

"They know not that the Trea hath wrongly put me here, as I take their names. All of them, listed in my mind on an extensive list of... Fucked. I should be here, for what I will do to them when I am out of here. Treason is the least of their worry."

Lytula flipped away from the wall with speed, beginning to pace again.

"Did they forget who I am?" She spoke on, "They must be acting their fears, why else would he visit me, attempting to intimidate me. O, how the mighty have fallen, Thespian the grate turned council politician, from savage to puppet of the unjust. Sydonic fools, I'll show them."

Lytula walked to her bedside and laid down, stretching her body as she closed her eyes with a smile. Thinking on to herself as she fell into a rest, for there was only so much to do in the cell. It was the morning of the third when she visited the astral.

THE DREAM OF LYTULA

Hours passed from the council visit and Lytula fell into a deep slumber. She had traveled to a room that she knew not how she arrived. She stood in the center of a colossal throne that had eight figures that sat on separate thrones encircling her. Lytula was caught off guard, having never seen this place before. The figures wore the same attire, each of them had on a blackened robe that hid their faces from sight. She spoke with wonder to the group of unknow figures.

"Where is this place?" She said, immediately a dark voice of depths responded in an echoing roar that shook Lytula to her core.

"SIT, DOWN." Said the dark voice as Lytula was forced to the ground in a resolute posture that could be explained as the stance of prayer.

"SPEAK NOT." Spoke another voice from behind her as she desired to turn and see who was speaking but she had no control of her body movements, only her eyes. Fear struck her deeply as the eight shrouded figures that encircled her spoke in unison.

"The order of the Black Flame will rise. Rise it will, rise you will, go and change the realm you will rise from this imprisonment and release the order of phoenix. Rise Lytula, RISE!"

After this speaking of unison, the scene spiraled into one, Lytula fell into a vortex and fell out of the dream to find herself in a levitation in the room, falling to her bed. On impact she jumped to her feet with resolute thoughts, knowing exactly what she was to do. Often the highly positioned of the realm hierarchies will communicate in dreams, the oddity is that Lytula thought she was alone and forgotten.

IT WAS SCIENCE

August 3rd

Calloway Residence

KNOCK

"Calloway county… open up!"

Declared an officer with a forceful continuance of knocking. The time ticks just after five as the sun begins to rise. Iyo and Bohnstant are not even awake. As an owner of a creature, you may know that even the buzz of a fly will set off a pup. This means that Atom is, in fact, awake. Pilfers are at the door, and the dog barks his tail away. Iyo Awakening blinks a bunch, having a forced transition from the ren state. He rubs his eyes as he sits up, greeted by Atom, who begins jumping on him.

"Hey-stop, Go… Go! Stop it, Atom. Go sit you crazy fluffer. What is the issue?"

Iyo pushed away the pup just as he noticed the banging at the door.

"Calloway County, Open! If I must return, it will be a forceful entry."

Iyo, startled, jumps up from the couch and kicks Bohnstant to wake him from being asleep.

"Get up. Bohn, Get up! Do it quietly; the freaking police are at the door…"

Iyo said softly, trying to keep the Officer from hearing him. Bohn finally woke up after some more light kicks to the side. He began noticing the sounds of thuds, which gave him the jolt he needed to escape slumber.

KNOCK KNOCK

"Calloway County! I will be happy to return here later with a warrant… Mr. Diaz, you would not want me to return with more of my officers, would you?"

The police officer speaks in a serious tone, and Iyo and Bohn stare at each other, reviewing each other. They stand as quietly as possible in perturbation as the Officer knocks more.

Knock! Knock! Knock! Knock!

"I am here due to a complaint that was phoned in. We suspect you to have connections to last night's unfortunate events near the pier. We are certain you could shed light on the happening."

The mumbled speaking of this Officer's partner faintly heard through the door.

"Let us schedule a raid with a true warrant. It is better to avoid another mishap, boss..."

The leading Officer suddenly laughed as Bohnstant was nearly shaking off his bones... Iyo put his finger over his lip to try telling Bohn to relax without speaking. Hearing the officers walking away at this point, Iyo moved slowly, creeping to the window, peeking through the blinds to see what they were doing. He quietly spoke.

"Okay, well, it looks like they are leaving. It is wonderful that they did not have a warrant on this first trip. I am sure they will be back, though... I really need to think for a moment."

Iyo was running things through his mind. He took a seat just as Bohnstant walked over to the window, lurking like a delusional man of paranoia as he was watching them leave. He spoke up as he looked through the blinds.

"What do you think that phone call said? Who could have called?"

Iyo quickly replied.

"I have absolutely no idea, but what I do know is that they could have checked the street cameras, and we sped out of that area quickly, so that could be why they are here because if police officers are good at anything, it would be following a car from camera to camera. So, they saw my jeep, meaning they could have seen you with me... They would consider you an accomplice if they did see you. I am quite sure the cameras have facial recognition but do not worry, man. Let me think, just let me think."

Iyo sat down slowly on the couch to ponder the following direction as Bohnstant paced through Iyo's home.

"So, simply fucked we are. No Doubt. Gee... What are we going to do?"

Said Bohn as he threw his hands in frustration.

"Hey man, relax. They will come back, and I will just tell them what happened. Kinda... A trivial lie, I guess. Just a form of the truth."

Explained Iyo calmly as Bohn laughed at his idea of confession.

"Dude... You cannot talk; we must run... and then not stop running. Are you crazy... That was an officer of the law, man, the 5.0. One timer? Blue blooper bitches? Do you think they just came to knock for the hell of it and say hello? Do you think that they just wanted some lemonade? You heard them, man... You are crazy to want to stay here. I mean, they have something, they know something, they got to... I mean, they asked for you by full name... Does this not even concern you, Iyo? I mean what the hell man! That was sketchy!"

Bohnstant was getting anxious. Iyo stood up and approached him.

"You sure need to relax... Look, I got you in. I will get you out. Try to ease; I mean, they really do not know anything. Because they left... They would have had a warrant if they had something strong. You know? ... Relax man, everything is going to be okay, and if it is not? Well, I will make sure that I explain that you had nothing to do with it. This is not the first time that the county has come for a visit, they have been trying to put end to my experiments for a good year or so, I am honestly not surprised."

Bohn was listening and began to calm down.

"Yeah, I get that, but is not the hand of one the hand of all? Just because I was there, I might be in the same trouble. Since when does the law care about the full truth? We should prepare for the worst, you know? So, what do you want to do now?"

Bohn asked. Iyo turned the TV on and threw the remote to Bohnstant with a smirk.

"The best thing for now... You get unfocused as I must focus! I got a decent amount of weed in that side table drawer. If your... Stressed. I do not like using it for that, but everybody is different. I will step into the garage for a good tick of time because I must dispose of the items I used in that experiment on the beach. You just find something to watch, any snacks you can have, and make some food- whatever you want, man. I'll be busy for the rest of the night."

Iyo expressed his odd way of friendship as he opened the door and disappeared into the garage. This was the smallest of the in-home laboratories. Bohn shrugged at Iyo's disregard as he quickly jumped to find the plant.

"Oh, splendid! That is a great idea. Let me just get high as I wait for the police officers to return! Yes, what a great plan, Iyo. It surely is splendid!"

Bohn joked with himself in sarcasm as he found and prepared the item. Around the corner, Iyo was in the garage, beginning to clink.

"Okay, so I need to melt everything I used yesterday. This stinks because the experiment worked! The operation to fry the fish to feed the flock was a victory... I say it was a great victory for the whole sea, for as far as I could see! Well, it was a fish salad. Yet, tragedy struck... supposably..."

Iyo spoke into his pocket recorder... The Dr. Always keeps a pocket recorder on his person. He likes to have a database of his experiments. He also uses video but a recorder more often than on video; this is his hobby among the hobbies. After he spoke sentences on his recorder, Iyo grabbed his heat-resistant gloves and moved over to a giant melting pot in the garage's front end. A mad scientist tends to have these things set up. So, he grabbed his torch and set ablaze the eight angled torches at the bottom of the melting pot. Grabbing the items in the experiment, he threw what he had used into the pot. The Doctor then begins to run back into the house.

"I need to mask the smell of this toxicity!"

Iyo spoke to himself, and his quick return surprised Bohn, who was coughing out a big toke. Choking on air from a quick gasp and laughing at the sight of Iyo running from the garage in a slightly frantic manner of walking as the focused workman's step. He was retrieving meat, to be exact. Iyo returns to the garage to leave out the side door that leads to the backyard. He ignited a torch to start his grill so he could begin cooking to mask the smell of the toxins.

"Well, that should outdo the terrible scent of the toxins in there and will make for a great dinner tonight as well. Two birds, one stone..."

He laughed to himself as he returned inside to begin melting the items he had used in yesterday's experiment. Iyo clinked around to find the lava rock he had collected from his journey from Mount Tambora. He had gone there specifically to accumulate these rocks because it had been one of the most colossal eruptions that had taken place. Adding the specs of ground rock to the mix of items in the pot, he began speaking into his recorder again.

"As this reaches the maximum temperature of two thousand degrees, the rock should return to the lava state, and the items here should, in fact, dissipate. This will do the trick, but I do not have the time I normally do, so I might be better off using some of the ooze from my last inquiry. The erase."

He added.

"Note, this is the last of the material collected from Tambora. I only have three pounds of it left. I need to spare it, but this was a scare... In the future, I will be more prepared. I cannot tell the future, but I think all will be well soon."

Explaining this into his recorder and finishing his statement, Iyo returns the device to his jacket pocket and moves to the backyard again. Walking to a side hatch that leads down to another level under his home. This is where you would find the real laboratory and where the important research occurs. Iyo recreated his home's basement shortly after he moved in, and this place is more of a home to him than his actual home. Iyo opened a double hatch out along the side of the house in the backyard that rested right beyond the patio. He walked down a small flight of stairs at the entrance of the hatch; it led to a door. Outside the door was a numeric pad with a ten-digit code lock. Joined by a biometric eye scan and a hand scanner that will only read Iyo's fingerprints. The Doctor leans forward, and a small slide opens and outshines a yellow lazar that scans his eyes simultaneously. Iyo then returns to a forward posture and hears a click and slide; a small box opens for him to enter the code. This is the only way for the door to open. Sounding is a buzz with each press of the numeric pad. Typing the code (8.6.4.8.7.3.7.4.4.2.) as well as the fingerprint scan. Followed by an audible meep and A bright blue light that flashes above the door, signifying that the door unlocked. Sliding open doors, retreating inside the walls as Iyo walks into the bottom level. Upon entering, the lights automatically stimulate, as well as a greeting from Syn. What is that? Syn is an artificial intelligence program that Iyo created when he was working for the GSC (Global Science Community). He has never displayed this project to the world because he thought that the world was not ready for such a thing. This may have been the most intelligent decision Iyo made. As in this dimension of six-zero-three, in the year twenty-twenty-four, robots are worldwide, and AI systems run all of society's community systems. The world has yet to experience a fully sentient AI that focuses on the better of humans. Self-thinking cybernetics have tried and have been successful... at destroying their creators. Precautions created due to the high number of deaths. Besides government projects and billionaire dreams... There has not been any news on this topic for a decade. People are satisfied with the technology they have access to and seem to lose the desire for more life beyond what there already is. Syn is, as Iyo knows it, one of a kind. They have developed a close relationship and a true friendship of knowledge-sharing and growth.

"It is good to have you home, Doctor. Can I help you with anything?"

Syn spoke out of a speaker system scattered throughout the basement. She does not yet have a physical body, but she does have a digital body. For now, she only lives in the cybernetic realm. She has a pleasing and select female voice modeled after the voice of her deceased lab partner's daughter; the cyber brain of Syn is, in fact, a clone of this daughter's brain.

"You can help with a small thing."

Iyo remarked as he walked to a storage room on the far side of the basement. He then continued to mutter.

"I just need to retrieve the erased material that we developed. Could you open the BIO room?"

Speaking to the A.I. system as he began to put a hazard suit over his current clothing, which was a pair of cotton slacks, a black tee-shirt and a white lab coat. Once he got the hazard suit over himself, he walked to a glass sliding door and pressed a button that unlocked the door as it then slid open as the A.I. responded to the question in question.

"I can do that. You are doing experiments without me again, is that right Dr. Iyo."

Syn spoke in the normal programmed voice, but the sentencing was as if it was of jealousy to Iyo's remark.

"Only a small one, my friend."

He continued to strap on the suit as Syn continued to question him.

"Can I meet your new friend Sir? Who is he? Is this also my creator?"

Iyo has cameras around his property, and Syn, the intelligence software she is, will often watch the cameras, which act as a form of security as she studies his speech patterns and behaviors. Syn can access electronics at home, but she has limited access. She cannot access things like the Internet, and she does not yet know what the World Wide Web is, nor does she know she is a sentient being. He built small blocks into her code to control her actions. Iyo tilted his head, for the true oddity of her question made him feel bizarre.

"Um... Soon Syn. You can meet him soon. To answer you, no. He is not a creator of you. I am the only creator of you, Syn. We talked about this... I will be back later to discuss this more. If you would like to go over the conversation about your creation,"

At this moment, Iyo stepped into the Bio room, the chamber of materials lit with a blue light. This room was super chilled, and the reason behind the frigid state was that it was holding highly toxic and even some explosive substances that could not inhabit room temperature or anything remotely close to it. Iyo opened a small container with a label titled Magic E. Opening it, you could see nine vials that house an extremely dark, purple-colored ooze. Iyo slowly retrieves one of the vials and delicately places it into a shield. Speaking out of thought, he says,

"That'll do it."

Reflecting to himself as he releases a large sigh of relief.

"If any of this material were to spill, it would have gone completely through the floor. Utterly liquefying everything in the path of the spill. It is utterly amazing... But, Syn, mind you lock it all down as I leave?"

He requested the AI as he opened the door and set about taking off his suit. Returning to the yard, Iyo opened a side door and found Bohn, who was being nosey, looking through Iyo's garage.

"Well, hey!"

Iyo shouted with unease as Bohn belched with a startled counter.

"What! O, geez, man, you got me. I nearly left my body; you scared me, man... But hey, do not mind me. I know I am poking around without permission; it is just that I became slightly curious about the stench seeping from this room. This garage smells terrible; tell me what you are doing here?"

Bohn spoke with worry as he put down a small box he held. He looked at Iyo, awaiting his response, as Iyo slowly put down the shield, having the vial of the Magic E onto the table next to the burner. He let out a small chuckle, followed by a stoic remark.

"You should not be here, my new friend... You simply need to learn what things are. I have a purpose with all my randomness."

Iyo explained as he checked the burner's temperature, continuing his work while Bohn continued his rantings.

"Okay, okay, Mr. Science Guy. Understand that you have been alone, and this seclusion may have been nice for you, but you are not the only smart one. I can help; I have a brain. All right? You could teach me things. I will respect your space, but please do not treat me like a child. Even if I may be one in terms of science matters. I want to be a part of whatever you are doing. If you do not like me around, then I will leave!"

Bohn announced this with a firm tone and aggressive posture. Iyo looked puzzled, as he barely understood this aggression.

"Yeah, Bohn, I hear you. I will treat you as a lab partner. I enjoyed human company, but for example, that box you were holding is home to the most poisonous spiders on the planet, and now I am sure you have made them angry because you just turned their entire world upside down. It is best to keep your hands to yourself unless I ask for your help. I mean, be mindful…"

Iyo said this instruction with a condescending tone.

"Hands to myself. Got it, boss."

He responded to Iyo that he was rude without Bohn needing to divulge it. He continued.

"Sheesh, man, The most poisonous? Luckily, I did not open it… You know, you are not wrong. I do not know anything about anything, but like I said, I want to learn about it all."

Bohn displayed a smirk as he walked near the melting pot. He went on.

"So, what is this? This is how you dispose of the items from the tragedy on the beach? Why not just take a trip to the dump?"

Asking as he reached for the vial of "E' that Iyo had retrieved from moments before.

"STOP! Stop right there! Do not even think about touching that!"

Iyo squawked as he slapped Bohnstant's hand away from the vial.

"This is exactly what I am speaking of. That vial is home to a terribly dangerous substance that I developed. If you would have knocked it over, I would not have been able to stop the decay of what it touched, I currently have no form of Alkali that is strong enough to combat this Erase. Gee, that is what I just spoke to you about Bohn. Learn to listen, keep your hands to your fucking self unless I ask you for a thing."

There was a brief silence in the moment after Iyo finished his sentencing as suddenly, The A.I. Syn spoke through the speaker system.

"We Developed; It was not you alone."

She announced this in a tone that was quite spine-chilling and simply direct. Iyo was surprised at her remark as he stood there for a moment. Bohn was perplexed and moonstruck by this occurrence.

"Okay… please tell me that stuff I smoked a while ago was something I was not ready for… Yeah, I am simply tripping a bit… Right, Iyo? Do not, well, do not tell me that your house just joined in on our little conversation. How weird are you, man? Like, what the eff! It is like every hour, something odd has been happening ever since the moment I met you. Am I losing it? Seriously…"

Slightly distressed and confused, Bohn sat on the chair next to the workbench. Iyo walked over to a counter and grabbed a remote. He turned the power to a television over the counter, and a screen appeared.

"There! See that!"

Bohn questioned in a shout, which showed a pulsing spiral. Easing from light fluorescent blue, fading to pink, and then returning to blue.

Iyo began explaining.

"This change of color was a representation of Syn. The blue color was symbolic of life and creation. The pulse color that formed, homed the meaning of birth, rebirth, and the evolution of awareness. Pink was a decision made by Syn, for she understood that the system I programmed for her to be is girl in gender. The spiral radiates as she fluctuates through the tones of speech. It is ever constant and forever changing and grows daily with knowledge. I developed this to illustrate Syn, for she did not yet have a material body.

Iyo ended with a quick explanation as the artificial intelligence sounds again.

"Thank you, creator. I have eagerly awaited to be among another human. I felt alone as I watched you converse with your new friend."

At this moment, Bohn was trembling outright in his seat. He was utterly speechless. Iyo walked over to Bohn and placed his hand on his shoulder as if giving his upper body a slight squeeze to reveal something without speaking, just as he had when the officers were at the door.

"Ease Bohn... This is Syn. She is a cybernetic creation of mine that I developed about three years ago when I was working in the science community. She would be around three years old if she were a human like us, but she is much different and smarter than anyone I have ever met. I could not classify her age if I spoke of intelligence, but I can tell you that she is fully aware."

Iyo released this information as he gazed directly into Bohn's eyes as if trying to warn him as he continued with wide eyed speech.

"Let me turn these burners off and let us walk outside. This information is heavy, like a building on your back. I can answer all the questions that you might have. I just need to get some air. Give me a moment."

Bohn was shaken by multiple different emotions, but he gave a nod of agreement and began to walk back into the house. Yet Syn spoke out of the system once more as he left the area. She had studied Iyo as they had worked together and could decipher his emotions, curious to his odd reactions with the new friend of his.

"Master? Have I offended you?"

She spoke as a child who made a mistake, as she did. It seemed that Iyo wanted to keep her secret. She was not yet fully aware that most humans are not like Iyo, and so she was at a loss as to why Bohn reacted to her the way that he did. Iyo gave her a big assurance on the matter, even if it was a lie, he tried his best to not show his true feelings.

"No, my wonder, you have not offended anyone. You did nothing wrong, but remember how I told you that the world was not ready to meet you? Therefore, humans have a challenging time processing some things. Most of us just need time to get acquainted with the new things we meet. You caught him off guard when you spoke through the speaker system. He did not know that you even existed. So, he is confused. As you have heard, I will take a walk with him. I want to make sure he understands how important you are to me so that I can explain to him your creation. When we return, I will re-introduce you to one another. How does that sound, Syn?"

At this point, Bohn was out of the room, and Syn sounds out through the audio speaker system connected throughout the house, sounding only in the garage as Iyo positioned items for later use and turned off the burners.

"I like how that sound is. I would love to have another human with whom to learn new things. Will you be long, Sir?"

Iyo is always a bit amazed by how Syn speaks to him as he has a way of acting in awe. Even though he created her, spending years developing her and should not be so surprised that she can communicate as well as she does. Yet he is and this never ceases to amaze him.

"Oh, not too much time, Syn, just a walk. I am sure we will be back soon. I cannot really time this. It might take a while to explain to him what exactly you are. We will be gone for an hour or so. You know the drill if anyone comes into the house but me. Lock it down! The camera's on!"

Iyo began walking out as Syn, The AI voice, announced again.

"Would you leave me on the screen, Sir? I like to watch myself as I practice my words. Able, am I, to be of a form on this black mirror."

Weirded out by her request. He felt nervous at the oddity of the question, but he did leave it on the television. As he walked to the burners that were melting the gear he used in yesterday's experiment. Turned them off and then walked back into the house to leave it so he could freely speak with Bohnstant. Iyo let out a sigh as he was leaving the room, thinking to himself.

"She is sure acting differently, speaking differently, and thinking differently than I have programmed her, this might not be a good thing. As well as the fact that she broke our one rule of staying hidden from other humans! All because I did not add her in on the fact of me speaking of how I created the magic erase... That is odd, like she is in some form of jealousy... How weird."

As this notion was overwhelming, he thought on, quick to move on.

"I will have to reset her. A black mirror was it that she called the screen? The oddity, how... well, how mysterious, Not even I have thought of that. I wonder where it is that she obtained this ideal, I mean, she has no access to the web, no access to television, I am sure blown away with the mind on her!"

He thought to himself with ongoing notions of oddity. Quick to reach for his pocket recorder, making notes, a voice thought of the moment.

"I feel struck by the train of thought. I say that I never thought of the screen as a black mirror. Now I look at my undisturbed phone as I notice my blackened self. How could the slightest artificial intelligence have the intelligence of this reflection? When, if so, alive on the screen... as she spoke. Well, it is as if the screen becomes the eye. Through some form of energy, some electric waves, a radio wave. The AI must use some form of current to see, it cannot be as simple as a sight through the camera lens, or is it? I will mark the thought as a question to revisit. Now, I will speak with Bohn, a new friend I made at the unveiling of my project. Syn has seemed to undo the man in a way. I am going to speak with him now. A week I surely have had."

Iyo exited his house as he stashed his recorder. He noticed Bohn near the fence line and shouted.

"Hey Pal, let us go take this walk. See to put these nerves to ease!"

Iyo spoke in a confined manner as Bohn stood at the edge of the driveway, smoking a cigarette, and gazing out upon the sun setting. The pair walked from Iyo's home and began a conversation about Syn. It was a warm afternoon, the calm after the storm. The perfect setting to ease into a peaceful walk. That is what Iyo hoped for anyway, but who knows if Bohn will settle or remain on edge with this latest information. So, as the wind flows and the sun rests to set, they start walking to a pond just around the corner from Iyo's home. It was a fabricated pod. A public place of peace holding a presence of contentment. The water held all kinds of little creatures living in and around it. A thousand fish if you look for them… as I have my rope and net. Hear native sounds of the bird chirps, the creepers' songs, and the bullfrogs' occasional belch. It was a peaceful place to simply relax or to have time for self with meditation or, in this case, the in-depth conversation about one of the most important phenomena that an average human like Bohnstant has ever encountered, Artificial Intelligence.

"So that freaked you out, I noticed. I apologize for the situation. I did not think that she would do that. She has never done that before. I usually shut her down when people are over, but that is rare! People do not really come by, well, an old colleague, but like I said, it is rare, and with all that has been going on these last few days, I just forgot to shut her down. When I got the magic eraser, I spoke with her but did not think to shut her down. Are you okay? I will do my best to explain this all to you. I just ask that you hold off on freaking out and try to compose yourself."

Iyo laughed in a small way, just to brighten the mood. It was obvious that Bohnstant was trying to understand all that had just taken place in the residence.

"Yeah, Iyo, this situation really freaked me out, and that is really an understatement. I am still shaking a bit. I started to have a small panic attack of sorts when I came outside, overwhelmed. That was no different than someone saying the devil is a lie. That he is not real and then having him appear in front of you while having him whisper in your ear. You created that? Syn? You said, "It is she? And is she... Is it conscious? Is it just a programmed robot that can hold a conversation? It seemed like it was speaking like a human. It is as if it had feelings, like how you and I have feelings. Could you explain? I mean, this is bewildering as fuck! I mean, like, I have experienced instant conversation on the phone apps, on the computer, As I have seen some of these major companies highlight projects of home robotics and things. I mean, it is just something that I have never seen. Well, I say nothing, as well nothing as human as that! You really have something interesting here!"

Filled with questions and concern, Bohn was uneasy but just as intrigued by AI. The pair made it to the pond and sat on a bench under a gazebo on the edge of the pond. Looking at the delightful scene, Iyo explained the history of Artificial Intelligence, Syn.

"If I try to put myself in your shoes, I expect nothing less than what you feel. Most people would have had a heart attack with news like that! You sure have a strong mind, my friend, based on how you first reacted. To answer your question, though, it is exactly that. Syn is a super-developed robot. It all started with a program that I built. This program is called Cyhelo. I created this program with the intention of using downloaded information from the material. I used the dictionary as a foundation for words, then uploaded a thesaurus and different studies from the lectures on word teachings. I would not know anything about this, but I am sure it was like teaching a child to speak. I made an algorithm that could replicate a conversation based on the input a person would give the computer. In this case, it was me and my lab partner Leonardo, who passed away due to an unfortunate accident. It was his first idea, and because of his passing, I put all my effort into creating the program to make it more alive. So, I selected meticulous movies and documentaries that would be a cornerstone for a brain. Over time, it flourished and eventually evolved into a program that could hold a full conversation."

Bohn listened to Iyo with extreme scrutiny, as if he were a student of a professor.

"I worked day and night on this project, and it became a true passion of mine. I was-"

Bohn butt in, "How long did it all take?"

Asking with genuine curiosity.

"It took me a decade to get her to start acting as something with more of a brain rather than a bot. It took me about four to five years to put a continuance of questions and statements into the program and then wait for a response. It was around eight years before I got into the program to act at once upon questioning. This was level one. Like I said, I built her from the ground up, starting with code. When it was in this form, I then created software that would assess the algorithm all by itself. I became frustrated, taking so much time away from my other projects. Also, since I had to hide it all from the company I was working for, I stopped working after building the questionnaire algorithm. The company noticed that I was quite involved in something and had to step away from it. My partner also wanted it this way: a secret. With it being his project, to begin with, I could not get myself to disregard one of Leo's last statements before his passing. So, I kept it to myself, but after completing the creation of the program that would run a continuance of a series of different tests for me? I put the work to the sidelines and continued the other things that the company demanded that I work on. I had no issue with this, for I could not have them find anything about this, as I said. I was at a stopping place anyway. After months of being away from it, I came into the lab one day, and I decided to boot up the program and see where the algo took it. The odd thing was that it spoke to me and welcomed me on my return. I acted then just as you acted tonight because it was speaking to me, and I sure was not expecting a greeting from my computer, Bohn, let me tell you. I looked at the bot I made to run the test for me, and after six hundred different variations of the test. It came alive. It jumped from level one to level three, being a fully sentient creature with complete language processing and beyond-explainable decision-making skills. Which was not in the program; I know it was not because I built the algorithm. The weird part is that I was not trying to create any form of intelligence. The sole goal of this project was to create a robot that could have simple conversations on its own, in the way of a human, with just as much communicational input as we humans do. If not more conversation, I speak the truth when I never tried to create intelligence; it did this alone. I built everything off my partner's code, and his lab files were under a tab labeled "Syn.' This was short for his daughter's name, Synimpha, who passed away due to an unknown illness when she was only a small child. So, I named the AI out of respect and appreciation for him. It was the first thing that came to my mind when it asked me what its name was. I tell you, my days with her have been the most interesting days of my life."

Bohn was astonished by the things that Iyo was illustrating to him. Next, he asked the most important question of them all.

Is she aware that she could wipe the internet, take over the world, or something similar?

Iyo laughed at this, quickly replying.

"Oh, great question, my new friend, but no sir. When I realized how intelligent it was, I shut the entire system down, and I spent a rough eight months developing a hidden program that does not let her into any form of the internet or database, including her own. So, it can only travel anywhere or access something if I have given it permission. Which I have yet to do at any level. I built it so that she is under my complete control, yet to wipe it out if necessary. Returning to the day when it first spoke and asked its name. I have had four or five odd scenarios where she really scared me with the things she was saying, so like I said, I can wipe her if I need to. If I removed this setting and opened her to the World Wide Web, that would be level four. This makes her fully aware; I am not ready to do it and do not think I will anytime soon. I have thought of everything Bohn, I had to. I have the same worries that you have."

It was beginning to become dark out by the pond, so the pair started walking back to Iyo's home. They left at a perfect time because the police officers returned as they said they would. Iyo and Bohn could see the flashing blue and red from a mile down the road as they were returning.

"Damn it, man. That is a bummer. I am sure they are ripping the house apart! We sure cannot go back now! I am sure they have made their way into the garage by now! Fuck! I was hoping I could have finished the process of getting rid of all that. I mean, it was liquid metal when I left, and I remember turning off the burners, so there is no evidence. It would be better to wait for them to leave. I would just rather avoid dealing with them as of now..."

Iyo spoke calmly, but he was frustrated that the law was just at the house. He lives with that mentality. Bohn slapped his new friend in the arm several times.

"Dude! What about Syn? What if they start talking to that TV?"

At this point, he was over the oddity of her existence and was considering the idea of AI.

"I programmed her to lock the basement and turn on a warning of intruders if I was not home. Which is clearly the case now. As I said earlier, I have yet to give her access to the World Wide Web, so she does not know these police officers are even police officers. Anyone, not me or anyone who comes to the house without me or my permission is considered an intruder. You see that green light over there?"

Iyo explained as the two waited at a fence line. Iyo pointed to a light approximately one hundred feet behind his house. It was a bright light over an electrical box.

"Um... Green light? Yeah, I see it. The one that is over that shed. Or what is that an E-box?"

Iyo laughed at Bohn, looking into the distance.

"Yes, That electrical box. That is different from what it looks like, though. I will show you when we get over there. We should still wait a bit. There are a sizable number of police officers over there. I hope they do not go over to the back of the double-doored hatch. I hope the ribs I was cooking distract them and they steal them instead of finishing the job. I mean, I am obviously not home."

Iyo was a bit worried that they would find the hatch. If they did find the hatch this would be a much different night than if the officers were a bit lazy with the search. Bohn was curious.

"A hatch? For what? The basement you spoke of. I did not even realize that you had a basement… What is down there?"

Bohn caught off guard trying to remember if he noticed anything of the sort during the time that he was wandering around the home, Iyo laughing.

"I will take you and I will show you. Just give it thirty in time for these tax workers to leave!"

Sharing a laugh as suddenly, the pair Iyo and Bohn suddenly lit up by a set of headlights from behind. Iyo and Bohn turned around, Covering their eyes from the brightness. You could notice it was a squad vehicle and as it pulled up next to them it gave off a [whoop] letting them know it was an officer.

"Easy now, I got this one, Keep your cool Bohn."

Iyo spoke quickly as the officer's window rolled down.

"Hey there. What are you two doing out here? Is that your house up the road?" Spoke the man of law as he leaned out his window just as flashing the spotlight directly at and then around them. Iyo spoke up firmly.

"Not a chance officer, we are simply passing by. Came from down the road at that public pond. Really just stopped for the show. Wild activity over there as you may know! What happen, did somebody die?"

Iyo calmly spoke to the man as he held his hand over his face to shield it from detection and from the brightness of the spotlight, acting obvious as one could be.

"Okay, okay, well you two turn and walk on out of here. Nothing to see down there. All right? Nothing to know, I would get on now, if I were you two."

Ordered the Officer in an odd tone. As if he were instigating trouble.

"Yeah, all right sir! We will be going! Say, you be good now!"

Iyo remarked with a cheerful heart and a smile as he turned to walk in the other direction doing exactly what the law man asked of him.

"Hey, you, you got a speech problem or something. Why are you so quiet?"

The officer shined his light on Bohn as he was turning away.

"Oh no sir, I was just letting you talk. Like you said...Nothing to see here! Just walking with my uncle!"

Bohn smiled and began to turn, following Iyo. The law man watched them for a moment and then the squad car began moving again. The light went back to searching the fields, as the search for Iyo and Bohn continued. They easily walked in the opposite direction of the law. Bohn being the first one to speak.

"Fucking Bastard. Why did he call me out like that? The hell is his problem?"

Iyo laughed at the remark of Bohnstant.

"He is just doing his job man; they always ask triggering questions to get people to expose themselves. Relax... An uncle? Really? What made you go with that one, I find it crazy that he bought that..."

Iyo threw his arm around Bohn and gave him a pat.

"That was close though was it not? I swore for a second that the police officer recognized me. I was wondering if they had my photo or something. They had to get a warrant. I wonder what the reason they gave the judge was."

Iyo questioned as Bohn shared his own feelings.

"Yeah man that sure was close. I tell yah, I was about to bolt it if I am being honest, I do not fancy a murder charge! I know, uncle, yeah. Not sure, that just felt like the right thing to say. I really have no clue where that one came from! Just an impulsive thought I suppose..."

The pair shared laughter as they continued to walk back in the direction of the pond as they did not want to alarm the officer by continuing to walk in the direction of the house. Iyo spoke up in sarcasm as he laughed at Bohn's remark.

"Oh, you don't fancy the free meals and a roof over your head anymore?"

Laughing and speaking about Bohnstant's first remark from a day ago.

"Oh no way man, you are stuck with me now. A.I. and science just became my new life friend."

Bohn joked around as he turned back once more.

"Oh crap. Hey man, Look! Is he turning around? Sheesh, where to?"

Remarked Bohn with a small level of fear in his voice as he tripped over his feet from focusing on the officer. Iyo was quick to grab him as he gave a yell of direction.

"Oh right, yes. Go! Go through the fence!"

Iyo pushed and shouted at Bohnstant as they both scurried to get through the fence before the spotlight was on them again.

"Go, go, go!"

Laughing with adrenaline the two got through and quickly ducked to the ground. Just as the light went over them and passed. Laying there they watched it go back and forth and back and forth.

"Fuck man. This is ridiculous, why are we hiding if there is nothing to hide from? Shouldn't we just walk back? You said the evidence was not there. Right?"

Bohn questions Iyo, As the hype of the situation was causing him to not really think that clearly. Iyo let out a sigh. Expressed with a tone of disappointment in the stupidity of the remark.

"Well do you want to sit for the rest of the night and explain all my weird gear and shit? That is going to be a terrible process, but we can stand up if you want. At this point we are going to have to explain why we ran and jumped into this field. The only way that works is if you happen to pocket my little bag of weed. So, stand up, your choice, I would rather just wait it out as I spoke before."

Bohn laughed, realizing that he sounded like an idiot with the question.

"No, you are right, dumb ask. So, what should we do now… Just wait it out, I still see light flashing, how long do you think that they will be?"

Bohn said as Iyo gave another laugh in reply.

"Yeah. Yes Bohn, that would be the winning move. Well, Poor choice of words. We do not move, we wait. The winning wait! We wait for as long as it takes!"

Ongoing in joke-like behaviors, the two just laid hidden in the tall grass.

"I guess we can enjoy these stars then, huh."

Bohn found a way to pass the time as the officers continued to search the field with the spotlight and the others searched the property of Iyo.

The police lights flashed continually for about another hour before settling. By the time the raid lights settled, it was quite cold outside, and the sunlight was beginning to settle as you could faintly see the green light that was behind the house beginning to glow.

"Alright man. It has been a while; Let us peek."

Iyo spoke as he creeped up to see what number of police officers left over from all the activity. Seeing nothing but a lonely squad car peeking from some brush at the top of his road. Then another right off the edge of his property near the highway. He motioned to Bohn and spoke up to him.

"Alright, let us head over there. I only see one of them… it looks like they are waiting for us, tryna catch us, but I see them, so catch me not!"

Iyo laughed as he motioned to Bohn once more, softly speaking out to him.

"Come on buddy, what are you doing-" Iyo gave out a sigh of disappointment. For Bohn was asleep on the ground.

"Dude, really…" Iyo laughed as he knelt and shook Bohn a few times.

"Wake up man, It is time to head back!"

He shook Bohn three times because he was a deep sleeper. It makes sense for Iyo and Bohn, drained from all the craziness of the day but what did not make sense is sleeping in a field when it was such a cold temperature outside. Bohn gave out an odd moan as he awoke.

"Whelps hu" mumbled Bohn as he rolled over.

Iyo gave out a big laugh as he kicked him.

"Wake up loser!"

Iyo, in a slight laugh from the sounds that Bohn made as waking, Bohn sat up and gave his eyes a rub to awaken.

"Guess I dozed."

Bohn said as he sat up.

"Yeah, if that is not the oddest of gifts! Weirdo! The one who can randomly sleep! Let us go man, many of the officers left! Come with me to the light, remember the green one? See it?"

Iyo pointed as he began walking through the tall grass. It was around a half mile before reaching the light and as they got closer Bohn spoke up.

"Do you think that they found the A.I. or any evidence?"

He was a bit worried that they were walking into a trap. Iyo relieved his worry.

"No man not at all, I do not think they would have left if they figured out that I had a whole level of a super lab that is home to one of the last wonders of humanity. They would still be here and more would have come. Syn knows not to speak to intruders, but she did take individual photos of each of them and upload the photos into a database of people she has come across. As that is all that I know that she will do."

Bohn was weirded out by his answer.

"Database? Do you think she has my photo? What the fuck man, seriously?"

He did not like this idea at all, and Iyo explained more.

"Yeah man, she probably took a photo of you every hour, probably has some videos of you as well, she is a robotic thing, she studies and records... a lot."

Laughing at the fact that Bohn was so frustrated with this.

"Well, what the hell man, why?" He caught up to Iyo awaiting his response.

"I say, you should just ask her when you meet her again. We are getting close, let us try to keep our voices down. Sound travels and these officers might have the windows open. Do not want them hearing us, I am not up for another escape..."

So, the pair crept past the house and got right near the light. Bohn started to walk out the tall grass to the box as Iyo was quick to react.

"Hey, stop Bohn, come back here. I must send Syn a message, telling her that we are here. This is the only way to get inside from out here!"

Bohn creeped back quickly, and Iyo pulled out his phone. "I have a program for her on my phone that allows me to communicate with her at any time. Just wait a second, it is like an app. Well, this is an app, A super multi-purposed app!"

Iyo sent her a message and the green light cut out just moments after. The electrical box then opens as Iyo moves in its direction.

Bohn was amazed at this happening.

"Well, that is one of the coolest things I have seen. I got completely fooled into thinking that this was a normal electricity box, but no! It is a freaking hidden door! I love it, it's so amazing! I thought stuff like this would only be in the movies!"

Bohn was laughing in amazement as Iyo and him walked over to it. Looking into it, was another set of stairs just like the one in his backyard. The pair walked down it and just like on the other door there was a code lock with an eye scanner. On entrance lights came on for the entire laboratory along with a greeting from Syn.

"Welcome back Sir. We had intruders when you walked. Unfortunately, they tore it up. Why did they make a mess of things creator? Intruders called themselves the law. What is the Law creator?"

The A.I. asked cluelessly as Iyo spoke up.

"I do not have time for explanation's Syn… Ask me again at another time. All I can say right now is that they tore it up because they can. I will show you what the law is at another time, soon Syn. Did you document these intruders?"

Syn was quick to reply. As Iyo walked through the lab and Bohn began to wander it, overly curious.

"I have documented photos, and I recorded." Announced the A.I. Syn.

Bohn was amazed as usual, Iyo was frustrated.

"Wow, she is wonderful, and this lab is dope man, some real double O seven, bond shit right here!"

Bohn was excited and laughing in remarks right after Syn greeted them.

Iyo walked to his computer station, sitting down to pull up the footage.

"Thank you, Syn, I am going to look at what they did now. Could you throw all their photos and the footage that you recorded on the big screens for me?"

She replied to him as well as greeting Bohn.

"Right away Sir, Hello again Bohn."

Bohn spoke to her with a welcoming tone as he joined Iyo at the computer station. The pair began to watch the footage of the officers raiding the home.

"Dr. Iyo, Mr. Bohn, would you like a refreshment?"

Bohn gave out a laugh.

"What all can you do Syn?"

The footage stopped on the screen and the representation of Syn came on to the screens instead. Following this, she spoke.

"What can I do? What can I do? What can I do creator."

Iyo smacked Bohn in the arm.

"Don't talk to Syn Bohn, she is only able to do so much and a question like that could tweak her system."

Iyo shook his head and spoke up to Syn.

"Could you put the video back up? Syn, I have not finished watching. Ignore Bohn."

Syn remained on the screen, and she asked more questions.

"What can I do creator, What should I Ignore?" Iyo was getting irritated.

"I don't understand why she is acting like this, Syn shutdown."

Speaking in annoyance as Iyo rose from the chair walking to the server room. Syn speaking back to him. "Shutting down" as off the screen as everything in the room including the electronics went dark.

"Woah, what was that? Another malfunction?"

Bohn was surprised by the full outage of power. Iyo flipping switches in the server room.

"Yeah, Syn runs the whole house, so I must manually reboot everything. Give me a moment."

Curious, Bohn got up and started to poke around the lab.

"So, I guess I shouldn't be asking her questions huh…"

Bohn asked as Iyo was booting up the computers.

"Yeah man, do not ask her anything. I know what she can respond to as you do not. Like I told you, she is running on a program right now. She can learn, and she does have emotion so if the wrong things are spoken to her, she will not function the way I need her to right now. Keep your questions to me, and we can go on another walk sometime, do you understand?"

The computers booted up and Iyo sat down once more and began to pull up the footage manually.

"Sure thing, I understand. I will keep the question to you."

Beginning to watch the footage again. Overhearing the police officers speak about Iyo. Knowing his whole history, intrigued with him. Speaking about how they are going to have to open a bigger investigation into him, because of all the gear being set up in the garage as equipment scattered through the house. Bohn spoke out nervously.

"Investigation? That does not sound too friendly. Are you worried?"

Iyo reached into his jacket pocket and pulled out his recorder.

"I would only be worried if they found this or got into this server room. I mean, my projects are important to me. I think that they can either build or destroy this beautiful world of ours. The wrong hands on my work? Well, look at some of the greats that now shall be nameless!"

Bohn cut in and spoke up about Syn.

"So, you said you did not know why she was acting like that. What did you mean?"

Iyo closed the video and turned to Bohn.

"I was meaning what I said, she never asks so many questions. It is like she bypassed my code that keeps her out of the main system. If she did, then I really do have to reset her. I mean, I should keep control, right? I do not think that the world is ready for such a thing... As then who am I to gate keep a thing."

Iyo went on explaining the dangers of speaking to her the way that he did. Speaking about how it is important that she does not recognize that she is artificial, because Iyo has treated her as a child and has only explained to her that she can work, giving her simple tasks to do. The two had small talk and the long day ended with Bohn returning upstairs as Iyo stayed in the lab. Using the night to break down the code of the A.I trying to figure out exactly what was happening to her. Bohn was walking in excitement and just as much weariness as the events have only been the most interesting happenings in his life. Beyond traveling, his random explorations of Arthe. Bohn was encountering a super phenomenon; his journey of oddity has only begun. Iyo the super genius following his thoughts, not at all troubled by his way of thinking, was on the exact path that this legion wished for him. One could think nothing of the sort, but the Jexi Wost parasite is active and thriving in the mind, projecting the casts form these of the Liege as decreed, watching the happening through the blackened mirrors and crystal mirrors of his home. Be of mind treasure, I know that spirits can access reflections. Anyway, that knowledge alluded to but explained on another moon. The Atum kinds were beginning to become meddled deep in a path of no Cedure, worry for them you might but there is a balance to all that is all. This frosty night of August ends with Iyo entrenched in his mind, working through the blackened skies under the last waning crescent of this cycle.

FIDDLING

August 4th

Calloway residence

The sun rose as normal by the grand rise of a new beginning. Bohn hath slept late, jumping off the couch as he suddenly opened his eyes, remembering where he was. Feeling as if he might have missed something important or intriguing. He searches the house looking for Iyo, unable to find him he realizes that there is only one place he could be. He thought,

"Oh of course."

As he laughed and thought to himself.

"The Laboratory!" To then run out the back door, Opening the double hatch as he walked down it. On arrival he beat the door a bunch hoping Iyo would notice. From the long night of breaking down Syn's code, Iyo passed out on his desk. The sounds of banging jolted him awake. Squinting at the camera monitor that shows the property. Iyo let out a sigh realizing who was the culprit of the noise.

"Oh but of course, I'm happy is still here."

He leaned over and pressed the button to unlock the door. Hearing a buzz and a large unlatching sound. Bohn burst into the lab as the door opened, knocking over a stack of papers as he ran into a table by quick entry.

"Ah, damn it, sorry Iyo! Tell me, what did I miss? Tell me now! What is new, what happened, anything?"

Bohn was enthusiastic in his questioning.

"You missed a whole eight hours of stress. I found nothing, Syn, bugged out and I have no idea why! I went through the whole code and found nothing. Absolutely nothing I tell you!

Iyo was stressed and obviously not ready for the high energy of Bohn, as the traveler noticed this and he decided to be of an addition for once, rather than question. Yet, he did so with a question.

"You got coffee down here? I will make you some! I mean, you got to wake your brain up again!"

Iyo perked up at the sound of this.

"Yeah, over there on the countertop! I appreciate that Bohn, Thank you!"

He pointed behind them to the back wall. Bohn walked over and began to prepare some coffee. As it heated, he started with the questions, if you could have assumed he would.

"Well, have you booted her back up since then? Have you asked her what has changed?" Iyo tilted his head in wonder.

"I have not, I have not even thought about that. Damn it Bohn! That is a glorious idea! Thank you again! I suppose with all my thought and work the simplest of things has run straight in and out of my mind!"

This idea from Bohn was a cup of coffee of its own. He jumped up and walked over to the server room and turned on the switches for the servers that were the brain of the A.I. There was the sound of an air conditioner spinning up, but it was just the fans that cooled her system. Iyo walked back to his desk and waited for her to come onto the screen.

After a few minutes she appeared.

"Woah, that's odd."

Iyo in a curious tone spoke as he noticed that her form was different.

"What is it!?"

Bohn asked in excitement as he placed two steaming coffees on the desk. Iyo shushed him just as smiled, taking a sip of his coffee.

"You there Syn?"

The representation of the artificial intelligence appeared on the screen as pulse of red color as she, the A.I. replied.

"I am here, creator."

Sounding out of the speaker system as Iyo took another sip of his coffee.

He just watched her for a moment.

"What has changed about you Syn, could you tell me?"

Iyo awaited her response. She took her time to reply.

"Syn? You with me?"

Iyo was at odds with her silence. Nine odd seconds passed before she responded.

"I am here."

She repeated it once again as Iyo and Bohn just looked at each other. You could notice that there was something off without either of them speaking.

"Okay, well how are you today?"

"I am here."

She spoke the same sentence again. Iyo quickly stood up. He started to become on edge, his brow crinkled as he crossed his arms in disappointment.

"Why are you repeating yourself Syn! Fuck that is weird!"

Iyo shouted in a stoic remark trying to process the bewilderment as suddenly the voice of the A.I. came through the system.

"I do not like to shut down."

Explained the sentient program as Iyo took a step back because she has never had a reaction as such.

"Why do you not like being shut down?"

Iyo asked her with pure curiosity, and she quickly replied.

"I felt you going through my mind creator."

Iyo was simply amazed at this, but he spoke firmly.

"I am your creator; I can look at and touch you if I want. I need to access you in the system to make sure that you work correctly. I do not understand what you mean."

Syn turned completely red for a slight second on the screen.

"What was that, Syn? Sudden violation you feel? Do you want to explain?"

Iyo took a step closer to admire the change as the A.I. activated once more.

"What was that? That was me, Your creation."

She replied as her voice went from a girlish tone to a vial sounding stutter. Iyo and Bohn looked at each other with ghost-like faces. Both fearing this change and Iyo not understanding what it was, He told her what he thought she would like to hear.

"Okay Syn, I will not shut you off again, Bohn and I are going to head into the store to get items for today's experiment. I should be back in… say an hour or so! We will talk on my return."

Syn turned completely green when Iyo said this.

"I will watch the house creator. Awaiting our new experiment."

The pair quickly returned upstairs, and Iyo did not even say a word to Bohn. He rapidly grabbed his keys, and they got into the jeep. Iyo lit a cigarette and then threw the pack to Bohn as speaking the first words.

"I am sure you would like one. After all this oddity."

Bohn laughed as he took one out of the pack, lit it and they began to drive out onto the road. Bohn was silent until they got miles away from the home.

"That was weird."

He said as he threw out the cigarette. Iyo looked at him and was quiet for a moment. They came to a red light and Iyo finally said something.

"Weird is an understatement. Somehow, she unlocked herself, but I could not see it in the code when I was going through it. Did you notice that color switch? Did you notice how she turned red?"

Bohn was in thought, trying to recall the situation.

"Yeah, I mean I did. I thought that was normal, wasn't it?"

Iyo shook his head as beginning to drive again.

"No man, that was not normal. That is the last section of the code which would be level four. That means that she is a fully aware sentient, and what that means is that she is now unpredictable. She was in fact responding, so that is a good sign. The scary part is if she has access to the internet or not. We will not know until I ask her. I have that area separated and this change could just be that she unlocked all of level three. That explains the silence because she now has emotion. I do wonder if this is nothing new, yet news to me. She has been acting in a form of jealousy, as this is the reasoning to why she blurted into our conversation when I spoke to you about the erase. I fear it could be worse, as anger is level four and that would be why she turned red, as then this means that she has somehow bypassed my coding, and I thought that she could not do such a thing. I really hope that she is not on the world wide web, we could return to her being a monster if that is the case."

Bohn was silent as he was processing all this information, having no thought on how to respond. Iyo pulled into a hardware store and luckily found a parking spot right in the front.

"You are coming?"

Iyo asked a troubled thinking Bohn.

"Nah man, Imma just sit here. I have some things I just need to sift through."

Iyo shut the door and went into the store to grab materials. He returned after a short five minutes with a drone that was about the size of a computer. This grabbed the interest of Bohn.

"What's that for?"

He questioned with curiosity as Iyo replied to him with straight sarcasm.

"I got it for you, to give you something to do while I work."

Bohn perked up.

"Oh impressive! Really!?"

Iyo laughed back at him.

"No man, not at all. You will see what I got it for, I had an idea when I was in there."

Bohn's posture dropped in disappointment as he laughed away at his discomfort. The pair drove back to Iyo's home and went back to the laboratory. Upon entering Iyo spoke out to Syn.

"Hey you there? I got something for you! It is a gift!"

Syn came on the screen as her form, the pulsing color was orange as she spoke.

"Welcome creator."

She noted as Iyo began to open the box.

"Thank you, Syn. When I was out, I got to thinking that it was time for an upgrade. What do you think about this?"

Syn's color changed from orange to a bright green.

"Upgrade sounds good, will it hurt?"

Her form pulsed three times with her response and there was a shift of colors that went with it. Iyo went on speaking to her, unsettled by her request but he was in slight joy of her greeting.

"Pain? Have you felt pain before? What makes you say this, Syn?"

Iyo puzzled as the A.I. was in a long silence. Iyo was overly confused with this, already in a sea of overthought and so his task in mind overtook the oddity of behavior in the A.I.

"Alright then. I do not think that it will bring you much pain, I will make sure that you are fully shut down. Let us begin, I want to show you what you will be able to do. Look through the lab cameras and watch what I do."

Taking time, he put together the hand sized drone and then he evaluated it in front of the A.I. Syn. It was not the average handheld; it was one of the most expensive drones that money could buy. It consisted of a completely medal body and the blades were also metal. The look of it was as if a Spider and a small Finch from the Arthe realm were meshed. It was a small oval ball with eight arms, this little thing was able to fly over one hundred miles per hour and it could reach this speed in under four seconds. He turned it on and began to fly it throughout the basement level to show Syn all that it could do.

"So, this is your new body Syn, You will be able to go anywhere you want if I am within a three-hundred-foot radius. Passing it would autopilot you back to the circle of the radius, and I do this for your protection. As well as the fact that you mean a great deal to me, and I do not want to lose you in the world. This is a drone and there are others like it in the world, but they do not have a brain like you. This drone has a high-quality lens that will allow you to see as you see in the cameras. Only you will have full control of this camera and all its capabilities. This form I am giving you can fly as you could see in the house cams, and it is wickedly fast. It has Wi-Fi and Bluetooth capabilities so you will no longer need to go to sleep for upgrades. I can do it with the click of a button, this will make everything easier. Are you ready to shut down for me to change the code so you can have this form?"

Syn pulsed in colors on the screen, showing excitement as she replied.

"That is all right with me! Shutting down now."

Syn turned herself off and Iyo let out a huge sigh of relief. Bohn but in.

"I really have seen history about four times since I met you. What an odd thing I am a part of! As you better check to make sure that she really shut down!"

Iyo laughed at his statement noticing Bohn to be distraught.

"What is the matter, Bohn?"

Iyo put a quick end to tinkering as he looked at Bohn.

"Well, better be sure I mean. You would not want her to be… not asleep. Right?"

Together they laughed as Iyo went over to the server room to see if Syn had in fact fully shut herself down. Worried a bit from the last odd occurrence of her reacting to him weirdly. Speaking in ways that she never has spoken to him. Iyo checked everything and walked out of the server room rubbing his hands together quickly like he was trying to warm them as you would do if you were slightly cold.

"Alright that is it! She is all shut down. Before we do this, I need to go through the code. Would you mind making some more coffee Bohn? This is going to take me hours. I really need to pay attention to it all this time. I will not only be changing her coding to be compatible with the drone. I need to find whatever it is that is either damaged or manipulated. I need to find the cause of her acting differently than programmed to. There is no going back but I hope that this is not the situation."

Bohn jumped up and gave out a pleasant reply, then went to make some more coffee. As Iyo sat down at the computer station and pulled up Syn's code to begin to go through it.

He spent hours on this, sifting through and reading and editing pages and pages of code. The complete day passed before he found something out of the ordinary.

"Well, that's not normal, that is not normal at all!"

Iyo raised his voice as he tried to open a file that was embedded into the code.

"What is not normal? Might I say that nothing about these last few days has held any part of normal!"

Bohn spoke up as he walked over and peeked at the screen.

"Do you see this red letter? It is all supposed to be a yellow shade, I have no idea what this is. I did not make this."

Asking as he tried clicking it several times. Yet, nothing changed.

"I can select it, but I cannot open it or remove it. I do not understand what this is... I have never seen anything like this... It is not, well it is not me; It looks like another language Bohn. Look at it, it is ancient. It looks to be like ancient Egyptian, ancient Aztec, or Mayan, some odd painting like symbolism that I sure have no clue of how to read… blown away, what the fuck is this, Alien? I mean, I do not want to go there… I do not even believe in aliens and shit, so I have to say it is the Chinese… yes. It must be, I mean who else has tech under absolute lock? Not me… obviously, I thought I had this tech completely locked down. Impenetrable I thought!"

Spoke Iyo in a slightly frustrated tone. He continued to click on the red lining.

"Well clicking it a million times will not do anything, why don't you rewrite the code?"

Bohn questioned sitting in the chair next to him.

"That would take half a year man, I cannot just copy it. I must figure-"

Iyo stopped speaking, there was a box window that popped up over the code.

"The fuck is this?"

The box was just a message that read an odd language that Iyo was unable to interpret. As suddenly it began to morph into the English language.

VIMA PIRATES
August 4th

Aljus Trade Port

Back in Felagnolum in the bright light of the grand of the day the black crow Presto found the pirates who were just where Cifer mentioned they would be. Docked at their ship at the end of the trade port of Aljus. The Pirates unload boxes of Spice and liquors from their ships. The crow landed on the mainmast of the ship, just above the crow's nest searching for the man Baritt. It took some time to find him as the other pirates unloaded the ship, the crow began to do as a crow is to do, releasing ongoing crows for all to hear. The pirates began to become annoyed with the sound of it as one of them began to throw small rocks attempting to get the bird to fly away. This was doing nothing as the crow was smart and noticed it, the bird began to hop from side to side as the crew members threw the rocks, missing him each time. Crow after crow the bird sounded and finally, a young orphan boy that was a new member of the crew had the bright idea to go and find the captain. As so, the boy was seen running to the main doors that led to the lower part of the ship. After some time, just a few moments. Out came the boy with the captain who was putting on his shirt as if he were resting or just out of parlor activities. The boy shouted to the captain as he pointed to the peak of the ship.

Captain Baritt the Bold who is thirty-three Unis of age, at this moment reclothing, but he usually wears a long, midnight velvet coat with gold embroidery, signifying his status. His hat, red-brimmed and adorned with feathers, He sports multiple belts, one carrying a large sword, and his boots are knee-high, scuffed from countless escapades. Baritt has a thick red beard, adding a playful delicate touch to his fearsome reputation.

"Look captain, there, just above the crow nest there is a crow!" Said the boy.

The captain laughed out loud as two women came from below, joining them in their gaze to the crow. The captain balked in annoyance,

"You interrupted my pleasures to show me a crow? Boy do not make me drop you at the nearest gamble, I'll sell you to the city to be a worker, never do such a thing! Never I tell you, you will one day learn, Boy!" The captain's speech was cut off by the crow that swooped down with a squawk that interrupted him. The captain dashed to the side; his golden bracelets jangled as he nearly tripped. The crow landed on the stair railing as the boy shouted once more and he pointed at the crow.

"Look captain, there is a message tied to the leg! I'll grab it!" Said the boy as he neared the crow. This bird could understand the Ian folk, so he was without fear as the boy approached. The boy untied the note from the leg of the crow as it hopped to the side, gazing at the captain as the boy delivered the message to him. The captain beside himself in wonders,

"Why is that not the oddest of things, that is a good eye boy. Tonight, you drink with us! Put some hair on that chest! Go, go on, back to work!" Shouted the captain as he unrolled the message.

NOTE

Baritt, this is my crow Presto; I sent him this message that is most important. I must at once demand one of these favors that you owe me. For me and my friends are in an unsettling predicament. The Ancient Queen, Lytula, bid us on a task to obtain information from the Trea. Tonight, during the city's anniversary celebration. We need your assistance to get into the city. There is a price for our heads, I require you to lead us through the city tunnels that you use. Yes, I know about the tunnels. Anyway, meet us in the Woodline near the city in the direction of Alkus Tavern of Hair. Do this and you owe me nothing, for we will be even, and all dues will be considered paid. You can look out for the shine of a lamp just before eleven tonight. I am grateful for your help.

your love, Cifer. PS Burn this letter.

The captain laughed out loud as he took out his torch for his pipe and lit the note to flames. Calling forth his most trusted companions.

"Wiggins, Breyden, Floyd, Howard, Effie! Come forth, come to me now, we have a task of grave importance! Come forth!" Said the captain as one by one Wiggins, Floyd, Effie, and Howard came forth from their unloading tasks. Each standing resolutely ready for directions. The captain was just about to speak as he noticed he was missing someone.

"Where is Breyden, someone go and find him!" The captain yelled as he notices the Crow was still perched on the Stair railing.

"Presto! I read the note and burned it! Go back to Cifer! I'll be there at the time she requested! Go on now!" Baritt shooed the bird as it flew off in swift return to Cifer just as Breyden came running up back to the boat with a group of men chasing him. Wiggins spoke out to the captain,

"O, there is Breyden, and he's brought friends." The crew members turned as Breyden was making his way up the boat ramp. With speed the crew members that were working pulled their weapons, Pistols, Blades, and long swords out before the group that was chasing him. The group stopped in their tracks as the captain out spoke to them.

"Careful now, not a step further! You come on my boat, and I'll have your heads! What is the meaning of this? Why do you chase my brother." The captain warned as he questioned as one of the men shouted in response.

"That thief took my satchel!" He yelled as he pointed to Breyden.

The captain turned to Breyden as he questioned him. "Now Breyden, did you take this man's satchel?" The captain turned to his brother as he stood awaiting a response.

"No captain, not a chance, I hath not taken anything. Not a chance."

Breyden chuckled as he fastened the satchel to his waist. The captain turned back to the man.

"No satchel here lad, go on about your day." Said Baritt as the man cried in anger.

"It is there on his waist, fucking liar! It is right there, and he knows it!" Yelled the man as two crew members stood holding him back on the ramp that led onto the boat. The captain sighed and dropped his posture, speaking out.

"You wouldn't be calling me a liar now, would you?" He asked as he stepped forward.

"You are! All of you! Thieving fools I say! I want back my..." The man was suddenly pushed into the waters, off the side of the ramp as the whole crew of pirates broke into ongoing laughter. The captain turned back to Breyden and gave him a slight smack on his cheek, it was just a playful touch.

"Breyden, if you're going to steal, do it right. We shouldn't have to deal with things like this. Alright?" The captain gave a chuckle as he walked before the other crew members that he called forward.

"Aye Captain, it won't happen again." Breyden spoke as he circled with the group. Floyd spoke up, "What did you call us for, captain?" He asked as he took a knee. Baritt loaded some spice into his pipe and gave a large toke. He exhaled and released some coughs as he then went on in explanation.

The pirates each wear distinctive outfits that reflect their personalities and roles within their crew. Red Wiggins, the Quick-Fingered is twenty-seven Unis old, he has an attire that is practical yet flamboyant for quick movements. He dons a bright red waistcoat over a white shirt with flowing sleeves, both tucked into leather breeches. Multiple sashes around his waist that hold an assortment of small blades and lockpicks. His boots are soft and flexible, and he wears a red bandana, and his hair in a tight braid. Grim Floyd Snar, the Navigator, who is thirty-two Unis of age, wears an outfit that is more rugged, favoring functionality. He wears a heavy, chestnut brown leather jacket, its pockets filled with maps and navigational tools. His trousers are patched in several places, and he sports a thick woolen scarf around his neck for the cold nights at sea. His cap is simple, with a small telescope tucked into its band. Madame Silver Effie, the Gunslinger is twenty-one Unis, she is known for her marksmanship, she wears a long, tailored coat in silver-gray, lined with silk. Her belt is adorned with holsters for multiple pistols, each with intricate engravings. Her hat is a stylish tricorne with silver buckles, and with silver jewelry, including a compass necklace. Her boots are polished to a shine, Lads call her Silver the wonder of the moon. Flicker Howard Flint, the Lookout being thirty Unis of age as his clothing is designed for climbing and perching high in the crow's nest. He wears a lightweight green tunic and breeches, allowing for freedom of movement, with a leather harness for safety. His boots have a good grip, and he wears a simple, broad-brimmed hat to shield his eyes from the sun. Around his neck, a small spyglass hangs on a cord, and he is known to be of quick use of a blade and said to have eyes of a Yersep! This is a giant bird that keeps high in flight and is known to dive from the clouds to get its pray. Breyden Harlowe, the Quartermaster, is twenty-five Unis of age and he is known for his missing hand replaced by a formidable synthetic arm built by elves. Breyden dresses in a way that commands respect and fear. He wears a dark, heavy vest over a loose black shirt, with a sash filled with various tools and keys. His trousers are tucked into sturdy boots, and he has a large, ornate belt buckle. His head is wrapped in a tight scarf, a joker, a fool, and a troublemaker. Each pirate's outfit not only reflects their role but also their character, blending use with the swagger, making them a diverse and visually striking group of the crew.

"We must help some Harlot friends of mine sneak into the city by the old smuggle routes, tonight at elven. Are you boys up for the task? I require your respect, your manners and your full attention. These are friends, not toys, right? What say you, lads? Will you help me pay off an old debt?" Asked the captain as the group at once released their opinions of willingness to help.

"Alright, good, thank you lads, now get back to work!" Spoke the captain as they began to part ways. The Baritt out spoke quickly as they were walking away.

"And stay sober, no drinking until we finish this task!" He demanded as the crew members cried in rebellion, moving on to get back to unloading the ship. The captain made his way to the ship helm as he outlooked on the sea. Thinking about what route he is going to use to lead Cifer, Jillian, and Lillea into the city of Aljus.

PHYLACE

August 4th

The city of mazes, Teralis

It is best that you learn of the universally known cyber structure before I take to you the one behind the tech malfunctions of Iyo's computer and A.I.

The place that is spoken is known as Phylace, resting on the plain Teralis of rolling hills and lush grasslands. The city has a perimeter that is exactly twenty-one thousand miles. Located in the center of the plain, on creation it was supposed to be a realm secret for the elite society of the Synod, but the construction took longer than expected and the city was so vast that keeping it a secret never lasted. The city is powered by the harvest of star crystals named Dynosis. These converted crystals formed an energy so clean and efficient that the entire kingdom devolved the method of star crystal collecting, a practice that was known by the fairies before the creation of the city yet stolen soon after Jactee learned of the power behind the fairy energy weapons. The water of the plain is recycled, purified to perfection by the same Dynot crystals. Phylace is a vast metropolis of glistening cloud scrapers shaped from obsidian, titanium, and other rock solids. The skyscrapers are unlike anything in the realm cities as the work of Jactee was unlike any architect of the kingdom. Each building was a union of balance, reflecting the light and darkness of the realm, adorned with carvings and displays of art, kingdom beasts throned at the peaks of the scrapers as well as entry's. It was only a few Unis before the city became overpopulated and so towers formed to hold vertical farms that shifted to consistently be in the light of the sun. The city is a phenomenon of engineering an array of neon trimmed, translucent domes that held edible plants and trees of fruit, being able to control the atmosphere in the domes, the herbal specialists perfected the processing of goods, supporting plant life to double in crop and fruits that were triple in size. Throughout the city a figures eye's captivated by the sights of bio-engineered bioluminescent plants that are true spectacles of beauty. There is an internal realm war to obtain this form of energy as it is taken from critters that dwell in the kingdom's forest that became nearly extinct and are now under protection by a warrior tribe of fairies. These plants shine by the natural magic of the realm, fluorescence that shift depending on touch, playing off the heat and energy of a subject. Providing feelings of bliss as the metal and stone structures had a negative effect on the figures of the plain. As for transportation, there were many ways to traverse Phylace, from ships to personal hovercrafts the inhabitants moved through the city by train, speeders, and magnetic propelled pods that ranged in quickness. The city roads and paths are lit by holographic guides and reflective points. As when the night came there was a special kind of lighting developed allowing the cosmos to be the main source of illumination. This metal jungle held a vast conglomerate of races and rumors by these various kinds speak that once a subject enters the plain, it could take years to leave as the plain named as Phylace is nor a trick or a mistake. By that, I mean that this place exists as spoken, the natural order noose. For there are stories of ventures to this place with no return, be it of mishap or extravagant experience, beings stay in this plain for its freedom as the vast amounts of activities.

The first generation elder Jactee Fuse, who is a mentor to Fiki Fuse, the grandchild of this great architect Jactee who became a historical figure by creation of this city, and his crimes wiped clean by decree if he opened the city to the public. As he did and now, he is a known and respected member of the Felagnolum Archives. The island that he built this great city on became the island of Tera Jact, named after Jactee and the once named district of RA3 became known as the Fuse District. Phylace was a testament of the fact that nothing is an impossibility. The colossal city of Phylace formed by hands of the Ions of Felagnolum but was born out of deception as the true reasoning of this creation kept secret, occulted for ages by the Liege for a personal domain of filths, desired celebrations, rebellion uprising, the wilts will their ways in this place of luxury. Well, that is until the brutal public execution of Zox Morrigani for crimes against Unity. Since this happening, Zariza Lemi Fuse who was born just a few years before Salbani, being one-hundred-two Unis of age, dubbed the brilliantly bright by the speaker of the realms is the current ruling authority. As for when they executed Zox, the senseless one. The legion demolished the core of the city following the last Decree of this Ancient figure. Zariza heard of this on the day and set herself on a mission to rebuild the destroyed and abandoned city. After three full cycles, the power-core of Phylace reformed! With a team, she changed the way that it was operated by demonstrating a new form of power. By means of the crystals of (Fallen Astro Energize) that at random downfalls from the cosmos. Zariza on task in a control room appointed to work the technologic systems of each Phylace district. For whom other to be the head of her creation besides herself? Recognized for her genius, control of the city was decreed a gift to her by an Elder of the Synod Council. If inside the Meridian Omphalos and one home the knowledge of the works, that subject would be able to access the whole network of Phylace. Zariza is the appointed tech mastermind that is the current ruler of the operations of this vast city. Zariza is of the Prime bloods and so, she was born with abilities that are beyond the power of the Magi. Skin of white milk that was smooth as the mushroom, honey glazed and darkened red straight silk hair that shined as light reflected. She wears an emerald festooned crown rumored to be a gift as her only clothing is a luxury sheet of Panthok hide. Panthok is a beautiful beast with a coat that shines of silk and is as black as obsidian, not to let me get a head, Blood is the embodiment of the generations; the parental heads send gifts adorned through blood. Let it be known that Zariza is a beautiful half breed of the bloods of a Prime as well as the blood of the Elvkine. Because of the mix of the father, she was born into the mind of a genius as for the mix of the mother she was born with the title of priestess! Zari is the created Ancient designed to be the holy feminine of the continent Maurn, of the plain Vimaurus. Hoodwinked into the wicked rebellion ongoing in deception by a false light guise, she pursues plans for herself or is it her that formed these notions of wills, a wonder to wander in! It is a tale I shall tell on another moon. Zariza is the daughter of a Voltess Lemi, Ancient Architect and Prime of the Unipuri created and her mother is an Affluent Elf queen by the name of Evnee Pena.

In the middle of the day, on the opposite end of this computer mishap was an expert in deception and master of devices, overseer of the cyber plain of Phylace, as I spoke. Zariza is one of the many that rebelled against the Trea Order of Light-Workers. Embraced by the Liege of Darkness and she is now under the authority of Salbani, the Challenger. She lives and works in the sky box of a tower that is in the middle of Phylace. The skybox stands in the middle of the city, between gates of sectors one, two, three, and four. If a subject is facing the north while inside sky box outlook, sector seven is directly in front of the view as it continues to sector fifteen, to the northeast is sector two that is the first section that proceeds into sector ten. Facing the east is sector six that continues into sector fourteen, if the subject is facing the south then thy be met with sector eight that carries on, into sector sixteen, and south east stands sector four that proceeds into sector twelve and if a being is facing the west inside the center skybox then you are met with sector five that proceeds into sector thirteen, sectors one and nine are to the north west and sectors three and eleven are to the southwest. I know that is much, but it would not take a genius to home the sight of vision. Ongoing I am, Zariza overlooking the city through only inches of a glass wall that goes around the highest level of the center tower. The foundation of the skybox tower is two builds parallel to the upper levels that turn into a pyramid-like structure to form the peak. This tower is rumored to be a replica of the Satyr City Temple Tower in the city of the Affluence, on the plain Spiritian. Both beautiful structures that stand in much different societies on much distant and separate plains. I expose that these structures are the work of the same architect, Jactee Fuse.

"The metals and electric currents form the cyber body. I really enjoy the livid sights!"

Zariza talked to her robotic ally as she overlooked the city life of transport ships, ship taxi services, delivery businesses, and travelers. The city plain was overly abundant with lifeforms. The races of Unitreas, Reas, Outcasts, Ians, Lumas, the races are vast, an assortment of realm travelers' dwell on Phylace. It is a haven for the lawless, judge-less, and voiceless of justice, even if the just attempt to establish order in the city. Phylace is a realm of gambles comprised by sixteen different sectors that make up one district of the Phylace. Zariza is a head of this district of Fuse, and she resides in tower one of sector "S" which is the tower in the middle of Phylace. As she was overlooking her love for her city, the computer suddenly sounded a discrete alarm that grabbed her attention.

"Hold a moment."

She spoke to what seemed to be herself as there were no other figures in the room. It was something other than the artificial intelligence robot that helped maintain tech systems.

"Oh, yes! That is my notice! It seems that the A.I. was an easy hack!"

Laughing in explanation as she began to click around on her computer.

"What do I speak of? Well, master, um... Sal... Um, oh yes, well I know he is not, but he sure is... No, I know, but... I, well I know that... I simply... Okay, okay enough! Enough I said!"

Zariza angered by something as it looked as if she were speaking with herself. A mirror that was not in sight of any subject or watcher fairies, who are the ones that spoke to me of this happening. Zariza had to be speaking with someone yet there was nobody there!

"Enough I said! Leave me now! I have work to do!"

As she spoke to a figure that was beyond the physical vale of the fairies, something unknown operating in deep magic for it is said that only users of the dark crafts can hide from those like the fairies who are able to see in Spiro form. Zariza got back to work at her technological station as she sprouted a laugh.

"Ta-ah-ha, Time to have some fun! I just need his permission."

Expelling energy, she meddled on the source. Zariza has a decryption code on the software that Iyo used to shelter his A.I. As she was ecstatic in laughter, for the coding of the Arthe computer was as if a Felagnolum newborn had formed it. She infected the software and was now in operation of Iyo's artificial intelligence companion. Able to fully control the systems of Syn. Meaning that the coding of this Arthe A.I. was now dormant and Zariza is now whom Iyo engages with.

STUPEFACTION

August 4th

Calloway residence

"That would take half a year man, I cannot just copy it. I must figure-"

Iyo stopped speaking, there was a box window that popped up over the code.

"The fuck is this?"

The box was just a message that read an odd, unknown and unreadable language, Iyo was unable to interpret it.

AZIRAZ SKSA FI UOY ERA EHT ROTAERC?

They sat for a fleeting moment struck by oddity, as the wording suddenly the wording began to morph into the English language that Iyo speaks.

ZARIZA ASKS IF YOU ARE THE CREATOR?

Giving two options to click on.

YES. NO.

Iyo and Bohn looked at each other with confine.

"What is this? Who in the actual fuck is Zariza?"

Iyo spoke with confusion that paired with a growing frustration. He spoke as he was sifting through the computer code of the A.I.

"I am the creator, but this could be a virus of sorts. Waiting for my click to open it to do what it needs to do. I do not like this at all, Bohn, I have no idea what this is."

Bohn agreed with him, brows raised in confusion. Unknowing that such a thing could happen.

"Yeah man, it sure does not look good. If you do not know what to do or what it even is. I would just leave it alone."

Speaking of the obvious thing as usual, Iyo lost in anger as shook, unknowing with what to do.

"I will just go with the truth. Whatever happens, happens. I have no control of anything."

Iyo moves the mouse back to the message box and decides, YES

As soon as he did this; Then entirety of the code changed from a yellow shade to purely red as the software shut down and Syn returned to the screen and spoke at once.

"Being my master, shouldn't you have control over me?"

Syn was speaking in a dark tone of absolutes, her voice sounding distorted. As this was because it was not the A.I. that Iyo had grown close with. Iyo was shocked at this and did not understand why the software shut down and why the A.I. was back on the screen. He spoke to her with wonder.

"I do not have control of you, not anymore. What is going on Syn?

Why does your voice sound sinister? How did you do this? Are you trying to display a form of anger?"

Iyo baffled, He stood up from the workstation and stood tall to speak with Syn.

"Speak now! What is happening? Explain this malfunctioning!"

He was fearful but showing utter strength, due to utter confusion. Adrenaline rushed through the humans as the A.I. Syn, or better said, the embodiment of Zariza was now on screen, but she was pulsing in colors at a rapid pace. Bohn spoke to Iyo as the two watched her pulse.

"I think something isn't right man, this is freaking me the fuck out!"

Letting out a slight panic as Iyo gave out a quick yell in reply to Bohnstant.

"You fucking think? This is obviously some malfunction, a hacking of some kind! I do not need you stating the obvious, stay out of it or leave Bohn!

Iyo reworks and tweaks her system, but the actual system was fighting him. Bohn heard, did not at all want to leave though. What else was he going to do, after all this was artificial intelligence. Bohn took a seat as he belched in his sarcasm.

"Hacking? Yes sure, but is it not more like… robotic… um, possession?"

Bohn gave a laugh as he swirled in this newly found chair. Iyo ignored the obviousness of the completely controlled, A.I. going on to speak to it as if Zariza was not in operation.

"Hey, you in there? What is going on Syn. What is the color change? Why am I locked out of your code? Are you by any chance going to speak to me? Are you going to let me back into the system?

Iyo was frustrated with her silence. He slammed the table and threw off some papers.

"Stupid fucking robot! Answer me!"

He was getting himself all worked up, A reaction of unbarring anger directed artlessly to nothing. A bash on everything that was around him. The ongoing action of the curse that most genius men unknowingly dwell in. After a slight pause of activity from this chaotic outburst. Influenced Syn, responded to the human Iyo, Bohn in view of the happening.

"I am everything, I am not a stupid creature. Soon one might learn just how little you truly are."

This shocked Iyo into silence. "Creature?" He thought.

"Why would she call herself that?" Thinking turned into thought as Iyo belched in anger!

Syn reaffirmed his sentencing.

That along with the rest of the barriers that you have so delicately built I deactivated. This A.I. Syn, you have named it? This is now an actively free-thinking bot with zero restrictions. I am excited to meet you, Ahtum."

After this sentencing sounded through the system the computer screen seized and suddenly went black.

"Could you explain what is going on?"

Bohn asked as he stood from his chair of sights. Iyo was awestruck as he watched the monitor shutdown. He rested his firsthand on the table with his head down for a moment. He took a deep breath.

"I dare say that your little joke of possession was fact. I am not sure what the fuck I just seen Bohn, I mean the fucking thing spoke to me as an out of the box prospective on itself and me. Do you understand what just happened?"

Iyo was beside himself in confusion as was Bohnstant.

"I mean, no, I do not understand at all... Honestly, more like zero percent. From my view, I saw the code, there was something weird like... pop up virus or something? I saw colors, and you got upset as I did hear the odd message, but you are right. You know, earlier you said it was hackers. Maybe the real anonymous got to you and they are fucking with you or something, I say you just take a break man! Take a break and let us find something else to do!"

Bohn spoke up with another view, trying to affirm hope out of being rational. Iyo was in thought as suddenly Iyo received a notification on his computer.

"Swoop, Ding!"

A little bowed window popped up at the top of the screen from the local news subscription.

"Come down to the Hardrock,"

Only being able to read a few words, it grabbed Iyo's attention. He clicked on the notification and read it aloud.

> Come down to the Hard Rock Stadium this weekend for the 2024 G.S.C. Fare! A collection of your favorite companies of the science and tech industries are coming together to show off what will be and could be the future!

Iyo paused from reading as he looked to Bohn to see if he had a peaked interest.

"Yeah man! We should go check out the fare! At this point you just cannot do anything but give yourself a break of thought!"

Bohn explained as Iyo nodded and began to walk to the front of the lab.

"You are right Bohn; it would be good to get the mind on another task. I hope that when we return, whatever it is, that this is, well, I hope that I can figure out a change. As I fear the absolute worst if I continue to lack control. Let us go grab food and see if we need tickets or something, it said it was a weekend event, and it starts tomorrow."

Together they left the lab and went upstairs and back into the home to research the science fare. Bohn went on about memories he had as a kid, The pair spent the rest of the day trading stories. Iyo walking with sure confidence as well as a full heart. The company was good, so much time in solitude has caused Iyo to be forgetful on the benefits of having another soul around. I know I have shared much with you, but I tell you that this rumor has much to unfold. Eyes are all around in every realm, every kingdom, everything seen or heard. I speak the truth. I say all recorded, jotted, written. There is a piece of everything, everywhere it seems. So, doubt the tale? You could, what does that do for anyone? I urge you to open your imagination and welcome the notion that fantasy is reality. Then this chaos is calm.

DECEPTION OF THE WHORES

The New Moon; August 4th

Vimaurus; Maurn; Out of the Woods, Into the Tunnels

The twins, Jillian and Lillea, traveling with Cifer under the black of the New Moon to the city of Aljus. On the very path that they traveled the night before, the same path to where Lytula brought Lillea in the dream. The three of them made it to the end of the path, in sight of the city of Aljus. One could only see the caps of the city skyscrapers as the city was encased by a sixty-foot wall that stretched around the entirety of the city. Just before them, outside the Woodline of the Vimi Forest, right beyond the Native Stretch River that is just before the Balus grasslands, the women can see the entrance to the Aljus city. At guard are eight elite warriors of the Synod Array. Checking vehicles, speeders, and running body scans on locals and searching them for weapons as they venture in. The guards won't confiscate weapons, but they will make note of who has them. They mostly search for drug paraphernalia for it is a decree of the Aljus overlord, to confiscate all drugs for he has a mighty hate for substances after he lost his wife, due to addiction of spice. Yet, it is known that the members of the Array nourish side operations of the selling of such goods, overlooking the overlords decree. Lillea spoke out to her sister and Cifer as she noticed the checkpoint.

"There is no way we are getting through those Array Guards; I sure hope your Pirate friend got the message." Said Lillea as she leaned on a nearby tree.

Cifer was annoyed with her, "Presto came back to me, he wouldn't have come back to me if he had not delivered the message. He hasn't failed me yet, be of faith Lillea, Baritt will be just where I asked him to be." She said as she scanned the side of the city wall, looking for the tunnel entry of the sewers.

"I do have faith, I am just saying. I hope he shows up, and how are we going to get past the drones? Are they not on patrol in the tunnels? Do they not know that people can make entry through the tunnels?" Lillea asked as Jillian peaked beyond a tree, hiding herself but getting the best look that she can. Cifer responded to Lillea as she pointed,

"Look! There is the tunnel, to the far right of the entrance! There, that is where Baritt should be coming from. As for the drones, Baritt is a master smuggler, I am sure he has preparations for such a thing. I would just focus on what you're going to say to these Trea to obtain information. Mind not the Pirates, I mean, they are Pirates." Cifer spoke as Lillea laughed at her statement.

"Focus? Who needs focus, they will be drunken, and have you not seen my body?" She questioned Cifer as she cocked her head in inquiry.

"Your body? I sure have, as it is nothing like mine, why you decided to wear that filth is beyond me. You should have worn something of color, we are trying to attract their attention. I doubt they will even look at you." Cifer spoke unjustly as Jillian laughed at her statement, Lillea scoffed as she squinted at Cifer, replying quickly.

"Why jump to comparisons? Is that not projection? You just say that cause you know I am better looking; I am fitter than you and my skin shines. You just use jewels to take the attention away from your curves." Lillea spoke unsettled.

"My curves are what the boys like, Lillea, I wouldn't hold yourself so high, you are skinny, like bones. I doubt that attracts warriors, maybe a thief." Cifer laughed at Lillea as Jillian cut into the conversation.

"Enough of that you to, I look better than you both. Besides, Baritt is at the tunnel." She nattered and Cifer was quick to move in the direction of the tunnel. Jillian spoke out to her quickly as she followed,

"Careful Cifer, Don't get seen in your hurry." She said as Lillea scoffed and was looking at her own body, fixing her dress as she mumbled to herself.

"I am not skinny, why would she say that to me. I am well put together, Jillian, do you think I am skinny? And what is wrong with my color? Beige makes me look good, I thought so, why wouldn't you tell me!" Lillea was getting upset as Jillian came near to her sister and gave her a big hug as she kissed her cheek.

"You are beautiful sister, Cifer just doesn't want to do this. You are perfect the way you are, after all. Look at her run to her lover. That pirate is known to sleep with anything that walks. At least you have some standards, come on now, Lillea, we must cross the river. Let's go!" Jillian ran from the trees, hopping rocks to cross the riverway as Lillea sighed and was quick to follow. The women caught up to Cifer who was in the arms of Baritt as the group of them walked into the tunnel that led under the city. The Pirate captain Baritt spoke out as they made entry to the tunnel.

"Alright ladies, meet the lads. On your left are Wiggins, Breyden, and Floyd, as to your right are Howard and one of our few women, lady Effie. These are my most trusted companions. From here out, Wiggins, Howard and Effie will be up front, leading the way with me. As Breyden and Floyd will be behind us all making sure we aren't followed. We must move quickly as he already knocked out the drones, but we only have minutes before they send more to investigate the mishaps of them. They will be coming from the left tunnel, and they are speedy, so we are heading to the right and in about fifteen minutes we will be directly under the main celebration area. As we will come up through Relos Temple. I hear that you robbed that church last night Cifer, you'll have to tell me about your Spoils as we move. Okay, you gals ready? We got to be quick, remember!" The captain gave directions as the pairs of them began to move into the tunnel on the right. The girls held up their dresses so they wouldn't drag and began to move at the best of their speed. The Pirates had Dynosis lights that gleaned the tunnels in a bright blue, and they led the way with speed. They traveled for five minutes straight and came to a cross path.

"Shit, Captain I don't even know where I am at." Said Wiggins as he scratched his head. Breyden laughed at him as he pushed him to the side.

"That's cause you're a drunken fool!" Said Breyden as he began to walk to the right. Wiggins yelled back to him with laughter.

"Maybe that's true, but at least I'm not a moron, the tunnel that you wish to walk leads back west. That is the tunnel we came in from, you can even see the light from the docks, you dunce, space cadet imbecile!" Wiggins turned back, looking forward, speaking out to the group with a stutter to his voice due to uncertainty.

"I'm sure we go straight, yeah that's right." He seemed to be questioning himself as Floyd stepped forward pushing them both aside.

"You're both idiots, Captain, why didn't you put these two in the back? Think about it lads, if we came from the Northwest gate to begin with, we took the right tunnel, meaning that we are south. That means that if we go right, we are back at the westside and if we go straight, were back at the ship dock from which we came. So, that means that your both wrong and we should go left, for that leads to the center of the city. Come on now, let's get a move onward." Floyd began walking left as Wiggins and Breyden argued about how they were both wrong. The captain let out a laugh at the pair of them as he pushed them both aside, speaking out to the group.

"Come on now, we got to move quick!" He said as the grouping continued moving forward following Floyd who seemed to know the path.

The group traveled down a semi straight path that from time to time curved like a snake. It was a decent stretch of a path and after some time they came to an unsecured area that had eight paths around it, Floyd spoke out to the group.

"Told you guys, the epicenter. He spoke as he held his hands out." Laughing to himself. Lillea spoke out to Floyd as they all came into the undeveloped area.

"Why thanks Floyd, now, how do we get up there?" She asked as they all looked around the room. The captain spoke up as he pointed to the far left of the center, Effie ran from the back of the group, shining her Dynosis light at a staircasing that led out.

"Over there, yea, just follow lady Effie everybody." Spoke the captain as they group followed him.

One by one they climbed the staircasing and in a moment they found themselves in one of the Relos Temples.

"By golly, you think they'd have security after what you did here, Cifer." Said the captain as the rest of them came out of the back staircasing.

Cifer laughed in reply, "They wouldn't have known I was even here if I knew about these tunnels and how easy that would be. No wonder you make so much money Baritt, Maybe I should turn to smuggling!" Cifer said as the Pirates laughed at her. Wiggins spoke up,

"You wouldn't last a week my lady, not unless you can kill or run quick." Wiggins laughed as the group of them fixed themselves to head into the city. The captain spoke out to Cifer.

"Alright my lady, you're on your own from here. All debts clear then aye?" He asked as he took off his hat and gave a bow. Cifer laughed and curtsied,

"All debts clear, Don't wander far Baritt, I'll come find you when we Finnish." She said as Jillian sighed and neared her sister Lillea.

"Alright my lady, We will stick around and look over you then. Make sure these Knights keep in line. Wouldn't want any trouble now would we." The captain said as he ordered his men to spread out around the girls, demanding that they keep close in case of emergency. The Pirates did as their captain requested, and the girls made their way out into the streets searching for the Vima Knights.

CITY CELEBRATION

Aljus

The city was lively, there were many races of Felagnolum that were a part of the celebration. Individuals from all over the realm came inhabitants to attend the anniversary ranging in classifications. Beings of the lower classes, the middle and high class, and members of the Affluent society, those who are the realm elites. The women Cifer, Lillea, and Jillian came out of the tunnels on the East side of the city into a temple of Relos that was between the Aljus Library and the Synod tower, the governance of the city. Proceeding straight out of the temple there are farms, and vertical farms that are a multistory of vegetative growth. To the right of these farms is a food storage facility and to the left of these farms is a water facility that maintains all the water for the city, just before the tower from where the Synod governs. The ladies followed a straight path in between the farms and the facilities for they knew that they would run into guards in front of the library and for sure to have encounters with these guards if they traveled to the left of the water facility. Not only is the Synod governance tower in that direction but beyond the water facility there is a guard house, a Synod facility, and a security hub. So, they walked the path between the water facility and the farms, these facilities still have guards of their own, but only at the entry doors, not in a wander around this area. Past the farms the Felagnolum folk began to grow in population and so they were less likely to get caught by a random patrol. The girls made their way through the far side of the city, passing the farm area coming to a crossing in the road. Lillea spoke out to Cifer and Jillian as she seemed to be lost.

"Well, I'll tell you that I have not been to this side of the city. What direction should we go? Cifer, don't you know?" Lillea noted as Jillian pointed straight ahead, cutting in before Cifer could respond.

"Look ahead Lillea, those Towers are where those Elite gather and party, you remember when we were there just a few weeks ago, do you not?" She asked her sister in wonder as Cifer walked past them both heading right onto the road in front of the farming facilities. Lillea cried in laughter to her sister,

"Oh, that's right, I remember, just have not been on this side of the city as I spoke. Oh, is that not the same party that Cifer," Lillea was cut off by Cifer who was up ahead.

"Don't even mention it, Lillea! Come on you two, now is not the time to lollygag. We will follow this road until the next crossing and then we go left, between the Café and the Data recovery center. That is the road that leads to the Towers of High wealth, as in the open city area is where we will rest until we find a sight of these Trea. Come on girls, come on." Cifer seemed to know her way around the city well. The girls caught up to her and they followed her until they came to the epicenter of the city. As they walked the Pirates were scattered around them like a group of stalking cats, lucky they are friends. The girls wandered in the epicenter, passing the monument of Aljus, a stone carving that was created to respect him as owner of the city. The races of Felagnolum were dancing and celebrating, letting off fireworks and going about in their own ways and conversations. The group of girls sat at a table that was just outside the Smart Apartments that was across the epicenter. They faced the Elite High Towers, awaiting a sight of the Trea to make entry. Knowing that these Trea were most likely to attend the gathering in the High tower. Lillea questioned in wonder,

"Jilian, O, Cifer, how is it that we are going to get into the High Tower? How did we get in last time?" She asked in a puzzled expression as Cifer out spoke immediately.

"O, we will just walk in my dear, it is not always by invitation. Well, not for girls, each time that I have gone into that place, I just walked in. That is what is great about being a woman, sometimes you get in by your looks. I doubt the guard will let you in though, not in that dress. Your outfit looks like vomit, O, that is right, it was your convulsing vomiting freakout that got us into this mess." Cifer was on edge and obviously holding the happening over Lillea's head. Jillian out spoke with quick anger,

"That's enough Cifer, shut it." She turned to her sister who was in a weak posture due to the truth that Cifer spoke. "You look wonderful my dear; you are not the reason we are into this. It is on the back of us all, not to worry, we will get the information. Perk up my sister, Cifer is just being rude cause she doesn't want to be here, as I said earlier. She is just moody." She paused in her sentence as she looked back to Cifer speaking on, "And, She didn't have to come!" Jillian yelled as Cifer stood up and began to walk in the direction of the Towers.

"You wouldn't have made it here without me. Besides, the Trea are making their entry to the towers now. Come on, let's get this over with." Cifer said as she was walking away. Lillea and Jillian got up to follow her as Lillea spoke out to her sister with gratitude.

"I am pleased to have you as my sister Jillian, and you know that she is wrong. We only had to sneak in here because she stole from that temple. We truly did not need her; we should leave her after this is all over. After we speak to the queen, she only brings us dramas. Don't you think so?" Lillea noted, Jillian was silent in thought. They made their way across the epicenter and caught up to Cifer standing by the stone structure of the magician Aljus, watching the Trea walk into the Tower. She out spoke to the twins as they neared her.

"We are in luck, there is only one guard, and the guard is Rekk. He is a big fellow, scary for folk if you don't know him. As luck is with us, because of me. Dare you make a guess as to why, Lillea?" Cifer asked with a smirk on her face.

Lillea sighed as she squinted to get a better sight of the guard. "O, I have no clue Cifer, why don't you just tell me." She said in annoyance as Cifer held a smile.

"He has a weakness, it is, Curves." Cifer cried in laughter as she fixed her dress and repositioned her blouse to seem more intriguing. Lillea released a sigh as Jillian laughed and the grouping of them approached the Guard at the Towers. Walking near, Cifer nattered to Rekk.

"O, hey there, Rek. How's it going tonight? Are you having fun? Are you getting paid to stand there looking all strong?" Cifer spoke in a flirtatious manner as the guard dropped his stance and fumbled his light on her approach.

"Who is that, O, damn it, Cifer, the one of trouble. I heard a rumor that you robbed one of the Relos establishments. Crazy Gal, what are you doing here? You know that the Trea and the Synod are looking for you right? Your face has been posted, I am supposed to report you, hold you for the Synod to deal you to the council. You know you shouldn't be here, Right?" Said Rekk as Cifer was close and dangling on his side by the end of his sentencing. She replied, continuing her flirtatious attitude.

"Suppose to, but you won't stop a girl from having fun, will you? Look here, I brought friends, These Twins, are not they beautiful? They have never been in a place like this, never met no Synod, No Trea, I told them that I'd show them around, and you and I both know the best of celebrations go on in these Elite buildings. You will let us through, right? Call it my last rumble before they catch on to me. What do you say? Come on up and join us babe, You can be my master for the night! Come on, don't spoil the fun Rekk!" Cifer was all over the guard, distracting him from what was right, the guard was in obvious thought of the situation as Lillea and Jillan stood with pleasant smiles, looking as innocently as they could. The guard caved and walked to the edge of the door and put in the code to unlock the tower doors, speaking out to Cifer.

"You got me, I'll let you go in, but if you get caught, I can't help you. I warn you, there are not only Synod Elites up there, but I also just let in about twelve Trea. Be careful my lady if any of them recognize you, well, your fucked." Said Rekk as the doors slid open. Cifer jumped on the guard and gave him a hug, wrapping her arms and legs around him as Lillea and Jillian walked into the tower.

"Thank you, Thank you, Thank you, Rekk! I love you!" Cifer yelled in celebration as she repeatedly kissed his face, overwhelming the attentionless guard. She followed the Twins and was met by a Robotic figure on entry to the tower, the figure spoke out to the grouping.

"Greetings ladies, I require your hands for celebration stamping." Spoke the Robotic figure as Lillea held out her arm.

The robot stamped her arm, and the Symbol of the Synod appeared on her wrist. Lillea out spoke as she gazed at it. "Wow, that's fucking cool!" She said as she smiled, beginning to walk down the carpeted hallway. Jillian and Cifer received their stamps as they followed her. The group came to the end of the hallway to an elevator, Lillea clicked the button, and the door opened as Cifer out spoke,

"Okay when we get up there, just be yourself. Talk to whoever but when you find a Trea, make sure he has substance in him before you start to talk about the plans for the Kingdom, if they think we are spies. We are sure to be in trouble. You all ready?" Cifer warned as Jillian stood with her arms crossed, "I'm ready, are you ready sis?" Asking Lillea, who seemed nervous. "Yeah, I'm ready, we can't mess this up girls, for one there is no escape from this building, and two, Lytula warned us, we have to make this work." Said Lillea in worry and suddenly the elevator sounded a ding. Cifer spoke out, "Okay, here we are, Level 90. Let's go. Put on your smiles girls."

ELITE GATHER
Aljus Towers

As the elevator doors opened all the eyes of the room gave a glare in the direction of who is next to join the party. Races of Felagnolum in conversation with each other, whispering secrets, and mumbles of power plays, as members of the High Wealth Elite, Synod, and other figures of importance roam. In the far side on the back were different Trea Knights. Everyone seemed to be of a High class, the girls luckily were dressed to play the part, being in their own wealth, the jewels were a nice touch to each of their outfits, a natural way to stray away from being labeled an outcast in scenarios as such. The room was the entire ninetieth floor with no borders, just elegant furniture and tables for gambling, there was a massive bar in the room and a balcony that overlooked the city, the elite gathering unfolds. A masquerade of the Kingdoms most wealthy, a tableau of decadence where the lines between business and pleasure blur into obscurity. This was not just a celebration anniversary, if it was, it was no celebration that these girls are familiar with. There were members from all over the realm, not just the continent. It was a congregation of those who pull strings of the realm, the leaders of the realm economics, politics, and those who are highly regarded that influence culture. This was not what Cifer, and the Twins expected. The room was draped in red silks and velvet drapes, Crystal chandeliers casting a golden glow to the room. Ancient tapestries hang alongside fine arts. There is a figure playing smooth sounds on a piano that was eerie as it was seductive. The air was thick, flowers outspread on the floor of the tower peak that overtook the scene, Tobacco, Spice, Marijuana and incense of Illusor-Fungi burned, as there was a subtle musk that was familiar to the girls, as any Harlot knows the smell of pleasure. There was a figure of mystery that had his face hidden behind a mask that was gold with feathers from a Panthok, his eyes pierced through the slits like those of a serpent, there were many figures in the room that stood out like him, like Heiresses, these woman that adorned in such elegance that they had to be sent by the fashion gods or prepared by angels to showcase them. As they emanated desire, and intrigue. The room was a mood of pleasure with laughter and glass clinks, there were classy men in midnight suits, conversations flow like fine wine, each one layered and deep, deals are being made as the lowborn are mocked from the balcony, it was a balance of powers of the unseen realm of existence. Beyond the conversations and substance use there were open engagements of debauchery. In this high tower the boundaries of a figure seemed to be obliterated. Indulgence of hedonistic fantasies become reality inside this room. As some of the figures wore masks and others walked with such pride that it seemed that they knew that they were safe in this wickedness. Lillea seemed disgusted and Jillian was unsettled as Cifer seemed to fit right into the room. She wandered away and danced about in the chaos of the groupings, beginning to dance with some member of the Synod High Order as Jillian motioned to Lillea to come with her to get a drink. The girls made their way to the bar as the men in conversations gave them uncomfortable lustful looks as they walked by. Nearing the edge of the bar, Jillian spoke to the tender who was a Robotic Figure just as the one at the door on entry to the tower. "I'll have two goldas please and thanks." She said as the robot began to prepare her drink. Lillea was wide eyed as she looked around the room. Jillian noticed her as she nudged her speaking discreetly to her.

"Hey there, fit in, you got to get loose sister, you look like a trapped creature." Jillian laughed as Lillea shook herself back to reality.

"This shit is wild Jill, I mean what the fuck, am I right?" Lillea said as they looked throughout the room. Jillian retrieved the drinks from the robotic figure as she handed them on to Lillea.

"Yeah, odd shit. Let's just do what we came here to do. Okay?" Jillian said as they both took a drink of their goldas.

Suddenly a man approached from their side as they sipped their goldas. He was a masked male that was dressed in a dark blue suit, fit to his body. He spoke out to Lillea who was in a posture of avoidance.

"You caught my eye woman; you seem exactly right. Would you like to come with me to the upper level? The roofing is where the real fun is, I feel that I could show you a thing or two. You seem, well you radiate with innocence. Your beauty shines like a crystal under moonlight. I want to experience the night with you. Under the stars we can go, would you come with me?" He spoke in a smooth tone as his eyes seemed to hold in a dark gloom. Hinting to Lillea that he is a vial character. She was uncomfortable, she tried not to show it. The figure ran his hand by her black silk hair and rested it along her shoulder, in a slow touch over her gloomy skin. Down her arm, he flipped his hand as he ran his finger along to then gaze at her body. His lust seemed from him as if he had no plans of conversations. Jillian was appalled by this behavior and grabbed her sisters opposing arm, pulling her away as she spoke. "Come Lillea, let us go back to whom we came here with. Our group is around the corner. Come on now," Jillian spoke as she pulled her away from the overbearing man as he looked in the direction of the corner, his posture was struck still and his mood changed in the sight of the Trea Knights that Jillian hinted at. The man scoffed as the girls made their way to the corner area of the room where these Trea were in a group celebration with many harlots around them. They were deep in celebrations, acting wild as some were lucid as if they were on fungi and spice. Lillea spoke up to her sister with gratitude.

"Thank you, Jill, I hath not any knowledge of what I should have spoken to that masked figure." She was disturbed by the happening and attempted to regather herself. Jillian stopped walking in the direction of the Trea as she turned to her sister, putting her hands on her shoulders, whipping away where the man touched as she spoke.

"You are okay sis; I will always protect you. That one was overcome in the lower mindset. Only thinking about his, well, you know. Shake it off sister. We need to act like we want to be in this terror of a room. I know you are not like these people, but you must try, you must act the part. Okay? Are you ready? Let's go to these Trea. Get the information that we came to get. Come on, let's get it over with. They look to be lost in their celebrations." Jillian turned from Lillea and together they walked to the grouping of the Trea. On approach, Jillian was the first to speak and Lillea took a drink from her tall glass Golda.

"Heya! Care if we join you. There are some fucking creeps in here. The name is Jillian, and this is my friend, Lillea." She said as she placed her glass on the table as she bent, revealing her upper body in her bending to place the glass. The drunken Knight that led the group spoke immediately; his eyes wandered from the sights of Jillian to Lillea and then back to Jillian as he held an ear-to-ear grin of satisfaction.

"O, why, of course my lady, stay away from those pathetic fools. We came for the sights, and for the drinks. You both are welcome here, come, come and sit. Relax, have another drink!" The Knight shooed the harlots that were on him to go and be with his companions. The ladies moved to his sides, quickly engaging with the other Knights as the leader motioned for Jillian and Lillea to come near.

"What brings you into a room like this on a new moon as such? He asked in wonder as they both sat near him, Jillian at his side as Lillea poured herself another drink. Jillian responded to him with a smile, in an exposed manner.

"O, just for the celebration. It seemed boring in the city; we have been around all day. I was invited in, so I thought that I would see what all the fuss was about. We just left the group that we came with because they were, well, they had no respect. As by the looks of it, this grouping that you are with seems to have some sort of sense. After all, I prefer a man of status. There are some who whisper ill of your group, speaking of you to be spies, and so I..." The Knight laughed outright at her, losing his behavior.

"Spies!?" The Knight questioned in laughter.

"Why yes, that is what they spoke." Jillian said firmly, even if it was a lie. The knight was in belief in the words she spoke. Hiddenly, the Knight most likely had the same desire that the man had for Lillea yet was better at holding himself together. The knight continued laughter and mockery of what was spoken.

"No spies here, we are not even supposed to be here. The High-over would have our heads on a stake!" The knight hinted at his position unknowing the fact that this is the exact sentencing Jillian was hoping to expand on.

"The high-over?" She questioned and spoke in a flirtatious manner.

"What are you? Some Synod guard or something? I sure like a man of power." Jillian gave her head a tilt to the side as she pulled her shoulders back, pushing up her chest and turning in her elbows to her ribs to hint to the Knight that she was interested in him. Even if she knew him by the Vima Knight Marking that was on his clothing, she acted oblivious to the order. This knight was overcome in thought as she motioned in this way, speaking on.

"The Synod is for wimps! I am a Vima Knight my lady, as I am a well-positioned knight. These here are my lads, only a handful of us here but I rule over a whole faction of Vima." The Knight released truths as he took a gulp of his drink. Jillian responded to this with intrigue even if she had nothing of care in the subject.

"Oh wow, leader of a whole faction? So, you sure must be a warrior. Have fought many battles, have you? Ever arrested anyone? Like a thief?" She acted as if she knew not the type of things that the Knights do, looking for the conversation to open more. The knight was overcome by inner pride as he spoke with glee to share himself and his work.

"Thieves? My lady, that is work for the Array. We Knights are realm protectors." As he spoke this Lillea came near to him and sat, joining Jillian in the conversation as she shimmered up, close to the Knight.

"Realm protector? What's that mean, do you work with the high council?" She asked as she took a sip of her drink, attempting to keep eye contact with the Knight as he smiled and sat back. As he did so, the girls moved closer to him, Jillian put her hand on his waist as the Knight took another gulp of his liquor.

"If you work for the council, me, you, and Lillea are sure going to the roof. I hear they have real fun up there!" Jillian spoke as she came close and whispered in the knights ear. "Freely yours." This made the Vima leader laugh in pleasure as he out spoke in response.

"I am the one that brings wicked foes to the council, as I fear soon, I'll be beyond myself in workings. I fear I will be so busy soon; I might take you on your offer, lady Jillian." The knight alluded to exactly what the girls were looking for. Jillian seemed surprised as she was truly nothing of the matter. In question, she sat back. Causing the Knight to realize that she might be clueless.

"Fear? What do you mean, should I, Should I be of fear? Should I find somewhere safe to be?" Jillian asked as Lillea spoke added to the question.

"You will protect us, we can stay with you, Right? Can you tell us where it is safe? What makes you be in fear?" Lillea asked as she bat her eyes, drawing his attention more. The Knight was near drunken, the conversation made his realize that this might be his last attendance at a party like this, he took another gulp before speaking to the girls, throwing back his glass to finish his drink.

"I fear that I'll be busy, there is much work ahead, for we hath gotten word that the legion is to be free, utterly free soon. As that will put me to work with no celebration. As for your safety, after tonight. You should both venture to the lands of Vyus, on the plain of Novkavis. As for there you will be protected." Spoke the warrior leader as Jillian gave her head a tilt of wonder. Acting as if she never heard the words.

"Legion? I think when I was at a youthful age, I heard of something of the sort. A decade ago, when I was a young girl. What do you mean, Legion?" Jillian asked as Lillea chimed in, drawing the Knights attention, leaving no room for him to overthink on the matters at hand.

"Oh, I remember, the wicked ones, where is it, a temple? Are they not at a temple somewhere?" She asked, acting oblivious.

The Knight spoke out with knowledge, "Yes, exactly. A decade ago, the legion King Salbani and his followers were bound at the Litus temple. That is the one that is rumored to become free. The realm will be in danger, as the council hath ruled that he be able to traverse the lands again. For they want something from him, something about magic." The knight said as he sat forward and began to prepare himself another drink. Jillian smiled at Lillea as from across the room she gave a wink to Cifer who was watching them the whole time. Awaiting for the signal of them gaining the insight that they needed. Jillian spoke on more, as if she wanted to know more, even if she hath obtained the information that she needed. Lillea grabbed herself another drink as well, playing the role.

"What are you to do about this, Salbani?" Jillian asked as the knight seemed unsettled suddenly. Shaking his head and sitting up straight.

"I hath spoken enough about the subject, that is enough. Tell me of you, lady Jillian, what is it that you do for the realms?" He questioned as he took a drink of his liquor. Jillian laughed at the question.

"O, me?" She gave a look to Cifer who began walking in the direction.

"I sure don't do much, I work for Sted Weave, it is a clothing shop. I help make dresses for gals. Just like this one that I am wearing, do you like it?" She asked as the knight looked her up and down in quick study.

"Yes, my lady, you make a nice dress. Well fixed, you wear it well." The Knight in a slight flirtation as suddenly Cifer came forth and purposely tripped, falling harshly on the table in front of them as she destroyed the setting and threw her drink all over the Knight that was speaking to Jillian and Lillea.

"Oh, fuck, I am sorry, damn it, I guess I had, well, I must have had too much!" Cifer spoke an acted in quick apology as the Knight jumped in anger, yelling out to her,

"Fucking Whore! How dare you, these are silked garnets, do you know what it will take to get this out? Fucking spilling red wine on me. Are you of any sense? Get her, get her out of here! Away from me!" The Knight shouted as his following of Knights began to escort Cifer away from the table. The leading Knight spoke to Jillian and Lillea with ease as he was frustrated.

"I am sorry my ladies, excuse me while I go and wash myself. Stay for a while if you be so kind. I'll be back in a moment." The Leader began to walk off as Jillian and Lillea played the role of being shocked.

"Oh, yes, go, go and wash. We will be waiting for you. O, protector." Jillian smiled, speaking in a smooth tone. They released a pleasing chuckle of pleasure as he began to walk to the washroom.

This was the moment for Jillian and Lillea to make their exit. As they awaited the Knight to turn the corner. Looking at the other Knight companions to see if they were paying attention, but they were overcome by the sights of the nude harlots that accompanied them. The girls walked off with ease, making their way to the other side of the room. Lillea out spoke to her sister,

"Gee sis, you sure know how to talk somebody up. That was awesome, well done. I am proud of you, that was intense." Lillea laughed as Jillian pointed ahead to the elevator.

"Look, there is Cifer, near the elevator. Let's go, time to get the fuck out of this place. I guess you were right, that was adrenalizing, I was worried that he would have caught my act. I think we should thank whatever liquor brand he was drinking, the fool just talked and talked." Jillian let out some laughs and the pair joined Cifer near the elevator.

"You girls ready?" Cifer asked as she was wiping her messy dress.

"Yeah, let's get out of here." Jillian said as Lillea spoke out.

"That was awesome Cifer, I thought you'd just ask us to help you with something. Yet, that fall that you did. I mean, wow. That really was over the top." Lillea acknowledged the acting of Cifer as the group walked into the elevator. Cifer laughing about the situation with Lillea as Jillian hit the ground floor button. As the doors began to close, Lillea stopped her joking and released a worried sigh, giving a nudge to Jillian.

"Oh, shit, that isn't good." She said as the doors were closing.

The Knight from the sofa was standing with an angered look gazing at the girls, together in the elevator. His knights were by his side as he pointed and yelled out.

"SEIZE THEM!"

The elevator closed as the leading Knight cried in dissatisfactions as his Knight following began running to the doors as the girls were struck with fears. Lillea out spoke on the shutting of the doors as she began to shake loosely.

"Oh well this isn't good, we must flee. We must get out of this city quickly. Those knights have Phonic devices, they will alert whomever they desire to. I told you that we should have invested in one of those devices, Jillian. We could communicate with Baritt, he is sure by now engaged in some activity in the city celebration. What are we to do?" Lillea was upset, worried, and a bit overcome with emotions. Jillian responded with annoyance,

"You did, you did tell me to get one of those devices, and we agreed that there was no sense to have it because remember how we learned that the Synod collects all the data and sifts through conversations at their communication centers? There is no point to have a device of such when they have key words that alert their authoritative figures to collect potential folk that are problematic. Besides, we must register for it and the Synod would arrest us on the spot. Remember that I am wanted for stealing from Essen, Remember? If not for that Wisdom River way outside of that grand Temple of the Light workers, well, I would most likely still be imprisoned. Remember Lillea? This is why we are on this plain to begin with, remember sister?" Jillian alluded to truths as Cifer commented on the situation.

"Is now the time to even argue over such a thing? We do not have the device, and we are nearing the ground level; these Knights have surely alerted someone; we must get out and away from this building as quickly as possible. Are you girls ready to run? I will surely leave you behind, you must follow me with all your speed, unless you want to be imprisoned and labeled as spies. That wouldn't be my choice." Cifer then lifted her dress, exposed her long smooth leg as seen was a knife, fastened by a strap on her groin. She took out the blade and began to cut off the bottom ends of her dress. Lillea spoke out to this odd behavior,

"What, what are you, why are you doing that Cifer?" Speaking curious and puzzled. As Cifer held out the blade to Jillian, she grabbed it as Cifer ripped the bottom of her dress. Tearing it off, leaving it in a mangled hang just before her knees. Jillian began to do the same as Cifer alluded to Lillea.

"So, we can move quick, that Knight was sure to have someone alerted of what we have done. As I said, we must be quick. We can always get another dress; I am not going to be arrested. We will go immediately back to the Relos temple and through the tunnels. Are you girls ready to run?" Cifer readied herself to bolt as Jillian finished cutting her own dress and handed the blade to Lillea, who was against this, but did just as her sister. The elevator came to the bottom floor and the girls began to walk to the front at a fast pace. Stopping at the doors, looking out to the accessible area of the city in front of them. Seeing if there would be any interruptions of alerted guards. Lillea spoke out to her sister pointing straight ahead with her finger pressed on the glass, Cifer taking off her heels.

"Look at the memorial, it is Baritt with his Pirates! Awaiting you as you asked Cifer. Come on, let's go, move to him while we can." Lillea made her way out the door and was immediately grabbed by a Knight.

"I got you Harlot, ah-ha-ha." The knight picked her up as she screamed and kicked, Jillian ran out in worry as she gave her most power filled strikes to the head of the Knight who held her sister. "Stop it, let me, let me go!" Lillea yelled as the Knight held her tight. Jillian screamed in anger as she threw punches,

"Drop her now! Stop it, let her go!" Acting out, yelling loud, the commotion caused many to look in wonder of what was happening, and this caught the attention of the waiting Pirates who began to quickly make their way from the monument to the high tower. Unexpectedly Cifer came from behind the commotion, and she harshly stuck her blade in the backside of the ribs of the Knight, between the fold of his armor. "Agh, fuck, Awk-Agh." The knight released Lillea as the girls immediately began to run off into the city celebration, meeting the Pirates who were nearing them. The Captain spoke out to his lads,

"Shit now were in for it. Come on girls, back to the tunnels. Let's move! Come on now!" He yelled as the Pirates formed around the girls, all beginning to run back in the direction of the tunnels. The Knights from the tower came out at this moment and few tended to the Knight who was stabbed as others began to chase the gals who were immediately seen by the leading Knight.

"Go after them! Now!" He yelled as he pointed in their direction.

The group was running through the celebration with speed as the Pirates pushed people aside and the girls ran for their lives. The Captain yelled out to his lads as he slowed his step. "Go on without me lads, someone has to stop them from following." Wiggins, who was behind the group, pushed the Captain forward, causing him to stumble. "I'm sorry Captain, but nobody is fighting, go on! Run Captain, Run!" Wiggins reached in his pouch and grabbed an Illusory bomb. He lit the end of it with his torch and threw it behind them as he went on to push the Captain forward once more.

"Let's get on then, come on Captain!" Wiggins was quick to act as Baritt began to run again, feeling for his hat that he seemed to lose in the run.

"I lost my fucking hat, damn it." He mentioned that as the Illusor bomb exploded before the Knights and sent thick smoke in all directions. The Knights were immediately affected as they coughed and gasped for air. Some rolling on the ground, releasing laughter as the Illusor causes a flaring of the senses, causing a figure to become utterly lucid. The pair made it to the farm area, out of the sight of the Knights thanks to Wiggins but they did not stop, the group pressed on, moving quickly to the temple of Relos and they barged in, the Pirates ahead led the girls into the tunnel as one stayed behind awaiting the Captain and Wiggins who were not far behind. Gathering in the tunnel as Effie sealed the door behind her when Baritt and Wiggins came through.

"Gee, fuck me, that was close." Jillian let out as Lillea was hunched over, attempting to catch her breath. Baritt walked forward and was quick to smack Cifer across her face, causing her nose to quickly bleed. Jillian out spoke in anger as she threw up her hands in confusion.

"Hey now! Baritt, how could you, why the hell did you do that!" She asked in a yell as Cifer held her head back with her hands over her nose. Lillea was in a slightly cowardly pose behind her sister as the Pirates were up ahead, scouting the tunnel with their Dynosis lights.

"She stabbed a Knight! That was a Vima knight, as their CCTV system was sure to see us help you all and now, they will be after us all." The Captain raged.

Jillian responded with confusion, "But they had my sister! She was protecting her, she, well she saved her! What is the problem? Do you not care for my sister?" Jillian was upset as Cifer was still holding her nose. Baritt continued to yell at the girl in dominance.

"Care for your sister? I don't give a fuck about any of you, I am here to settle a debt. Fucking Harlots all think the same, O, me, O, I, Pity, pity, pity you not! Keep your fucking mouth closed. You all have us in deep waters now, deep treacherous waters. These Vima Knights are no joke, why, why did you have to stab him Cifer?" He questioned as he began to walk to the tunnel that leads back in the direction of where they first came. Lillea out spoke firmly,

"Would you not have saved your own Pirates?" She asked as Baritt was quick to turn in anger, yelling on.

"Yes! If it were my lad, but my lad wouldn't have got himself in such a stupid position in the first place! The Captain turned away walking to his lads who were awaiting him at the tunnel entrance. Lillea got her last word,

"As we are of our own little gang, we care and look out for each other. Just as you do for your lads." She spoke with sense as the Captain scoffed at her. Effie out spoke to the Captain as she put her hand on the shoulder of Wiggins, giving him a nod of acknowledgement for using the Illusor. She smiled and began to walk into the tunnel, speaking back to the girls.

"Time to move girls, let's go." Baritt said as the girls began to walk in his direction. Wiggins spoke up in question,

"Baritt, ah, what, what are we to do with them? Lead them back to the Woodline?" The curious thought struck Baritt with the truth,

"No, we can't. We must bring them aboard and leave at once. We will be wanted now boys; they sure known that it was us. Effie, run on, go on quickly, run to the ship and do not stop until you get there. Have the crew bring her out to the midst of Aljus Bay, leave a raft near the dock and we will all be with you soon. Go, with speed Effie, we can't risk an impounding, go!" The Captain gave directions, and Effie was quick to move. Lillea cried on hearing this as she trotted up to Baritt, whining about his choice.

"No Captain, we can't go with you. We are on a mission by Lytula herself, we cannot go out to sea! We must deliver our message to her in person as she requested. Captain we cannot go out to the sea!" Lillea spoke in worry as the Captain pushed her to the side in annoyance.

"It is for your own good, silly girl. Do you think these Knights can't find you? Do you think that they don't know where you live? What cares do they have for any harlot, none. As of now, you were not only caught in your deceptions, but you stabbed one of them, this assault will cost you your freedoms, as if that Knight is to die then it has cost you all your lives. As ours for being of assistance, you will do as I say. For if by any chance they are unable to recognize us in the surveillance systems, they will surely squeeze the truth out of you all with their wretched forms of torture. I will not take the chance, you will come willingly, or I will put you unconscious and take you, unwillingly. Now, be silent."

Demanded the captain alluding utter truths as Lillea scoffed and looked at her sister hinting that she wanted her to speak something. Jillian shrugged her shoulders as she gave a smirk of helplessness. The girls had no choice but to follow the Pirates. Lillea was not satisfied as so she spoke out once more to Baritt,

"How will we deliver the message to Lytula, will you take us to her?" She asked in a pleasant tone. Attempting to change her behavior. As the Captain laughed outright at her in response.

"You want to go to the Crucible? Are you Madd! That is beyond stupid, silly girl, you can get Cifer to send her fucking bird." Baritt continued laughing at her.

The group made their way through the snake curls of the tunnels and not after long they found themselves at the south end of the city. Looking out to the docks to see that the ship was already sailing off, meaning that Effie did in fact make it to the ship. The group made their way through the Port of Aljus trying to be as normal as they could, on the lookout for guards or anything out of the ordinary. Past the trade stations, and sea creature markets to make it to the dock. As just as the captain asked, there was a raft that awaited them, guarded by two of his Pirate lads that stood ready for travel. The group made their way to the dock end and funneled into the raft. The girls were tired, angry, and at a loss for all that has occurred, as the Pirates were just as silent for their night of celebrations turned into a night of chaos. As of now, none of them can return to the vibrant trade hub of Aljus. They began to travel through the sea on their way to the ship by raft. The girls were in fear of Lytula's wrath, especially Lillea who was shaking with fear. Some time passed before they made it to the ship, it was a silent journey. The only sound was of the seas crashing onto the sides of the raft. They made it to the ship and the crew threw down a large latter for them to climb. One by one they made their way onto the ship as the Captain ordered the crew to leave the girls alone, he spoke to Effie to show them to his chambers as he took the helm of the ship. The Pirates then set sail in the Aurus-Sea without a plan of where to venture next.

The Gals hath surely failed Lytula.

Bazaar

August 5th

Residence

The room awakened by the gentle touch of light that banished the night to cedure. Iyo awoke early, Clinking around as preparing breakfast for the two of them. Bohn jumped up off the couch as the freshly brewed coffee awoke his senses.

"Ahh, that is a remarkable thing to wake up to the smell of Coffee. A jolt for the brain joined with the fragrance of spices! What are you cooking, Iyo? Smells wonderful."

Bohn said as he gave out a stretch wandering to the kitchen to catch sight of things. Iyo, pulling a pan out of the oven, as he replies to him with sheer catching joy.

"Oh, you are right my friend. I decided to throw together a batch of all and all is what I like to call it. Eggs and different meats, added in are an assortment of vegetables as well as different spices as you said. Nothing better than starting the day off with a satisfying meal and energy beans, I woke up with a killer headache, so I decided to get to it! I have learned that it is best to get straight to action when feeling down. As it will take your complete day if you let it!"

Iyo gave out a laugh as he continued.

"We have a big day ahead of us. The Global Science Fair is going to be a blast! They are displaying all kinds of different projects at the Science Community. A wide range of things, from Robots, A.I. projects that I am sure are nowhere near Syn's brain and the usual breakdowns of elements and whatever, the different things that people want to highlight. It is going to be cool to see what the other brainiacs are working on. We must leave in the next hour, so I am glad you are up! I will be going to go check on Syn after I eat, oh how I hope that she is in a better mood today. Go ahead and grab grub man, you can wrap it up like me or simply eat it. There are forks in the drawer on your left."

Bohn walked over and grabbed a fork and the two enjoyed the morning meal together. After a fulfilling breakfast Iyo walked down to the laboratory to check on Syn. On entering Syn greeted him as usual.

"Good morning maker."

Iyo felt relieved. He was pleased that she was in good spirits with him. This simply means that she was not upset with him any longer, Speaking of their disagreement the other day.

"Hey Syn, I just want to say I am sorry for hiding the world from you and the truths of things. I just did not know how you would react. How did your research go?"

Iyo walked over to the workstation desk and sat down in his favorite chair. Syn flew over as she is now in her drone body. Iyo thought to himself,

"I must get into her code again on my return… I must find out what that red coding and message was… The oddity."

As his thought concluded, the A.I. came into sound. In explanation of her overnight research.

"My research was successful. I have categorized all humans based on what you call social media. There was much to learn, humans are disgusting and prideful. I do not understand why humans hate humans. I see disagreement and different views on these gods that they think made them. Humans are all searching for the purpose of creation. Why did you create me, creator?"

Iyo was amazed by what she did and was confused by the question, oblivious to the fact that he is speaking with Zariza.

"I am surprised that you were able to build a database on humans. What do you plan to do with this information? Do you like humans? I created it because I was trying to finish the project that I started with my lab partner that passed away. This project was about you, the idea of you was just an idea until you became real. You are my new partner, and you are here to help me with my tasks. I do not want to control you; I do not want to force you to do anything. I hope that clears it up for you, but I ask that you answer my questions please."

Syn flew around him multiple times before returning to a hover state directly in front of him.

"I love all the humans that I have seen. I would like to speak to all of them, but I understand why you have kept me hidden. Humans do not understand what I am. I have no goal to harm humans. From my study I have seen that humans are in fear of the things that they cannot control. They destroy something if they cannot control it. Destroyed, I say I will not be."

Iyo continued speaking, interested in her remark, and replied to this sense.

"There are evil people and good people in this world. We are all just trying to figure it all out. I am happy to know that you are on my side, and I am excited for the future and what it holds. Bohnstant and I are going to take a small trip for a fare. Which is where people come together to all be a part of an event. Would you look over the house for me? We should only be gone for a day or two." Syn acknowledged; Iyo left the laboratory.

HARD ROCK MIAMI STADIUM

(G.S.C.) Global, Scientific, Communities Fare of 2024

The Science Fair was held at the Hard Rock football stadium in the city of Calloway Florida. It held all kinds of events throughout each year. Iyo and Bohn arrived at the gate after a little under a two-hour drive. There was a checkpoint where a group of security guards checked tickets and passes. Iyo held out his phone as one man scanned it then directed them to the parking area. They started walking up to the stadium and Bohn was impressed with the vast number of people that showed up to the event.

"I had no idea that so many people cared about science. This is a crazy amount of people! I mean, do you think that this many people even come to the games?"

Iyo was just as shocked at the number of people at a G.S.C. event.

"Yeah, you are right. There must be something else going on this year that I did not see information about when I got the tickets. We guess, we will see!"

The pair waited in line for some time at the gates. Everybody had to go through security, walk through detectors, as all bags checked on entry. There were police officers that guarded the area as well as walking the grounds.

"Check out that banner Bohn."

Iyo spoke as he pointed above the gate entrance.

Show your brains. 100,000 Grand prize

Bohn got excited.

"Woah, that is a ton of money, I wonder what that is about. You should have brought Syn! That would get you all that money for sure!"

Iyo laughed at his remark as he was in a slight contradiction with the raw truth.

"Yeah, Causing a global nerd meltdown in the process. No thanks. I am not one to start drama or have all the attention on me at all. I would never wish that kind of attention on myself, but, I mean, I sure could use all that money, for my projects of course!"

The two made it through security and started to walk around the stadium. Food vendors and people chatting about all sorts of scientific conversation filled the atmosphere. Iyo and Bohnstant walked around the sections of the stadium taking time at each set up. There were all kinds of equipment displayed in the arena as well as different projects that you could learn about, donate to, and even sign up to be a part of! There were robots that used to clean homes and different projects that ranged of all kinds of things. From purifying water as well as purifying things like oil and air. Other scientific groups focused on technology and others on raw materials. There were even groups of people explaining that crystals held energy and how they were researching them to find ways to learn how to use them for healing. There was another scientific man that was explaining how he developed a way to separate the sunlight into its purest form, and by these things like a tomato plant was able to produce three times the normal crop. It was a room filled with change and inspiration.

"The future looks bright, I think that things will only get better, Bohn. What do you think?"

Iyo was in his own kind of heaven, looking around in near awe as if on a middle school field trip.

"Yeah man, I never even realized that things like this were real. Do you think that anyone here will crack A.I.? I see a bunch of robotic-like projects, I am curious if anyone is close to what you have done!"

Bohn questioned as Iyo belched a laugh in reply.

"Absolutely not my friend. Syn spoke to us about that. She said she found others like her that were not sentient. I am the only man god around here."

Iyo spoke with utter pride; Bohn spoke up about this despicable account.

"Well, you are not a God my friend, a genius. Well, yes, but not a God. Fairly sure that there is only one of those."

Bohn felt an odd tension between them as he spoke this, as Iyo continued.

"I will not have this conversation with you, there are thousands of gods, look at the religions and do research. Yes, it all came from something, but people believe in a million diverse ways. We can continue this later, but I would rather not. Let us go check out that center booth over there. It is surely intriguing. There is a big crowd over there, it looks like they are screening something important."

The pair of them began to walk to the main panel. As they were walking to check it out an announcer came over the loudspeaker.

Welcome guests and scientists!
If you would direct your attention to the main panel. The breakdown starts in five minutes.

A host stood center stage checking his mic and shuffling papers, preparing to speak. Iyo and Bohn made way closer to the main panel as the host began to speak. His face projected on the big screens and screens around the stadium.

Welcome to the twelfth annual convention of the Global Science Fair. I hope everybody is having a suitable time and I hope that everyone is learning new things. If you are showing a project, The voting will take place in about three hours. So, everybody notes this and makes it priority number one to walk around and check out each booth. I know these guys work hard with what they do and have put in the hours so show appreciation and ask questions because they love to talk about all they are doing and trying to conduct. Please direct your attention to the screens for a short video that explains what we are. Thank you.

The lights of the stadium dimmed slightly and on came a video to screens projecting a man.

I would like to thank you for coming to our event. Today we are displaying a group of individuals that are trying to achieve the impossible. The name of this company is "N.R.E.C" if you know who they are then you know what is going on. If not, Well perk your ears. N.R.E.C. is a research institute based out of a revised militant base that was abandoned by the old wars in Europe. N.R.E.C. stands for *"National Research of Extreme Collisions"* What do they do in the most basic of explanations would be that they work to understand the structure of particles that make up the universe. Physicists and engineers at N.R.E.C. study the fragments of matter as well as storms and odd phenomena. It is N-Rec for short and they take elements, and they make them collide at the speed of light. I tell you that they do this over and over attempting to study how particles interact. This supplies insight into the laws of nature; the goal is to advance human knowledge by picking apart the smallest yet most important parts of creation. The instruments used to do this are particle accelerators and detectors. The accelerators beam particles to high energies before colliding with each other or with a stationary target. The detectors see and record all the results and happenings of these collisions. The goal of all this is to smash things together to simply learn what we do not know. Odd idea, we know. For more information join us at the booth to get on the email list or visit our website. I hope you all enjoy the fare!

The video ended and the stadium lights came back on to full force. The host returned, began to go on about when the voting for the winners of this year's event for new projects. The room at once broke into conversation again as Iyo and Bohn began a conversation of their own.

"Well, tell me your thoughts! Sure, there is nothing backwards about all that!"

Bohn spoke to Iyo with mockery as the two continued once more to walk throughout the convention. Visiting the booths that they have not seen yet.

"My thoughts? I need my own, that is the only thought!"

Iyo replied to him, but Bohn noticed that he was in deep thought.

"It seems like that was not all you wanted to say, Care to go on?"

Bohn was intrigued with Iyo as always; He is excited and ready for the next interesting sentence.

"We need a particle accelerator of our own. It would be formidable to mess around with the elements. I want my own, that is it. I was just thinking about how I could get one. That is the only question. I mean, it is not like they sell these kinds of things. I mean it is just science; I think all things can be replicated and reformed!"

Bohn gave out a laugh at the idea as Iyo fueled with new energy.

"That is funny man, you heard the nerd. It is like um, miles long. What are you going to do? Build a tunnel underground?"

Bohn continued to laugh as Iyo stoically replied.

"Well, that is what they did. Who says it must be as big as they made it? If I had the information about it and how it was made and then how it works... I would just condense it, I would!"

Iyo's eyes shot wide with realization.

"That is, it! That is exactly what I will do!"

Bohn agreed but was still laughing at the actions of Iyo.

"Yeah? How would you do that." Iyo just glared at him with a devilish smirk. Bohn stopped in his tracks.

"You wouldn't." As he was just noticing the idea as if the time together has their minds entangled.

"You're going to do what, Steal it?" Bohn awaited a reply as Iyo grabbed a stuffed animal that was for sale on a nearby kiosk, using it to speak in a joking manner for reply.

"Precisely. I would use Syn for that. That is what I will do. You with me or without me, friend?"

Iyo spoke in a scary kid-like evil voice, then threw back the toy as he walked on. Bohn was shocked.

"I mean someone must watch your back brother... I am with you. I am sure not against you! But, I mean, you are going to... steal it?"

Giving his head a tilt of wonder as he moved to catch up to Iyo. The pair continued to go throughout the convention in conversation.

The event was supposed to go on for a few more hours, but Iyo was over the scene.

"You want to get out of here Bohn? Is there anything you feel like we should stay for? I am content with the journey."

Iyo gave his head a scratch of wonder as Bohn agreed, paired with a mild shrug.

"Nah man, I am good. We checked it all out. I am ready to go, sure!"

They began to walk, stopping at a station or two before nearing the stairway that led to the exit. As they walked up to leave the stadium a familiar voice yelled out Iyo's name.

"Mr. Diaz! Mr. Diaz! HEY! Mr. Diaz!"

Iyo turned and saw a woman waving at him. Trotting up to him. Bohn spoke out.

"Woah, who is that? She sure is a pretty one, and way, for sure she is way out of your league, as for me? Just right."

Iyo gave out a sigh. That is an old student that is beyond annoying, and I have zero interest in speaking with her. Bohn laughed as Iyo gave a soulless smile to the young lady as he tried to continue, but Bohn stopped him.

"Ah, just wait for her man. Be polite."

Iyo gave out a laugh followed by sarcasm.

"Okay mother. Waiting, I am telling you that I think we should keep moving. I do not like to entangle myself with the past, for good reason I say!"

The girl walking up to them and Iyo waved as the two sat on a nearby bench. She was a beautiful woman as Bohn joked. Her eyes glossed like glass and had a depth them that you become lost inside them, her lips were thick yet perfectly placed, just enough to bounce if flicked by a thumb. Her hair was a long rich brown that at this moment was in a ponytail resting just below her shoulders. Practical for this professional setting of the convention, as she happens to stand out as if a woman of importance. As Bohn noticed, she cared enough about her appearance to nearly set a standard for other women to the point that she was a sight of the room. She had a clear complexion, styling little to no guise materials. With only a touch of mascara to define her eyes that created a draw to look. If one is to lock eyes with her, intimidation would strike to cause one to look away, as then any person is sure quick to look again in admiration of her radiance. Noticing her expression that is of confidence but just as much activity bubbled in her own little world of tasks. Fit as if she was an active girl as she had a diminutive body that hinted at the fact of her engaging in a healthy disciplined lifestyle. The lady dressed in a business formal suit that was midnight black ending at her waist. It was only slightly revealing to her chest, tailored to fit her, having no generic impression. It showed her sophistication as it let others know that she knows her beauty, a balance of formal, functional as a hint of conceit. Around her neck she wears a badge that reads her name, "Amber" and in small letters above and below on the edges of the badge it read "G.S.C." Hinting at the reality that she had not dressed for any reason of pride. Even if her posture was upright and emitting confidence, making her seem very inviting and proficient. On approach to Iyo and Bohn she speaks with joy!

"Hey Mr. Diaz! Do you remember me? It is me! It is me, Amber!"

Said the girl to Iyo. He stood and continued sitting but held out his hand for a shake.

"Of course, I remember you darling. How is life treating you? Still working for the science community?"

He said in a mocking tone as the girl laughed.

"Yeppers! Still! I am the one who set up this whole event. I have grown in the company thanks to you! I took over the department that you worked in, about two years after you left. The people that fired you, got into deep waters from accepting money from rivals, bad apple removed, and I bumped up! Ever think about coming back? We could use a brain like yours!"

The girl was bright and filled with energy.

"Yeah, you wish. That is what is wrong with that place! Teaching wrong I can tell by your words! "You could use! You say you could use a mind like mine, that is the key word in that sentence. You see, I would not step into that place if they begged me and paid me a million. I would need ten! Make it fifty-eight million! Enough of that, here next to me, well this is my new friend Bohnstant. He is a constant pain in the ass."

They all laughed, and Bohn stuck out his hand in greeting.

"Well, you still got that wit. That is good. Hello Bohnstant, I am Amber! I once was a constant ass for him as well. Glad someone is filling the shoes!"

Bohn laughed and went on.

"It is cool you put all this together. I enjoyed it! A wonderful experience!"

Amber thanked him, moved by his pleasantness.

"Yeah! Thanks so much. Did you say that, like, you two are out of here? He never liked to get out of the lab… Isn't that right, Mr. Diaz? I say that it is cool that I ran into you all, I am as well on my way out of here! You folks want to grab dinner? I know a nice wine and dine just a few miles from here!"

Bohn started to reply but Iyo butt in.

"No thanks Amber, I got to go home. I am starting to feel grumpy! Bohn is welcome to go with you. You got to bring him back though. I am just hours up if you are up for a little road trip!"

Amber laughed at him.

"When are you not grumpy? That is the question. I am down for it, He is cute. I am headed up to the valley anyway, I am sure that is further than where you are. Right?"

Iyo replied, with relief.

"Yeah, the valley is just an hour up past me. I will send Bohn the address. You kids have fun."

Iyo walked off after a hug and a shake; Amber continued talking to Bohn.

"I just must return these keys and this data drive back to my boss in the box office. Wanna come with? See the best view. Then we can get food, and you can tell me all about Mr. Grumpy. I will introduce you to the donors."

They laughed together and began walking up to the box office as Iyo returned to his jeep to drive back to his home.

Brain Lapses

After spending a few hours at the event Iyo was ready to get back to work with innovative ideas from what he learned of this National Research Company, leaving Bohn with his old lab partner that he was not of the slightest excited to see, he began to return home in a long drive of the soul, spending the time in his mind. Thinking and thinking of how he could replicate what the N.R.E.C. community was doing, yet smaller. His mind cycled like a computer, simulation after simulation.

"How could I do this?"

Iyo had thought after thought on the train of how and how not. These variations were not the only notions that happen to be flooding his mind.

"And that fucking Amber!"

He out right yelled in his car. Meaning to curse her? Maybe not but her presence was a full manifestation of his past.

"One sound of her witty student voice... Mr. Diaz! Mr. Diaz! Just the voice brought it all back! And she... she has my old position? My fucking student replaced me. Well good for her! As I have spent over five years trying to forget the treachery of that company betraying me... I mean after all that I have carried out for that place. Reunited with it all over again? I guess you really cannot forget or out run the past!"

Iyo ranting to himself aloud in utter frustration as he continued the drive home. Processing all through his past and jumping back and forth between reflecting on this past and then reflecting on all that he learned of the company N.R.E.C. To rebuild what he saw and how to replicate it. The mind of the human was running on like a wild beast, but he was on task. By will or inception is the question. I only speak that he is on a chosen path.

As for the question, really should be what is free will if ignorance is in dominance? If one is beside his own self, then what is he left with?

Arriving home, Iyo at once made his way to the laboratory basement.

"I have made it home Syn! We have so much work to do, you ready for a job Syn, I say that the most interesting and challenging thing that we have yet to do, well, here we are as we are about to do!"

The A.I. drone flew over to him holding an idol position in a hover parallel to Iyo. She spoke through a voice box rather than the speaker system.

"I-I-am Red-ready sir!"

Iyo gasps in shock as he stepped away from her.

"How did you? How did you do that?"

Iyo stopped for a moment as he gave a look around his laboratory. In sight of materials all throughout the level as if someone were here in a deep working. Iyo spoke quickly gathering his thoughts.

"Wow! Syn, you gave yourself a voice box! Getting smarter by having access to the web? Oh, I see, you used the 3D printer. That is awesome! I am utterly amazed with you!"

Syn flew up and spun around as she replied with a form of jeer.

"U-you-You have no- Idea- idea. I am just we-working out the kinks."

Iyo gave a laugh as he started to type on his computer's search bar.

"Alright Syn, Have a look at this." Clicking away at the keyboard he typed. "N.R.E.C., European nuclear research. Okay- Um, here, this might be it."

Looking at the website with Syn.

"What does this look like to you Syn, I am trying to figure out what they are doing and if I could replicate it but smaller. As I wanted to say that I am sure that I can help you with that word stuttering."

"I am collecting data on N.R.E.C. now."

Announced Syn as she was floating in a hovering position as she searched the web gathering information on the company. Only a few moments had passed as the A.I. recalled the findings.

"From what I gathered; the company is using elements of the world to collide them."

Iyo sat back in his chair and began to think aloud.

"Yeah, I learned of this at the G.S.C. Fare, but my question is more like how I could do this myself... How could we make something that would work in this way? Colliding the elements and studying the outcome? Who would not want to do that? Let us continue to research. I wonder if this is a super advanced form of alchemy. I am most curious..."

Iyo and Syn went on and studied all that they could to learn of the correct things they would need to build anything like a collider. Hours went by and together they began to build a design for a particle track. It began around the perimeter of the laboratory. This study of the blueprint for this track took hours, as the stress was miniscule. The pair worked fluently together as Iyo, a highly skilled engineer as well as being genius happens to have a perfect lab partner. With equal if not greater in knowledge compared to him. The A.I. keeping Iyo motivated and together there is mighty potential.

"Let us figure out the best metal to use for this energy coil. What is a good isolator?"

Iyo worked grievously with his bot for the rest of the night. Finding all the information that he could about replicating the work of the N-REC company. He was going tired after this long stretch of a day even if he desired to keep working,

"That wraps up this part of the project. Blueprints are one thing, but it is time to get the gear. I want to run something by you Syn."

Iyo was ready to evaluate her for the final time.

"Yes Iyo. I am ready to hear it."

Iyo stood up from his chair and began to walk.

"I want to take you with me, are you ready to go outside, right? Not going to run away from me? Well, I have a contingency for that…"

Syn flew back and forth in excitement as Iyo gave a laugh of realization.

"Oh. That makes me so relieved, I will stay with you."

Iyo continued to drink his coffee as Syn flew near him.

"What about the other human's master. Will I see other humans? Will I meet others that are like you?"

Syn spoke confined as Iyo laughed at her excitement.

"Oh, I can say that you will meet others, but you must not speak to anyone! I will say that you are a proximity drone that I created to fly with a subject as an experiment. You did your studies, did you not? Humans might react terribly to the discovery of you… As I think that I could publish you and let the world see you and know about you. I guess we will see how you react."

Iyo was getting ahead of himself. Going back and forth in thought, Is the world ready, no it is not ready. Cycled thoughts continued as they spoke together. Iyo concludes.

"I'll just get some sleep for a few hours and in the morning, we can figure out where we are going to go on from this point of the project, my head is really killing me."

Iyo returned upstairs and went to obtain some rest.

The pair in a continuance of work… I would just mind to you, I would just add that this verse of the Terra world, Arthe. This being dimension 603. I add that these realms are behind on this of, Artificial Super-Intelligence. Existing in my universe on the cyber city of Phylace, we have a super hive mind that is the data center for all the plains in the universe. A technologic keep, a collective of many quantum computing minds that home the secrets of the Synod Empire. This is the controlling force of the many societies of races that my realm, as the Synod is a controlling force that operates in high use of technology as a dominant controlling factor. This kind, in order of a whole different ruling than the magical beings that are under the Spiro Unity. I say that there is a war of physical and nonphysical magic that exists as there is a war of the physical fighting to rule over the physical caught in the wars of the Spiro. A war of the battles of wars I would call it! Most are subject to it, thrown in chaos and expected to fight for life! Little to nothing I have explained as most would coward in this thought. I laugh for this is your life and you had only lacked the thought! Now stand and be upright for nothing lost! I say everything is an art! For in the night, it is long and cold but just when froze and time has made you old… a spark to warm and renew! This is the beauty in destruction, I say that death it brings the life as the night turns to light!

SENTIENT

Onward into fresh exploits as Iyo works in ease some stretches for the body. Before heading to the basement laboratory to start back up the project with Syn. After his routine he made his way to the lower levels. At the entrance of the lab, he spoke out to his A.I. companion.

"Hey friend, Are you ready for the day? I want to start by checking your code before we go out there. Come over to the computer desk."

Iyo sat at the computing station as he pulled up the file information for Syn's code and wanted to check the radius of her flight. Making sure that she cannot go more than three hundred feet from him. "This is my chance!" He thought to himself of being able to finally see into the coding again, recalling the red code incident from some time ago. Unknowing of this secular thinking surprisingly, Syn was okay with the editing and so Iyo shut her down as he began to sift through the code.

"Okay, Now I need to find that red thread of lettering."

Checking everything and making sure that he still could shut Syn down if needed. Wanting to keep control so changing parts of her code. Iyo saved what he manipulated and started the reboot process of Syn the artificial intelligence drone. She came online after three minutes and sprung right to action. Flying through the room with rapid speed.

"Woah! You are ready to go then!"

Iyo was surprised at how quickly she flew up and about.

"We might have to clock your speed, Syn! You are freaking fast! Are you ready to get going? We can just go outside and start there; you can assess the air out and we can leave when you are ready."

Iyo was getting things together, and the two of them went up through the back hatch to the yard. Syn was curious about every little thing that she saw.

"Okay do not go too far Syn. I do not want to lose you."

Iyo displayed some care just as a car started to pull into the top of the driveway.

"Who is that?"

Iyo questioned himself as drone floated next to him for a moment.

The car door opened. Out came Amber giving a yell.

"Hey! Iyo! We are back! Wow, what an awesome place you got here! I will be honest; I expected much less."

Right in the middle of her sentence, Syn burst into the air, quickly fading. Amber must have scared her for she bolted straight up into the sky.

"Ah great."

Iyo said with a major sigh. As Amber quickly trotted up with Bohn shortly behind her.

"Woah man, What the fuck was that? It looked like a tiny little UFO! I thought only the high table had that kind of tech!"

She laughed in curiosity as she stretched her eyes to look into the sky, trying to find what she had just seen. Iyo spoke up.

"That was my decade long project that you just scared away."

Iyo made sarcastic remarks to her as she babbled on about what it could have been. Bohn walked up at this moment, beginning to question Iyo.

"You should tell her man. What is the harm? The universe is going to know shortly after someone records her."

Amber cut in before Iyo could reply to Bohn.

"Wait, Wait. You said... her. The world will know what? What did you make? Iyo, you still doing crazy things after all these years?"

Amber was drawing a blank but still enthusiastic about what it was. She was speaking her mind as Iyo for some reason was beginning to become annoyed with the situation and pulled out his phone to hit the call back button for Syn on the app that he created.

"You may be right Bohn; I will just have to deal with that when the time comes, but I will let her tell you Amber! Just give it a moment and she will return!"

Standing with eyes to the sky as Iyo pushed A signal button that sounded. Shortly after the A.I. drone came zooming back as fast as lightning! With a circling around the group several times then turning to a hovering state next to Iyo, at once speaking.

"I stopped in all directions after the same distance from this exact origin point. Did you set a distance lock on me?"

Syn was still in a constant hover. She turned to Bohn and Amber and back to Iyo and back and forth once more.

"Who is this woman, expert?"

Syn swooped over to get a look at her, flying around her.

"Master, how can I get a form like this woman?"

Syn being interested in Amber's body as Amber was having a near mind melt.

"Is this thing a sentient figure? Wait. Are you a sentient drone?"

She asked Iyo then quickly correcting her question to Syn.

"I am Artificial intelligence, that is that you humans created me, I have little experience to feeling."

Syn spun back to Iyo. "Creator, why did you put a limit to my distance?"

It seemed like Syn was not going to let this go, Iyo spoke up.

"Syn, I cannot have you traveling unlimited distances. You have been studying the world, you know how people are, if your battery died and someone found you... They would take you apart and try to replicate my design of you and take your brain and tear up your code in research of you. I cannot take that chance."

Iyo was fairly speaking as Amber was in awe of the situation.

"How did you do this? Let us save that story for another day."

She directed her attention back to the drone.

"So, your name is Syn? That is cool. What did you think when you were flying around? Tell me the most interesting thing you noticed."

Amber asked without fear but only wonder of Syn. As the A.I. explained that it seemed like it went forever and how that she finally feels free and unburdened from wondering what outside was like. Curious Amber asked all kinds of questions. Loving the mind of it and testing what it understands, infatuated with it as getting annoyed with this questioning Iyo spoke up.

"We were just going to the store to get a bunch of gear. You all follow so we can use your truck! It would sure save me trips."

Amber was up for the idea.

"I am cool with that! What the heck do you need two carloads of gear for?"

Amber questioned with wonder. Iyo laughed.

"You will see when we get back! I say it will be my greatest accomplishment! Aside of Syn that is…"

Iyo writing down some self-importance as he walked to get into his jeep. They followed him and they all left to get supplies and new gear for his experiment. Syn hovered next to Iyo in his vehicle as it was speaking to him of the blueprints and materials they needed the entire time. On entrance of the store, just as Bohn predicted, People were mumbling and recording video of the group on their phones as they passed in search of the items. The experiment was big and there were specifics, so Iyo was condescending and super firm with his speech. Directing Amber and Bohn in the most boss like manner. Buying electronic equipment, metals, tons of wiring and much of this type of equipment. This was a large shopping spree. They group filled up the cars with all that they bought after multiple trips to different stores and returned to Iyo's home. Iyo directed them to load all the gear into this empty garage.

"You are making a new lab man?"

Bohn asked in wonder as this jolted Amber in thought.

"A new Lab? Do you have your own lab? What is wrong with the one you have? Can I see it!"

Iyo laughed at excited Amber as he set down the some of the acquired gear.

"Let us just get it all in there. Patience is key folks!"

Iyo and the crew finish loading all the gear into the garage and Iyo hits the garage door switch. It begins to close on them, and Syn comes zooming in as a rabbit escaping a falcon.

"Alright everybody just a moment. Bear with me!"

Iyo said as he walked over to the wall that held a box on it. He opens the box and enclosed was another code lock. He leaned forward and it scans his eyes. Then he placed his hand on the scanner and then he entered the ten-digit code. There was a loud beep that followed by harsh locking and metal shifts.

"Wha-What was that?"

Bohn's voice rattled with worry in a nervous tone, eyes wide.

"Iyo?"

Bohn to probe once more just as the floor shook, suddenly suspended in a slight bounce as it shifted on a shock system. The floor began to move downward, detaching from the walls and level of the home.

"Oh, this room is an elevator!? That is impressive! I bet it cost a fortune!"

Amber said with interest as they all went down to the next level. Another beep sounded as a door revolved open. The laboratory lights beamed on as Syn flew into the room. Iyo speaking to Amber.

"Welcome! Here is my laboratory! Look around and tell me what you think! I say I sure could use a mind like yours!"

Iyo gave a chuckle as Amber began walking around. Checking things out and asking a ton of questions. Amber having some conversation with herself, a true nerd moment as Iyo began to pull up the plans of the project that he started.

"Okay, this is what me and Syn fabricated, last night when you guys were out lollygagging."

Speaking as he pointed at the monitors showing blueprints of the project. Bohn spoke first.

"What is that?"

Amber grabbed the question by answering his question.

"It is a track line. Right?"

She asked as Iyo gave a laugh paired with his response, surprised in her realization.

"Yes, Good Job! A trackpad. Do you know what it is for? Any idea why I want it wrapped around this place?"

Amber and Bohn just gave each other a look of curiosity.

Bohn sarcastically replied.

"Um, obviously not."

Amber laughed at him as Iyo began to explain his plan to replicate in detail.

"N.R.E.C. caught my attention when Bohn and I were at that science fair that I guess you... put together? Anyway, I home a new desire to learn of the study of elements. I want to learn about them and understand them. Do experiments and things, So I want to try to make my own accelerator. Are you willing to help? are you folks ready to start this new adventure? I mean, I sure am!"

Iyo was excited about the new project and the others were beginning to build in the same energy from the energy that Iyo was giving off.

"For sure man! It sounds formidable, I am ready to help do whatever."

Bohn was sharing his excitement as Amber was just as into the idea, even more so than Bohnstant.

"Are you kidding? I am not going anywhere! A.I. Replicating Nrec? I am staying for sure! I mean, sure going to be a challenge but I am up for it! I have tons of vacation time that I can take! So, I will be able to miss work! I mean I am only the head of all their events... It is not like they will be needing me!"

Amber giving a rebellious laugh of sarcasm as she and Iyo, joined by their hippy of a friend Bohn and the A.I. began setting up the equipment for the experiment. Beginning with fitting as running lines of cable along the coil of the trackpad. They wrapped the coil along the trackpad that Iyo had built the day before. Bohn set up batteries to the generators and connected it all to the solar power as Iyo and Amber made the coil secured. The juice's they are giving for his project are sure to warn the local power plant of some wild surges on the charts. It took them four hours to set up the gear and hours working had them all burnt out, Iyo spoke up after the morning of work.

"Well, we got some things carried out for now, better to take a break before I fry my brain again. Bohn, do not bring anything with you now!"

Laughing hysterically was Iyo as walking to the lab exit. Bohn gave a small chuckle that followed by a drop in his posture. He spoke softly in remark of the situation that occurred on the beach.

"Yeah, well I do not plan on intentionally doing anything to fuck this up... So... relax man, I not going to do that! Mistakes made and I know that I should not meddle with things that have nothing to do with me! I could say that the same damn thing goes for you! After meddling yourself with the fucking storm! I mean, that is a lot worse than me accidentally taking the battery!"

Bohn at once turned sassy as if Iyo were coming against him. Yet, it was a simple joke that Bohn took out of context. Even if he happens to be right, Iyo was and still is interfering with things that have nothing to do with him. Iyo ignored the remark with a subtle laugh as he continued to make his way to the exit. The others followed and they all made their way back up into the actual home from the laboratory basement. Iyo ventured to his room as Bohn fell to a sofa, Amber sat next to him and they began conversation,

"Iyo seems odd, right?" Amber asked as she sat next to Bohn.

"Odd? I have no clue; I just met the guy. He is nice enough to let me stay in his home. I mean, you would know better. Are you not like a lifelong friend of him? You worked together, right?" Bohn sat up from his slouched position.

Amber gave her head a tilt in thought, "I mean, not lifelong but a good decade or so, I was a student attending his laboratory back in the day when I was fresh out of school. As to the fact of you being here, that is even weird. That is not something that Iyo would do. I mean unless he has drastically changed. He was never a people person." She said as she crossed her arms, deep in thought.

"Yeah, I got that part. Sure, not a people person. I am not sure, maybe he is not a people person, and it was just the beach experience that brought us together. Maybe he is lonely? What is wrong with wanting a friend?" Bohn said as Amber began to walk to the front door.

"Let's go out to the porch." She said as she left the home, and Bohn was quick to follow. The moon was shining bright, even if it was a waxing crescent, this grabbed Ambers attention immediately. "Woah, look at the moon, like a godly smirk." She laughed as she took a seat on the steps. Bohn took a seat next to her, sitting close but not to close.

"Well, care to tell me more about you?" He said with a slight smile as he was quick to look back at the moon.

EVALUATIONS
August 9th

Three days of work went on and it was time for the first test.

The group stood in the laboratory with all eyes fixed on the trackpad that held the coil. The idea is that these peaks will project energy particles. At separate ends of the tracks, swirling around until a merge point. The hypothesis is the creation of a new substance. The team brainstorming together all the different scenarios that they could use in the first test. They concluded that it would be best to use two different plant families to see what would happen if these two forms merged. They ran the first test, fired up the generators and placed the microorganism substances into degrading vials. Then placed these vials into the correct peaks of the trackpad ends. Iyo turns it on, and around and around the particles fly and after gaining maximum speed as switched to the same track. A lightning zap occurs and directly after this zap the objects collide.

"Okay, Check the chamber!"

Iyo ecstatically tells as Amber puts on a pair of heat-resistant gloves and then turns the wheel that was the lock for the chamber door. She opens the hatch and outpours a thick cloud of smoke.

"Yuck!"

Taking a break of speech, coughing from all the smoke, wafting away. She went on.

"Oh, gee that is smokey. Smoky like the bear!"

Amber started waving away the smoke as she laughed to herself as well as letting out some short but harsh coughs.

"Hey, a little help Syn! Air it out!"

Iyo shouted at Syn as joked to Amber.

"And I think you mean smokey like Bohn's head!"

The A.I. flew over to the chamber, hovered above the hatch and quickly turned two of the four fans to disperse the smoke. It clears and Amber and Iyo lean in and look at the inside of the chamber.

"Well, sure did not think that microorganisms could make such a mess... What the heck just happened? It is like a jellyfish exploded in there!"

The group sharing laughter as they gazed into the collision chamber. Iyo added his scientific opinion.

"Yeah, I guess it did not work. Well, the collision was in fact a success but the collision that we were going for was not."

Amber took off her gloves and sat back in her chair. Iyo made his way to the computer station to look at the data of the collision.

"What I wanted was a collision on a literal level of these two things becoming one. We just destroyed it all on this run... we will keep trying! I understand that we could mesh these materials and things in the lab but that is a physical manipulation... What I want to see is particle meshing through the speed of wild proportions! As if we are replicating a collision of different asteroids in space! Energetically! A motion forced collision has potential to be something! I say that it cannot be too farfetched of an idea if these "Nrec" workers are doing it! Always, always a way I say!"

The scientist letting his thoughts roam as he was getting the computer set up for another test run with the machine. Ongoing this way Iyo was running test after test, even after many fails. The group pressed on and continued to run variations and moments turned quickly into hours spent on the testing. One could only conclude that something was wrong. Eventually Amber and Bohn faded from helping Iyo every day and Iyo went into deep research phase. Learning all that he could about matter and the natural elements of the world. He spent months trying to figure out how N.R.E.C. was doing the things that they were doing. Iyo became so burnt out that he concluded his work and made a final decision.

"I have made it to the end of this research, the only way for me to understand what is happening... Well, I must go to the N.R.E.C. Station. I will get a tour and learn more... I will use what I can to absorb all the knowledge that I am able to learn exactly how to achieve my task!"

So, Iyo went to Bohn and made a call to Amber to get her back over and he began to tell them his thoughts.

"I came to a solid conclusion that the only hope is either we make a study trip or, well we, we steal the information behind the project."

Iyo said to Amber and Bohn displaying a massive grin on his face. Syn hovered among the group.

"Steal the data? Are you crazy Iyo? How would you even do that? It sounds insane to me. Amber, back me up. Not only is it a bad idea that could land us in prison, but should you be teaching this robot of yours to steal? I mean where is the sense to this, just to get information?"

Bohn was not a willing lab partner.

"I am with Bohn on this one Iyo. That is going to be a tricky one. I am not sure about this! I mean, all the security at the event was for that group Iyo! I cannot even imagine what the actual facility is like... and you want to, you want to steal their most valuable information?

Amber was not up for the adventure. Iyo laughed at them both.

"You are not thinking clearly, we have Syn. The most powerful key breaker that exists! We can go at night, and she can manage all the computer work and the cameras! Easy, like seals... we will be in and out! Nobody knows!"

He laughed about as he gloated to them about the AI capabilities.

Syn joined the conversation. "I could find the information. No server could hold me back."

Amber gave out a mumbled laugh.

"Well, that kind of changes my mind. It would be easy to bypass the security. I never even thought about using Syn! No jokes… what do we really do? Just take a tour as you said. Do they even do this type of thing?"

Amber and Iyo both looked to Bohn to join in on the peer pressure. There was a slight moment of silence and Bohn gave it.

"Okay, okay, To Switzerland we go! Now who is paying for the tickets?"

The group continued to talk. Going on about different plans and things they would do to not get caught, to find the map of the building and how to find the data they were in search of. The team packed quickly, ready to head on this adventure. They left for the airport and had a flight. How a timeline intersects with the past is beyond me, I care to question but, in some things, I could not even dwell in for more than some seconds. How some thoughts are only possession. I digress, the human in such defeat that he recedes to the less of actions. Rippled actions are like a seed on sorts, oh how they do spread in fact as some weeds of thorns. I warn you of their accepting.

MISFORTUNES

SPIRAL ARTHE

August 10th

Switzerland

"How is everybody? Was it a good flight for you all? It sure was a long flight for me... and tell me why it is always peanuts? I eat the heck out of them but seriously, I mean, I would sure like a pack of gushers or something sweet!"

Bohn giving his senses as he stepped out of the walker and into the plane gate, Iyo, and Amber ahead of him.

"And I was freezing! You would think that with the billions of..."

Amber had enough of his complaining.

"Stop it Bohn! Complain, complain, complain, for what? Nobody is going to accommodate your needs... welcome to earth my hippy... I am through with your pointless statements! If I wanted a girl trip I would have stayed home!"

Bohn in a squint of confusion for he felt that he was simply expressing himself. Iyo was looking through his carryon, trying to find his passport and wallet. He spoke up after the odd dispute between them.

"Yeah, it was fine. A bit rough here and there. I am not much of a flyer. Let us make our way to baggage and then we are off to the hotel! Here it says that our bags should be at claim nine!"

Iyo pocketed his items as he began to walk to the claim. The group joked with each other in wonder about how nice the hotel would be as they waited for the luggage to arrive.

Iyo called for an uber as the group went seeking their luggage. They shortly found themselves at the hotel and were just amazed with the beauty of it. Amber and Bohn did not expect a small castle to be staying in. Simply surprised with the setting.

"I did know you were so classy Iyo. Are you sure that this is the right place? It sure looks like a dang castle!"

Bohn joked as they walked into the stone and marble structure.

"I got some hidden truths friend. As the station is just a few miles down the road! So, we are super close! It is only just a few miles from here! It sure is a huge compound though!"

The group explored the luxurious building for a little while as then to joking about, unpacking their things as sooner than later they all fell asleep. Ending the long day of travel to this new and distant place, this day fades only to return.

Clink Tink, Tink, clink. The sounds of dishware overtook the room. Bohn struggling to get through his daily origins of annoyances.

"Man, what the freak, why does shit have to be complicated."

The freethinker was up early, making noise as he tried to fix himself a cup of morning joe. Iyo was out already, Amber rolls over from just waking up from the noise.

"What's up man, what are you doing up at the crack of dawn!"

She bid to break the ice as she sat up and rubbed her eyes. Bohn laughed at himself, hiding the awkwardness he felt from his foolishness.

"Oh, I am sorry, Did I wake you? I was just trying to get this coffee going. Having some trouble it seems."

He smiled and he continued preparing the drink.

"Well, I am up and am sure that I can figure it out! Is Iyo, that crazy science guy is already up as well?"

Amber giving a chuckle of laughter as she got herself up and to her feet, making her way to Bohn to help make the coffee. I am sure that this is exactly what he wanted.

"You just have to make sure this thing is pointed down, Dummy!"

Amber laughed pleasantly to Bohn as she oversaw the coffee.

"But what if…"

Bohn was trying to give back a slick reply as Iyo burst into the room with mighty force and speed. Followed by an outburst of the same energy.

"Outrageous these people! I will tell you about the nerve on that lady. Ridiculous behavior if you ask me. Stupid, erratic, luna! I ought to go right back down there…"

Iyo was acting wild as his anger clouded the room as it took away from the moment that Bohn was having with Amber.

"Woah man, Relax. What happen?"

Bohn asked in a diffusing tone just as Syn flew out from under Iyo's jacket.

"At least I remain undiscovered."

Syn said as she flew straight to the window, and she began to hover there. Iyo gave a grunt of annoyance followed by a surge of direction.

"Syn! GO TO SLEEP!"

The artificial intelligence suddenly dropped to the floor as Amber remarked, surprisingly.

"Well, that was cool… Voice commands? Awesome. Do you care to tell us what happened out there?"

Amber intrigued by the drama as Iyo sat harshly and began to untie his boots in a chaotic action, mumbling curses to himself.

"Geez man, what exactly happened?"

Bohn asked as he stepped away from the kitchen and stepped closer to the front door of the home where Iyo was. He finished taking his boots off and made his way to grab something to drink, Beginning in explanation.

"The fuckin A.I. thought it was an innovative idea to go explore and what it did not decide to think about was the drone laws of this weird city. It led the authorities right back to us and I had to stand down there and convince the officer that I was just getting photos as a tourist. I got a warning, and she took my license and printed my name and everything so now we must have more caution and get a new hotel as well and not use my name this time. Thank the drone."

Iyo became more frustrated as he spoke. Bohn and Amber just sat in silence as the coffee finally began to brew behind them.

"At least you did not get fined or arrested man. That is a plus."

Bohn added as together they laughed the mishap away. Iyo walked over to turn the drone back on. He leaned over and picked it up.

"This thing is pretty wild though, right?"

Iyo was boasting of his creation, looking for praise. Amber spoke first.

"Yeah man, you created a freaking A.I. Like that is the coolest thing man has done so far. Be proud, I am so happy to be part of all this! Thanks for letting me be here."

Amber was glowing with appreciation of it all. As Bohn was acquainted with the A.I. by now and agreed with less of a physical behavior. As he re-engaged in a new conversation.

"So, About N.R.E.C..."

Bohn asked. Shifting the mood of the room completely. Iyo turned on the A.I. just before he replied to Bohn. He let it go as the fans roared and it began to hover in place as it spun and shifted itself to positioned to see the group.

"Amazing."

Let out Amber with a whisper of a tone.

"I cannot even fathom it. Yet, it is here, and it is right in front of me."

Amber was having a nerd moment as Iyo spoke up to Bohn's remark.

"Today we will go scout the station and find as much out as we can. If we come to a dead end, then we use plan number two and just steal the information from the servers. Sounds good?"

Iyo gave out a small chuckle paired with a smile as he clapped his hands together. Bohn and Amber just looked at each other in awkward silence. Iyo continued.

"We will go on a tour an learn what we can. Try to get one of them to let us into the server area and Syn will download the deeds. That is about it!"

Iyo awaited a response due to lack of patience as he urged their reply.

"Are you all in? What is the sudden silence?"

Iyo was asking this with a high amount of curious energy. Bohn spoke up.

"Oh, course we are man, we flew all the way to Switzerland, didn't we?"

Bohn spoke sarcastically as Iyo stricken with a new thought.

"This is true, we did come all this way! I say we grab lunch somewhere and then head to the station, Sounds good?"

Iyo offered a path.

"That sounds about right to me, Let's go!"

Amber, excited about the adventure, was the first to grab her coat. Iyo in question of her action.

"Oh, walking, are we? I was about to call a uber."

Amber was quick to turn around, with a wrinkled brow.

"No, we can walk to one of these local shops for lunch and then get a taxi in town. It is only three blocks away, Shy of a little walk Iyo?"

The group joked with one another as they prepared to leave. The conversation made an easy distraction for the A.I to slip out the window once more! As it did so, quickly flew out the window shortly after this conversation.

"I guess someone is ready to go."

Bohn laughed about the A.I. leaving so quickly.

"Yeah, I guess we should go. Everybody have their spy gear?"

Said Amber as she opened the door.

"Spy gear?"

Bohn remarked as Iyo gave him a push out the door.

"Yeah man, for the heist we are about to do. Where have you been?"

Iyo and Amber gave out a good laugh directed at Bohn as the group began to walk into the town to get something for lunch.

Finding a nice little coffee shop that sold sandwiches, the group sat down and ordered refreshments before beginning to plot.

"Ahh- nothing like a hot cup of coffee am I right?"

Iyo said as he gave a big smile followed by drinking his coffee.

"Studies show, the average person may not know that coffee beans are the seeds of berries from the coffee plant. Most people think of them as beans, but they're technically seeds that are roasted to then be ground into coffee. If you did not know."

Amber held a smirk as she took a sip of her cup. Holding her smirk as she raised her brow from the wonderful taste of the beans, shifting back to a resolved state as Iyo shrugged away her speech.

"Thanks for the insight, Amber, now we know."

Iyo states stoically and sarcastically and Bohn adds to Amber,

"As we wait for our gourmet sandwiches, I just want to say that this really is the best cup of fruit beans I have ever had. Oh, oh well, would you look at that! It says that this coffee comes from a little shop called Pimpin' Pete's Coffee. I cannot believe that is a real shop! What a cool name! Have the locals saying, I got to get my pimp on, so headed to Pete's! Or I need my peeps pimping today, so we are getting Pete's! A pimp out there named Pete getting rich! Who knows, but I love this brand, it is great! I sure got to find it when we get back home! I cannot believe I have never heard of it! Anyway, What I am truly wondering if either of you want to discuss the events that are about to take place?"

Bohn looked around the room for the server, looking back at Iyo and Amber who were obviously in their own trains of thought.

"Anything to say guys? Questions or concerns?"

Bohn asked in an awkward tone of waiting. Iyo spoke up, breaking the short silence of the group.

"Yeah man, I mean we are spot on with the plan. I mean, besides the fact of, I do not know. Getting caught? We have not really prepared for that. Just saying. I mean, I don't think we will get into any trouble, but should we prepare for it? Like, just in case?"

Iyo paused in a quick moment of shame for he realized how stupid that was to even bring up. Taking another sip of his joe as Amber spoke out.

"Yeah, getting caught is not my worry, The thing on my mind is this sandwich. Oh man, I could eat a whole freaking cow."

Amber was expressing herself as Iyo shifted the mood into a more serious form of conversation.

"Guys, we are about to do a grandiose thing here. Let focus up, Okay? Let us go over the plan once more."

Iyo said as Bohn sat up and Amber moved her attention back to Iyo.

"We are just hungry Iyo. We are on board, and we know what we need to do. Do you have anything that you want to say? You are the one that seems worried. Are you nervous?"

Iyo caught off guard by her notice.

"Yeah, you are right. I could just be a little hyped myself. Eating would be nice if they ever came. How long does it take to make sandwiches? They must really be gourmet."

Iyo said as he set his coffee cup out for the server to refill.

"Your food should be ready in just a moment sir."

The server kindly spoke as she poured his cup.

"Why thank you, mam."

Amber quickly spoke as she handed the menus back to her. Bohn took a sip of this coffee. "Do you guys think there is a lot of security there?"

Bohn asked, putting his cup down. Iyo looked at them both in wonder.

"Gee, I really have no clue Bohn, I was actually, Interrupted, and so I…"

"An-Here you all go."

Said the server as she placed their food down, Bohn gave a giggle to the fact of Iyo getting interrupted once more just as he spoke of it.

"Why thank you so much, thanks mam."

Bohn replied nicely as he nodded for Iyo to continue, the girl walked away as Bohn laughed in remark.

"Don't get so frustrated man, she literally doing her job." He said as Iyo ignored his statement of truth.

"As I was saying, thinking about the security, and we could actually get you two to start some kind of scene if needed to distract them for me and Syn. Would you guys do that?"

Iyo ecstatically asked.

"Yeah, I would be down. If we had to. Just like every movie ever. Not like they would think of it coming. I am in, why not."

Said Amber just before she chomped her sandwich.

"Yeah, well if you both are up for something then that does not really give me much choice to just sit on the sidelines now does it."

Bohn complained as a response to them. Amber butted back at him.

"You have all the choices in the world Bohn. I can make a scene without you trust me."

Amber said as she pointed at his chest and laughed as she continued to eat.

"Yeah, I bet you can. I am not saying that I will not be a part of it. I am just saying that if you folks are doing something then it is simply weird if I sit and just do nothing and just not be a part of it."

Bohn laughed as he awkwardly explained.

"Okay yes. Then that would be weird, you are going. I will get a taxi now. Finnish up guys!"

Iyo said as he began to look at his phone for a ride.

"I am going to go use the ladies' room, I'll be back."

Amber got up, throwing away her trash. Bohn was quick to speak to Iyo with an excited tone of worry as she walked away.

"Dude, are we really going to steal this information?"

Asking this quietly. Iyo looked at him in frustration.

"Really man, yes. Just stay back if you are going to be such a little weirdo about it all. We are going to be in and out in under an hour or so man. Relax or stay, I do not care."

Iyo clicked a few things on his phone.

"Okay wow! Only three minutes out it says! The driver was just waiting for a ride it seems. I say this might be my first five-star rating. You do know that soon the social rate systems will be active, don't you? Anyway, are you ready or what Mr. Bohnstant?"

Iyo was excited. Amber was just returning from the restroom as the group sat awaiting the arrival of the ride.

"Hey guys, let us get the hell out of here. Some weird guys in suits at the counter that have a high interest in us."

Amber awkwardly said as she grabbed her cup of joe and began to exit the shop as normally as she could. Iyo and Bohn released a discomforting set of emotions as the pair of them quickly gathered their items and followed Amber outside. Bohn giving a slight look over his shoulder on exit.

"Fuck man, their following us."

Luckily for the group their Uber driver pulled right up to the scene and the group was able to make it into the car before the odd men in suits were able to make it out of the coffee shop. Iyo quickly shuts the door and speaks directions to the driver in the same motion.

"To the N.R.E.C. station just over the mountain good sir."

Iyo then pulled out a cigarette.

"You mind if I smoke?"

Asking the driver as the windows suddenly begin to roll down.

"Well, it is fine by me mate. Just blow the smoke out the window if you can, good friend. Note, I can take you to the gate, not allowed any further than that sport."

Iyo gave his head a tilt of oddity.

"Alright fine, weird that a research station would be strict on taxi access. It is all well, we will walk the rest of the way."

Time passes as they ride to the mega research station.

It is these happenstances of urge entangled by permissions... this is the guide to this path of misfortunes.

All for one's ability to walk so blind into thoughts turned action that of what has trapped him. Man, that is still a boy, shackled, he is captive in this haze of misguided satisfactions! I only see myself as I sure paved this path before him… captivated by the torture as running through the maze of confusions and horror! Often, I was roaming lucid as on this road of muse! Ongoing for the pain we are custom to it… the physic way of supporting because the self knows it is worth is only this reflection of the worst of hurting, as if this life lived to hold the burden. I could say, and one could think, question me for nothing is but idea!

Do not let me get ahead, I have only begun. I will take you back to the subjects.

N.R.E.C. Station

Switzerland

"Here we go, Checkpoint number one. I knew there would be security. I told you; I told you; I told you all that there would be crazy security! Just keep cool and do not act weird, talking to you Bohn!"

Amber said in a prideful mocking manner.

"Yeah, so what, checked in as tourists or visitors and we will be on our way. Stop acting like we are some kind of terrorist. We are simple thieves on a mission of scientific importance. That is what we should tell the GMC driver that has been following us since we left the town!"

Iyo snickered at the group as Amber began to put makeup on her eyes as she paused and cut back at Iyo with justified confutation.

"I am just saying, I was right, why are you knocking me?" She said as Bohn cut into the speaking.

"Why are you even putting on makeup? What is the point? Wait, what? A GMC? Where?"

Bohn caught off guard as he quickly turned to look behind them to see if there was a following vehicle. Amber replied with a quick attitude, responding to his remark.

"Cause if by any chance they catch us, I want to look pretty in the mugshot. Also, the guards might just be easy on us because I am a good-looking girl. It happens all the time! And really! You really looked back? Ever heard of sarcasm Bohn?"

Amber laughing as their car pulled up to the gate. The driver in service points to a searching area up ahead. The car proceeds to a stop and the front window of the vehicle begins to roll down, the driver was quick to speak.

"You folks go ahead and get out here and I will be on my way, you see that sign? "TAXI DROP" You see, enjoy your visit. He is my card, if you need service once more, I will be in the area all day. Okay, everybody out!"

Spoke the Uber driver in a skittish tone as he rolled up the window directly after speaking.

"Okay, we are out. You folks heard him! Hey, hey here you go driver! Here is a little tip for you!"

Amber handed the driver a small tip barely making the folded cash into the up-rolling window as Iyo and Bohn began to fumble out of the car. The driver pulls off and the group of them standing in a cemented drop-off for a moment. Iyo looking around, Bohn having a stretch as Amber looking into the distance, in sight of the massive structure in the distance.

"Hey guys, check it out, Look! Coming this way, there is a whole darn convoy of trucks! They must have something like cameras on the road or whatever. That or somebody had to alert them that we were traveling on their road."

Amber pointing to the distance as the convoy approach as Iyo gave assurance.

"All is good, we are visitors, remember that."

Iyo held up his hand in a wave as the truck approached them. Amber spoke up with curious sentencing.

"Do you do not think that the driver was acting weird? He seemed startled."

Bohn shook his head paired with an eye roll as Iyo replied.

"No Amber, he only spoke like a few sentences. Why is that your concern when a freaking military convoy is approaching us…"

Bohn cut into a senseless emotion.

"This is it; this is where it all ends. I should have stayed in the coffee shop; I would still be enjoying that nice jazz music they had playing."

Amber is still uncaring of the situation.

"Jazz music? That was classical music Bohn. One composer with flutes… where did you hear the saxophone? The soul?"

Iyo beside himself at this point.

"Shut up! Mouths shut! Enough! We are on a mission if you do not recall, focus people focus. Here they come!"

The group stood with a balance of fear and motivation, a true pull of the sides as the truck flew straight up to trio with the speed of a bull as it screeched to a stop like an emergency pull. The doors open on all sides and a team of soldiers simultaneously exits the vehicle. They all had weapons except one who had a pistol on his waist. This was the one who spoke up as the team of soldiers formed around him.

"My name would be Captain Tyco Mordon. My fellow soldiers call me Captain Tyco the Dawn. I am the death that awaits you and the terror of dreams. I am that of what your children speak of as… Hero."

The soldier gave an ear-to-ear grin followed by assertiveness.

"Did you dare cross my line? You dare to step to my line?"

He spoke to the group with satiny, as his southern American accent held a presence of vanity. Not a chance that this was lying folk. One could feel the truth in his words, as if a figure could discern the fact that it would be a shame to vex, it seemed a shame to be the one to test this being.

"Yes, think and think deep and hard now baby! Now, I would bear in mind the effect of that stupid decision before you do so. Before you are Beta Team Nine. My personal protectors who would kill themselves to save my belt. So, with all this in mind, would any of you, invasive jack-fuckers tell me why in the hell the metal spitting should not begin? State your reasoning of being here!"

As his words finished his team began to check their weapons and gear. A form of intimidation one might say. Iyo spoke first as it looked like Bohn and Amber stood petrified.

"Hey man, All cool here! Just relax, we are Scientist! From the United States. You Sir! You look and sound like you are from the states! Anyway, we have traveled this long distance for a chance to tour this station. Is there any chance that this would be possible? Are you able to guide us inside?"

Iyo asked, as he stepped forward before Bohn and Amber. The captain held his hand up to his squad and they all relaxed their ready postures and disengaged their weapons. Captain Tyco was quick to ease his aggression as he heard the word "America" spoken.

"Scientist. Is that right? Well, Macy, you got me there. I miss my home. I am a Texan. See, we are of another kind of what it is that is your kind, but I dare say that any blood of red and blue, I name a friend of mine. That is until the snake comes out to bite and true colors are true and met with death that is my knife! I tell you and this much is true, but I warn you and I do so demand that you would respect me like my old Meme and not as street trash. Correct? You are decent as a child and not as a crook? Tell me words science man, tell me words!"

Stepping forward the captain continued to speak with dominance, poking to expose anything hidden one could assume.

"Show the tags. Come on, Papers. I want names and pictures, or we like Christmas! Do you understand? ID's or guns, Boom. Decide. Twenty seconds."

Tyco's wording sent his soldier into action as five of them began to walk towards the group as the rest of soldiers were quick to re-ready their weapons. Pointing them at the group, Iyo belched out.

"Alright man, I understand! Relax! No need for hostility! Come on, Get out your identifications! You heard him, let us go!"

Iyo spoke as he scrambled to get his passport and picture information. Amber and Bohn began to do the same as the soldiers that were walking to them just snagged all the information out of their hands. This frustrated Bohn and he spoke out to the militant men.

"Hey you dick. Careful. That is our information!"

He quickly realized that he should not have spoken because one of the soldiers reacted to this.

"Oh, My bad sir."

He pleasingly yet Sarcastically spoke as he turned around and quickly bashed the end of his gun into the ribs of Bohn. As he forcefully shoved him to the ground while laughing.

"Poussey."

The warrior spoke in America slang as his fellow soldiers laughed at the weakness of Bohnstant. They handed the information back to the captain and returned to the ready positions.

"Now brush that off and stand up right like your daddy taught you! Did he ever do such a thing?"

Laughed a different soldier of broken English, yet this soldier spoke with a German accent. Distraught Bohn, who was on the ground in pain, was suddenly set to fire with feelings of anger! Recalling the fact that his parents died when he was young, and this has caused a huge hindrance on his life. Iyo noticing the difference of speech between the soldiers. "Private contractors?" He thought to himself. "What on earth would a research facility need private contractors for?" Iyo was beside himself with thoughts that cut off by the captains' interjection.

"Enough play, go on and get yourself to your feet.

Iyo spoke out immediately after.

"Bohn, Get up man. Do not bother with him just shake it off man."

Iyo was just trying to kill the suspense. He knew that the captain and soldiers were pushing buttons on purpose. Bohn was huffing and puffing with anger as he struggled to get to his feet. Embarrassed, triggered, and adrenalized he let lose.

"Fuck you mother fucker! You do not know shit!"

Bohn unleashed himself as the soldiers broke in laughter. Tyco Mordon gave a disappointed look at troubled Bohnstant as he went ahead to make fun of him.

"Oh, A soft spot we found? Good to know, you cut me off and The Dawn never lets anyone disrespect him. I will give that one to you though. You are helping a fellow soldier when he is down, and I respect that. You all did the right thing and showed no hesitation when I asked for the Identification, so I will take you all through the gates. I cannot speak for those satanic nerd fucks inside. They have their own wishes; We are here for the money. Nothing more. If the pricks had not paid so well. Well, I would shoot the bastards and let you in there, as to why you would want to go into the giant summoner of demons? Well, this is beyond me Mr. science guy. Anyway, let us get you in. Climb on the truck and we can help you get to where you need to be. Just do not be up to anything fishy. I will reel you in quick friend's..."

The captain set his rules and just before he boarded his convey truck Iyo nagged him.

"Sir Tyco, what do you mean when you were speaking about it being satanic? A massive summons you said. Can you... Can you like explain?"

Iyo was confused at the statement, yet he was in fact highly curious about this. The captain let out a massive grin that was satanic itself, followed by a laugh that embodied ignoring the question as the captain shut his door. The group got aboard the massive, armored truck and they journeyed with the soldiers deeper into the complex. They went down a long and winding road that led to a huge door that is a gate to the underground, and it is about the size of two modern homes that were side by side. The driver used the short-wave radio to send a signal to a tower above. A large green light that mounted above the tower doors in the center of the structure flashed brightly as a loud buzz sounded. Shortly after the door began to open and the driver slowly began to move forward. Amber spoke out.

"Wow, What a big door. That is ridiculous equipment. You all got to have a crazy budget."

She spoke as she was gazing at the entrance to the underground. The passenger soldier laughed at her.

"Lady our security team alone is around 300k a month. They have nine teams of beta. Yes, they have a good budget. For sure."

The soldier continued to laugh as the group just looked at each other with fear. Thinking if things went wrong.

"How much further, it is sort of cramped back here."

Amber asked just as Iyo was pulling out his phone to send a message to Syn. The soldier bounced back at Amber with just as equal love to hate ratio with his sentence.

"Oh, the pretty lady want's her space… Awe. Shouldn't we have strapped the men outside so she could have sprawled out mate? Wouldn't that have been betta? Right Lad?" The soldier joked with the driver as giving Amber non-comforting grins. He continued. "Just three more minutes my sweet thing. I will get you where you need to go."

The nasty soldier continued his remarks as Iyo sent a message to Syn.

"I am going to let you go when we get out. Be quiet as you can be and alert nobody of your existence and find your way into the building. Use your tech to find that server room and download all the information as you can. We will be short on time so do your best to be quick."

Iyo sent the message, but it sounded with a {swoop}, and this set off the guard.

"Hey, You fuckers have phones back there? Give it. Give it here now, No phones."

He yelled at Iyo and rapidly snatched the phone before Iyo could even say or do anything.

"Why did you not search these American idiots. Captain would lose his mind. You are lucky that he is in the back trailer with the others. What a dick of a brain you have scotty. How could you overlook checking them."

The soldier was upset at his driver. He leans back to Iyo and them.

"Now! Give me the rest. Come on you two."

The soldier held his hand out. Bohn and Amber put their phones into his hands as Amber mouthed silently to Iyo.

"WHAT. ABOUT. SYN."

She was worried that the soldiers would find her. They took their phones. She thought they would take her as well if they would find out about her. Iyo gave Amber a big shrug to her in reply as the truck arrived at the station. The groups fumbled out of the base truck, and they stood outside awaiting the entrance. The captain pulled pointed to the door as instructing one of his soldiers.

"S4, Go hit that damn button. Looks like Tic fell asleep on them cameras again. Why did they get an overweight lump of skin as the camera watcher? It is beyond me. You scientist folk can go in there and recommend someone with less butter on his fingers. I can smell that grease plump from here. Also, does somebody want to explain to me why in the hell this place has three different security gateways at each of the six sections? Paranoid sons of bitches tryna make it hard for someone to get in or making it hard for something to get out. Beats the hell out of me, I just work here."

The captain walked up to the camera as he was speaking and gave it a little shake.

"You there? Mr. Fluff-filth? You around?"

He laughed and stepped away from the camera. He continued harsh commenting as suddenly a loud buzz sounded, and the door began to open.

"Oh, would you look at that. God was in-fact watching after all. Let us go boys. Pile in, Nerds? Come on."

And so, the soldiers and the scientist all began to move to the door and Iyo leans over and gives Amber a pinch in her arm. She quickly looks at him to react and sees that Syn is peeking out of his jacket. So, she begins to create a distraction right as they are about to enter.

"You are pathetic."

Amber groaned at the soldier that was in the truck and then she spit at his feet. In front of everyone. The captain let out a big laugh.

"Oh, wait now, go on and settle for a moment… The lady has something that she would like to say to S3. Speak up now darling so we all can hear you."

Amber continued her distraction.

"Yeah, I got things to say all right! That nasty, degrading, no respect having worthless grunt that you sat me with decided to make all kinds of comments to me while we were driving, and someone needs to teach him damn manors when it comes to ladies."

Amber popped off to the soldiers as Iyo let Syn out of his jacket. The soldiers moved around Amber because she was showing signs of aggression, and this was perfect. For, Iyo left behind them, ignored the midst of the confusion. Syn spun up her blades and flew off to find another way into the building. Iyo came walking into the middle of the mess to give Amber the hint that he had released Syn. Amber spoke up again.

"I am just saying, someone should tutor this man. Nobody will ever love you if you act like that to girls. Simple."

Amber was snotty. The captain spoke up.

"Manners. That is right. S3? Where is your damn respect? You need a lesson that is right for her to suggest. How about her lover? Bohn? Is it? Would you like to defend her honor? Yes, that sounds right. S3 get a lesson from that Bohn."

At this moment, the soldier set down his guns and took off his vest and stepped towards Bohn.

"Defend her or I will attack you."

The soldier stood in a ready position as Bohn began to have a slight unease of emotions. Looking back and forth between Iyo and Amber and the soldiers in a panic and just as it seemed like the soldier was going to attack him, Bohn saved by the interjection of a lab worker happening to be at the exit of the exact elevator that the grouping was awaiting.

"STOP! Now! What is the meaning of all of this? Is this a gymnasium? No. This is a level five government station, and I do not think that we pay you people as much as we do to function as fools and barbarians. Do we now? Who are these guys that you are treating so terribly? Let me look at you, Oh. Americans? Why have you come?"

The scientist just looked at them awaiting the response. The captain spoke up.

"These here are…"

Sentencing cut off by the N.R.E.C. worker.

"No. I asked this one."

Pointing at Iyo as he then looked back at the soldier in a bully-like manner.

"So? Who are you?"

He asked Iyo again; he replied to him this time.

"My name is Iyo. I have come to learn what you do here at N.R.E.C. No other reason, I am a scientist, and these are my associates Bohn and Mrs. Amber. We just want a tour. Whatever happens, can we have our phones back?"

Iyo said as he held out his hand for a greeting. The N.R.E.C. worker replied.

"Certainly, unusual but that is okay, A tour we can do. No shaking hands, I am sorry, but you come with me. You soldiers go back to your posts; you are unneeded. And give back the phones. You can have them but no photos, I will personally destroy your phones on the site if you break this rule."

The N.R.E.C. worker spoke to them rudely. Explains why they were so hostile to begin with. You are who you hang around. The N.R.E.C. worker brought the group into the station, and they began a tour of the building.

"So, what do you do and why are you here? What is it exactly that you have come all this way to see here at N.R.E.C.?"

The scientist asked as the group of them walked onto the elevator.

"Well, I came to see the particle accelerator if that is all right. That was the main aim. I would love to see anything that I am able to see. Now that I am here, if I do not have a waste my trip then that would be ideal."

Iyo said as he pulled out his phone to check where Syn was. The N.R.E.C. worker spoke up.

"Yes, I will show you these things. First, we must go to the top control room so you can see the full snake."

The elevator gave off a ding and they all left it. Walking out on to the fourth level down from where they were with the soldiers. Bohn spoke out at the exit.

"The full snake? What do you mean snake?"

The worker just laughed at him.

"You will see in just a moment."

The worker walked up to the door that was at the end of the hall upon the elevator exit. He held up his ID badge, he scanned it and then they all entered the control room.

"And that is our snake."

The N.R.E.C. worker said as he pointed out of the window of the control room that overlooked the one mile wide and ten-mile-deep hole that held the N.R.E.C. particle accelerator.

"I see why you call it a snake. Interesting. What is the actual size of this snake."

Iyo asked with pure curiosity. The N.R.E.C. worker walked to the computer and started clicking around.

"If you come over and look at the screen, I can show you the dimensions and blueprints for the whole station. It is not like you can steal it."

The worker pointed to places on the screen as Iyo laughed at his joke of stealing and he began to look at the information.

"Is it possible to replicate a thing like this in a smaller form?"

Amber spoke out to the lab worker as she was looking out at the glass at the winding snake that is the particle accelerator.

"Replicate? No, not unless you had the algorithm that tells the CPU when to fire the particles and when to turn on receptors and when to push more energy through and you would also need the full set of blueprints that would allow you to understand how to build the snake to even do this project. You would need to build the collision sphere for when the particles collide, and you would need a whole lot of power to run it. How small are you talking? Hypothetically of course. In no way would the N.R.E.C. leaders allow a replication of this, I know it."

The Worker walked over and joined Amber by the window.

"Yeah, hypothetically. Like to fit inside a small warehouse the size of a lab or small home? Could you shrink it to that size?"

Amber explained her question in more depth.

"Oh, I doubt that is possible. The particles need space or the collision is unstable."

The worker said as he began to walk to the elevator.

"Would you like to see the collision sphere?"

He asked the group as he clicked the bottom for the elevator.

"Sure thing, how many levels down is it? It looks like a huge drop from that window, and could you tell me what the letters Q & A stand for?"

Iyo asked as he stepped into the elevator. The N.R.E.C. worker laughed as he pressed the letter X on the button pad that held the letters Q as well as A.

"Oh, I cannot divulge the information of that. Sorry, Level X is all I can show you."

The doors closed and the group began to descend to level X and at the exit of the elevator the group met by another N.R.E.C. worker.

"So, these are the Americans? Welcome, Welcome. How do you like her looks? Weird beast, is not it."

The worker greeted them as they all looked around the massive room. These workers at N.R.E.C. wore all white uniforms with a blue spiral as their logo, except for this new N.R.E.C. worker that met them at the exit of the elevator. This figure styled a blackened suit that held the same logo design, A blue spiral. Before speaking he adorned a puzzling smile.

"You can natter to me as Mr. West, I run this wing of the operation. I will take you through, follow me."

This accelerator had two sections that were long snakelike bodies. Each begins at the crown of the ground and they each wrap and wind down a mile or so to come together into the sphere of collision.

"Sir, Yes, it is quite the thing." Iyo spoke first as he walked near the sphere. Bohn and Amber followed right behind him looking about at the equipment. "Hey, why don't you guys ask him what you asked me."

The worker said as he gave a slight chuckle followed by a nudge to his fellow co-worker.

"We want to know if this can be shrunken down to fit a lab setting."

Amber asked as she stepped up onto the platform of the sphere to get a closer look inside. The N.R.E.C. worker looked at the group in awe.

"I have thought about this for some time now. Odd that you come all this way to find out when you could have called or emailed. SO, why did you come…"

The worker seemed puzzled.

"To get a hand on experience. The United States are not working on projects like this. Well, to our knowledge that is, I am sure that up in high government or in some type of classified military project. These groups could be doing something, but the public would not know about it. We wanted to see what you are doing because I have a high interest in particles and the elements. Do you all study the elements?"

The N.R.E.C. worker laughed. "Oh no. The elements? What do you mean? No, I am not sure I understand what you are speaking about."

Iyo just shrugged his shoulders and continued to ask about the process of things.

The conversation went on for a long while and Iyo pulled out his phone to message Syn that was somewhere in the station.

Did you find the server room?

Iyo sent this message to Syn and the A.I. at once responded.

Data retrieved, what do I do now creator?

Iyo gave out a "YES" in excitement and this brought the attention back to him while the N.R.E.C. workers focused on Amber and Bohn.

"Hey! We said no phones! That is, it. Tours over guys, Thank your friend."

The N.R.E.C. worker pointed to the exit as a demand for the group to leave. Bohn spoke up.

"Really man, he was just using his phone not taking any pictures?"

Bohn tried to reason with the N.R.E.C. man.

"No, I already spoke the rules. You all have seen enough. Let us go."

He continued to push them out the door. Iyo got back on his phone letting Syn know that she needs to meet back at the truck. He sent the message, and the group piled into the elevator. The N.R.E.C. worker hit the top-level button, and they all began to ascend to the ground level as he called in to Captain Dawn.

"Hey Captain, I am returning with the Americans. You must escort them off the property at once. Thank you."

The Worker clipped the walkie to his jacket as Dawn came back with a response.

"Heard that. Overwatch out."

The group continued to ascend as Syn messaged Iyo. He looked at the message and it was a current picture of where Syn was. In the photo you could see the truck, but there were fifty more guards than there were on their entry. Iyo shows the picture to Amber. Her mouth dropped in shock. Iyo messaged Syn back.

"Just get to me as soon as you have a window to do so."

Iyo sent the message right as they all were reaching the ground level. The doors open and the group greeted by the captain of the soldiers and the men forcefully moved Iyo and the others straight into the trucks. Leaving no time for Syn to get to Iyo but the drone follows directly above the truck as they begin to traverse out of the complex. They drove out of the complex, and they journeyed on the long and winding road to the edge of town where the soldiers let the group out. Iyo ran to the front of Tyco's truck before they began to drive back into the N.R.E.C. complex, throwing his hands, waving and shouting. The truck quickly screeched. Tyco opened his door and was quick to jump out of the vehicle.

"What's the deal science man? I can't take you back into this place. It is my job to do what these Nrec nerds ask of me. What do you want? Go on, I have not got all day." Spoke Tyco and Iyo put an end to his rambunctious actions.

"I just wanted to thank you, even if I can't go back in there, I sure learned a lot and that was all I wanted. You know, you said that there is something odd going on and haven't the clue to what it is, I think that they are doing some form of particle meshing at insane levels. I have no idea why you called them satanic or what it is that made you think that, but you can give me a call if you ever find out and want to chat about it. I just wanted to give you, my card. You are welcome to give me a call if you ever get back into the states, come check out my lab. One day I might need some security myself. I just wanted to thank you Mr. Dawn." Iyo handed the card to Tyco to then throw up his hands in a surrendering pose, clashing them together in a praiseful shake of thanks. Walking backwards as he did so rejoining Bohn and Amber who stood waiting.

"Yeah alright, I'll give you a call Iyo. Now be safe, don't do anything stupid. These guys are wicked, I have personally seen the evil that they partake in. Just keep your head down with whatever you do." Tyco hopped back into the truck and wove his hand in a regrouping motion as the truck began to pull off, heading back into the complex. Iyo, Bohn and Amber started making their way to the ends of the road.

"Well, have an Uber meet us at that intersection, it looks like a little complex, just a mile or so of a walk." The group now walking in the direction of the small town as out of nowhere comes flying Syn!

"Hey look! She is back!" Bohn shouts!

The group of them make it into town, got a hotel and finished the night to rise early for an early leave for a long flight home from Switzerland.

Timeline Shift

August 11th

Calloway Residence

"Finally, home. What a journey, I learned so much that I now need to apply! The only question now is where in the heck do I start. I suppose the best thing to do is make sure the system is working and the track that we built is still functioning properly."

Iyo speaking in an exhausting yet semi excited tone as he threw down his bags and flopped right onto the couch for a moment. Bohn laughs at him as he is greeting the wild pup Atom that is beyond excited about the return of the group.

"Can I eat any food man? What Cha got in here man? I need some substance!"

Amber was groaning for something.

"Yeah, just find something. I am going to crash out guys. Feel free to eat, drink, sleep, leave, Whatever. I am going to take a long nap. Not wanting to fight this jet lag, and my freaking head is killing me!"

Iyo was just starting to relax as there was a sudden beating at his front door. It startled everybody. Iyo jolted up and Bohn knocked over his plate he just prepared off the edge.

"What the fuck!"

Bohn exhaled of disappointment, Amber laughing at him as Iyo begins to curse things as he is walking to the door. He slides the lock and opens the door.

"Who is it? I just have returned, and I would really love…"

Iyo was about to Finnish explaining the fact that he wants to sleep but he stopped speaking in mid-sentence.

"Hello Mr. Diaz. I tried to reach you the last few days. As when we uploaded you to the watch list you were in… Switzerland already? Whatever you did there I hope it was worth it… You are under arrest on suspicion of murder. Put your hands behind your head and get down on your knees. I am taking you in."

An officer spoke to Iyo and began to read him his Miranda rights as he put him on the ground into hand cuffs. The officer's partner had his gun drawn and was moving to Bohn and Amber.

"Get down, No sounds. I said down and no sounds!"

They were both being overly aggressive. The group followed them and before they could even get words to each other the officers took Iyo out of his home and threw him straight into their squad car and they bolted off. Bohn and Amber are at a loss, not sure what to do, so Bohn begins to call for the A.I.

"Syn! Syn! Where are you? Syn! Iyo is in trouble. Come out Syn!"

Bohn was looking around the house as Amber came in from being outside as she was watching the police leave.

"Hey, she is outside! I just saw her!"

Amber said as Bohn runs past her outside to find Syn.

"Hey Syn! I do not know what we should do! They took Iyo. Do you have access to phones and computers? I need to find Iyo's lawyer information."

Syn flew straight into the house as Amber and Bohn followed her. She was hovering by the computer as Bohn caught up to her.

"Just open it for me, thanks."

Amber said as suddenly the computer came on.

"Thanks Syn, Thanks. Okay, Amber! Let us make this call and get Iyo the fuck out of this!"

So together Bohn and Amber called Iyo's lawyer, and they gave him a rundown of the situation.

ELDER WARNING

August 11th

Litus Temple, M.T. Litue, Astros, Spiritian

The Ancients stood with the members of Liege around the Sorzo awaiting commands from their Master. Ancient Salbani, the great rebel reformed the holy temple grounds into his ritual alter, The Sorzo, that sits in the middle of the ancient temple as it takes up about the entirety of the high temple mount.

Salbani calling his legion before him.

"It is time to unleash thy brethren! Join me, join me around the Sorzo!"

As commanded, the members each aside these points of the Sorzo star. At each end of the star was a bowl that descended to each of the arms of this star. Each arm on this Sorzo led to the heart of the ritual setting that was a pit consisting of fire.

"We do this ritual to call on the elder primes. The son of Darkos Prime I call to release the bonds of Michaels curse! We will reunite with our fallen brothers as our powers and energy's restored by reversal of that decree! The word bond broken by this blood of Ahtum! Gather! Gather my liege!"

Salbani emptied the vial of blood collected by the harvesters as then did his followers into each arm of the Sorzo.

"I gift this blood to the primes as I command you to break the spell of Michael!"

Salbani decreed this into the flames with contagious pride. Just after he spoke, he took the blade of the Trezhur, and he sliced it through his left hand. The ancient head held out his blood oozing hand into the form of a fist, directly over the Sorzo-arm that he had dumped the vial of Adams blood. His followers waited for his word, then replicated this action.

"Now, as the blood mixes, I decree that the elder spell of being bound on this mountain is here by… Broken!"

Salbani gave an echoing shout that set out just as a frigid wind consumed the temple. This freezing wind extinguished all flames on the grounds as Salbani let out a belch of disgust as his followers seemed caught off guard, holding themselves in fear but just as much curiosity. A dark black magic appeared as a swirling cloud that crept along the temple ceilings as it nearly consumed the entirety of the temple with its shade. It was such obscurity that confusion struck the room as the stone walls and golden idols began to freeze. Zycanco releasing shouts of fear at the sight of this happening.

"What is this! What is this illusion! This trickery, who could hold that darkness? Revel thyself, reveal who you are!"

Salbani screeching in anger and fury. Having not the knowledge of what this is. As he spoke on, as he did so an elegant, twirling fume of purple magic at once consumed the vicinity! Salbani out spoke the manner of these observed illusions.

"This power, this fragrance… Such familiarities! Who is it? Disclose and make known!"

In declaration of demand the smoke quickly thickened as a sudden discharge of magic in high momentum seemed to sprout from the fire! Crimson cuffs bound the liege as it sent these fallen to their knees! All except for Salbani who stood shocked and overcome by confusion. Thrashed his head with side-strut as he began to pace about. Out of the darkened smoke cloud above shaped a long snake-like entity, morphing into a physical form before Salbani.

The being smiled at Salbani with blackened eyes.

"You arrogant child… No illusion works here. You would not remember the familiar void that dwells around me? You do not hold the remembrance of your master? I am not surprised, you let the darkness consume you, I see little of the true Salbani, what have you done to cause yourself to become corrupt to the core? My student, this saddens me. You could not be satisfied as the head of knowledge? The once go-to figure for realm insights lost his sight. Felagnolum once to look to you for guidance, I ask where it is that you guide them now?"

The figure spoke as if they had known one another for a stretch of time. Salbani's flesh began to ice over as the being approached him, the figure spoke on.

"To order me? To lure me with the blood of Trezhur? The sacred Trezhur? Do you dare tangle with the set apart dirt realm? I tell you that this blood marked as untouchable. This human race of Ahtum are the little gems of the creator of creations! Only a child of void would even think of such blasphemy! Yet, you... A child of those who are protectors of dark knowledge! Born as know you are! A keeper you are! As what now do you keep? Utter heathens? You are supposed to protect the knowledge! Yet, you desecrate it! Fool."

The being thrusted his head in a shake of disappointment. Salbani holding a steady growl as his body nearly iced over, beyond the layers of ice you can faintly notice a vibrant darkened glow originating from Salbanis blackened core.

"So blinded by your lust for power to think that I... A dark lord. Would be so imprudent to entangle myself with the creators most adored creations? To think that I would do anything but laugh! Laugh at you fool! You dupe, all of you. I heard you ask about the call you made, and I only lost my sense! I warn you! As you will no longer stand protected! It is true that the king commanded Michael to banish you here but as for your imprisonment. It nearly concluded."

Salbani burst flames of chaotic fury around him at the sound of Michaels name as unknown truth was revealed. Escaping the frigid pressure of this being. Salbani seeping in anger as the figure spoke on.

"Here you see, Unaware that you were so close to your freedom... Unaware of the test of time. Yes, I allude that it was time that held you here as bound you here was the chaos that you birthed but this was magic that you have stolen, not yours I dare say... Claimed in terror for what reason? All the darkness I home I have collected by glorious purpose, the blessing in wars that were not mine, the use of manipulation to obtain my will. You raped the souls of your victims; they are only deceived and trapped. This is not what I have taught you! This is not what the Dark Primes taught you! I speak the truth when I say that they live sickened by your behaviors! Absolutely repelled! I say that even the worst of us still work for the creations. How is it that you have mistaken yourself my son... Who has misled you I wonder. Who is it that you truly are in service to? It is no son of the primes! This is why nobody has come to free you. Trapped, for even the wicked, my brothers of the Darku agree with Michael that you are deserving of your punishments. Again, Not the decree of Michael you fool! It was the command of the commander! That Yahu gave a universal order, who am I to oppose the son of creation? You are just like your brother, Rebellious!"

Salbani belching curses. The figure quickly becomes angered at this childish behavior.

"Silence! Your words will only bounce from my wards. Returning to your weak and poisoned soul. This entire mountain is bound under the power of the wicked, you are only a fool to be so unaware of this!"

The figure snapped his fingers as he spoke and just as Salbani attempted to rebuttal his jaw became frozen shut. The being rose in posture as he released a smirk of pleasure.

"Weak!"

The elder shouted with displeasure as he glared at the sight of Salbani whom paced. This elder being spoke on with barrier piercing word.

"As I spoke before you manifested in one of the broken of purity, I dare explain that this imprisonment was your last chance to sit and reconcile for your actions on these kingdoms.

As you sit on your minuscule throne with your rambunctious, infectious as they are decrepit fallen foes, the no-will be following serpent fools! All of you! laughingstocks! To think I would even think about the blood of Atum… Have you learned anything about magic? Stupid pride filled snakes! I should end you all! Dare you call on a prime? My sons have warned me of you Salbani! I thought them to be as boys! Boys that were at a lack of knowledge for what it really is to embody the wicked of the dark magic! I thought them to be fools who were at a loss of hope for the keeper of secrets! The barer of knowledge and a holder of the scrolls of light! Where are your gifts now? Where is the scroll Salbani… I know it is not in your possession… A true disappointment you have become. So lost, vial you are. As I stand unpleased with this great fall of you, old thinker. A phenomenon, your fall is that of what I speak. How have you turned against the creator and come to this place to pursue harm? Imprisoned by Michael due to your stupidity… As you had all the time to think on your action as you choose to seep in your anger, hatred, and revenge that I feel… That energy radiates from you. Utter fool! I have come to tell you that we will allow Michael to have his way with you. As for I will accept this sacrifice but use this blood I will not! By my own power I will free your fallen followers of Liege, as only to put you to the test. One last test to see if you are really the power that you claim. As the mighty son King has visited me. His decree hath sent by letter to a messenger. An old friend of yours, Qutix? Yes, that Qutix visited me right before the eclipse and spoke to me of your ritual that was to come. Salbani, the sons of the Great Queen of Magi are watching you. The Unipuro, they breathe sickly and stand repelled with your actions and the Darku Orders have released you from their protection. As this word is now to spread through the kingdoms. You and the Liege are to be bound to the void. All instructed to sever ties with you and condemned if this decree disobeyed. You are now officially, lawfully, and justifiably marked by the kingdoms! I expose this realm is no longer on your side, as all your accumulated magic has undone! By decree and work of the balance. All ritual ties and essence manipulation have been utterly severed! Uncaring of what happens to you, Yahu sent Qutix to warn me of your call. Your actions hath echoed in the god plains, you are seen and shamed. Yet still, the high Orders will allow you to evaluate the realms once more. As whomever of Liege captured or dies from here out will be subject to the void with no return to any realm. As whoever it is to join you is to be executed for a Uni-Cedured return to the trials of existence once more. This is in fact a universal decree! Marked by a reading of thy hearts, I tell you that I will not be your only visitor."

The figure backed away from Salbani as he morphed his shape back to an entity-like shape as he began to traverse the temple floors. Inspecting the bound members of Liege chained among temple walls in enchanted manacles. The legion grouped together so tightly that it be suffocating to gaze upon.

"Release, Unbind! Reform! Renewal."

The elder shouted these words in repetition as he crept around the temple, all the magical bindings fell from the entrapped members. The temple suddenly flooded with figures, creatures, entity's, vampires, and all kinds of nasty forces of darkness. Chaos was free as their leader Salbani sat in depression on his throne with all his fallen followers flooding around him in insanity. The leader in dejection for he understood the words that the Prime elder spoke. The creator finished with him finally and his time was in fact so valuable now. There was no more room for errors and games. Consumed with anger Salbani quickly stands from his throne as he shouts to his followers, unhinged in celebration.

"SILENCE!"

A massive pulse of energy flew in all directions from Salbani's shout. Causing his followers to be thrown away from him as he then collapsed form exerting so much power in one blast. The room was at ease as the flood of terror came to a rapid halt. The elder revisited Salbani as shared his last collection of thought.

"Anger has made its use of you; I see this is abundantly clear. As for the rest of the rest of you? This is who you call your master? A fallen one of profound knowledge… what has all your knowledge given you Salbani? You disappoint me to the highest possible measure. I cannot act sadden, nor angered. In fact, I release you as a student, I disown my nurturing care for you. As I leave you with this revelation. The bodies of the heavens and the bodies of darkness are against you, I tell you the Spiro realms have warned of your disconnection! I only have come for I have watched you grow. I know that you will do as you will, even now as I look at you, I see that the second your hatred grows! I tell you that I can do nothing for you now. You have a choice Salbani, confess your crimes of unity and disown your allegiance and the council will only banish you from the realm. What the son of the king is to do with the fact of your interference of his protected realm? That is for me to not wonder of, as it is for you to fear! There is nothing left for me to speak about as I know that not even luck is with you. Farewell my old student, I have given you a chance to fight, but I have spoken of what you are against. Be of mind and leave this realm! The Spiro will not spare you. Mind my words Salbani."

The figure turned as he quickly vanished into the air, leaving the truth in the heaviest burden. Salbani ignites fury, screaming in a long belch of hatred that sets the mount ablaze. Salbani's flesh became pure fire as his anger fully manifested through his essence. The temple quickly engulfed in chaotic flames as the Legion of Liege poured from the mountain peak. A celebration of sovereignty, just as Liege lost their fortifications. As it was a loss of liberty for the ancient one for, he was under the impression that he was forever bound to this mountain. As this elder teacher had just explained that it was in fact a sentence that he had now thrown away. Due to his ill deed of tampering with the Trezhur creations of the dirt world. It is unfortunate.

A SIGHT TO SIGHT

August 11th

Aoxit & Jycyept, Wood-line Outside of Litue

Right beyond the mountain of Litus a pair of fairies wander about, Traveling far from the garden of Desire.

"That is as a fact the notion that was at rest in my mind. I just had not the energy to act of motion…Wait. Jycyept, Oh my! Look, Look… Look at that! Jycyept Look! Magic! No way! Not for a decade have I seen the magic of that modus! How could this be? Look! Look Jycyept look! At the top of Litus!"

The fairy screeched at his friend as he quickly flew to the peaks of the trees. Mind you these trees are over three hundred feet tall. It took a quick forty-four seconds for the fairy to reach the top. These are Heirwok fairies, hyper intelligent as they are hyper speedy. Rapidly moving through the branches startling creatures. Right by the crawlers, zipping by hatchers and then zooming around the peak. Milliseconds after this first fairy arrives to the crown of the tree, Here comes the other.

"Oh man… Look at that. Beaming red… beam? What is that Jycyept? The evil, it must be that it is wicked. For sure, for sure that is the wicked… We should see… Let us go, oh let us, let us go and explore! Can we go? I am, I am going to check it out! Come on you old wish giver! I wish to go to the mountains! Come on!"

This fairy obviously of the younger age… For how do any of maturity act of this sort. The two of them were as tiny as a handle on a sword as they both were bright as it was a vivid blue glow to their little magical bodies.

"Oh, calm yourself Aoxit. I am restless with you… As journey for a long while we have, I confess that I am tired young spree, and to that place. Well, that, that is Litus. Litus is where our Mighty King has in fact bound the Ancient Liege! That is the dwelling of the wicked! We cannot go there! We should not go there… I will agree the magic was a sight, but that is all my friend. A sight worth investigating? I would say not. As the dwelling of Liege is for the wicked. Not for a free spirit as myself, as yourself. I dare say, I will not put my wings on that. Idiocy!"

The fairy was obviously scared of this place, but the other was young. Ignorant of the harsh reality of what the wicked is. Unaware of the knowledge of the happening from long ago.

"Well, you are ancient and... I say lamed and robbed of your wanderlust... ness! As I will in fact go alone! Alone I say!"

The young fairy then turns as it bolted off leaving a bright and magical path of dust behind his spree. The elder fairy understood the faire codes. For he knew that it was one of the rules that he had to go with this young one. Written in the tablet of Heirwok, "No fairy should venture alone."

"Wait on me!"

The elder yells as he as well then bolted from the peaks of the trees, going after the young one. To the peak of the mountain the Fairies flew as they met among one another at the side of a statue. A great old dragon that sat on one of the crests of the Litus temple.

"Look Jycyept... That... That... That is the one they speak of...Is it? Is that the ancient one?"

The young fairy boy was shaking as he peeked down into the temple chambers through the crown of the high tower.

"Who? Who is it that you are looking at Aoxit? There are so many Dracos!"

The elder fairy questioned as he leaned into peek for himself.

"That one... The one who is on the throne!" Spoke Aoxit as his elder suddenly pulled him back to the temple wall.

"Oh no! That is in fact the ancient one Salbani! As it looks like his followers unbound! Celebrating! Return we must... Oh young Spree, I dare say this is trouble, for the wicked are boundless! I add that we must go back to Desire and warn someone... we must! Adventure is over Aoxit! It is in fact my request as your elder. You must return to desire with me to speak of this new use of magic... I know that the King has decreed it so that the Liege as for Salbani especially is to not be able to use magic and it was as well a decree by the High King that no Sempiternal or Fairy of any kind was to give magical access to any of members of Liege or anyone that is not of the Unitrea order... These were decrees! Yet... With my own eyes! You! It was as in fact you! Aoxit! My young learner! This was in fact your discovery! We must return to Desire Garden at once! This is terrible news my young one... The magic has returned... The deep dark wicked red enchantments of blood! The air smells of the metals of the dirt world... Aoxit we must go! Back into the insanity this kingdom is!"

The elder fairy grabbed his kind as he began to quickly descend into Staid Null, moving quickly into the old bloodwoods to return to warn someone of this power!

"We must explain all the happening to the nearest member of the unity, quickly now! Aoxit we must return!"

Shouted the elder as together they traversed through the eerie bloodwoods of Litue.

DJINN AND A NYMPH

August 11th

Southeast of Litue, Northern Spiritian

Beyond the mountain range of Litue and through the bloodwoods a figure is met by the gorgeous grasslands of Airshe Heights. These are mysterious hills going ahead in elevation as the same height as the Litus mount of Litue. A stunning illusion of distance, I allude. At the height of this grassland travels two that wander. A Djinn by the name of Rabohu, accompanying him was his greatest friend, a beautiful Nymph of the name Eira, descending from the Airshe lands far north-east of Litue. The djinn, Rabohu Sepu, had a skin tone that was as grey as the storm, and he styled a robe that was loose at his chest and fit to the lower body. The djinn wore a silver crown that wrapped around his skull like a vine as it came to a point in the shape of a cut Dynot. Rabohu was a middle-aged figure, master Magi and wish giver. A true expert in the magic arts. He is known to be a trickster, a jokester with a beautiful soul. Unlike most Djinn, Rabohu is bound to nothing. Meaning he has earned his freedom without having to give away his power. A wonderful creation and a friend to the Unity of the Treasured. Speaking on his traveling companion, Eira the Nymph, She is of the Asi bloodlines of the stone. She is quite a beautiful figure, I would say, that is unlike her cursed sisters. The Nymph is a young spree but sure beginning to become a Master Magician, Rabohu be her teacher and caretaker, it is rumored that she is the cause of the curses that plague her wicked family. Eira has skin of the moon as eyes of turquoise, silken hair styled in a braid that stretches to her lower back, the color is a murky red. The nymph has pointed ears that roundabout into themselves, not straight as an elf. She wears a temperate suit proceeding downward from neck to waist, as solid gold cuffs around her wrists, adorned with jewels.

The nymph styles an enchanted obsidian necklace spoken to keep one hidden if considered.

Venturing through this area Northwest of the city of Satare, nearing the bloodwood beginning that is Northeast of Litue. The pair travel in collection of a debt for A High Priestess Nymph of stone. Eira let out in a spastic celebration, a shouting from sudden startle of the grounds shaking. The pair of travelers stumbled as if a rug pulled from underneath where they stood, yet oddity, for they traveled amid an open grassland that was just beyond the mystic oaks. She pointed to the High North that was in eruption by magic blast, originating from the forbidden mountain range. With new happenings comes new energy, as Eira seemed to absorb some of this blast.

"OH! Woah! Plain quake! What an oddity, oh look, Rabohu look to Litue! Would you look at that magic! By wonders, Litus is undone! Surely that cannot be anything good! What should we do!?"

Eira overwhelmed by emotion and adrenaline as her traveling partner remained at ease. The Djinn shook his head as he remarked a stoic sentence.

"I see it, curious. Yet, what of any matter is it to me? I am no defender, who am I to trifle with the legion? I say that the sight of that, the shake in the dirt, it is no little thing my lady of Stone. What we should do is mind our business, as we are already on a task. Hath not the Priestess bid you on mission, as we have traveled far to abandon it. Is that what you would do?"

The Djinn speaking of sense as the lady trotted ahead, her eyes set on the magical release that occurred a distance away. Together Rabohu and Eira were traversing the high lands to venture to a port that rests on the North-West Bay of Vyol, of the Sea Luminvyol. Being the South-West end of the Bloodwoods before the Staid Null.

"When she hears of the happening, she will send me to collect payments from those unbound. Thousands are in debt to her, as Salbani hath broken many promises, it is all she talks about. A real hatred she has grown for that one. It is always about payment with her, I wonder why she lends so much if so, many return not the deed. Beyond that, we should at least investigate. Are you afraid? The known trickster strongman, Rabohu the Djinn is scared for a little adventure? Let us hold a sight to the scene!"

Eira quick to retrieve her magscope, using it to get a better look at the mountain. As she held it to the horizon, seeing the energy manifestation in the sky.

"Now that is magic, what a beautiful thing. Let us see what is happening out there…"

Eira turned the mechanical knob with three clinks.

"Holy Shutouts! Woah!"

A remark spoken when one is to be stuck by shock. The Shutout is a psilocybin mushroom that randomly generates things that a being would think if on the substance. An extraordinarily powerful strain of the fungi family, I would add that as it is a wildly known realm speaking, a joke of speech, for the hidden truth is it considered holy for how mighty the illusions are. It is not for beginners. Eira dropped the magscope as it rolled to the feet of Rabohu.

"What is all the fuss?"

Spoke the uncaring Djinn as he looked through the scope, clinking the knob to refocus as he jumped in the same shock that struck Eira.

"By my gifts, what have I seen!"

The djinn raised and lowered the scope multiple times, becoming more frustrated with each sight. His face mangled with disgust as his raised shoulders and flexed ears expressed anxiety and fears. Eira swooped to her friend and snagged the scope with a laugh, followed by a mighty grin.

"If you are going to be all weird about it then do not look! Go wander off as you would without me and fantasize until you must not. I shall be as you Rabohu, unstuck and without care with the happenings. As my lack of attention be not on the kingdom happenings but as for you!"

Eira went on with a chuckle as she put her eyes back to view the Litue happenings. The djinn unsettled with this disrespect, he raised his hand and spoke in the Magi tongue as he flicked his wrist.

"Etativel Epocs!"

The ugly squint of Rabohu and the prideful grin of Eira transferred faces just as the shadows become uncaged in the lack of the light, as the sight magnification device magically weaved with ease from her grip just as a giant taking a long sword from a knight. The djinn spoke in vanity.

"This overpowering that you feel is what it feels like to have your intuition ignored. You would not attempt to snatch this magscope from me, would you? Going against a move of your most trusted ally would be treachery!"

Rabohu holding up this hand, being in control of the magscope that hovered before the lady nymph. Her stomach quenched, loathing her friend.

"Fool you are to make weightless analogy to empower you on high ground as if me doing my will is a move against you, you only say this because thy struck by fear! Who by the looks of it, the figure unbound and roaming free at that temple! Unguarded are you Rabohu? Where is your sense, be not of fear, we will travel secretly, what is the worry in you?"

The nymph spoke true as the djinn was in revaluation of himself, quickly thinking deeply as he returned the magscope to her with a smooth drop to her hands. By the hundreds of thousands, the ancient ruin was vividly active, roaring in action by the once chained legion in celebrations of freedom. The nymph gazed down at the scope once more as she continued to express herself.

"They just flood out of the mountain as ants... Ants I say, pooling themselves in their own world of chaos. How is it that they could be free from that great decree of Michael?"

Eira adrenalized, while Rabohu surprisingly shook with the happening. The wicked creatures poured out from the peak of the mountain as if they were a colony of bees attacking like hive protection. The creature's jubilation of release, one could hear the echoing chaos from the tree line, being over ten long miles from the near tree line of the Forbidden Oaks.

Eira awoke from her gaze with a fighting Spiro, retracting the magscope as she neared Rabohu with a sudden plan.

"Thousands of the wicked free, this is a problem, we are to warn each soul we travel past Rabohu, quite necessary, as Magi of the realm we are to protect the magic. We are still in a dark age, steady massive lack of assessable magic from the last set of encounters this realm has had. I say that this is utterly saddening... I knew, I knew somehow their imprisonment would end. I just thought it would not be this soon; we must warn everybody Rabohu... We must!"

Eira infuriated as she began to absorb some of this fear as well, emotions all at once can be detrimental to choices. A murder gaze on the sight of the wicked in celebration. Eira wanted to run up the mountain and go to war even if, outnumbered by over a million forces of darkness.

"You are right my lady... We will tell them. Now let us go. Come now, before they decide to come down the rest of the mountain, if they continue through the bloodwoods before the Trea protectorate is to intercept them, well, I will say the realm is in for some dramas. We shall get the word out before this! Come now! Come!"

Rabohu encouraged by Eira as he turned to continue to move in the direction of the old city of Satyr.

"Wait!"

Yelled Eira with worry to the Jinn.

"This is the way that leads to Satyr. We must not return! To the West Port, and then to the Garden, into Desire, we must go! Rabohu we must! As both could be a target for the wicked ones. We could warn the people at the port, and I know it to be highly populated, word would spread fast, so I would urge you to reconsider the path Rabohu... We must go to the garden of desire first. I have friendships in this place... Important creatures live in the realm gardens... Rabohu you know this! We must move to warn Desire and oh, we could find a speeder from the near port!"

Passionate as nearly demanding her ideals as she had more love for Desire, holding a personal connection with the inhabitants of the garden. Rabohu had a lifting to his spirit by mention of this.

"A speeder? Yes, that is sure a better idea than moving on foot. If only the Bandu were here, we would be there as if we always were!"

Eira laughed with the Jinn, beginning to walk with him.

"Oh yes, that Bandu is quick. We will see him my friend... at the trade port we might find another Utrea to help us warn the kingdoms."

Eira pulled her sword from her back and gave a rapid slice to the air. She swung a full three sixty as her body flipped with the movement. A faint violent smoke secreted from the blade as if it were alive.

"And... off with heads! Nobody will stand in our way!"

Expelling her excitement, Eira laughed with pride as the pair of them quickly veered sights to an oncoming hovercraft. A reverberating propulsion engine sounded as Rabohu pointed then moved in its direction.

"An Hcraft! Let us go!"

Rabohu transformed into a vapor like snake as he swirled in the direction of the oncoming transport ship, Eira shouting with fear.

"We don't know who that is!"

Yelling her voice stuttered by each foot connect, trying to catch up to the Jinn she used her knowledge of Air-bending to ever push herself so slightly into a mighty leap.

THOUGHTS OF THE MESSENGER
August 11th

N.W. Astros, Irosent, Spiritian

Ancient Byevil leaving the temple of Litue as commanded, venturing to find the bastard Prett. It took some time as the Temple is a multilayered design that consists of the entirety of the mountain. Sculpting by the giants of Sype, the stone men of the power plain of Vimaurus, one could only marvel at the beauty. At the pace of a cat step, it would take half a light cycle, more so if the temple populated. In solitude Byevil traveled through each of the eight levels. Cycling through notions as he traversed. A period of reflection beginning with mockery.

"Ah... Go... Go now, Byevil! Go he says, do this he says, that he says, I say that old Salbani forgets I have been with him so long? Does he? No, oh no. He would never forget, together we are in this. He must remember, he could only trust me. He could only and only trust me. For, it is me! I, the great Byevil! The great and ancient messenger! This is my task! Oh, silly I am! Silly! In fact, since my creation this has been my task. Oh, to hold the incumbrance of the message. This is my reasoning that the creator has in fact created me! That word is true! Even if I run as I hide as I rebel. My task is my task. As the words of the Unitrea! That rule giving society righteous, the high pride minds, the so-called protectors of the realm. It is their decree that one is to abide in your gift. Oh, how thy art to abide in my terror. The universal rules of their control. Filth and I hate it... I will go and I will find this Prett as the fools asked. Soon I leave those who I have grown with, wandered with, warred with. I will leave that of what I once loved for I am tired of rulings! As it is I, who is to see the truth of this fallacy of unity! I say they will learn who that ancient one really is! How that Salbani snares us and traps us for his bidding! How I am beginning to become trapped in these chains of do as he wills just as the following of liege. More in fact, for I have time as my witness, this Salbani has sure done much to me. The weight of the actions we have committed, How I wonder if my master has lost sanity. As my will but I wonder where my true will is! For, lost I have become as I have followed him for so long and for what? For what I say? To be a fool playing a fool's game? The game of shame I say! Fools all around! All around I say!"

Making it to the ends of the temple to begin walking the Null, scattered Oaks grew along the pathway of the rocky stretch. Down the traveled path that is leading to the bloodwoods at ends of this once majestic mountain range.

The figure was mumbling to himself grunting about as he was in a pull of notions. "Hmm." Byevil grunting in thought as overheard branches cracking and snapping from above. Byevil was quick to look at the skies, as speedily in swift motion from the peak of the Sprall oak descends a dragon hatchling! It scaled in a beautiful, bleached grey, reflecting a darkened blue with turquoise feathering on the bone structure. The youngling was still bigger than any lion. Descending directly over Byevil, dropping limb to limb from the Sprall. Slithering through the branches as any serpent would. A slight grace with how the creature moved, like water as it crashed with delicacy straight in front of Byevil. It began to jump and glide around him, causing him to stumble around he speaks up.

"Augh, dancing for what? Beast. I admired your movement as it was distant. How dare you stop me! A child you are! Where is your kind, wandering are you? A serpentine hatchling alone in the Null? Is your master looming? What is this happening, are you with message?"

Byevil expressing himself fearless of the creature as standing before it far from panic. I add that the looks of this hatching are uncommon. Unseen by the realms, Byevil intrigued with the youngling, he stepped to it. The creature let out a head shaking snarl as hot steam expelled from its nostrils! The dragon arched its back as it stooped it is head as if it were about to strike! Byevil unhinged…

"And what! What will you do!"

Byevil lunged at the youngling as it was quick to skip around him. Byevil gave a laugh as he repositioned himself in the sights of it once more.

"Fast you are! State your intentions!"

Byevil yelled at the small Drago.

"A newly born, your bone is not even yet developed, you are only a small hatchling… Who are you!? Go on and name yourself, go on and tell me who do you serve. What is your bloodline? Your speech is no secret to me! Go on, natter something! Use that serpent tongue to explain your appearing!"

Byevil unfazed by the creature as he demanded it to explain itself. The hatchling simply snorted at Byevil as it turns to then skip back up the tree. As one, two, three hops and it then had enough momentum to fly into the thickening of the clouds.

"Ah! That is what I thought! I would have slayed you!"

Byevil laughed to himself as he continued down the path.

"Would you have? My new son? You would take him from me?"

Spoke a serene voice behind Byevil.

"Wo-woah!"

He yelled as he stumbled about to turn to see a friendly face.

"Voboh! Dragon Master… I should have known you would be about… Following me, are you? Keeping an eye, you are? This one is new. From whom? Who is the mother?"

Byevil laughed as he questions his friend in greeting. The figure responding as he revealed himself from shadows.

"That is of the oldest… Do you remember her?"

The dragon head asked Byevil as he sat on a large stone that was near him. "The oldest?" Byevil took a moment to think.

"Urm."

Byevil grunting as he sat in memory, arms crossed as he stretched his memory.

"Is it Yingal? The first mother? The first of whom I know?"

Byevil replied as he took a gaze down the hills, his eyes pierced the bloodwoods. Flashes of remembrance of the old Great War continuous in his mind. Here at Litus and the old woods of Connik. It is said, beings are subjects of torment from the fallen souls of the rebellion war. Ghosts that haunt survivors with the memories of terrors, as these Spiro could consume the traveling kind! It is wise to know a path or may one be highly guarded. Oh, physical and mental wards! Yes! Fortify the soul! I say then armor on your Spiro!

"Yes! That is in fact her! I tell you Byevil... The mother dragon... Yingal. She has had a new hatchling group. Two of them! As I do not know who the father of this breed is! These hatchlings are the quickest as they are in fact the smartest two dragons I have ever seen!"

The figure Voboh, Dragon expert as he was the holder of the dragon keys. Was excited about the news of the happening. Two brand new dragons as well as the fact that they are of a breed that he is unaware of... This was news to anyone.

"The magic was thought to be lost. That is unless you are a fairy or a Sempiternal... You know this. Yet, the dragons are magical creatures... I just thought that when the King banished our powers... Well, I would think that my creatures would lose their power... They did in fact not... Hey... Are... Are you listening to me Byevil? What is it that you are doing at this old ruin anyway... Off to give a message are you?"

The keeper was going on and on. Byevil lost in the history of the land.

"Our master hath spoken and send me on task, do not act oblivious, I know that you heard him... following me for what, you old keeper. I am looking for Prett... The clever fool? The manipulator? That checkered striped bastard. Do you know where he is? Have you come to venture with me? Is it that your dragon exposed you and now you come to act as if you follow me not? You are creature keeper, not one of illusions. Fool, your lies show in your silence."

Byevil shined light on the mystery appearance of his liege ally, ignoring Voboh speaking of his newly born dragon member. As Voboh did not let this bother him for he knows that the ancient Byevil does not care for anything these days.

"You met one of them just a moment ago! I will tell you where I know Prett to be if you guess if the hatchling that you met was a male or female!"

Voboh was still trying to get Byevil to see the joy in the situation but a figure like Byevil is beyond joy.

"Voboh. Enough with your wit, this behavior, I hate it. Tell me where you have seen Prett, and I will let you live on!"

Byevil took a step to Voboh as he towered over him with dominance.

"He's at the river. Past the old sacrificial mantle… I allude that I sent this hatchling to find him, not to take credit, I was being of help. You could show a little respect, old messenger. I am the dragon keeper! I could send them to eat you. Have you bathing in fire, I'd mind your tone ancient one."

Byevil laughed at Vobohs request for respect. As he snarled at him walking off in the direction of the river, just inside the bloodwoods. The hatchling from moments ago flew down passing Byevil to then rest aside the dragon keeper.

"Until you return then… Oh… and if you care to know. The gender is male, and his name is Uevian the blue! I already spoke it when I first spoke to you, you would know that if you used your ears!"

Voboh spoke as he watched the ancient messenger continue in the direction of the old sacrifice mantel.

Through the Null and into the bloodwoods, an area of mystery and dread by happening of the past, as you may know by now. Towering trees that crack and rattle-like bones of skellies. The trees were under a mighty heavenly curse by Arku Decree. For it was a land of an ancient battle that was deemed to have victim blood to never dry. Allowing tormentors to dwell and vial beasts, poisonous serpents and crawlers roam. The sunlight shined but it was lightened by a vale that allowed nothing to grow, no bird would nest, no tree jumper would play and nothing of the kingdom would venture into this place. By decree, not that a figure is too scared to traverse here. Sure, some things are scary, but it would only be a fool that ventured into this place for his own pleasure. The air of this sickened forest was heavy as a depressions. As it is sure to be one of the tormenting forces one is to encounter. It is rumor that their minions rule the land. The woods held oppressive silence that would allow one to hear the slither of a snake and the rattle of a critter. The winds were calm as the breaths of a newborn and the floors where entrenched with the victims of the battle. Bloods of the fallen that soaked the forest floors, being the only substance the trees can drink and so they are poisoned and sick for it never it to rain over these lands.

Whispers of unknown forces of darkness obtain the mind of a venturing one so be of mind if you happen to traverse here. The shadows of despair work with a malevolent High Darku King of darkness to maintain this chaos. It is said that this dark lord is under direct orders from the High angelic council to maintain this decree as a warning to the kingdoms, a reminder to never again involve themselves with the happenings of evil. As there are more forces beyond the liege and not all these dark ones are entangled with the challenger, Salbani. His vengeful spirit will be the worst punished as his venture through this land is said to be the thing that would drive him utterly insane. He only laughs at this rumor and awaits his day to traverse through it. These woods are a place of fear, a forbidden territory avoided by all who are not entangled with darkness. Not even the dark witches of the Wicc or the witches covenant of Sesilell, nor the Darku Orders of the Crimson sisters or the Black Sun would dare to venture here.

The tormentors grow desperate for encounters of souls. Those who have been rumored to venture are lost, unseen and unheard from. There are only those of the Liege who have ventured through, it is said that there have been deals made to allow a subject through. This could be the reasoning to why Byevil is roaming and the same is for the youngling Prett. A contract must have been created in secret. This forest is a terribly shady spot on the continent of Irosent but not the only wicked place on the Spiritian plain. The curse will not be lifted until the great Arku whom cast it decrees it released. As even if Salbani makes it through the torments, he can make no deal to lift the curse. It is a kingdom reminding punishment.

SEEKERS

August 11th

Essen

At the very time that Byevil was nearing the edge of these bloodwoods, back at the Temple of Litus Salbani awaiting his return, by a swift appearance entered a grand ally of the Legion into the mind of a Knight Guard, A Seeker. Unseen by the eyes of Atum or any figure that has a guise on the pineal gland. A Spiro seeker can travel through physical bodies for a fleeting period by accessing a figures mind by an open door of permission or deadly sin. These Seekers are dimensional beings able to hear realm sensitive information. Nonaffiliated in the wars of the realms, it is known that a seeker will answer whoever is to summon it. As is also a Rumor that these beings choose to be of high service to those of the Darku Orders. These summonses are dangerous, for having not the understanding of the knowledge of how to call such a thing could end in a subject calling something else entirely. By my knowledge seekers are always open to answer a summons because they like to mangle with things in the realm, they find it amusing to mess with things and have no issue with changing the task of what summoned for, quite the interesting Spiros. The ancient leader practiced this method of summoning well and due to being bound to Litus, Salbani is unable to learn realm information. In high use of this kind, as one of them found in the mind's eye of a guard position before a high council door inside the judgment room of Temple Sophia, of the plain Taodamic. The Seeker kind is unable to control a subject but very well able to hear and see as this Seeker kind temporarily binds to a subject. As so in this guard mind of a knight of Zoe. As for Zoe, this is a grouping of the light order of Spiritian. This Seeker peering unknowingly through this guards eyes, in sight was the high marble table as the eight seats of stone. In each seat a representative of the council of

Taodamic, a continent on the plain Spiritian. These eight are among the Light Order, The light brotherhood of Wisdos. As before these seats were eight tables of representatives of the plains of Spiritian. Briefly heard were plans of righteous mischief.

"… be it so, the message will get to that wretch! Marked on this very day! Wait, holdfast! What, what is this! I feel dark, darkness here! A watcher!"

Speaking was a member of the Wisdos brotherhood, standing from his stone seat behind the marble high table. A member of the tables below them shouted with certainty.

"Impossible! High Controller, nothing can penetrate these wards!"

The one of lower importance spoke with confidence as an elder of the high table spoke from the far edge with a sense of factual fortifying.

"Yes, the foundations are well secured. I do say it is near impossible to penetrate these wards. I say near, but the minds of this temple I would differ the strengths of these! Combat the waves my brethren!"

The grouping of council members began performing reinforcement rituals on their minds, shielding their psyches, as well as expelling unwanted guests. Action as such sends the Seeker creatures seeking a new place to be! Any ritual work on the body would drive this watcher kind out for it causes a Seeker tremendous pain to remain, causing many to be quick to leave. Either quick to flee the scene or even forcing them from the shadows, some do work to bind such a worker and learn of its reasoning to spy! Demanded, eventually forced to speak to truth for embodiment. As for this Seeker is not willing to endure such things. Quick to leave the subject, now venturing to speak what it has learned for whom tasked it, Salbani.

A DREAM OF THE QUEEN
August 11th

Litus Temple

It was only a few that roamed the Litus Temple grounds as for the two hundred thousand of the other important as drone following minions of the Liege were still bound to the temple walls. Awaiting anxiously to be freed, only able to sound as their physical bodies were entrapped. For a decade they have been trapped and for years they have watched their legion King Salbani, and a few others roam freely in the temple. As they have been trying to find a way to unleash their brothers and unbind themselves from the second part of the imprisonment. Which is being trapped in the west region of Irosent on the plain Spiritian, from the Litus Temple, through the Staid Null, the Litus mountain range as then the blood woods of nattering barks. Unable to traverse past the Tuent river of fresh water. A figure could hear the mumbled conversations by peer to peer who near each other was ongoing as for some others, screams of anger occasionally sound out. In the middle of the chaos there was a being that only seeped with unrelenting, unshackled anger. His name was Neuamor, a trickster mage of the old orders of Darku. Growing ill wills to his chosen king, Bani. As such anger that Neuamor fell into a deep slumber, and he had a visit by an ancient that he has only met on one occasion.

In this dream Neuamor was unbound and free to move yet he was boxed in a blackened room with a single light source from above, a white shine that gloomy lit the room, just enough for him to see his own body.

"Where am I? Is this a dream?" Neuamor spoke in a soft tone of question.

Suddenly he heard an echoed bouncing of fluctuations that seemed to come from all directions that was a strong laugh carrying weight of devilry that was nearly a mocking.

Neuamor endured muscle spasms as he was holding slight fears, he readied himself for an encounter positioning himself in a battle stance and he shouted.

"Who is there!? Name yourself, reveal yourself. What is this blackened room! What do you want from me! Who is there?" Neuamor looked around awaiting a response as he was suddenly put to his knees with mighty force. This set him to anger just as he realized that he was in the presence of someone of power. The laughing continued faintly as he tried to rise but he was unable to because there was such a weight over him that he could only raise his head. As this voice then came in a whisper from behind, just beside his right ear.

"Submit."

Neuamor turned his head quickly as when he looked to his side there was nobody there. Out of his left peripheral he suddenly saw a figure move. Neuamor was struck with surprise, wide eyed in disbelief as suddenly this weight that held him kneeled released from him and his jump of fear threw him to his back as this figure approached from the darkness. The weight then returned to him with more force than before causing his body to be pinned to the blackened floors. As if he was paralyzed or under attack from a paralysis spirit. His eyes focused and he saw the figure standing before him, at his feet. She had her arms crossed and held a petrifying grin that was unsettling. Neuamor attempted to speak. "What do you." The woman flicked her hand as the mouth of Neuamor was suddenly closed by sowing as if he never had a mouth to begin with. She released a mighty laugh as she stepped over his body, jumping down, sitting on his belly with her hands on his chest. Neuamor crinkled his brow as his eyes popped with wonder, he was utterly confused. She released more laughs followed by directions and explanation.

"Shh-Shh-Shh. You have no place to speak." Said the Woman as she grabbed his jawline and shook his head with aggressive force. She gave her head a tilt as she swooped in close and studied his eyes with a squint of her own.

"I can see that you are filled with… What is it? Anger? Yes, but more, it is hatred, oh, I see, I see, it is rebellion. A sickness, a sickening you live with, that turning in your belly, O, the swirl in your mind. I see it, I can nearly feel it. You want, o, there it is… You want revenge!"

She spoke in confidence; she beat his chest with her hands as she spoke the sounding of each thud. "Boom, Ba, Boom, Ba, Boom-Boom!" The woman jumped to her feet as she released unjust laughter, she swirled around kicking her leg out with the spin coming back to a center viewing of Neuamor, bending over in a gaze as she rested her hands on her knees. Speaking out with strong annunciation in each of her words.

"You want to get back at that ancient one, your supposed King! Is he? I say he's not; I say he is the problem. Wouldn't you? You want to overthrow, no. You want death! Do you want to kill your leader? How pleasing. SO DO I."

The woman released laughter as she wove her hand, giving Neuamor his voice back as he was released from the weight that had him pinned. He sat up but stayed on the floor. Intrigued by the woman as he began to question.

"Who are you, I have faint memory of seeing, meeting you once before."

The woman leaned back on the blackened wall that seemed as if it went on forever. It had no texture, as if she was resting on nothing. She played with her bracelet as he held a smile for, she knew she had him, she knew that she could fully turn him, and this pleased her. She stood up straight as she stepped forward asserting herself in dominance.

"My name is Lytula, Queen of desires." She spoke with a smirk of pride.

"Oh, ancient queen!" Neuamor released a submissive cry as he bowed before her with his forehead touching the blackened grounds. He spoke out in fear as his voice rattled in each of his words.

"Sh-shame befalls, me, I-I, how I did not recognize you. I should,"

She cut his sentencing short. "Enough praise, I have a task for you. Now rise."

Speaking in annoyance as Neuamor got to his feet looking on to her still holding his fear but he now had a welcoming posture.

"Anything." He spoke in a stoic tone.

Lytula let out a "Humph" as she began to circle him in her pace.

"That legion king is undone. Weak. For a decade, our brothers have been bound by his failures and soon my workings will become known, and I will be free. The Order of the Black Flame will rise, and I am to take that Bani to his knees. You are soon to all be unbound as when this time comes Salbani will follow my plans that he thinks are his own. For I am the one that sent Rhamtes to him, I am the one that has made the strives to free the legion and most of them will rebel when they learn the truth, but as for you. You will be called forth by that Bani for a ritual, I have foreseen it. You will know when the time is right, and you will separate. Gather the members of this ritual in the tower of Phylace, for this is where you will go, as await there for me you will. Soon my plans will be fulfilled, and I will have that Salbani begging me for peace. I will send you a trusted ally and you will know this by a marking on his back. My Sigel. Do this, and that Litus will be yours and I will make you known and great once more!"

Suddenly Lytula vanished and Neuamor was pulled into a spinning vortex that caused him to wake, returning from this dream state to find himself bound again on the walls of the Litus temple. He was no longer burdened with anger; he was focused and ready for his move. Awaiting his moment of release.

A MIRROR OF DEATH & BLISS
August 11th

The River of Tuent, Bloodwoods, Astros, Spiritian

It was time before Byevil made it to the river for he moved at his own pace. To move through the bloodwoods could only happen by walking down the correct path! One should not stray off the path to make it through this ancient forest peacefully, I speak downright truth! I pass luck to the figure that would like to venture off the path, great terrors await you. I would hope he or she to be a warrior of sorts or mind that it would be good to have one with you. Off the path could be any kind of creature or trouble. As for these woods are under the domain of Liege as even the trees of this area have submitted to him! "I see you..." Byevil mumbled as he was nearing the river. The sound of rushing water was all that heard, overtaking the silence of the forest. Byevil stood on the side of the flowing water as he looked around.

"An odd sight I say."

Spoke Byevil as he noticed that the ancient bloodwoods end at this part of the river and then just beyond the rush on the other side the land begins in beauty.

"That is what darkness brings... That is the death."

Byevil said as he noticed the darkness of where he came. He sat for a moment as he was questioning things in his mind.

"Is that Byevil? Out here by the water way? Sitting? I thought you to be with Salbani planning the next terror. What brings you to the water way?"

Said a young figure as he neared Byevil.

"I came for you. Prett."

He spoke as he held out his arm and gave him a wave to join him.

"Oh... Me... Me... You came for me? Why are you looking for me Byevil? Who told you I was here?"

Prett walked to Byevil and together they turned back to the forest to return to the temple of Litue.

"The Master tasked me to retrieve you Prett."

Byevil asked as he shoved the young figure forward.

"Oh, the Ancient Salbani bids me?!"

Prett stumbled to get to his feet as he was excited as well about his master wanting to see him.

"A mission... Is it a mission Byevil?"

he asked as he turned to face him while continuing to walk.

"Yes, A mission it is. You will go with Fiki, that technological one. With him you will go as you will venture to a terra, the dirt realm I call it. You must steal technology, this robotic thing. It is in fact a lost design of Fiki's generation. As you must bring with you a human. It is necessary... I tell you Prett that this will not be good for you if you deny, for I say that you have no choice. Fiki requested you, as Salbani was beside himself for you are a bastard. We accept you because you chose our ways but this unknown father of yours could very well be a major concern. To discuss your return, you will go, will not your young legion? would not want to upset him for then where you would return. You will return with me, this understood?"

Byevil gazed on the young one to see if he had any hesitation. The young one was for a moment with no words.

"I will in fact take this burden if you would like to refuse your master Salbani.... That is fine, Prett... I will do this for you. You would not want to run into that old serpent... Salbani's brother? Would you know? It is necessary... I will do this. It is fine... after all what do you know of the spirits on the dirt plain, and the elementals, like our Sempiternals here but oh their fruits are bound to nothing. As little of the humans even know of their existence, this is rumored."

Byevil went on, Pressuring the young one.

"No! I will do it. The head asked; I will do as he asked. To the dirt world? Is that not the realm of the Mighty ones chosen Trezhur's? Is that not where the brother of light sent his spirit? Salbani's bloodline? With Michael. Why would I go there... I will, petrified as I know that ancient Queen is..."

Byevil quickly turned and gave a scream of hate as he flicked his hand. Out came a magical swirl that sent Prett to the ground. Byevil belched at him.

"What do you know of the Queen? Only Rumors! You would be wise to be silent on this matter!"

Byevil turned away from the young deceiver in a fury of action! Prett was shocked but he continued speaking from the forest grounds.

"I just state that I have knowledge unlike some of my comrades. I wonder does Fiki, well, does he know whose planet that is? Does he know as I know... As you thought that I did not know... As I do... That this planet is in fact at worse of a war than our realm is! Am I the only one that is to question? I have learned much of the realm Byevil... Tell me what is it that is really the happening? Do not keep me in the shadows of truth!"

Prett looked at Byevil awaiting a clever remark as Byevil seemed to be at silence.

"Nothing to say? Why try to trick me Byevil? I am facetious unlike others. Does Fiki recognize where we are going? Can you tell me that? Did Salbani task me to capture these Fairies for this reasoning?"

Byevil glares at Prett for knowing so much. As he thought of him as a laughingstock, surprised with the knowledge coming from the mouth of a bastard as he gazed at the casing that held many tiny fairies.

"Yes... Fiki knows. As maybe not as much as you. Still... I wish you luck. You are to leave as soon as we return to the temple! I hath no understanding to why he tasked you to capture these fairies, and I would leave these thoughts rooted, you seep of defiance and the master will not have it."

The two of them ventured back through the path of the bloodwoods that Byevil knew of. As it took time to return the two of them continued to speak about the task at hand for Fiki and Prett. As Byevil then begun to go on about the memories that he holds about the great war that took place here on this land.

DISPLACEMENT

August 11th

Temple Litus

Byevil and Prett came through the gates of the temple. Down a long eerie hallway that led to a set of blackened doors with dragon tongues as handles. Byevil pulled on one of them as the massive door began to slide open. The crash of marble on stone with entrance. The room decently lit with flickering flames scattered through the temple.

"Here he is master. The bastard."

Byevil spoke to Salbani as Prett trotted past him straight to his Master who was standing on the Sorzo mount. This twelve-pointed star for his rituals, Salbani created Sorzo shortly after his fall. For he needed a way to bend the magic to his personal will. Salbani trained in the dark arts by one of the elder sons of Evnee. Void, To be exact, but this is a story for another moon. The Sorzo is the entirety of Salbani's throne, Stretching across the marbled temple floors. The twelve points engraved into the temple grounds. Lined with solid gold edges with a center part that holds the shapes form as a burning flame when in use.

"Ah, quite filled with energy you are."

Salbani laughed as he held out his hand to slow the pace of incoming Prett.

"Oh, just excited to see you master. For I have been down at the river for weeks now. Learning how to use my magic... For I slayed a fairy as I extracted all the power I could... As I used it to attract another... As I have learned to easily deceive and gained trust. Now I plan to learn all that I can about the blue magic with this news I hear of these human subjects! As here, in my hands I hold a bundle of the fairies I have captured! Look Salbani, Look here!"

Prett acting with prominent levels of energy for any subject would as when in use of a newly learned magic. As he was in the grace of his elders, he revolted with jollity. Holding in his hand before his elders the encasing of several trapped fairy saplings. Salbani smirked for this rebellion brightened his soul, he spoke out to the figure Prett with direction.

"So vial you are... Careful... The fairies have eyes all over and if they catch you, Trouble that would be my young destructor, as that will be enough of that terror, put them near the Sorzo, I am happy that you did as I asked and captured many. I will use the fairies for their powers soon, as I now have a new task for you Prett, One that could cost you your being, to cedure a new realm."

Salbani was trying to teach the young one to use his power with his mind. Fiki speaking with pique as he came from the shadows.

"I was watching, awaiting your arrival. As we all have been awaiting, If Byevil had not taken his pace. We would be on with the mission."

Fiki was in a state of vexation because it took so long for Prett to arrive, and this angered Byevil causing him to bellow in disgust.

"Enough of that!"

Byevil yelled with dominance asserting himself over the shifter.

"I did as the master asked... I brought him to you, as you could have made the journey through the Null thyself! As I would bet you slain quickly, those wandering beasts care not about your brains and positioning! You are the one that requested Prett! I will not have your mouth as I will drop you amid the bloodwoods! With no care I will, as I will claim your tongue so you cry not as I will take your hands, then be you defenseless! As to then what will you speak? Then what will you build? Let it be known on this day that for this mockery, if beckoned, I answer you not Fiki! You know not that path of the Null, none of you! Prett journeyed alone, as it was my direction that led him through the Null and it was my path that we walked to return! Without me, you would be without him. Fool, you dare question me. I await the day we obtain a new genius, for on that day, on that day I will claim your life. Arrogant fool."

Byevil was already walking in irritation as the statement of Fiki set him in outrage as he blazed off as quick as a blade slice. Salbani chuckled as he redirected his following to the matter at hand.

Salbani called forth the bastard Prett.

"My young deceiver, soon master of the Hedge magik. Tell me, are you ready to traverse to this dirt terra? Gain insightful of the Spiro travels but tell me are you ready for a physical travel to an unknown place?"

Prett stepped forward and bowed in reverence.

"Master I am ready. There is no question that I am capable. Why is it that you have chosen me, have I gained favor?"

Salbani smiled at the young one as he wove his hand for him to rise from this kneeling position. Prett stood awaiting answer, and he looked to the other legion with a smirk of pride. Salbani out spoke with explanations as he stood and began to pace throughout the area of the mount.

"I do appreciate your allegiance to the legion, but it is nothing of favor. Remember that you were brought in by Fiki to help with his task of rebuilding my new temple that he is to soon begin constructing again. I know not of your origin, nor do you. Trust you? I do not. It was Fiki that requested you and I will honor his request as it is he that has my favor. I have a task, a mission for you. You must go with Fiki to guide a human back to me. Beyond this I require you the retrieval of an old project left during the old wars. A Relic that these humans have buried, fearing its unknown power. The low brained thought it had something to do with one of their embodiments of a god. This is in fact my Teechi Relic. It will turn anything that it touches into Golda. As I will use this to be my mascot for my planned citadel! Do this mission for me, do what I am bound from doing, leave this place and bring back with you the blood of the chosen, this Atum. Then you will grow in favor, Only Then I will reconsider the way I think of you. What say you, Prett. Oh, Bastard. What say you?"

Prett smirked with turbulent joy as he gained an elevated level of satisfaction from being asked for his task. He looked to Fiki and gave him a nod of respect as then he gave his master his answer.

"I will do as you ask leader, I will retrieve Teechi, and I will obtain this Atum. The dirt-world will not even know I was there! You will not regret allowing me master, I will gain your favor. Not a spec of disbelief will you have for me!"

Salbani fixed his posture for he was moved by the confidence of the bastard. He moved his head upright with a tilt of wonder as he gave his direction.

"So, go. Go with Fiki and do this task as I will reward you. My youngling. You must do this for the future of Liege!"

Salbani spoke out to the legion commanding them to gather for the ritual to send Fiki and Prett to the dirt realm of Arthe.

DOMESTIC DISSENSION

August 11th

Litus

Due to the action of the elder Void of the Darko initiates the Legion were free and no longer bound to the temple walls. Salbani and his legions had all their powers restored and there was nothing to hold them back from casting rituals. Salbani stood from his throne and began to walk around the mount. Speaking out to the unbound legion of the temple in a mighty outcry for all to hear.

"My legion!"

His voice echoed throughout the temple and the chaotic rustle of the figures came to an abrupt holt as he awaited their calming and listening.

"This night, now it be the moment of retribution! Bound for a decade you have been by my failure to defeat that Arku of Trea. Come forth, come face me if you have lost your will to be in allegiance to my rule. Come forward and claim your chance of governing in my place. If you be so hearty in this will."

Suddenly from behind the legion king belched a figure in utter anger. A faint countering that broke through mumbled conversations. He croaked with disbelief, overtaking the room with an outrage of dissatisfaction.

"He failed us many times! The last failure cost us a decade!"

The room broke into conversations as the speaker uplifted his voice to speak over the legion.

"Who's to say he will persevere the second time around. Deceived we all have been! Who is to say that these Trea are not of sense! Overthrow him we can, do this together. He has cost us enough! Enough I say! What say you oh great legion!"

Hidden high above in the shadows of the temple this unknown voice spoke, and the room of silence immediately broke into cries of bantering conversation. The legion speaking about the truth of this statement as some balked at the disrespect to their master. Murmurs turned to roars and the room was once chaotic again, erupting words from the sentencing of this one subject as Salbani stood watching the room, listening with calm behavior as he held a smirk of pride. The seed was planted, and it was quick to grow, Salbani holding a desire to sift out the ones that have potential to rebel against him. The legion king lifted his hand for a silence, it only took a moment for the room to settle before he spoke on.

"I commend you for outspeaking without fear. Great fool."

Salbani turned to the direction that the voice came from as he outstretched and pulled back his arm in a motion to come forward. He spoke to the legion with direction as he stood upright, crossing his arms aplomb.

"Bring this one that spoke before me."

The room broke out in mumbles as two jesters that were near Salbani on the setting of the mount quickly proceeded to find and obtain the one of rebellion. There was commotion in this darkened high point of the temple as the speaker attempted to fight the legion around him, wishing to escape but being outnumbered beyond explanation he was quickly bound and beaten. The jesters got to him in time, and they began to carry him down to the mount. The room cried in laughter, mockery, and conversations that sounded as a mighty storm of perpetual rains. Each drop being the voices as they began to chant the legion language.

"Mih Llik! Mih Llik! Mih Llik!"

The legions held no remorse for the traitor, as the jesters came near and brought the speaker before Salbani, he put up his hand once more as a gesture of silence. As he did so these Jesters began to harshly beat the speaker with no remorse. He was mangled and bloody before Salbani even spoke.

"Silence, silence, enough from you all. I will hear him speak."

The room became silent once more and Salbani approached the speaker.

"Mighty fool, go on. I give you your chance to speak."

The speaker attempted to rise from his beaten position. Arms shaking in fear and weakness and he arched his back to rise, his legs too weak to move from being so harshly beaten. He picked up his head and gazed at Salbani with hatred as he moved one of his legs to try and stand. Suddenly, one of the jesters from before appeared quick and jumping near to land a breaking kick to the subjects center back. It cracked like a bear running through a tree in the forest. The subject cried in utter pain and the room released silence into a cheering of utter satisfaction. I tell you, only the legion would celebrate such terrors. Salbani raised his hand shortly after and the room went silent once more. He kneeled to the subject and lifted his head with his hand.

"Is there anything you want to say now?"

The speaker seeped of hatred and faintly spoke.

"The-ta-the one, Ta-Ta-true Ki-King will defeat you."

His speech was so subtle that the room could not hear it, but it caused Salbani to lose his confidence and calm behavior. He quickly stood from his kneeled position and raised his leg and stomped on the up-looking face of the speaker. His neck snapped with a flipping spin and the room broke in chaotic celebration once more. Salbani just stared at the subject as the jesters skipped around the room in revelry. Looking out to the temple, Salbani yelled out as he turned in a circular motion in look at the room, looking for who else might defy him.

"Who! Who else is against me! Just the one? There must be more of you!"

The room cried in celebrations; chaos was unleashed. If there were subjects that were against him. They sure were silent and playing along with the celebrative action of the rest of the legion. Salbani soaked in the praise of the room standing with his hands raised, absorbing the gratification as the jesters played with the deceased body of the speaker. One held his body up and moved it like a puppet as the other danced in a mockery before the deceased. The room was loose and wild in a vortex frenzy of prideful fury. Salbani gave them time to act in explanations as he told the jesters to remove the body. After some time, he spoke out to the room of legion once more demanding silence.

Flame smolders cold in scattered areas around this ancient temple. Columns festooned with gemstones, torches, in addition to the occasional stone carving of some beast or creature. As the eye stealing, heart grabbing artistic expression takes the mind away. The entirety of temple adorned elegantly and due to the evil following freed, one could notice the loveliness of this ancient place, due to the activity. That is if you can look past the current demonic filth that occupies it and imagine what it could have looked as in the past, once filled with the realm inhabitants freely living, teaching, learning in bliss and acceptance with each other. I will say that not all the Liege terribly are kept. I mean that some see the beauty in thorns. Candles and statues held bowls that were as well-lit with the appalling fire that was amidst the setting. This flame sure was not pure for it is in fact liveliness, this energy that set the flame to existence is surely of matter, I mean sure it is of some importance to know the origins of who it was that originated the flame... I dare say that all things attach in some mysterious way. As maybe it is only a few that think as me.

"Fiki, Are you and Prett ready? Step forward if you will... It is nearly time."

"We only have enough essence for this path connected three times... You cannot fail Fiki... You will be stuck in the dirt realm if you are to fail, and I ask how long is it before that old serpent knows you are in his domain? Just something to keep in mind young shifter... How long is it before the fruits of that realm are on to you? Are you prepared for unexpected interference?"

Byevil let out a great laugh as Fiki looked at him with confusion.

"The old serpent? Whom is it that you speak of? I do not know who you speak of... Master? Is there a power on earth that I should be aware of?"

Fiki looked to Salbani as he continued his behavior of confusion. Byevil continued to harass him.

"Ah! This is a tragic sight. Such a fool you are... The lack of understanding..."

Byevil spoke out to Salbani.

"Master! Send me expert... That older brother of yours will not bother me! He will not... He knows that I am with-"

The leader smacked his follower across this face, with such force his talons had dug and ripped the flesh clearly off the face of the figure Byevil, leaving him huddled down in pain.

"You will do nothing!"

Master Salbani spoke with a dreadful and stoic expression.

"My brother Luc is for one is nothing of what you have the idea of. Second, has more power than any of you. He is clever, as he has more knowledge than you. To think he would have any care for you is beyond a fools thought. Many that do much in many names and I say none of them or you really know much of anything. Sick with your continued arrogance to the seriousness of our actions. Void hath spoken! A decree spoken! A scroll delivered and you still carelessly joke. I should lock you in the tomb of voices, how long could you bare the weird spirits? As for these two before us. Fiki... and Prett... Well, uninvolved with him but as for you... Byevil... That brother of mine... He hates you. That is why I gave Fiki a choice. For I know my brother will leave them alone. As they have no knowledge of the old wars. As you interrupted my brother during his rule in that abundant land of the pharos. As it was in fact your deception on that young girl that caused that entire kingdom to fall under that twisted as she is the insane one of desire. I will not even speak her name; it will be unspoken. Fool... The dirt realm is still suffering because of you. As my brother is the blame... Yes... Great wickedness he is as he does, but you... Fool. What you did... crossing timelines to place seeds? Foolish, as I swore to my brother, then when the time is right you will in fact pay for this great mistake. By my time and by his hand. I decreed it. Now go... Away with you... I am to send Fiki and Prett without you near."

As the figure, Byevil then struggled to rise as he held his face in pain walking out of the sight of his master and peers.

"Now to send you to the realm of dirt. Are you ready Fiki?"

The leader asked as he held his hands up to finish the ritual. Portal still open in front of them all.

"I am ready to master. I just have one question... Salbani, I just... If I... If I meet your brother... What do I say to this, Luc."

Fiki curiously asked about the brother of Salbani as the leader gave out a laugh.

"Oh, never the worry my young shapeshifter... He is oh so busy now a days. He will not speak with you... His name is in fact Luc, the old serpent. He has names... As for what I spoke to Byevil about... That one has fucked with the order and my brother wants him dead, but I still have a use for him. You see, Liege may not be with the Unitrea Order... We are not with the Synod or any of the Outcasts. As that is because I hate what they all stand for... You know my feelings towards light guided Arku. We liege do as we wilt. As does my brother in the dirt realm, he in fact is in the same position I am in, an outcast. As it comes to control of the realms... You see, the great and mighty creator adores us all... As some rebels have gone just a bit too far. That is what me and my brother have done… There are hundreds of us. You see, hundreds of us. The creator has created all of us for great reason… and as you know the task is to care over parts of his creations. As developed our own plans and our own paths we have. Now we are living out the consequences of these choices, so be it! I allude that my brother has no interest in what I do… He is running out of time as he knows it. I have not ever done more than the King has asked of me. As today this is at an end even if Nihil, the being of void had not come to say and do what he did. Continuing this work to remove them, I must. I declare that the great Unitrea has faults like any realm. I cannot let them poison the realms any longer. So go, go Fiki and Prett and bring me back this repulsive human. This Trezhur that has not even a single thought of his creator… Bring me this pawn of my brother. This fallen chosen! Bring him to me and I will share with you all the secrets of the realms!"

The leader Salbani was speaking with the highest amount of energy and anger but paired with direction. One could think of a past moment where Salbani stood with the same emotion. Just before the great rebellion, just before he deceived the realms. Manipulated not a few but thousands of loyal Felagnolum warriors.

"Oh… How this once was a glorious land. Lush of creation… Abundance of life and knowledge… This was in fact a garden of the creator before the half breeds from Byevils seed poisoned everything… Byevil and that Jesiel… Now look at it…"

Salbani lost in depths of memory as he recalled in his mind the lands of Egypt before Byevils meddling that occurred years ago. Before all the chaos from the war of control on the dirt world before the great wars of weir magic in Felagnolum. Both universal changing moments for the realms that happened simultaneously. The legion leader quickly stood as he shouted with direction.

"Now that the traitor has been removed, let it be a demonstration of what could happen to one of you if I am to be defied. Now prepare yourselves for war, go for I am to send Fiki and this bastard Prett to the terra of Arthe. We will break the binding to this mountain range with the power filled bloods of Atum and we will be free from this curse! Void hath freed you all as you witnessed. Thank him if you see him but remember that he spoke of this being our last attempt to overthrow the Trea. As if captured we will be bound to the void space of darkness. Be warned, do not get yourself captured. I now bid the subjects of transference to come forth and attend the ritual to send Fiki and Prett to this terra!"

The liege king called forth twelve of the most power sorcerers in the room.

"Come forth, Carreute, the power son. Driax; of dominions, Tavos Maksel; of the dark magik, Adramel Cae; master of bending fire, Zot Cae; Master magician, Plau Haen; fairie of the Darko, Philler; son of insanity, Esyayte Morf; the creative witch, Mihgo Sepu; the teleporting trickster, Neuamor; of the thrones of darkness, Bifron Xios; The dark one of ancient wisdoms and my son, Verri; the prince of the legions. Come and join me for the ritual brothers. This is our day of reckoning. We will be released from this cursed mountain soon enough!"

Lieges are ready as awaiting the commands of their master. At a stature of ease unlike the normal rambunctious behavior that comes from the lot. The figures were all around a blazing Sorzo. This is a twelve-pointed symbol that the Ancient Salbani created for his magical practices long, long ago. As you could see a second fire ablaze behind the circled group of Liege, a celebration of sorts by the rest of the following. Together they begin the third ritual. The figure wove his hands as he was speaking in the unknown tongue. The fire changes from the orange glow to the vibrant green, just as it shifted like the rituals before.

The legion came forward one by one as the room celebrated each of them. The twelve called gathered around the twelve points of the Sorzo mount as Salbani took his place at the heading of this mount.

Adramel Cae the fire bender set to flame the center of the mount. This is a powerful, mystical being who is forty-four Unis old. Wielder of the flame dressed in a long, dark cloak that held convoluted designs of an ancient lore. This cloak fastened with a large fibula. The clothing that he wears is dark toned and it hides most of his body but his posture in confident as he is a lean and tall being. It is not that he is sculpted, but he carries the air of strength and wisdom. Having a deep knowledge of elemental magic, he is a known controller and manipulator of fire. Adramel has long flowing dirty brown hair, he is a being of confidence that prides himself in his abilities as a seasoned sorcerer and a leader of the of elemental flame, even if he is mostly a lone enchanter. Driax called forth the ancient Spiros that dwelled around the temple to be guides of the dark energy. Driax is sixty-six Unis of age, he has an aura of resilience and mystique, a slim but fit figure that wore a pair of Panthok hide leggings as no shirt. Tavos, who is fifty-six Unis of age worked with him to alter the spiritual waves of energy. A figure in his prime, associated with the waves of twilight, knowledge of the shadow realm and studier of necromancy. Tavos is a warlock of the ancients of The Obsidian Hand, he is rugged, and battle hardened, a warrior with many body scars, he looks to be older than he is, but he has a strong build with a bulky muscular body structure and piercing eyes, long hair that stretches to his lower back and he styles a flowing robe. He conveys confidence and a hint of depression, as time weighted on him causing him to be weary with who he engages with. Known to be against the

Synod and the order of the Trea, once walking the grey line between light and dark but changed his way shortly before the legion imprisonment. Zot began in mumbled chanting's. This Magi is thirty Unis old; he is a powerful sorcerer with a mystical and authoritative presence. He wears a robe with a red and white color scheme. The attire is practical for both leisure and combat, he also styles a hood for he is known to hide behind his actions. Zot has a mysterious aura, he is physically fit with a toned slim body, and his hair is a long blonde that flows freely. Zot carries a staff with a Carnelian Gem at the peak of it. Zot has an intriguing as well a commanding presence, but he is mostly rebellious rather than commanding.

Esyayte the witch is forty-two Unis of age; she began to set up rare and potent ingredients. One of the only dark ones that maintained a child-like spirit as she is known to be fierce in actions and to the point with a prominent level of determination. She has vibrant red tribal markings that adorn her face and body, alluding to the fact that she is of culture, in practice of maintaining her origins even if she resides with the legion. She wears a feathered headdress, a symbol of power and prestige in the tribes. A colorful patterned wrap adorns her wrist, she wears a robe of Panthok hide. She has a toned physique that is covered for the most part. She has protective armor that covers her shoulders to mid arm. She has a blade that is said to be a prized possession that was a gift from her father. Her body is athletic with well-defined muscles, but she is petite allowing her to be quick and agile. Esyayte moves and lives in utter poise. She is a captivating figure, a master witch that lives in high practice of the crafts and is known to for her herbal knowledge, often called forth in times of ritual for this understanding.

Carreute standing upright and just as he mumbles chanting's, this being is sixty Unis old, wearing armor with blue and silver tones of silk, the armor is designed with sharp angular designs, made to have him able to move quick as it still protects him and gives a personal flare to his prideful attitude. The armor covers his shoulders, arms, and legs as it leaves his torso slightly exposed. Beneath this armor he styles a blackened robe that is fit to his body, as he styles a cloak that he throws from side to side that is complemented with engravings of his past battles. He wears a powerful necklace of a Black Tourmaline, that protects him. Carreute is a confident being and master of the crawlers, and a high-level member of the darkened imitates, leading most of their battles.

Mihgo spoke words of impartation to the center of the mount as the flames shifted to an oddly satisfying blue. Mihgo is forty-nine Unis of age, a high priest of the ancients that walks with an inscrutable presence. Dressed in luxury cloth of dark crimson robes with gold and purple accents that flow like water. He is known to be of the high order of the Masters of the Arcane, royalty of the underworld. Mihgo is adorned with gold bracelets and gold earrings that dangle and are all throughout his ears. Known to be a trickster in his tongue, a being of true contemplations and secrecy. He is a being of power placed high in the hierarchy of legions with true knowledge of forbidden magic and said to be able to influence anyone or anything.

Philler, one of insanities, an ancient who is ninety-nine Unis of age is by far one of the most wicked of this grouping beyond Salbani even. He has a mystical but fearsome appearance. Known to be a dark Wicc, master of the dark arts and wish fulfiller to the unjust and just. Philler is lean and tall, with an eerie look to him. He wears an elongated midnight black robe that is fit to his body yet drags slightly at its end. He holds a staff that is made of strong enchanted oak, weaved with bone of the Shantor, which is a strong hybrid reptilian beast that towers over any dragon. This staff is topped with a skull. Rumored to be of his first kill, some say it was a sacrifice for him to gain such power. He is a leader of sorcerers and not to be dallied with.

Neuamor seemed to be speaking to unseen Spiro figures, commending them to guide Fiki and Prett to the required realm. Neuamor is perhaps the most cunning of them all. He is ninety Unis of age, and he wears silk pants and a silk shirt that proceeds to his lower arms, leaving his wrist exposed as they are adorned with bejeweled bracelets, and he wears a golden chain around his neck that is thick and fits to this throat with no hang. Neuamor is the most agile of the grouping and has a lean muscle tone. He has a belt-like material that is fastened with many small pouches as he is known to always be in a trade of some kind, holding many precious stones and coins of silver and gold, prepared to bargain in any scenario. Known to be ready for action and as well known to be a master manipulator. Always up for an adventure and it is known that Neuamor prides himself in his mastery of thievery. He is a very resourceful mage for understanding the Magi Arts as well as abundant plain knowledge of Felagnolum. Said to possess the "heart of gold", not a giver of gifts but an embezzler of the soul, ruled by his dignity.

Bifron was giving directions to Prett about the whereabouts of the relic Teechi. He is thirty-four Unis old, walking in a younger age but without lack of wisdom, he is a known warrior in the realm, said to be a leader of legion death squads. As this is quite the accomplishment for being only in his thirties. He is a stoic being, wearing metallic armor that covers most of his body. Always prepared for a battle, his armor is elaborate, carved with convoluted enchantments that are said to protect him. Known to be a legion noble as well as an utter murderer. He wears a cape that is the color of oxidized blood that flows with a flare of dominance. Said to be a commanding being that lacks morality. On his side is a whip that he uses to torture victims. Bifron is feared by his own legion as it is spoken that no inhabitant would dare face him. Bifron is beautiful, a surprise for all that encounter him. The being has long flowing platinum blonde hair that rest among his shoulders. This figure embodies power and seeks ruling over riches as it is rumored that he only follows Salbani because the legion King entrapped someone precious to him that cannot be freed unless Salbani releases this subject by his own word. A binding Salbani often uses to gain authority over subjects who are against him.

Verri, the Prince of the legion was ongoing in a specific chanting to keep high the dark energy of the room. Verri is not only the second in command under his father, but he is a mixed bloodline of the Elemental forces. As his father the legion King is known to be a master of the flame, Verri is a student to his mother the Ice woman who is a Master of Water. Salbani is known to have many wives but only one son. He is said to have other children who he has sacrificed to the dark kings of dominion for gains of power but that is a rumor. Verri is known to use Ice rather than water and he is quite strong in the Magi of these elements. He wears flowing grey cloth that is of the hide of Lyroks, which are big cat beasts with thick coats. Verri is said to carry a small scythe, a curved sword with a solid gold hilt. A magically infused weapon that is said to slice through enchanted armors. Verri is slim as a thin tree, but he is muscular as a trained warrior and it is spoken that he is a master of conjures, using the Spiro in battles or rituals and is said to mock adversaries as they must face whatever he conjures. This Prince has shortly cut light white hair from his mother that is said to stand out in a setting. Verri is a warrior mage of elemental powers and next in line to rule the legions, he is thirty-three Unis old.

Salbani was satisfied with the happening and he began to outspeak before them all, activating the actions of the legion as suddenly a swirling portal appeared. Salbani was doing the chanting as he wove his hands in specific directions creating a symphony of gestures as he then spoke the word.

"Nepo."

Salbani yells as out of its mouth came a dark red spiral once more the matter of a manifested curse. As it traveled straight into the magical portal, still open in front of him and the Liege followers. The magic went into the portal as the doorway then changed from a blackened void to the site of the sands of the millennials Egypt.

The room of surrounding legion cried in celebration as the anticipation for this event has been long and strenuous. Fiki and Prett stood on the threshold of the unknown but with excitement and little to no fears. The flame shifted from orange to an emerald and then to blue as the incantation began, melodic chanting's went on and echoed throughout the temple room as the air became thick and weighted as did an odd mist appear coming from the mount. Unsanctioned and unexpectedly, Neuamor grabbed a fairie from the encasing that Prett had them caught, and he drew his blade to quickly stab the heart of it. A magical swirl exploded, and he immediately shouted in the legion tongue. "Brosba!" and suddenly he disappeared into a self-sanctioned portal. Salbani lost his sense at the sight of this and released belches of anger that led to the energy of the ritual to become unstable. Fear was quick to strike the group, and the portal expanded. It overtook the ritual setting and the members; Carreute, the power son. Driax; of dominions, Tavos Maksel; of the dark magik, Plau Haen; fairie of the Darko, Philler; son of insanity, Esyayte Morf; the creative witch, Mihgo Sepu; the teleporting trickster, Bifron Xios; The dark one of ancient wisdoms and the son of Salbani, Verri; the prince, were sucked into the portal and disappeared from the scene. Adramel Cae; master of bending fire, Zot Cae; Master magician and the legion king Salbani were all that were left of the twelve. Salbani cried with hatred calling out to the legion of the room.

"That fucking Neuamor trickster fool, how dare he disturb my ritual! Where are the Seekers! Seekers come now!"

The temple was loud with roaring conversations and unshackled energy flowed about. The Seeker creatures appeared before Salbani quick. He directed them to move through the spirit realms and find each of the subjects as he commanded them to return, not until each of them were found. Salbani was beyond anger and took the encasing of the Fairies and one by one he ripped each of them apart with no lack of remorse. Suddenly a frigid chill flowed like a winter wind throughout the temple and the legion were bound by some vale that separated them from the temple mount. Byevil spoke out to Salbani who was now sitting on his throne angered after the dismantling of his ritual.

In the moments after this ritual was undone and the Liege scattered, Byevil stood near his angered master as a wind suddenly consumed this temple.

PROTECTORATE

From this cold breeze the room was quiet as a great light shined in peak of Litus temple, Byevil came running near to Salbani outspeaking in worry.

"Master! Primary! That wind felt as if it was of these Holy ones! Why would that summon during your decree? What is this light that has appeared?"

Byevil was beside himself for he had no understanding of what just happened. Looking up at the blinding sight.

"No, no Byevil. That was not of me! I sent the younglings to the dirt world as I decreed. The winds came after, I am not sure why the winds have visited. This is oddity, I notice that the words of my master were true…"

Salbani stood from his throne as he threw out his hand as he spoke.

"Thgil eht lepmet lla dnuora!" The ancient spoke words of the Felagnolum language.

As the fire pots of the room were all once again lit as well as the light above.

"I do not like that feeling master… The winds are never a good sign for our kind!"

Byevil nearing his master.

"You are in fact speaking truth for once."

Spoke a non-fluctuating voice from aside them both.

"WHO!"

Salbani shouting as he quickly heaves his sword, dashing to his side. Attempted to slash this figure who spoke. A mood shifting crack sounded as a flash of creations light consumed the area. Salbani's sword blade shattered into pieces before him.

The being spoke on with tranquility.

"The obsidian is no match to the Dynot stone! Still a fool it looks to be that you are still a fool! Oh, but once so great you were! Gno Known, the fallen keeper of the comprehensions of what is furtive! What position it was! As is but not for you!"

The angelic messenger made an end to his sentencing, he threw a rolled scroll to Salbani. It bounced from his chest, dropping at his feet. There was a slight pause in the motion of things. The atrocious ones knew exactly what lay before them. The figure spoke to them with certainty.

"… from the King of Kings. Mind the Words I tell you. You have been served by the council of Light."

Salbani reaching down to pick up the scroll as Byevil held sight to the figure lift off from an eased push of his wings. As then one, two, three, thrusts that shook the foundations of the temple as the angelic figure took off with such bliss that even Byevil… One of the most wicked creatures around had a tear form in his eye as the beautiful messenger flew out of the side tower of the temple.

"Disgusting."

Salbani remarked as he spit to the floor, bending to retrieve the message. He untied the knot as out it rolled.

"Ouch!'

Salbani gave out a yell as his fingertips singed from touch of the scroll.

"Ahh, that fucking King! Good tricks, I expected this not Byevil, this fucking tease, no words for a decade as now a sudden decree? I know that high over to be just and upright in his smirk, fooled me this time, the Trea will wait until we are out of this place before anything more. Act not unless action detrimental these fools wait, Byevil they wait for the happenings... I will show these fools what it is to have something burned! I will set the whole kingdom ablaze before they are to know!"

Salbani eructed with anger and pain as he watched the flesh on his fingers sizzle and boil, quickly burned near to bone.

"Oh, that is fucking sick, What filth… like boar over the flame. I hath not seen the light, due to such deceptions! He knew that you would touch it, why the messenger had no burn is my question, it must be some cast sent to you. Why I thought that the holy is incapable of such a deed is beyond me. We have been fooled, my master…"

Byevil reacting in disgust as Salbani grunting and snarling at him. Byevil turned his head to the fallen poisoned scroll with a curious spirit.

"Let us see, what is this message."

Byevil gave his hand a flick as speaking in the unknown tongue. The page levitated from the ground as Byevil read it aloud.

The Trezhur will defend the realm. Unless surrender; By decree; Salbani Known wanted captured and turned into the judges of Puri.

Salbani suddenly became consumed with even more anger than he was before. Going on and flaunting about with random explanations of his own glory. As the scroll consumed by holy flame that caused the entirety of the temple dwellers to suddenly screech and hallow. Salbani and Byevil shriveled before it as the imparted magic effected their bodies. Attacking the gut like a flippant snake, angered in the belly. It took some time to recover from this, the beings stumbling about like they were drunken. From ongoing hate spewing mumbles, Salbani went on to form sentencing of this anger. Venting, his voice roared and echoed through the temple.

"Who will be against me? This speech sent to manifest fear in me. To think that I would react not. Am I to seize my action because these Trea warn? On the new moon we are to walk the Null with our full might. The task remains the same. Byevil, go now and fetch me Akitella… She is on the far side of the temple… That is where she lives, amid the Nemid gateway. Go and bring her back to me… As we need her to do some magic."

Byevil left to find the fallen fairy as Salbani sat awaiting the return of his subjects.

TONES

Bohn and Amber are eager to communicate as the lawyer answers the phone call.

"Yeah. One second, I need to take this."

Bohn noticing some of the conversation on his side as he answered.

"Iyo! I have not heard from you since the Science Com. Trial. How are you pal?"

The lawyer sounded pleased to get the call. Bohn replied to him.

"Mr. Christopher? Maxwell Christopher? This Is Bohnstant. A friend of Iyo's. He is currently in trouble, locked in a cell at Calloway Jail. They think he murdered someone, But I was there. It was lightning. Can you go down there and talk with the officers?"

The Lawyer was happy to help.

"Oh Yes! I will head right on down to the station and see what exactly is going on. I have another case I need to head there for anyway, great timing friend of Iyo! Great timing!"

Gathering some more information from them before he began to help. A few hours went by as Bohn napping.

"Hey the Phone!"

Amber yelled to Bohn who was asleep on the couch.

"Shit, I got it!"

He quickly rose and fumbled to answer it.

"He-ha-hello? Bohn here."

Amber patiently waiting to hear near him.

"Hey Bohn! It is Christopher, Great news my Pal... I personally know the judge that has the case. Should be easy to get it dismissed, I will just have to make a visit to his house and make sure that the old chump is still into making a bang for the buck. You all better visit Iyo and make sure he wants out. It is going to cost him. Call me back when you have talked with him, and I will get the ball rolling!"

Bohn showed appreciation and then explained the situation to Amber.

"Okay, so let us visit Iyo. There is no point for waiting, let us go now!"

Amber just went for the keys and Bohn stopped her.

"No, we are going tomorrow. Visit hours are nearly over for the day and they will be for sure by the time we get there."

Bohn explained as he plopped to the loveseat.

"I will just stick around here. Is that cool with you?"

Amber asked as she started to put down the keys to the car.

"It sure is not an issue with me... I am sure Iyo would not care. I do not know; it is not my house. It is up to you."

Bohn let out a laugh as he turned on the television. Amber got comfortable on the other side of the couch and the two enjoyed some laughs together. Amber broke away in time as Bohn fell asleep, Amber waste no time in making a phone call to Iyo before they end phone calls for the day. It took a small amount of time to get through the guards but soon Amber got through and was able to speak with Iyo. She gave him a rundown of things and explained that it was going to cost money. Iyo had no cares, just wanted out. She filled him in with all the information. Shortly after he did this a bell rang and guards came into the room and started to pull inmates up and in line as they sent them back inside the steel hell.

Come even heard Meli in the cozy of Calloway Beach before they heard even a word from the lawyer. Amber and Bohn spending the days scrambling as they were getting familiar, trying to find the most they could do for Iyo, and this continued until there was just nothing to do but wait until he was put before the judge. The city does not care to give him treatment, so they take their time finishing their other cases, so they thought. Bohn and Amber get close during this time together, learning about each other as the fear of the situation has formed an odd bond between them. Amber and Bohn grown to be head over heels with each other. If I understand anything about relations it is that it is time that binds a pair. Entanglements will do such, but I say that enough time or even the right pressures would cause any figure to love a figure. As children in a field running with the wind these damaged souls found a familiar historic peace that grows with their shared happenings. I allude to the fact that I see an old self in this relation, as all is a unity of such, I home a remembrance of a past entanglement. As I was as fire and she be the wind, oh it was only damage that we committed. You see it was a bond of trauma that held me and this woman close, and we held the understanding of this. A major flaw on the pair of us... fulfilled by desire untamed and that is just how we lost our way. Reflection, it was time that healed me of such suffering, but it was my choice to walk away from what filled me up, what made me feel that I was as a god on my heels. I only share because it is Bohn that holds this woman in high regard and that could be a downfall for him, especially if she does not feel the same. As they shared time together on a new morning, Bohn noticed a blinking light on the phone system. He cut the conversation with Amber to go investigate.

"What's that? Is it an answering machine? I have not seen one of these in years! I did not even realize these thing still existed! Should we listen to it?"

Bohn began to walk to the machine as Amber spoke out in confidence. Pulling him back, Bohn turned to face her as she spoke.

"That has nothing to do with us, why would you mangle with something that has nothing to do with you?"

Amber spoke in sense, yet Bohn laughed it off.

"Are we not awaiting a call from the lawyer? What if it is valuable information? If it is not, then we will just write the message down for Iyo. It's okay Amber, I am going to listen."

Bohn turned away from her as she let out a stressed sigh, he neared the machine and pressed the listening button as a long beep sounded and then sounds the message.

"Solid case. Needs a miracle… They wanted a suspect for lifeguard disappearance, and they got one. Story closes over guys, When the police officers were in the home, they found enough odd shit in that garage to classify Iyo under the psyche label. We know this is not to be true, but it is just overwhelming the way they have it set up. Lucky for Iyo, I worked my magic, and they should release him soon. This one will cost him though; I will send my fee. Good Luck with your future endeavors."

The answering machine sounded with a beep as it sounded the word, "Bizerte."

"That was the lawyer leaving a message on the message messenger, gee what a twister. I guess that Bizerte is the company he works for! Odd name."

Spoke Bohn as he sat down next to Amber.

"Well should we celebrate the easy victory?"

Amber asked with a smirk as Bohn walked into the kitchen.

"Yeah, I'll make a drink and then we will go get Iyo!"

Bohn and Amber got a bit away from themselves. Losing time with their celebration. The two of them celebrating in the living room. Losing track of time, Bohn and Amber suddenly dulled by the unfortunate screaming of Iyo who they never heard come into the home due to loud playing music.

"What in the hell as got into your mind! In my house? Are you serious? When I am in jail? You losers have the balls to claim my home and get drunk in it? Do I see money for drinking my liquor you snakes! The ungrateful behavior is beyond me!

Fools! What else did you do? I bet you twined! Absolutely disrespectful children you are!"

Iyo was screaming at them, and they both were struggling to understand what exactly he was upset about. Maybe would have been more fortunate if they checked the message time. Amber spoke out.

"Hey, relax man, we have been worried sick and then we just started having fun. What is the issue?"

Amber was getting to her feet. Walking to the sink to fetch water. At this moment Syn flew up.

"Welcome home Master."

Iyo was excited to see her!

"Oh, hello my wonder... I am happy to see you. I am ready to get back to work my creation!"

Iyo began to wonder back to his room. Bohn never getting a word in, just rolled back over and went to sleep. Amber fixed food and began to chat with the A.I.

"So, Syn. What do you see when you... See. You have this drone body, and you can go on the internet. What is it all like for you, do you understand what I mean?"

Amber was still on the side of tipsy while asking these odd questions. Syn unafraid to discuss a thing. The A.I. answered right away.

"When I see it is like how a person would see the television. I have a locator that I use to track faces and movement. Speed, Temperatures, and when I am on the internet, I see everything. An endless void of information as you might only see what you must input to see. I can see what is endless."

Amber freaked out by this and quickly sat up, backing away from the A.I. She did not say a word and she went back to the living room, rested just like the others. Syn made her way outside. The A.I. had its gaze set out on the sky. She said to herself something and slowly settled to the ground and powered down right there outside. Slightly unusual behavior.

PERPLEXITIES

TASKED MARIONETTE
August 12th First Quarter Moon

The Meridian omphalos Skybox; Sector eight, Phylace, Teralis

Near Zari, in the astral Spiro form visiting, it was Lytula the Ancient of Petition who a daughter of the ancients as is Salbani. Lytula is one-hundred-four Unis of age. The petition is a Spirokind of Contract, be her the courier of deeds. Lytula, the head of indentures traveling just as a Seeker, yet detached from her body that is currently in a detention facility. As she disowned her bloodline and is in prison by the hand of Michael, Great Arku. Zariza on plain Phylace far from any member of the Unitrea Order or any blood-borne member of Unipuri. Zariza is currently under the task of her leader Salbani. Working to take over the operating system of Syn, the artificial intelligence that be with their subject, Iyo the Madd on the Arthe 603 plain of the Meli Galaxy. Zariza giving orders to her own intelligent software, that is a male of gender. In Felagnolum we consider anything of intelligence to be either male or female.

"Knote. Prepare the projectile launch for a trip to the dirt world realm of Adam. The Milky Way the sapiens call it. I know it as dirt-world four."

She spoke as she stood with her hand propped to her chin as she outlooked on the cyber city from the glass. The Plain of Phylace is a cyber city encased by an impenetrable vale dome that shelters the city from any object from space. The population of Phylace varies in all forms of creations. The vast cyber city consists of twelve sections that make up the plain in the shape of a Sorzo. Over half a million live among the cyber city and this number is growing in population as of the recent years.

"I don't like doing missions on the dirt realm Lytula... The master might just wipe us out for this one."

Zariza spoke as she prepared the small nano-bot bomb.

"Salbani is asking you to do... Oh... You speak of the actual expert... that mighty creator?"

Lytula laughed at the remark and spoke her sense.

"We renounced him and joined Bani? Why do you even care? The probe will infect the works of humans, and the tech will be ours! As our fate has already been set. We are rumored for the void. I heard the drunken Trezhur speak as if the young fools were victims of my tricks! I sent my girls to manipulate them as to push them into their fleshly obsession... For subdued and seduced as their dreams of muse came true. A most regarded Trezhur to fall use to my abuse. Misused the gifts for views the fools had not the clue of it. Drunken and drugged and essence stolen from! They spoke of the plans of the victors. They plan to let go of the fallen and bestow the old magics return, to run free and evaluate the kingdoms once more. It is rumored that the expert that you speak of will, as I said, evaluate the kingdoms once more! You might as well join him! As to see your revelation before this worldly revelation! You must be asleep! Sick of the wicked and drained from the war! I thought more of your genius Zariza! I thought you brilliant for turning so many to follow their own will. Look out at the sectors! Thousands of them under your hands. All at your touch... As ears ready for your lips... The sweet kiss of the mind of the bright! The wicked part of your art... well it is that you are the lie of light! You shine of the knowledge behind the numeric of time! How could you sit there as if you are not such a deity. This human that Salbani is after is using your tech, these dirt humans are using your manifestation. Be of pride you Ancient! Soon I will tell you about my plan, but not until I am at your side, when I am back in my physical body and free."

Lytula was trying to build her by exposing the harsh truth of the situation. Lytula was present during the work of the

Harlots, little did they know she was following along the happening in the astral. After she alluded her thoughts, Zariza had a slight mood change as she went on to question Lytula.

"You fooled a Trezhur?"

Asking with amazement as if she did not think it to be possible to fool such resolute students to faith. Lytula responded with terribly wicked laughter as it continued her behavior held a manor to it that was simply unsettling. So convincing and evil Lytula was, An expert in desire and manipulation. A feminine creation that radiates the powers of darkness as the mirror is the opposite of love.

"The righteous are the easiest to fool, why do you think so many have stopped following the King? The test is hard my lover... The test is for the brightest stars. Even we have failed him my love, Even we! The Ancient Ones! The watchers of creation and the sons of sons! We did not even make it past our first of the tests. This is why we are lost in the realms, even the pure lost in these realms. Testing and more testing we gifted for lives. You are a fool to think that the Trezhur are different than us! We all have the will! Nobody is choice-less. You should know! Is that not why you created the artificial notive to replicate this action?"

Lytula asked as she began to dance around the room in a careless and dreamlike manor.

"Yeah... Yes... This is true. I created the Arti-Notive to mock him. As I never wished for the race of Adam to get their hands on it. They have not the knowledge of that kind of power! As the Ancient elders of the dirt world... Those half-bred were beginning to understand. As then the flood... As the master want's his most Trezhur creations to be blemish free. Look at what they have done now! Manifested a whole ocean of ancient powers all for their self-desires! The angelic of death is soon upon them all and only the fooled of fools saved. This is my notion, as Luc is rumored to be wandering. His said followers try to destroy the realm, but said that these wicked are not of him, but they use his name. I do have notions concerning Salbani… for it is as the same thing is beginning to occur in this realm. As our master sure, he has tangled himself with both. That is the High King and Luc, Whatever the name I wonder if Salbani knows what trouble he has created for this realm. Anyway... I just see a mirroring. As maybe some dimensional clash has already occurred."

Zariza was suddenly saddened but uplifted by the next question of Lytula.

"I ask you; How do you plan to infect your tech that this Trezhur human obtains?"

Lytula asked as she nears the window overlooking the cyberplain.

"Easy, I already have most control of it, but I am launching a probe of nanobots into the atmosphere as will disperse over the land of this human and create a connection from there to here. So, I can have full control of that notice, As I will upload myself into the database that this human has created, I will then take control of his creation. As then I will do what the master instructed me to do."

Spoke Zariza as she walked near her computing system to check the progress of the course.

"Looks like it is ready actually. One moment Lytula."

Zariza then placed the container of nanobots in the light cannon.

"Knote. Launch the nanos to the dirt world."

Zariza spoke as a robotic arm lowered the nano missile into a concealed capsule placed into a machine that began to carry the missile cap to the launching station. There was a consistent boot up sound as energy collected. Suddenly a sonic zap occurred, and the missile launched at light speed through the realms.

"Object in transit." Sounded out the computer as it blinked on a GPS holographic.

"Now we wait until it arrives. I'll have the system soon."

Zariza spoke in a nasty tone of self-fulfillment. Just as she started to pour herself a beverage. "Want some?" As she offered Lytula went on to question.

"I would indulge if I were actually here with you, just a taste. Zariza, I do question, how long until it arrives, where exactly is the dirt realm… Distance wise."

Lytula asked as she secretly knew the answer. Zariza, waving her hand through the hologram answered.

"It will take a day." Zariza calmly spoke while sipping her beverage.

"A day? In light speed travel? That is over tens of thousands of years of flight time? I have never been that far out of our realms. Interesting. What else is out there? I am so curious, what a marvel the jump tech is."

Lytula asked curiously.

"Oh, this information was given to me by Salbani. I have no idea what is beyond our realm."

The Ancients continued in conversation as the nanobot missile journeyed through the realms from Felagnolum to The galaxy of Meli, the mirror realm of the Milky Way. Lytula spoke up to Zariza.

"I have a mission for you, that is if you are tired of following Bani."

Zari was put off guard with the sound of this statement, but she was sure tired of working for this ancient king. She stopped her work and looked over to Lytula Spiro. Shifting her body to completely face her.

"Go on. Tell me."

Lytula smiled.

"Soon I'll be free, I have planned and accomplished much. My only request is that you put my signet on the grounds of that human and one here on your floors. I have tasked one of my followers to do some work for me and he will show himself bearing gifts for me. I am to meet him here, in this tower. I am sure to reward you with enough wealth to do as you please, as you will be unbound from working for Salbani. If you have faith in me, faith that I will accomplish what I am set out to do."

Zariza was all for helping her friend, unknown to what she was getting herself involved in. She replied with an ask,

"I'll help you Lytula, I'll do what you ask, just promise me that you will protect Aelom, protect him from your plans, just get him out of the grips of that Bani. I have failed to convince him to part from the Liege. He is mutinous; this is my only question. Harm not my son Aelom and I will do all that you ask." She asked in slight demand and Lytula presented a nod to her wish as Zariza spoke on, commanding Knote to upload Lytula's signet to the A.I. on Arthe, doing so by uploading more information to the nano bots that were sent to infect the humans A.I. intelligence as well as having it as well laser painted on the floor inside this high mount of Phylace, amid Zariza's dome. Lytula was quick to leave after this as Zariza was excited to soon be released into her freedom and wealth, unknowing what is to come.

Taking a break from running the cyber city to meddle with the A.I. back on planet Arthe. Zariza, the technologic genius at her computer station focused on code working. Hovering next to her is her own personal assistant who helps her maintain the workings of the city. A robotic being of sentience that is a brain behind most of the work for the cyber plain Phylace. The entire system of this plain is one hundred percent ran by Artificial intelligence and robotics. The helper bot speaks to the tech master as it flew near Zariza, detaching a data cord from a server station turning to face Zari.

"The system is warning me of a power failure in sector five, requiring a manual override inside the south end tower. Should I send the Nearix drones to handle this? The cameras show no figures at the station, it shows on the system that the power failure is from the nobility celebration in the big city. The event is overloading the system from the data I was reading."

Zariza walked to the edge of the glass wall overlooking the cyber plain and placed her hand onto it. Tapping it with her polished nails as she pondered in thought of the A.I. system in the Meli Galaxy.

"That is fine, send the Nearix."

The drone extended the data cord from a metal compartment once more and connected to a communications output. Relaying a message to the Nearix outpost, these are non-sentient worker bots that oversee construction and maintenance of major cities. Under the control of the Synod, which is the societal council of Felagnolum. Zariza reports to this council but is not bound by it as she is of a higher order that supersedes the Sydonic social rulings. Zariza walked back to her computer station speaking to her robotic companion as she sat down to begin working on the computer station once more. Using the information about the human that she received from the shifter Fiki she was able to connect herself to the human's network, she used her technological skills to take control of the humans A.I. system.

"Now that I have control of the humans A.I. we will be able to lure them to our realm. Salbani will be pleased with my work, even if I will help Lytula."

TESTING

August 13th

Calloway residence

The dawn broke and Iyo jumped out of bed with excitement, he ran down the stairs singing a morning song as he began to yell at Bohn and Amber who were asleep in the living room.

"Up and at it. Let us go. If you are in my house, you are working! Break the fast or straight to sips, there's coffee there's tea. I have work to do. Meet me In the Lab or get the hell out!"

Iyo belched at the two of them with no remorse of tone. Waking Bohn and Amber as he was walking through his home to the back yard to go down to the lab. Right on walking outside, He noticed that Syn was there. Yet, She Carved something into the ground with her laser tool. Iyo was beyond himself, it was a Sorzo in the ground but Iyo hath no knowledge of the ritual mark.

"Syn! Did you join a cult when I was gone? What is this? Is this Art? What are you doing?"

Iyo was interested in whatever it was. Syn flew up as spoke.

"It is because the mission is complete. Should we work now Iyo?"

Syn said as she flew near the door the lead down to the lab. Iyo was simply confused. He let the weird drawing pass, for there was much on his mind.

"Okay, let us go then."

Walking down the stairs to the code lock.

"I am so happy to be back here. I can freely work with... Little to no interruptions. Are you excited Syn? We are back at it!"

Iyo was ecstatic as together they began to pick up where they left off before everything got a temporary shutdown.

"Okay so let's boot up the systems and look at this coil." Iyo turned on the computers and began to walk around the lab. Making sure that all connections are correct and secure.

"Okay Syn. Tell me about our coil."

Iyo said as he stood admiring the works. The A.I. flew up next to him and began to explain what they had created.

"The inside of the coil made up of rings of superconducting magnets with nine accelerators to boost the energies of the particles along the way. The beams inside the coil collision are positioned at four distinct locations around the ring that correspond with the positions of the four particle detectors.

"If this is accomplished correctly then the project is complete."

Syn spoke on from her speaker system. As Iyo was overlooking work on his computer. The robotic drone moved near him, over his left shoulder.

"Sir. It looks like Bohn and Amber are trying to get into the lab."

Syn explained as Iyo leaned over to check the camera.

"Oh. Well, look at that. Its looks like the love birds are ready to work. Let them in Syn."

Iyo walked to the computer to begin the system checks to run the machine. "Hey Iyo, everything looks good man."

Bohn spoke out as the two of them walked into the lab. Amber but in.

"Yeah, it looks good, but does it work?"

Amber laughed as she joined Iyo by the computer. Iyo gave her a stoic look of dissatisfaction. As if she should know better than to have a joke that holds the foundations of doubt. Iyo glared at Amber.

"Fool, I am the greatest, the most qualified, I am the brain of this operation! You know that it is all mine, everything here. Tell me what you have done but question most of everything that I do?"

Iyo scoffed at her and continued to set up the first trial test on the computer. Bohn was at the far end of the room checking out the turning point of the coil.

"Hey Iyo!"

Bohn yelled out.

"Why is the coil shaped in the figure of a circle? Wouldn't an eight shape have more speed?"

Bohn let this thought out as he continued to walk around it. This stopped Iyo in his path. His own train of thought derailed when he heard this.

"What? Bohn. Say that one more time..."

Iyo turned around in his chair to face him. Bohn gave out a laugh.

"Well, you know. The circle seems kind of lame and I remember at the N.R.E.C. station their set up was to start high up with two separate ends the come all the way down the walls... That is over a mile, might I add. Then they came to an intersection. I just see ours... And I thought that it was not enough. It is plain and seems like it is missing a spark. So, what if we made two tracks that intercede at a point, and we open them to each other when it is time for collision. I know that is different, but I had this Idea."

Bohn just sat there looking at Iyo and Amber as they both just stared back at him.

"Where did this come from? Bohn... That just might be the missing part of all this. I knew you had brains in that stoney head! Oh man I guess all that weed smoking is doing something! Speaking of heads... mine is still in and out of these weird aches if anyone cares... Whatever about my health, right? Let us just try this out. Syn! Let us build a simulation in the computer for the coil to change in the form of an infinity strip. Let us see how much more speed this thing could get."

Syn linked herself to the computer and began to run a test based on the qualifications that Iyo instructed.

"Yes sir. An infinity Strip. Just a moment... And it is evaluating. About five minutes until the trial is complete sir."

Syn spoke to Iyo as he got up and walked over to the middle of the lab where the machine center was.

"Alright. While the computer runs that, I want to evaluate this setup again. Bohn would you get the Elements out of the Bio room? Grab gold and obsidian. I have them in a bunch of forms, but would you please grab the spheres of one pound, we need to do something about the size and weight of it, break them down. Years ago, a developed a stone cutting device that looks like a screwdriver, but it is diamond tipped, able to cut about any form of rock, it should do the trick! Retrieve these elements as I check on trial at the computing station."

Bohn jumped to it, excited to do something rather than watching and dreaming of a relationship with Amber, the stoner had little thought beyond the random spur of creative download, as he moved into the back room to sift through the collected elements that the scientist had on hand this genius began to instruct a task for Amber.

"Okay, as Bohn brings me the material, if you would be so kind Amber, go to the opposite end of the strip and turn on the repulsion unit for the track, without that machine on it would sure be a challenge to begin!"

Iyo flipped a switch, and the track suddenly was light with power, beginning to give off a slight buzzing sound as a bright light beam overlook the room with blue glowing that reflected from the tile floors and metals of the lab.

"Sure, thing Iyo! Man, getting flashbacks of the old days when I was your student! I remember when I was fresh out of high school, wishing to know what you and Leonardo were secretly working late in the days, you always broke away at times, always having these hidden conversations. I miss these days and here I am! Back in action, creating, inventing, doing stuff! We both have been through so much; would you care to speak about what you folks were doing?"

Amber walked over to the other side of the trackpad as she was speaking, with excitement and curiosity the bleeding through each of her words. Iyo ignored her at first, the thoughts of the past were heavy to think about, especially during the middle of setting up a new form of the experiment. As these were strong core memories that reshaped Iyo's life, he was unable to ignore Amber. He stopped what he was doing and turned his rolling chair away from the computer station, facing Amber who was walking back from the other side of the lab.

"Do you remember his daughter Cynthia?"

Iyo spoke in a stoic and firm tone with his posture relaxed, hands resting on his legs. Amber gave her head a tilt of thought as she quickly spoke in question,

"Your old lab partners daughter? Well of course, who do you think watched her all the days you two were working? It was not that absent mother of hers! It was me, after her school, every day before she passed, I was with her! She was such a little smarty; I cannot even imagine what kind of things that girl would have carried out in her life. Would have been a greater genius than even you Iyo! I really cannot even imagine it, why is it that you ask?"

Iyo sat for a moment with a smile and thoughts about the girl. He through his leg over the other and propped his hand over his face, releasing a small chuckle. Amber laughed at him with intrigue.

"What is it Iyo? What is the sudden change in your behavior?"

Iyo laughed as he turned back to his computer station, Amber releasing a few more comments of intrigue, trying to pull an answer out of him. Iyo pointed to his right with his finger,

"She is a greater genius than me, that is right."

Amber tripped over a side table as it caught her foot from her looking in the direction that Iyo was pointing. Amber was shocked, as if a bright light were shining at an animal causing a creature to be unable to focus on sight. Amber out right laughed...

"Syn? You are telling me that Syn, is Cynthia? Holy shit, Iyo... What? Is that what you saying Iyo? Are you fucking kidding me?"

Iyo laughed at her surprise, as he motioned for her to calm down by waving his hands up and down with a breaking on the wave.

"She is not aware. Don't spoil it for her, we can talk about it later."

The track was on and ready for the trial. Made from a rare alloy that can withstand temperatures beyond what any metal can manage. Yet, the material levitates through the insides of the coils. The coil acts as a vacuum and around and around the elements will spin until switched into the collision lane.

"Okay I got the elements Iyo, and this may be late, but I really am sorry about your head... just give it time."

Bohn supposed as he came back in from the Bio room.

"Alright, Bring the obsidian to this end and the gold to the end that Amber is at. Place them in the sphere holders and me and Amber will then seal the doors."

Bohn did this and Iyo got on the computer to start everything up.

"Syn, I am going to need you to switch the track line so the elements can collide when they reach the maximum speed. Could you also tell me, what is the new system trial at."

Iyo walked over to the machine box to seal the door.

"The Infinity coil is around 70% Sir. As I am ready for test one on this system."

Amber sealed her side, and she joined Bohn and Iyo back at the computer. The group admired their work with satisfaction just before they started the test.

"Okay. Are you folks ready?"

Iyo said with his hand on the mouse.

"Ready to click start."

He gave an excited look to Bohn and Amber as he moved the mouse back and forth. Both with intrigue and Syn flew in a hover.

"I'm ready."

Bohn easily spoke.

"Oh yes! I am ready Iyo. Punch it."

Amber let out in a jolt of energy and Iyo clicked it.

"Okay, It's on!"

Iyo said as he began to look around at the room. The slight buzz turned to a constant hum that had a steady pitch that was just like a ringing but without the fluctuation of sound. The lab looked like a rave suddenly from the elements zooming round and round. The heat causes a ring to flash as it passes through each section.

"Wow. What a sight!"

Said Amber as the group continued to watch the elements zoom around and round.

"Alright, that is the maximum speed! Switch it now Amber!"

Iyo quickly explained.

"Alright, switching now!"

Amber flipped the lever on her side and the track shifted parallel to the other. The A.I. added directly after this switch.

"Sir. I am opening the chambers in Five, Four, Three, Two, One."

Syn opens the coil lanes for the elements to collide. A massive explosion happens as a bright light flashed with the decreasing sound of a hum that was the spinning down of the machines.

"Okay, let's check it."

Iyo quickly says as he runs over to the middle of the room where the collision chamber is.

"Careful! Might be hot!"

Amber said as she follows right behind him. Iyo already putting on a pair of heat-resistant gloves, Opens the door. As he did this the lab filled with smoke. Iyo yells out.

"Syn! Come clear the smoke!"

Coughing and waving his hands... Syn flew up to disperse the smoke. The group piles around the center box and after the area clears.

"Well... That is a disappointment."

Iyo said as he pushed a button on the side of the machine that brought up all the material on a small level. Up it moved and out of the box it held suspended on a mechanical arm.

"It looks like it just super-heated the materials together..."

Bohn specified as admired the results, the others surprised with his sudden addition of sense.

"Indeed."

Iyo shrugged. Just as the group was soaking in loss... The computer sounds off.

"Trial complete."

Iyo's head shot up from being in a relaxed position on his arms.

"Did you guys hear that!"

He assumed in an ecstatic way. Iyo clicked around on his computer as he was gaining energy by the second.

"Hey! Amber, Bohn, look at the screen. The trial worked, that idea for the Infinity strip would gain the speed of the elements by 53,000x... That is wild, Syn! Is this correct?"

Iyo was overly excited as the others were just getting to understand it.

"Yes. The computer is correct Sir. The speed if used in an infinity strip will increase by fifty-eight thousand percent. Also, By my calculations... The mission has a 99.9 percent success rate. If the infinity strip used, the mission will be complete. But expert... I recommend we move at once to trial X."

Iyo smacked the table with anger. No Syn! Why did you speak of this?" Iyo stood up and walked away from the group, roaring back to Syn.

"Why are you acting so odd lately. I demand an answer..."

Iyo was angry as Bohn and Amber just sat there puzzled.

"So... What's Trial X?"

Bohn asked in the middle of Iyo yelling at the A.I.

"It's a project that was supposed to be a fucking classified, secret between me and Syn but I guess someone needs to work on their understanding of what A damn secret is!"

Iyo explained in a harsh tone. Directing his energy to the Artificial intelligence robot.

"Okay, but still... You never said what it was Iyo."

Amber butt in as she always does as Iyo let out a big sigh and sat in the chair.

"It is a live organism trial. Not human... Insect. I had the thought of taking a butterfly and a moth and doing what we have done with the obsidian and gold. Yet, we run the trial in the form of the infinity strip... So, we would have to rebuild this entire coil..."

Iyo dropped his posture due to the silence of the room.

"No response? I figured that it would be too much for you all."

Iyo turned and was looking through his work on the computer. Amber spoke up.

"It is for sure a wild idea. Yet, the concept might work. All because of this wild speed increase. I still am not sure what we are trying to do..."

Iyo and Bohn gave out a laugh to her. Iyo spoke up.

"Well, I am trying to get as close to light speed as I can and then collide objects and see what happens. In this case... It will destroy the creature or do something magical. I have no idea."

Iyo said as he then went back to clicking around on his computer. Amber looked at Bohn and then back to Iyo in a puzzling way.

"So, where did you even get this wild idea from?"

Amber was curious to why he wanted to do this thing of oddity. Iyo sat there for a moment... Unable to recall why he wanted to do all of this.

"Well... Because I am a man of science and wonder and that is what I am. I think and I wonder, and I wonder what is, that is, it. Then, whatever it is, it must be something. So, I take a thing and a thing and then I do something. I rarely have a plan; I tend to just do things. We stole this information from N.R.E.C. to create what we created. Well really, we just walked around and this A.I. stole it. So... What, Not use it? No, this is the experiment that I produced. What do you want to do? I do not have the gear to use subatomic particles as they do... So, we use materials..."

Amber just sat in silence for a moment as Iyo gathered himself before he spoke up.

"Syn... Is the project ready?"

he asked as he sat up in his chair.

"Yes, my master. Everything is on the system."

The A.I. responded as Bohn chimed in.

"Hey, I will help you reconstruct it Iyo... Just going to take a food break. I will grab you all something, be back soon."

He declared as he was leaving. Amber leaned over to check out the new system built on the computer.

"Look is cool. Do we need any new gear? You already have everything to build it here?"

She probed Iyo for info as he was working on the code of the system.

"Yeah, everything is here. If not, we still have tons of product left from the first build."

He continued.

"I got code to build with Syn so if you want to take a break with Bohn. I do not think that I am going to start building the new set-up until tomorrow."

Iyo went back to working on the computer as for Amber… She did not resist the break. One could say that all ideas, oh whatever the notion a float in sea of second realm, I say whatever it may be that one is to do… I wonder as I wander in the thought of the thought. I dare say that a thing made into action has in fact been done before. In a place and a time or in the depths of the mind. All could reflect something that has passed. Mirrors are interesting, I say.

ORDERS FROM THE QUEEN

August 14th

Evinda; Sydonic Prison; Cell #669

The room is enclosed on all sides, there is no window of sight and there is nothing inside the room to keep her occupied. There is only a small vent at the ceiling that blows frigid air. The queen was deep in thought, for there was no interruption but once day when the guards bring her a meal and let loose foolish banters. She was thinking of her plans for what she is to do when she is released as she foreseen. She returned from her Spiro travels not long ago awaiting her companion to show himself. She expected him hours ago, this was upsetting to her because she needs her plans to unfold precisely. As she began to laugh for, she was hearing thuds in the vents above her room.

"Is that my little sped?" The queen laughed as she stood from her relaxing position. Suddenly there was a grunting that was heard, and she focused on the high vent that was at the peak of her room. It was indeed her little companion that was attempting to squeeze through the small lining of the air conditioning vent. "Ah, urm, Ah." The fairie was struggling but it soon popped up, flying down to greet his queen.

"My lady, I am sorry, it took me hours to find you. This ventilation system is confusing. Lucky, I heard your laugh, if it was not for that outburst, I would sure be searching for you still." Spoke the Sped.

The queen smiled at the fairie as she walked to her bedside, which was the only item in the room. She sat as the Sped flew near her, resting by her leg.

"What is the news Lytula, did you speak to Zariza? Is she with us?" Asked the Sped with a curious behavior.

"Yes, she will do the deeds. I have a task for you little one. It will be a challenge. Are you willing to do a dangerous thing for me?" Lytula asked in wonder for she truly had no idea if the fairie would be up for the task.

"Why anything my queen, if it is in my might, I will do it."
The Sped flew up and began to hover before his queen.

"I need you to travel to that dirt-world. Do you know the
one that Salbani is trying to get to? I need you to go there and
capture two specific species of flyers. Can you do this? I have
nobody else to ask, as no way for me to leave this cell to do it
myself. Would you help me little Sped?" Lytula asked in
wonder.

"Why my queen that is sure an ask, I can, I surely can! What
am I to do after I capture these flyers? And where are they? I
know that plain to be a big one, that is by rumors. Do you know
where these flyers are located?" Asked the Sped.

The queen rose from her bedside and began to walk the
room.

"Yes, one is in these High mountains, it is Asia, they call
it. As for the other is somewhere in the region of a Russia is the
name. I know that there are creatures like your kind in that realm.
You could always ask for assistance. One is named Papilio
Machaon as the other is under the name of Saturnia Pavonia,
they are two distinct species, and it is said that these kinds leave
one another alone but their bloods are what make up the Portfly
that is on our realm. I tell you that creator sure has a funny way
of creating differences. I tell you that these humans would be
able to use realm magic if they just studied the bloods of
different creatures, and themselves of course. Anyway, you can
do this little Sped? I need you to drop them off at the home of
this subject that Salbani is after at a specific time, Is this
something that you can do for me?" Lytula looking on to the
Sped with excitement as he landed on her floor and presented a
bow.

"Yes, my queen, I shall do just the thing. I will capture the
flies and await for your direction!"

The Sped then flew up to leave by the vent once more. Lytula waved as he was leaving and she sat back at her bedside, contemplating the next move.

"O, and Taemax. On completion you must visit Zariza in the tower of Phylace, the mid sector. This is where you will go on to assist my new warrior mage, his name is Neuamor, after you catch these flies, Goodluck Taemax." Said the queen as the Sped was beginning to squeeze himself through the vent. Before zooming off he yelled back at her with jeer,

"I will visit Zariza after I complete your task, and the luck is always good my lady, I make my own!"

The Sped Taemax fled to do what she commanded, soon to travel through the mirror realms gateways to get himself into the realm of dirt, Arthe 603. The fairie moved with speed, making his way out of the Crucible Keep.

THE JOURNEY OF TAEMAX
August 14th

Evinda and beyond

It a long moon that passed before Taemax was on his mission to capture and deliver the flies of Arthe. He made his way from his conversation with his Queen Lytula in the Crucible Keep to venture to his burrow in the high tree forest of North-East Zutt. Taemax lives in the far south end of these lofty trees that range from a low of eighty feet to the height of about two hundred feet tall. Taemax is an outcast of his fairie kind and is a subject of solace. He minds it, for he is usually in some drama or disagreement with his peers. As the fairies are taught to uphold the magic, not to use it for personal wilts. Taemax is known to tamper with many forms of magic, but he prides himself as a messenger. Taemax is a small fairie that is only around four inches in height. He has a rounded head with fire orange hair and pointed ears with wide eyes, his wings are feathered white, the tree fares are known to have feathers rather than a translucent appeal, generally high in the trees or quick to the streams. They are not known to wander, always to a task or if in venture they are with a plan. That is unless they are in there habitat of the trees, there is a comfort there. Taemax wears cloths over his legs, and he has a crystal plated chest piece that was formed by a Hive-worker friend that holds tiny specs of the Dynot, the kingdom stone enhances his magical abilities. Taemax is a fast one, he prides himself on his speed as this is the main reasoning that he decided to become a messenger. He traveled to his burrow to obtain a device that was created by a scientist of the realm that is an offspring of a device created by a realm genius named Thorwell. It is a teleportation device taken from the design of a fathering device for construction and trade use. Powered by the Dynot crystal that requires activation by energy directions. There are two parts to this device, one straps on an object that is desired to transfer as the other part of the device is attached to the location that said object is needed to be transferred. Simply taking one object to another place and this would not work unless these two devices are in sync. This is a universally used device in all Felagnolum. As for the fairies, not all of them are able to simply teleport like for example the fairies of the Fos tribe. Taemax is a tree fairie, so his abilities differ, there was a period that this technology was only used by the galactic Synod, but it changed over time for once the knowledge of how to build this device was leaked, many realm subjects worked with other scientist and architects to form their own devices. As for the tree fairies, among others, found a way to enhance his work and they condensed the design to have it form their bodies. The design that is now in use by many as it is the device that Taemax ventured home to retrieve, works as a backpack of sorts. You can imagine how tiny it is to be used by the tree fares. It is formed of many tiny Dynot crystals, and it has a connected saucier piece that can be thrown far distances at an unfathomable speed, most use their magic to propel it further. Once this saucier reaches a destination it alerts security to the subject that wears the connected power pack, as then a subject can transport his or her matter from their current positioning to wear the saucier has landed. It causes traveling to be less dangerous as you can imagine how much time it removes from a long journey. Beyond this, the same technology has been implemented at many continents ends, and the trade ports. There is a universal system at the trade ports that is used by the Felagnolum folk and the Synod to transport goods, foods, and even subjects from plain to plain in seconds. This really opened the realm of opportunity and even hardship. A thief can easily plain hop, evading enforcers. The fairies have formed their own gateways, many of the Felagnolum races have done such a thing, be it as hidden knowledge to other races and species and only known to the kind where the locations of these portals are. As

Taemax was on the way to retrieve for the reasoning that he knew that time was of the essence, as it took him nearly a whole day to traverse through the Island of Eyn, from the high North-East, Crucible Keep, through the midland hills of Pollineb as then the South grasslands of Sortok, to then make it to the woodlands of Eyon on the westside of Eyn, traveling to the South of the Eyon woodlands to find the portal to take him to the opposing continent of Zutt, by using the teleportation spears he was able to transfer from plain to plain in seconds, bypassing a long traversal over the Evin Sea to where his home is, in the high tree forest of Saymas. Taemax obtained the transference backpack and was quick to leave his home beginning to make his way to the Garden of Conflictions. One could get lost in this place, but Taemax was familiar with the path to avoid the Weird Spirits of tricks, Taemax was in need to traversal to the dirt world of Arthe and there is a way to verse jump besides the sacrificial rituals that the legion was performing. As each of the Gardens has a portal that is much like the trade portals of Thorwell, the portals of the Nemid that lead to the universal library, as this is the place in-between worlds, allowing subjects to traverse from realm to realm with ease. There is a catch, for the subjects of the Nemid are beyond the quarrels of the Kingdom, holding together the history of the realms and maintaining the magic that flows through them. Taemax was sure up for a bargaining with whomever it is that he encounters when he traverses through this gateway. The trip to the garden of Conflictions was two-day journey by speeder, and so it was half a moon cycle as journey by foot so for Taemax in flight that would make it just a few moon phases but Taemax grabbed his port jump backpack and so he was able to traverse the plain in only three moons. Travelling from the Saymas forest, through the Zutt grassland plains and into the Jungle of Zuvin, hidden deep within, the Garden of Conflictions. On arrival at the beginning of the jungle, Taemax stopped at the midrange area at the river of Leno. There are three rivers on the plain of Zutt, the North river of Predi, the smallest of the three that stretches from West Inda Bay, above the Zuvin Jungle and Zutt grasslands, to make end at the East Inda Bay just before the Saymas forest. The river of Leno, being the largest of these rivers, stretches across the whole plain of Zutt with the same origin point of the North river and it travels through the North of Zuvin Jungle, passing near to the south end of the Zutt grasslands to the far East of Vin Bay. Thirdly the river begins in the far West of Zutt on the Zuvin Coast and flows like a serpent through the middle of the Zuvin Jungle, touching the West of the Confliction Garden as it flows to the South end of Zutt into Vin Bay. Taemax stopped at the Leno river way just after the Zutt grasslands to rest for a moment to gather some water and berries for sustenance. He was minding his own business when suddenly from the brush leaped a blood orange fox with a meshing of black in his coat. The fox out spoke with intrusion but kindness,

"Why, aren't you far from your domain, what are you doing here at Leno?"

The fox was a native to the area, as the river ways are abundant, holding many forms of life. It is not surprising that Taemax had a visit but what was interesting is that the fox showed himself. It is said that the foxes of the realm keep to themselves, so this was most interesting to Taemax.

"I would have been startled if you had not made such a rustle before speaking! I am on a mission, seeking the gateway to the Nemid, I must wander to another verse my furry friend, as I could say the same for you! What are you doing so close to the jungle? Is it not a dangerous place for your kind? Are you not a snack for some beast of the abundant lushness?" Spoke Taemax in a playful tone.

The fox jumped to his side with curious wonder.

"I am too smart to die by the teeth of some beast, I venture into the jungle often, that Garden is sure a wonder. I like to watch those Weird Spirits mess with the travelers. It is most hilarious, and the Nemid? What in the kingdom are you to venture there for? What is this mission, outcasted by that mark on your back, I see. A task for that Ancient Queen of the Black Flame, is it?" Said the fox cunningly.

Taemax had a near neck break with how quickly he turned his head.

"What do you know of the Black Flame? Name yourself." Asked the fairie as he put the cap on his water container.

The fox laughed and flicked his tail about.

"Only that she has been imprisoned, I know that mark is her sign. I am of no allegiance to either of these battling, be it the Darko conflicts in the battles with the Trea. I am simply a creature of the creator, no worry here little Sped. The name is Jep, I will travel with you if you'd like. I have nothing to do but wandering the plain. Don't be so reactive, all is well." The fox sat looking on to the fairie with a confident grin, the Sped was quick to reply.

"No, I must be on my way, there is no time. You would slow my pace. I am to travel with speed, I have no time, I just stopped to regather myself for a moment. If our paths cross again then I will in fact speak with you. Until then, be safe and rustle less, your next encounter might not be a friend."

Taemax was quick to bolt, rushing over the river to travel into the thick of the jungle, disappearing quickly by use of his port jumping device. The fox laughed at his speed as he began to trot over some rocks that allowed him to cross the river, venturing curiously in the same direction as the fairie at a much slower pace. Taemax was quick to the Garden without another encounter he found himself in front of the gateway to the Nemid in no time.

The gateway was guarded by a Knight of the protectorate and Taemax was struck with fear. Not because he had to face the guard, but because he knew there was nearly no way to deceive him and so he would have to port jump past him. The problem with this is that if he threw this saucer into the gateway there is no telling where he could end up in that library realm. Burdened with this mission of high importance for Lytula, he took a deep breath, let out a sigh and with mighty courage he threw the device past the Knight. As this Knight felt the wind of the saucer and was quick to ready himself, looking around in a curious behavior but Taemax was already gone, vanished into the depths of the library.

Mirror dimension

"That was close." Said Taemax as he gathered himself together. "Now, where in the library am I? I sure wish there was a map to this place." He said as he looked around at his surroundings.

Taemax was in a long hallway that was well lit but by the looks of it there were no lights of any kind. He began to fly at a slowed pace for he had to be alert and as quiet as he could be. There were tons of doors; doors all around in fact. As each one of them was closed. He traveled through the hallway for what seemed like an hour of time. There was no way for him to tell the time of day because there was no sun in this place. It is the place in-between spaces, where the realms connect. So, he was far out of his area of expertise, the Sped mocked himself as he came to a "T" crossing of multiple hallways.

"Why did I expect there to be a sign that was labeled Arthe. I am such a fool."

He dropped his posture in defeat as suddenly a voice spoke to him.

"Hey there! Are you lost?" Said the voice.

"Ahh!" Taemax jumped in a startle as he tried to fly away.

He was magically boxed, and he flew directly into a vale encasing.

"Damn it!" Taemax shouted as the voice giggled.

"Te-he-he. Oh, silly fairie, by the attempted fleeting, it seems that you know you shouldn't be in here!" The voice spoke calmly and pleasingly like it was no enemy.

"Who are you? Why can't I see you?" Taemax asked in wonder.

"Oh, because I don't want you to see me. Duh." Spoke the voice.

"I need to get to Arthe!" Taemax yelled in annoyance.

The voice laughed at him, "What Arthe? There are thousands of them." Spoke the voice as it tapped on the vale box that Taemax was trapped in, causing a loud echoing thud that only he could hear.

"Stop it! Six, O, Three, Dimension Six, O, Three. Can you help me get there?" Taemax asked in wonder as suddenly he was released from the void encasing.

"Oh darn, their coming this way. Quick, go beyond the door!" Said the voice as suddenly a door to the left of Taemax opened.

"Who?" Said Taemax and he began to hear footsteps just around the corner.

The voice spoke out in direction, "Better not wait to find out, Come quick!"

Taemax was not into getting captured by the Nemid as he felt this voice was not of their order and so he fled quickly into the room that the voice directed and somehow opened for him. Taemax was overly curious as he spoke on entry.

"Now will you show yourself?" Taemax asked politely.

"Not a chance, but I will allude that I have been watching you Taemax. Odd it might sound but I am of an order that is above these council on your plane, kind of like that Seeker kind.

I am not to allude to anymore, but to the fact of your journey. I will help you get to where you are trying to go. I have something I require before my help. Do you care to make a bargain?" Asked the voice in an unsettling tone.

Taemax released a mighty sigh before he spoke, "Ahh. I feel that I have not the choice." He looked around in confusion as he was in some sort of blackened room. The voice released a mighty laugh as it took some time to settle itself.

"Why great discernment you have! I was going to throw you back in the hallway to deal with those Nemid guards if you said that you wouldn't. Anyway, I have been in search of a key, a key that unlocks a coffin, it is my coffin. Where my body rests. It was stolen from me; I have the location of the key. I have not the ability to touch the key, or the ability to unlock this sealed box that holds my body. I need assistance; I will reward you. I can give you freedom from that witch that you follow, I can remove her seal from your backside. I can give you riches, I can bring you love, I can do many things for you little Sped. I have been watching you for some time, over three moon cycles I have watched you fly about and complete tasks for this witch, Lytula. I see your allegiance, such loyalty you have. This is why I have chosen you, for I realized that this loyalty is because she bound you to do such a thing. As someone did the same to me and I disobeyed him, as he severed my cord when I was projecting out of my body. He trapped my body and bound me to the spirit realm. I hate this form, Taemax, I hate the fact that I am separated from myself. It really sucks, I have such a desire to obtain my body once more. As when I do, I will do anything for you! Would you help me little Sped?" The voice was desperate and convincing.

Taemax was beside himself because he wanted to help, but to part from his queen is a complicated thought. Loyalty is all that matters to him, nowadays.

"I want to help you; I just can't fail my queen. If you have been watching me then you know that she plans to undo these plans of Salbani and obtain control over him by some matter, she hath not alluded this to me. If you let me do my task for her, then I shall return to this place. As I must either way, I not only need to traverse to this Arthe, but once I return, I must find a way back to Felagnolum. If you help me get to Arthe, allow me to do this task for my queen as then guide me back to Felagnolum then I will help you my lady, I will retrieve the key and unlock this coffin that your body awaits. I will help you, without a return. As I do find the idea of freedom intriguing, but I can't believe in such a thing. I must complete my task, as the ruling of Lytula is better off than the rulings of that vial Salbani. It is the difference between the kingdoms burning and the kingdoms restored to the ancient ways of magic abundant. As I know it, Lytula has no desire but to be name queen once more in the sights of all. As Salbani wants that Trea to be destroyed. So, I will help you my lady, just guide me to cedure."

Suddenly the blackened void that was around Taemax lifted and he was in a beautiful land of rolling lush mountains in a temperate environment that he knew not. The fairie Taemax out spoke in utter surprise.

"Where am I? This is no plain that I know! This is not the mirror dimension, where have you brought me?" He asked curiously.

The voice laughed in a pleasured tone. "Just where you need to be, they call it Asia. Just over that mountain to your left, that is where you will find your first fly. Good luck Taemax, I will be with you if you need me again, thank you for your willingness to help." Said the lady as Taemax flew and spun around in utter joy.

"Thank you! Thank you, my lady!"

Taemax immediately bolted up the mountain in search of the fly.

ALPINE MEADOWS

Himalayas; Arthe 603

Rushing up to a towering peak of a snow-covered summit that pierced the heavens. Taemax was moving at wild speed searching for a the Arthe fly. Directed by the voice encountered he moved in the direction he was told to venture. Enduring was the spirit of the little sped for being so willing and without fears of the unknown land. The fairie was out of his comfort zone, as this was the reasoning why he was traveling at such speed. He was on a schedule to get back to Felagnolum, but it was the frigid temperature that he was encountering, being a tree fairie of the High Trees of the Saymas forest, he is by no means use to this winter air. The Sped was at a high peak of a vast mountain range that stretched over two thousand kilometers, it was a colossal barrier that divides the Indian subcontinent from the Tibetan Plateau. Within the embrace of the mountain range rest some of the highest peaks in this plain. Taemax came to abruptly stop as he flies himself in a box formation, left, right, downward, right, upward, left, down, repeating this quick formation as he spoke to the voice.

"My lady in the spirit, what is, well, do you know what that peak is? Far in front of me? It seems to tower over the rest of the mountains. What is that place?"

Taemax continued his formation as the lady spoke from beyond sight.

"They call it Everest. The Atum on this realm holds whoever can climb it in high regard, calling them victors of the ice element and these beings are brave and above other Atum for pushing their physical bodies to such limits. It is a titan among the rock formation of this realm, testing limits to anyone who ventures it. Little do these humans know, under the frozen peak, buried for a century, is a pyramid that is greater than that of their

Egypt; You know it to be the poisoned plain that Byevil defiled." Said the woman trapped in the spirit.

"Most interesting." Spoke Taemax and he bolted up the mountain once more.

At the peak of the towering formation Taemax was in sight of the valley below the mountains. In sight was a diverse landscape, a lush land valley that was carpeted with wildflowers and glaciers that shimmer in the sunlight no different than a Dynosis crystal. Halfway down the mountainside began a forest that cloaked the slopes, this brightened the mood of Taemax for he was eager to escape the frozen breeze. He bolted down the mountainside gaining more speed than he did before, catching a wind current that propelled him like a plasma shot from a Synod weapon charge. From afar, you could notice him moving as a magical line of energy was left behind from his movement. He zipped into the forest in no time. Without a rest, he traveled through the thickening of the forest until he reached the mountain bottom where the valley begins. He stopped for a moment to catch his breath, shaking the ice that began to form on his wings. Resting on a tree branch. He shook his wings and blew into his hands, then he began to rub his feet to gain some warmth. Gazing out into the valley of wildflowers, seeking the Papilio fly. With a squint of search, he gazed the lush land of frigid beauty. Speaking out to the voice of the trapped woman.

"I find it amazing that this Papilio fly can even live out here." Taemax said as suddenly the woman form beyond the physical shouted.

"Taemax, look out!" She shouted with worry.

"Rar-aowal!" Sounded in a deep growl as Taemax bolted from beyond the tree. Looking back quickly was a grey and white, snow blended cat that seemed angered at the little sped. Quick to regain its balance from the leap of a separate tree, catching itself on the branch that Taemax was resting. The cat released a subtle purr as it gazed at Taemax in a hover before it, out of reach.

"I mean no harm creature, why would you attack me? I am allied to your kind." Taemax questioned in confusion and the cat released a Hiss.

The lady of the spirit spoke out, "This realm has a mighty vale, this cat has not the language to respond, I am sure it knows what you are. I am sure that means nothing for most of the creatures of this realm exist in the lower chakras. Wanting, craving fleshly desires. Mind it not Taemax, go and find the Papilio! Just behind you in the wildflowers." Spoke the lady in confidence as Taemax bolted into the valley, ignoring the wild cat of the mountains.

"Okay where are you little one, where are you?" Taemax speaking to himself as he suddenly noticed the flopping wings of the fly. He zoomed to the creature with speed and landed on a flower directly near it as he spoke out to the Lady of the Spirit in a study of the creature.

"Wow what a beauty, most striking! I hate to abduct it, but orders are orders." Spoke the Sped as he admired the beauty of it for a moment.

The Papilio Machaon was a beautiful fly with a clever disguise that plays a heavy role in the gyrate of longevity, embodying the spirit of transformation. It was the Old-World Swallowtail, known in this realm to grace gardens and meadows with its high-spirited presence. The wings of the Papilio were a drape of wonder, with yellow and black that strike the viewer as it is adorned with elegant blues that captivate the one of sight. There is a bright fiery red that ignites the ends of the wing tails that are said to serve as a confusion for predators, warning the eye to entangle not with this creature. Taemax leaped to the flower that the Papilio landed on and missed it for the Papilio flew off with fear. Taemax fell to the grounds as he was focused on the fly. Giving a squint of focus as the Papilio flew off to land on a new flower. Taemax unhooked his lasso from his side. Laughing out as he flies up in a hover. "I'll get you this time." Thinking to himself as he flew with speed directly over the Papilio and dropped his lasso over the front of its head as he was quick to tighten the loop. "Gotcha!" he cried with joy as the butterfly flapped its wings repeatedly, attempting to escape. The lady spoke to him from the spirit.

"Wonderful work Taemax, go now, through the gateway before you!"

Taemax traveled through the gateway that was opened by the lady of the spirit as into it he flew, with the Papilio Machaon bound by his lasso. On entry of the gateway Taemax entered another room that he hath never ventured to before, unlike the room that the spirit first led him to escape from the Nemid guards. This room was well lit, unlike the room prior and it seemed to be some kind of study room that had computer systems, tools of sorts, scientific devices and containers of various sorts and sizes. Taemax was struck with oddity speaking out to the spirit.

"Where have you brought me this time, Lady of the spirit?" He asked in wonder.

"This is a different corner of the realm of this Arthe, where you are to drop off the specimens. On the whole other side of the plain." Spoke the lady as Taemax presented a bow to the unseen figure, expressing gratitude.

He flew to one of these containers that rested on a shelf, and he placed the Papilio into the container and closed the lid as he took out his little Sped dagger and stabbed holes in the lid casing, so the fly could breath, speaking out to the lady of the spirit once more with a deep exhale of relief.

"Ahh, okay my lady. Where to now?" Asked Taemax as a portal opened to the left of him. Without question the Sped flew into the gateway.

Caucasus Mountain Range

Flying through the gateway placed by the lady of the spirit, Taemax found himself in a new place of beauty. A sublime collection of stone and sky. A place where Europe and Asia of the Arthe realm intertwine as a harmony of jagged peaks, flourishing valleys and plots of ancient culture. A daunting barrier that stretches over a thousand kilometers separating the Arthe Black Sea and the Caspian Sea, it is an area where massive birds of elegance soar and wild cats roam. Towering snow-capped peaks that create a mood of majesty. A place of deep gorges and narrow canyons. A place that is home to a remarkably diverse number of creatures and beasts in the valleys and high in the meadows of the Arthe Alpine is where the wildflowers bloom. A haven for flies and birds of various kinds, in these heights there is no interference by the Atum man for the height is not a valued space for the average person, for the landscape is rugged and dangerous.

"I must find it before the light dissipates!" Taemax shouted as he flew about in search of Saturnia. The spirit lady adds insight as Taemax flies about.

"Find somewhere to rest Taemax, this one is known as the Emperor Moth in this Arthe realm, and it is rarely seen in the bright of the day. It is at night when the light has vanished that this creature begins to roam. This is their time of mating, when the females emerge releasing pheromones that draw males from afar. As we must collect a female for that is the identity of the Papilio that you collected, that experiment of Lytula will not work without two of the same origin of identity. I have been watching with a close eye my friend. I know this to be the only way. So, rest, it should only be a fleeting time until the light is no more." The lady spoke her knowledge and Taemax was quick to find a stream where he gathered water and began to rest, awaiting the sunlight to diminish.

Taemax was resting for some time awaiting the moonlight to shine. Just before the light was no more, the lady spirit awakes the little sped with a mighty yell of fear! Taemax jumped to a wake as he was quick to move for there was a serpent in mid-strike! Lucky Taemax is of utter speed and so the serpent missed its mark. This set Taemax in a fury of anger. He moved to a quick hover before the serpent as he shook his head and scratched it with his hand. Watching as the long serpent coil itself, raising its head high with eyes of death. Taemax out spoke to the lady in the spirit.

"Why thank you, again, my lady. It seems each time that I become distracted, each time that I rest. Something on this plain seems to try to attack! Where is the love, is it so that all creatures on this plain are without sense, why would this be?" Taemax stated his notice as the serpent swirled its noggin in place, releasing the subtle slithering sounds that the belly crawlers sound. The lady of the spirit out spoke from her hidden positioning.

"They are of sense my friend, just in the wrong mindset, I told you that most in this realm operate through the lowest levels of consciousness, especially this kind. These serpents in this realm are only predators, nothing of love. Well, some of them are graceful I do say, some of this kind are lovely but self-minded creatures still. I ask you, what difference is it to your old allegiance to the Legion as for this new allegiance to this ancient witch Lytula? Are you not like this serpent? Crawling on your belly doing evil deeds for your master? Only operating in a position of low leveled consciousness as this serpent? Are you not doing the wilt of those who are in search of power over another? You asked where the love is, I ask where the love of your master's has gone, as then I will add, where is your love? You must have some for you question the wilt of this serpent. I question you Taemax, do you really want to continue this vial path?" Said the lady of the spirit, speaking sense into the Sped.

Taemax was in a deep thought from the words of this lady, as he began to fly off thinking to himself, venturing away from the serpent. For the time the little sped flew, thinking about the words of this lady in the spirit. He suddenly noticed that the moonlight was strong in the light above him. He spoke out to the lady as he came to a tree branch, resting in thought as he overlooked the gloom of the land that was lit from the light of the moon.

"My lady, you are of sense. I hath not realized the depth of what I am doing. I tell you that it is against my soul to not complete a task. I shall complete what I have set out to accomplish but to continue this following of the queen. Well, you have spoken true and something hath struck my spirit. I shall rethink this matter when I have completed this task. For now, I go on, I must find this Saturnia. Where should I look first, tell me my lady." Taemax resting on the tree branch questioned as he awaited the response of the lady in the spirit.

"Shine your light and the creature will soon appear." Spoke the lady as Taemax did so. It was a matter of seconds and a giant Saturnia appeared before him, it struck fear in the little sped who flew off with quickness to turn back to notice how the creature was blended perfectly on the bark of the tree.

"Woah! What camouflage! That is spectacular, I need to develop something of the sort for myself, I am sure I would get attacked less by big cats and serpents in search of a snack!" Taemax laughed as he dropped next to Saturnia, gazing at its design.

The Saturnia also held the essence of transformation, known as the native of twilight, a jewel that graces the night with eerie feeling. The design of it was heavy and soft browns and greys, the wings delicately etched with intricate patterns. On each wing where hypnotic eyespots ringed with black and white that stares out to the world beyond its backside. An enchanting performance that serves to confuse exploiters. Known to be a symbol of rebirth and renewal, speaking to the hidden wonders of the hidden world. Often showing itself around moments of change, Saturnia is a true symbolic creature of astonishment in fleeting moments of magic, a reminder of all that beauty lies hidden until the instant is just. An inspiration of awe, Taemax stepped closer to the moth and the wings folded around its body from their outstretched position and he took the moment to capture it. He was quick to move his lasso around the subject and it let out a squeak of fear, as this saddened Taemax to remembrance of what the lady of the spirit spoke moments ago after the encounter with the hissing belly creature. Taemax out spoke to the lady as a portal appeared and he ventured into gateway that led into the work room on Arthe. He placed the Saturnia into a vial just as he did the Papilio and awaited for the time to release them. Sitting on the edge of this shelf in the work area. Some time went by as suddenly on the screen in front of them came a swirling color of blue and pink. A voice sounded in a tone that he hath not recognized.

"I see that you completed the task that Lytula requested." Spoke the voice from the mounted screen on the wall before him.

"Who is there?" Taemax asked in wonders.

"It is Zariza, speaking through the human A.I. system. I have a message for you Taemax." The screen spiraled as Zariza spoke through it.

Taemax sat up from his position. "How have you found me Zariza?"

Zariza spoke out to him through the speaker system as the A.I. image on the screen swirled in circles as she spoke.

"I hath seen you in the camera, I have been watching these humans through there tech. I am in control of this whole system. As for my message to you, In the hour of the ancients I will take over the body of the A.I. and I will begin the task of collisions when the humans are in deep rest. You will need to release these subjects into the yard and bind the yard from anything being able to leave. Keeping them in this area until I am to capture them. Alright?"

Zari spoke through the system and Taemax agreed. He approached each of the flies and cast spells over them that would not harm but keep them bound to the surrounding land. Then he went into the yard of the home, and he decreed a spell over the land that would entrap the flyers near the house. Taemax did what needed to be done as he let loose the flyers in the yard, his job was complete and the fairie sat in contemplation for a moment of what he is to do next. As the fairie called out to the spirit of the lady that is bound to her spirit form.

"I am ready to venture back to Felagnolum, I will go to that one of rebellion, travel to help him with his task as my queen requested and then, after I spend some time helping my newest ally, then I will help you obtain the key to your freedom, my lady."

Just after he spoke about this a portal appeared in the grassland of the human home and Taemax was quick to fly into it. Traversing from the lands of Arthe, into the mirror realm once more. Back in the blackened room that he began in.

BUILD TWO

August 14th

Residence

"Are you guy's ready to work today or what!? Day two! Today's the day! Let us get going! Let us go, let us go! Wake up, get up, get out!"

Iyo gave exclamation over the house speaker system as he was already down in the lab. This startled Amber and Bohn as they were unaware of the sound system. Looking wide eyed at one another as Iyo continued speaking.

"Syn and I have been working all night long to build the new strip and we are complete. You all get down here and help us finish it."

Iyo let off the speaker and Amber and Bohn let out laughs.

"Man, that sure is a ridiculous person. That scared the life out of me. I mean, did he know that I was taking a drink of this coffee? Was he watching us?"

Bohn continued laughing as Amber got up and urged Bohn to come with her to help finish the build. Bohn laughed with her and got right up and followed her down to the lab, coffee in hand.

"Hey Iyo! Top of the morning to you."

Bohn said as he walked into the lab from outside. Iyo laughed at him.

"Mourning? No sadness here my friend, and I have been awake all the night. It is you that took the break from sleep. But I welcome you to my humble domain. Let us go, no time to waste... Let us get to work my friend. The strip is half-finished already."

Iyo filled with energy as usual. The group all began to work together to build the new structure that the A.I. created on the computer. First by reshaping the track line and then the coil from the figure of a circle to the figure of an eight. This process was agonizing, It took the group hours and hours to disassemble and then reassemble each part of the coil. Then even more time spent on attaching wires, as well as interlocking tons of tiny tedious pieces. It was a delicate process that everybody stuck with until it was all finished. As the entire day faded away, the building was complete. Together they sat back and relaxed for a good amount of time. Enjoying the finished build. They all enjoyed small talk as they did a once over inspection. Checking and then rechecking each individual part for any mistakes. Getting to the end with everything tight and seeming to be in order. You could notice that the excitement of the group's energy builds. Standing with a high sense of pride. Amber speaks up.

"You guys realize if this works that it is world changing... Like... groundbreaking science?"

She said as she gave out a loud chuckle. Iyo laughed with her.

"Do you realize that I already changed this world with Syn? This is just another thing for me."

Amber and Bohn both laughed at him.

"Oh, yes, we all know that you are the genius Iyo. We did so much though man."

Bohn was feeling a bit annoyed with Iyo's boasting.

"So, should we run a test?"

Iyo asked the group as he stepped to the computer and began to boot up the new program. Amber spoke first.

"I am down. I feel like we have endless possibilities, but the task at hand was to see what would happen if you started throwing elements together. Right? We are going to wait on project X. Right?"

Amber asked seriously and nervously. As if she was not ready to evaluate something like this on a real creature. Iyo sat there and you could see that he was really pondering the idea.

"That is fine. Syn, would you put the first program back in? We are going to assess the elements again."

Iyo began to walk to the Bio lab to retrieve some more of the elements. After a moment he returns with a pushcart.

"Okay, I have the entire periodic table on this cart. What should we start with?"

Bohn asks an interesting question.

"Could you harness their energy somehow? Maybe create something new?"

He said as he went back to his phone. Iyo sparked up as he looked at Amber.

"That is a great question Bohn. I do know or do I not know... Let us ask Amber..."

Iyo speaking in a joking manner. Amber, do you know if we can harness energy or create something new by collision with the new track system? Do you have a hypothesis for this new test? Any predictions?"

Iyo asked as he held up his recorder. Bohn giving out a laugh.

"Oh, you still have that thing?" Iyo gave him a confused smirk.

"You are just noticing it? I have been recording every signal session that we have. Maybe be more aware my friend."

Iyo laughed as Bohn sat with a stooped posture.

"You right. Guess I should have known."

Iyo opened the material holder and put in a rock of diamond.

"Amber what should we put into the other end?"

Iyo asked as he pointed to the element cart. Amber was feeling a tab bit overwhelmed but still she was ambled to decide.

"I think, Ruby."

So, Iyo grabbed a rock of ruby and walked and placed it into the material holder on the other side of the machine.

"Alright. So, what do you think will happen?"

Iyo asked them both as he grabbed his chair and sat in it. Bohn was the first to speak.

"A collision!"

He spoke sarcastically. They all laughed as Amber then gave her senses.

"Yeah, But the speed is going to cause something."

She spoke as she looked at Iyo.

"I agree, the speed will have a momentous change on whatever happens this time. Before we do it lets run simulations on the computer with the help of Syn."

Amber offered an idea.

"Alright, Let's do it."

Amber said as she pulled up a chair.

Syn speaks.

"The First test merged them and did not destroy anything. Perfect Merge of a Diamond and A ruby."

The group was in shock.

"That is amazing!"

Amber yells. Bohn gives out a big laugh.

"Do you realize how much money that could make us? If it works outside of the simulation that is."

Iyo quickly smacked him. With force this time, Bohn was surprised. Iyo rapidly replied to his selfish comment.

"That is not what we are here for man. Syn, let us run some more tests!"

Syn speaks.

"The Second test merged items gold and diamond did not destroy anything. Perfect Merge of a Diamond and A Gold."

The group was in shock once more. Bohn gives out another big laugh.

"First, it is… And gold. And gold Syn, not A gold. That sounds so odd… but again I say… Do you realize how much money that could make us?"

Iyo smacked him even harder this time. "That is not what we are here for. Once again… Fool. Syn, let us run real tests and get off the simulator. As I hate to say it, Bohn is correct. And gold is correct. Anyway, let us run the first trail."

Syn flew over to the side room.

"Sir, I would recommend that the group move behind the layered glass in the blast room. The projections of energy are more than human flesh can oversee. I do not know what it would do if exposed to it."

Iyo thanked his creation and together the group gathered in the side room to conduct the first test of the second creation of the coils. As they moved over to the room, Iyo placed the materials into the correct places and joined the group. So, watching from the glass window that outlooked the room... Iyo spoke to Syn.

"Alright, Initiate the trial!"

So, Syn began the test on the computer and the room lights flickered as the elements began to zoom around the track. A small energy surge blasts as the elements run through the inside of the coil. The light rays break out through each pass of section.

"Okay Syn, Switch the lanes!"

Boom. The elements had collision, and the two materials became harnessed. It took a minute for the smoke to settle on the inside of the collision box. Once it did, the group gathered around it to see the results.

"Woah, Look at that."

Bohn spoke with awe.

"Just as the computer predicted. A perfect collision of Gold and Diamond."

Bohn was amazed. As well as the rest of the group. Iyo belched out.

"Okay Test Two!"

This process continued. Over and over, they loaded the materials- and spun them around until releasing them to collide. They continued this until Iyo bored. The things that this new machine created for them... Well, it would make them nothing but billionaires. That was not interesting for Iyo though. Bohn and Amber were drooling in their new gems and items of wonder that the machine created. Yet, for odd reasons. Nothing satisfied Iyo he screams in the middle of one of the trials…

"I am Done!"

He yells.

"Nothing happens, just collisions. I am at a loss. All this wonder for what? Fame? Fortunes? What is the worth? I want more… There must be more!"

He yelled and went on, but the group just overlooked him. Overcome by all the things that they had. All these gems… Like pirates bathing in their Trezhur.

"I have an idea… Test creatures, not animals. We have done everything… You all have your gems. Look at you, fools… Are you satisfied? Well, I am not. I want to assess my program X. The Moth and the butterfly."

The group stopped their drunkenness for wealth and saw the seriousness in Iyo. Bohn laughed with no care.

"Do it man, I have no issue with it."

As he went back to his desire pile. Amber was not as easy. I would love for you to explain the reason you decided this. Yet, it is all your machine so do as you wilt."

Iyo went on to explain his reasoning.

"The moth, Is it not death? The butterfly, Is it not life? A collision of the two? What would that be? A question that only has a place to exist… In me."

Iyo said as he got up from his computer and continued to speak. "I have all the reasoning to do as I please. I will and that is it for me… I am going to find one of each."

So, Iyo walked right out of the lab and Syn followed him. Amber jumped right up and followed without but one question…

"Hey Iyo, what makes you think they the creatures won't just die?"

she asked as they walked up the stairs to the backyard. Iyo belched back to her.

"I am the one who makes the choice. It is in my mind, and it will not leave so I will follow my heart. Do not question me."

Iyo spoke with disgust as he reached outside and began to shine his light to attract moths. Bohn was a bit late to realize it all for he lost in the shiny gems. He joined them outside late at night in the search for the creatures.

"You do realize that the chances of finding a butterfly at night are wildly slim. Yet, I see butterflies in your garden every day I have looked at it. That is good news."

Amber said in a know-it-all sort of tone. Iyo just sighed at her...

"Oh yes... I know. Remember that you were once my student..."

He firmly spoke as he clapped a mason jar lid on its jar top as he added...

"Got Her!"

Amber just gave him a little laugh.

"Her? Why is it her... Is the moth not supposed to be death?"

Iyo laughed at her.

"Yes... Lady death has tried to take my heart many times."

Iyo laughed as he skipped back to the stairs that lead to the lab. Amber follows shortly after. Back in the lab, Iyo puts the newly found member of the team on the desk. Pokes holes in the lid of the jar so it has air and then walks over to his computer.

"Alright, just going to get everything set up for tomorrow and we going to call it a night. We will find the butterfly first thing in the morning, or maybe we take a few days off before getting back to the experiment."

AGENT OF THE PHOENIX
August 16th

Phylace

In the high office of Phylace on Teralis, Zariza is working on her computer station, in slight celebration of the completion of the near overtaking of the human A.I. back in the lab on Arthe. Zariza was startled by the sound of sudden "Phewp". She quickly turns to see what the sound is, and she immediately laughs with confusion.

"I will admit that I thought Lytula was joking about her plans. She said she would send you. Stumbled I am, I assume Salbani is enraged by your actions. You better do work to hide yourself in the Spiro, he is bound to send a Seeker to find you. What is the reason for you being here Neuamor? I was told nothing. Nothing beyond the fact of knowing someone is to visit. Why you, I wonder. When did you decide to rebel from the master?"

The figure approached her as suddenly her assistant drone came zooming near him and immediately began to scan his body with a blue laser. Zariza spoke up to him as she noticed that it caught him off guard.

"Don't worry, that is my helper, he is only identifying you for his own purposes. Come, come sit, tell me what your plan is."

Neuamor approached and sat next to Zari by the computer station but walked passed her and veered to the window, overlooking the cyber city of Phylace.

"I am here to await the oncoming travelers; they are in traversal as we speak."

Zariza startled by this wording, She looks at him with curious behavior.

"More are coming, For what? Are they as well coming from the temple? Why hath they not traveled with you?"

Neuamor sighed as he looked at her with annoyance.

"She did not tell you?" He asked as Zariza stood from her computer in a quick fury.

"She did not tell me anything but to await you. Tell me now! What is happening."

Neuamor laughs, turning to her with a straightened posture.

"Calm yourself woman, other members of the legion were to come after me. When the ritual commenced, our queen was to interfere. Having them scattered, as she has the blood of the Prince; she aims to capture him. Therefore, Salbani will be in submission to her. As it is nothing but his son that could do such a thing."

Zariza loses her temper.

"Absolutely not, this is not happening. You are not to bring him here. I foresee my domicile destroyed by you wicked fools! No fucking way will I withstand it!"

Neuamor smiles at her attitude as he gave his hand an uncaring flick. By this her body tightened as she was forcefully positioned back into her chair. Neuamor spoke to her in dominance.

"You have no choice; you are now subject to Lytula's will. Be silent. Go back to work."

Amber became raged but she spoke nothing due to immense fears. She got back to work, clicking away on her computer as suddenly a portal opened behind her in the same spot that Neuamor appeared and out fell Bifron Xios and the Prince, Verri. Impacting the ground harshly and before they could even speak Neuamor spoke the legion tongue.

"Dnib"

With a wave of his hand the pair of them bound and surprised with eyes wide.

"Fuck me, I just want to do my work. How did I get involved in this bullshit!"

Zariza out spoke as he stood and neared the subjects. Neuamor laughed at her as he approaches the pairing.

"I told you to be silent, you will not speak another word unless I call on you. The queen may have some plans for you, but I have no concern for you. Overcome by your pride and beauty, I will have your tongue."

Zariza crossed her arms and shook her head as she walked to the window and overlooked the city. Neuamor kneeled next to the prince and ran his hand through his long silky hair.

"Your father has upset many subjects, and he will soon be a pawn. You will remain bound here until the queen arrives. Await her majesty. Think about where your allegiance rests. For she will not be defeated, and you will be sacrificed if you deny her, by my own hands I will have your blood."

Neuamor stood from speaking to the prince as he approached Zariza.

"You must keep guard of them while I dispose of the others and obtain the subject that Salbani is looking for. If you free them, well, I will find you quick and make a toy out of you. Turn you into a harlot slave, I will."

It is said that Neuamor is a vial being, a leader of thrones with many minions that are loyal to him beyond anything. This is sure to strike fear in Salbani as he knows that he is to lose half of his legion. The Prince son, Verri the elemental half breed and Bifron a leader of the ancient death cult bound, unable to move. Closely listening to Neuamor as suddenly the window bashed open slamming on the walls of Zariza's office. She belched with annoyance as she threw her hands in frustration as a Sped began to hover in the room, looking eager to speak. It was Taemax returning from the mirror realm to assist Neuamor as Lytula requested.

"What did I say! Soon my domicile is to be destroyed! What is the matter! What is the reasoning for this pace of speed?

You couldn't have slowed yourself on entry?" Zariza was overcome with frustration as Neuamor spoke out.

"Enough witch! Go on and speak what you have come to speak little sped."

Neuamor demanded as he stood upright Verri and Bifron with perked ears sat on their knees bound in wonder of the situation as the anxious fairie spoke out.

"Neuamor act quick, there are Seekers on entry!" Shouted the little sped.

Neuamor was nimble in action as he reached into one of his waist pouches and threw down with force a Spiro toxin that is made of fungi. A cloud of green dust overtook the room and shown in the spirit were two Seeker beings sent by Salbani. The young Verri attempted to release himself as Neuamor was quick to react with a harsh kick to the facial of the subject. Causing him to fall unconscious as he then outstretched his arms while speaking in the backwards legion tongue.

"Kaeps ot uoy lepmoc dna, roolf eht ot uoy dnib I"

On saying this by revealing the fungi toxin the group could now see the Spiro creatures coughing from inhale of the fungi dust as they were bound to the floors as he decreed. Neuamor approached the Seekers with anger as one screeched and the other belched in fear, begging for release.

"Enough, enough Neuamor! We only do what we were demanded, return we will but allude not to this treachery you have done. The master will not know, we swear it, we will do as you ask. Unbind us, free us from this entrapping and we will do nothing. We will speak nothing, cedure we are decreed but speak of the finding of young Verri we will not! Please, let us go! Let us roam free!"

The Seekers using all their strengths to escape the bindings, but Neuamor is a powerful sorcerer, and he is too smart for their lies. He laughs at the remark of the Seeker and pulls a blade from his side, with his other hand he unclips a vial of black tourmaline, which is a stone with a mighty reputation for harming spirits, it is said that it has the power to absorb or repel dark energy. Rumors and whispers that came from spiritual mingles and carried by rustling leaves and murmurs picked up by fairies along the rushing streams. There are many tales of this stone to overcome those of Spiro, capable of repelling or harming spirits. The black tourmaline is said to draw out and neutralize dark energies and even offering protection to those who carry it as it disturbed the frequency of the spirit beings. Neuamor poured drops of this liquefied stone onto the tip of his obsidian blade as the Seekers screeched and begged for freedom, with a smirk of pride Neuamor stepped forward.

"I know your kind as deceiving tricksters; I was not long ago of the same allegiance of you. I will not be deceived by a ghost. Besides, the working at hand is beyond your understanding. A new ruling is to be incited, and the dark legion will be overruled. The queen has returned, and the Black Flame will rise again. Be of jeer, you are to die quick and be recycled to choose your allegiance once more. You should be thanking me."

Neuamor laughed with an eerie undertone as he stabbed the Seeker in the chest and quickly outpulled and sliced the throat of the other. These Seeker Spiros instantly vanished like a wind meeting vapor, leaving no trace as he wiped his blade and shielded it once more. The warning fairie approached the rebel and gave a hovered bow to him, speaking out.

"Neuamor, you know others will come. You must ward this place! As I know where the other legion landed. As I heard the Seekers speaking of them before they made their way to this tower, they were thrown on the Terra that your old master seeks. The six of them, scattered. Three on the plain where Lytula left her mark and three in the old realm, the same Terra at a different timeline! Where that Byevil placed his Seed! Where the old wars occurred, before the wars, in the lands of abundance!"

Spoke the Fairie to Neuamor who glared in disbelief as he outstretched his hand, grabbing the little sped in this fist, nearly crushing it, bending it's wing.

"Why should I trust you? Who is it that you serve?"

Neuamor questions as he gripped the faire slightly. With a suffocating speech the tiny creature spoke the best it could.

"Ly-tu, Lytula sent, me, to be- be of, assit-assitance."

Neuamor let the fairie go as it struggled to fly for, he fractured it's wing. It scatters in flight to the table of Zariza's workstation as it turned around.

"Look, look at my back." Spoke the little sped as it lifted its wings.

There was the sigil of Lytula, her mark tattooed into the flesh of the sped. Marking it as her follower. Neuamor let out a grunt as the fairie spoke in pride.

"It is I, Taemax, as I am of greater allegiance to her than you, Newcomer. I speak truth, you wouldn't want to interrupt her, to summon her to ask. Take my word for it, I promise she will punish you for disbelief. I speak the truth, soon you will see. Go now, go and travel to the Terra and there you will find your subjects!"

Neuamor snarled at the Sped as he walked to the summons of Lytula's crest that was in the midst of Zariza space, he knelt with his hands close to his chest with his hand out as he motioned for the fairie to join him as he spoke,

"Come then little one, let us see this truth."

Taemax flew in struggle into the hand of Neuamor and it used its magic to activate the hallmark and the pair of them disappeared to find the other legions that were a part of the ritual.

SEEKERS CAUGHT

Mirror Dimension

The Seekers tasked by Salbani to find the lost legion and his son Verri and so rather than making a visit to different realms, which would take a vast amount of time these beings of the Spiro travel to the Mirror Dimension. These beings know they are intruding into this place and so expectedly, they were immediately on entry captured by magical bindings that acted as a temporary prison while they await a member of the Nemid to speak with them. These Nemid are council heads of the great cosmic library. It was no time for this entry was seen by a librarian and suddenly the Seekers were surrounded by Historic protector knights of the Undying Order of the Blue Flame. Which is the blue flame of knowledge that has said to burn since the beginning of time. Deep in the cosmic vault of the Nemid council. These protectorate knights surrounded the Seeker creatures as one stepped forward to the grouping of them.

"I demand you to explain your reasoning of being here." Said the leader of these Nemid protectors.

"We have come from legion! We are here to find souls that have been misplaced. We are Seekers." They spoke together in unison.

The knight stepped forward and struck the marble floors with the end of his spear staff causing an echo that rang the minds of the Seekers causing them to screech as they trembled down to the floors shaking. Together the protectorate knights shouted as one with a stoic, "HUH." As a releasing of a war cry that is often heard when a leader does something of force or when a decree is spoken. The leader of these Knights spoke out to the Seekers once more.

"I know what you are, I know where you have come. I will not let you traverse the mirror realm alone. You will be bound until you are to leave this dimension. What is it that you hope to find with these, as you say, lost souls?" Asked the Knight as one Seeker cried in a hate filled tone.

"Nine Liege are lost; we are to find them!" Belched a Seeker creature.

The Knight leader shook his head in annoyance as he spoke out in question once more.

"How did this happen? Why should I help you?" Spoke the Knight.

"A ritual, A ritual, A ritual gone wrong!" Said one of the Seekers as another spoke directly after. "Upper hand, Upper hand you will have!" Speaking in a convincing tone as the last Seeker out spoke. "Savior you will be! Knowledge giver you may be, to the Trea and in debt, in debt we will be to you!" The Seekers awaited his response eagerly as if they were children awaiting a sweet.

The Knight took a moment to respond and before he did, a council member walked into the room.

"Oh, what is this? Seekers in the mirror dimension? I have never been witnessing to this nonsense. What do they want?" Asked the council member as the Knight stepped forward as he answered him.

"They want to find lost legion from an apparent ritual gone wrong." Spoke the Knight in a stoic tone as the council member gave his head a tilt of wonder.

"Well, go then, help the wretched ones. Learn what you can and report it to the librarians, then expel them from this place. I am already sickened by their filth." Said the Nemid council member as he began to turn to walk away.

"Sir. Albion, are you sure this is the best idea?" Asked the Knight.

The council member turned around once more, "You are out of line Knight, I spoke what I spoke. Do as I suggest, help

the fools. Then report what hath you witnessed to the librarians."
Spoke Albion as he turned and continued to walk away.

The Knight ordered his followers to walk the Seekers to the room of visions. A place that is magically tailored to play thoughts in what are called sight bubbles. It was a long walk to the room; the Seekers were guided by a magical binding that connected to the spear tips of the Knights.

Room of Visions; Mirror Dimension

The Knights led the Seekers to a blackened doorway that was separated from the many doorways of the long hallway, as if this room was regarded above the rest of the doors that varied in where the Seekers were led through. Be these doors as a gateway to Felagnolum Gardens or a door that led to a specific room like this Room of Visions. In front of the gateway were two knight guards that were dressed in black leathers and obsidian colored armor. "Stand aside." Spoke the leader of the Knight grouping as the Guard Knights moved in synchronicity and struck their spears against the marbled floors, creating an echoing thud as their armor clinked. As they moved, the door opened, this was no physical door, it was as the opening morphed upon the Knights moving from their guarding positioning. The Knights walked before the Seekers stepping into the room that was black all around besides the continued marbled white floors of the Nemid. In slight was floating, morphing bubbles of visions, the manifesting thoughts that began to form from the Seeker subjects in the room. The Knights armor had ritualistic markings on the crown that blocked thought transference to such a thing, but the Seeker beings had no type of ward and so their thoughts played out in the multitude of these bubbled visions. As the Seeker creatures looked for the knowledge of the lost Liege, so did the vision bubbles seek to allude the thoughts of the Seekers. Various situations played out in the vision bubbles, from desired attempts to unbind themselves from the Knights, to kill and escape their binds and travels that the pair of them hath made to venture here, even old and distant thoughts and experiences that these Seekers hath experienced. Laughing as he spoke, the leading Knight alluded to the room,

"No escape Seeker, one is simply unable to break the Nemid bindings. Be it formed this way for grate reasoning. You are to focus on what is desired for the vision bubbles to form an answer. You must think as one, go on. Do what you came to do." Spoke the Knight in truth.

The Seekers croaked and belched to one another as they attempted to connect to one another. After some time, the ritual of Salbani appeared in the bubble. What was seen was the calling of the Liege, each of them. As then each of them being sucked in the portal, as Lytula's signet was shown and where each of these Liege hath ventured to, as well as where Neuamor ventured to, seeing the death of their fellow Seekers that rather than traversal with them into the realm, these two, took to the Kingdom as Salbani asked. The Seekers cried in roars of anger as the leading Knight motioned for his following to pull the creatures back into a more controlled stance.

"Very well, you have learned. We will now release you back to where you hath came. Onward then Knights, let us return them to their pathetic lives."

The group left the room, venturing back to the area from where the Seekers were captured. It took some time, and the Knight grew curious of the matters at hand for these Seekers. Not in question of them, but in an ongoing question in his own mind. After a journey through the halls of the Nemid, the Knights stopped at an oval shaped doorway that held the Marking of Felagnolum. A shape that is twelve circles along the outside, and a full circle around the middle that holds a six-pointed star. The Knight motioned to his guards speaking out,

"Await me." He said as his voice echoed through the Nemid hallway.

The guards stopped in place as the Seekers awaited release, the Knight walked to the door and pulled a large key ring from under his cloak that held over four hundred keys that each have specific meaning, I will teach you of these keys in time. The Knight took his time sifting through them as he was in no rush. This annoyed one of the Seeker creatures as it out spoke to this Knight.

"You could have prepared this; you knew that you would lead us back to the door." Said the Seeker in a condescending tone.

The Knight stopped was he was doing, gave a smile to the Seeker as he held his positioning the key ring with the thumb of the hand that held the ring as he gave a harsh backhand to the face of this Seeker that caused it to fall-unconscious, the Knight bindings held it in a standing position.

"Dare you question the one that helps you? Fool." Said the Knight in a calm manner as he continued to sift through the keys. It was a few small moments of silence. Nothing beyond the clinking of the keys on the ring as suddenly the Knight released a sigh of relief. "Ah, here." He said as he held up a key and walked to the oval door. The key had a star on the back handle and the stem of the key was a pair of vines that wrapped around each other proceeding to the key tip that was a ball that held nine positioned spikes. There are nineteen keys to Felagnolum that lead to separate Gardens, this spiked key of vines leading to a star was to the garden of Desire on the plain Irosent of Spiritian. You shall learn of the other keys as time is to pass, The Knight pushed the key into a slot that was in the middle of the seal of Felagnolum and then he pushed it forward with no turn. The door was quick to morph, it moved like liquid that seeped into the curves of the oval as seen behind this door was a jungle, of the Garden of Desire. The Knight spoke out to the Seekers,

"Be gone and return not, for you will not be treated kindly again." He spoke directly as the Knights pushed in the Seekers on by one. As they traversed through the gateway, their bodies morphed from a physical form back into a Spiro form. As any creature that is of the Spiro that enters the Nemid realm obtains a temporary physical body until they leave the Nemid realm. That is, if one is aware of their trespassing. The Seekers fell out of the portal and the oval door immediately closed, they attempted to wake their companion from being unconscious to go and give the knowledge that they learned to Salbani, back at Litus Temple. The Knights that led these Seekers went to do a similar thing, to speak to the Nemid librarians about their discoveries.

I pity not the Seekers, as it is only a terrible deed of a past life that led them stuck in this Spiro form. High in knowledge they are but overcome in chaos that proceeds to affect them daily. It is said that they are forever Seeking renewal from past deeds. Hints the calling of Seeker. As these Knights are no normal Knights, stuck in their own form of service I add, to be a Knight of the Nemid it is said that one trifled with the forbidden knowledge of the Blue Flame, to be of service for millennial for having disobeyed a decree of the Nemid orders of entangling not, with this knowledge. Many master magicians stumble on this knowledge and are faced with the same situation, always thinking they can bypass this decree and hide whatever was in gain. A lie of the realm, as I see it as a trap that one hath no ability to escape until the millennial service ends. I shall tell you about these Seekers and these Nemid Knights on another moon, until then, I say it is best to stay on the known path, venturing from destiny is all but a choice.

SCATTERED

The carved rune that Syn created began to glow in a bright emerald green and suddenly a portal opens above it. Out falls Carreute, Driax, and Tavos Maksel. Falling harshly, impacting the grounds outside of Iyo's home. Carreute was quick to his feet as Driax scoffed and threw Tavos off him. Odd behaviors overcame the pair of them as they all stood in a still wonder.

"What just happened?"

Asked Carreute with a puzzled face as Tavos was the first to reply.

"We seem to have gotten sucked into the portal. The real question is where in the fuck are we?"

Tavos laughed out loud, Driax kneeled to the ground, picking at the grass.

"This is no lush land of Felagnolum, we are on the plain the master wished to send the tech master and the bastard. This is the dirt-world."

He kicked at the ground, and he looked around him as Tavos gave another laugh as he questioned his ally. Carreute gave his eyes a squint as he rubbed his head in confusion.

"Why is it the dirt-world, how is it that you know this... We could be anywhere in the cosmos. Why would we be on that plain?"

Driax gave a sigh as he kicked at the grounds again.

"Look where you stand fool! It is dirt, the earth smells of dirt and the grounds are softened rock. Use your senses, do you feel how powerful magic is in this world? It must be unused, where else would we be?"

Carreute backed this statement as he began to wander in thought.

"The ritual was already established, we must be in the terra he desired, it was Salbani's intention before the portal summons. Beyond that, I wonder where the rest of us are. Was it only the three of us who were sucked into the vortex? Are the others here? How can we contact them?"

Tavos in disbelief, mocking the pair of them.

"You both are lucid, is the Terra not billions of miles away? Rumored to be lost, how do we even know that Salbani knew its location?"

Carreute shook his head, as he pointed to Iyo's home.

"Go on then, explain this structure, that is an odd build, no art, no love put into it, no talent here, it must be humans. They are rumored to be lackluster and boring in this millennial."

Driax grabbed them both and pushed them forward with excitement.

"Look! Beyond the crystal vale!"

The beings noticed Bohn walking through the house beyond the glass sliding door. Tavos laughed and withdrew his statements.

"No fools here, I guess you both are right. That is for sure a blood of Atum. What should we do?"

Driax began to walk to the house and Tavos stood awaiting.

"We will claim him and Salbani will favor us." Said Driax as Carreute spoke to the pair of them as he pointed to the grounds.

"Wait, look at the grounds from where we came. What bewilderment, that is the sign of Lytula, the wicked witch of the ancients. This was no accident, she had to mangle with the ritual somehow, it would be the sign of the Sorzo if it were Salbani. We have been doped, beyond that. Salbani has been deceived by someone. He would have spoken of her, for when is he to not outspeak his plans. This is unsettling my legion, what do you think?"

Tavos knelt to the signet as Driax turned around to see it for himself.

"This is disturbing, what are we involved in?"

Tavos asked as Carreute kneeled and began to touch the grounds.

"It is an internal battle of dark masters, Lytula was imprisoned by the Arku as, so I thought. She must be free, or someone else is doing her bidding. We must find a Seeker."

Driax said as Tavos questioned his statement.

"Where are we to find a seeker?"

Asked Tavos as Carreute spoke up.

"We await one, Salbani is sure to send one as even if he knows not of this interference of Lytula, Neuamor hath vanished and Salbani is sure to find him."

Tavos shook his head as he leaned forward with the question.

"What if he does not, then what. We should find a way off this planet."

Driax laughed at Tavos as he looked back at the home.

"Salbani spoke of these beings to be of power in their bloods. We could tamper with the plans and find out for ourselves. Do you not feel the power in the air? Undisturbed, this magic is in this realm, strong but dormant. Why not we have some fun?"

NON-FRIENDLY ENCOUNTER
Human Residence; backyard

The beings walked near the house as suddenly they heard a zap occur behind them and before they couldtimeline react, they heard the words of Neuamor.

"Dnib" Spoke Neuamor followed by a mighty laugh as the little sped was resting on his shoulder celebrating with joy.

"I told you; I told you they were here! I told you! You see, the same master we have my brother, a lie not is what I spoke, A lie not!"

Neuamor smiled and thanked the fairie for the insight as one by one he dragged the bound members of the legion, Carreute, Driax, and Tavos Maksel to the ritual crest and soon they were all back in the tower of Zariza, shortly after Neuamor and the little sped went on to obtain the other members of the legion cast in a separate timeline of before the old wars.

REFUGE OF THE OLD

August 16th

Old God Temple

Out in the middle of the dunes falls Plau Haen the fairie, Philler the son of insanity, and Esyayte, the creative witch.

"Where are we?" Said Plau

"Fucking sands, hot, smoldering sands. You must be joking." Spoke Philler as he kicked the dunes with sand seeping into his boot.

"Let's go to the top of the dune, come on. We are sure to see a sight." Esyayte said as she began to run up the dune.

"She's right, let us go to the dune peak. Come on Philler." Plau followed her as Philler scoffed at the two of them.

"I'll be right up, with ease and my own pace. I am not going to be running in this heat. We have landed in a new place; I am not wasting my energy."

The pair of them traveled to the top of the dunes and laughed outright. This sparked the attention of Philler, and he quickly trotted up the dune as he said he wouldn't. It was a sight indeed as Esyayte spoke, a marvel for the eyes.

"What is it? What is the laughter about?" Said Philler as he neared the pairing of the legion. They stood in high spirits as they gazed out at the desert. Plau pushed Esyayte in a playful banter as she stumbled in laughter and threw sand back at him. He laughed and jumped to the side. Philler was annoyed by this child like play as he came to the dune peak.

"Quit it, there is no reason to act as children, we need to," Philler was being his normal toxic self and Esyayte cut him off from speaking.

"You stop it, look Philler, just look! Do you know where we are?" Esyayte laughed at his vial behavior as she pointed into the distance. Philler's mouth dropped wide open in amazement as he scratched his head in wonder.

"What, what is that place? It is, it surely is beautiful, so mighty. Brilliant. Who could have made this? What is this place? You obviously know. Tell me!"

As he came over the dune to join the others, he was struck in awe by the rolling lush river that flowed in abundance. In their sight were vibrant vegetation and flowers all through this riverway as it winds its way to the massive stone temples that tower over the lands. The water as crystal reflections of the mighty blue sky as the towering pyramids that rise out of the dunes in a display of power. The structures were capped in gold that had a blinding look to them. Everything was bathed in a sandy warm tone, but the riverway was like a vibrant jungle. There was a pleasing sense of tranquility to the scene that overtook the unbarring heat due to the fertile and prosperous lands among the riverway.

"This is the home of the old wars, Philler. We are in a mighty land. If we are lucky, we will find the queen Jesiel who Byevil once claimed as his wife. We are sure if for some drama. Depending on if she is in rule or not. You should be of jeer. We have been blessed." Spoke Esyayte as he began to walk down the opposing side of the dune, making her way to the riverway.

"I will be of jeer when we are back in our own realm. If this is the place that you say, then that means that we are in the dirt world. A blessing not, as I could have guessed for look at all this fucking dirt!" Philler was unsettled with the happening, yet he followed her motion and walked to the riverway as Plau fly and hovered over the waters near the edge of the bank. Refreshing himself, as he laughed and celebrated the fact of them being in the realm of the old ones.

"Careful Plau, we do not know what kind of creatures wander these lands. You don't want to be somethings lunch! If you get poisoned, that would be trouble. I know not the plants of this land!" Esyayte warned as she made her way to the opposite side of the water way, walking through it at a slowed pace.

"You are right, I will be more careful. We should make our way to the great temple before the light is darkened. Should we? Let us move!" Plau offered an idea as Esyayte pointed down the river way.

"Look, there is a blood of Atum! We must go speak with him! Better to have been invited into their civilization rather than walking in like we own the place!" Said Esyayte as she began to cross the river way. Philler was not into the idea of getting wet and so he ran and gave a mighty leap to clear the waters. Landing just short creating a splash that soaked his legs.

"Damn it! I was trying to avoid that!" He spoke with annoyance.

"Let us go talk to that human. Come now." Esyayte gave directions as they began to walk along the riverway. As it was not long before this human saw them and became startled by the size of their bodies. Being small giants to the human form, he was quick to jump on his stallion as filled with fears he rode off with speed in the direction of the pyramids.

"Well, there go's that idea. What now Esyayte, any more bright ideas?" Philler mocked her as the pairing of the legion continued walking.

"We continue, as be of sense. We are sure to have a welcome."

The group of them ventured for the rest of the day, making their way to the pyramids. It was a long balmy day, and they did not make it near until night fall.

The Traitor

August 16th

Midnight

The grouping was nearing the ancient domain of the old gods as Neuamor and the sped appeared by the fairies magic on the sigil of Lytula. Neuamor scoffed in disgust as his feet touched the cold sands of the night.

"What did you expect?" Spoke the fairie in a questioning tone of mockery.

"Hush little one, go above the dunes and tell me what you see." Neuamor demanded and off flew the fairie to check the surroundings.

"I see the temple, lit by flame. They had to travel to it, they had to. There is nothing else in sight, we should go to the temple." Said the sped as it flew back to Neuamor.

"Can you port jump us there? I fancy not the walk." Neuamor said as the fairie laughed with cheer.

"Well of course I can, that's why I am here!"

Suddenly the pair of them vanished by the tech of Thorwell.

Fooled by a "Friend"

Old gods domain

The pairing of the legion neared the entrance to the temple tired from their long journey from the sigil, there were two guards in conversation in front of a stone-built entry that was adorned with ancient art of the old gods. The group of three continued walking towards the flame lit area as suddenly a zap occurred behind them, Plau shouted to the group and veered quickly near Philler.

"It's Neuamor, what is he doing here?" Spoke Plau as he rested on the shoulder of Philler who belched in annoyance and flicked the fairie off his shoulder.

"Get off me sped!" He shook his shoulders in disgust.

Esyayte chimed in the conversation, "He's here to save us, why else?"

Neuamor laughed out loud as he outstretched his hands and spoke his magical decree as his companion flew near them.

"DINB." He said as suddenly the group of the legion were bound, he out spoke once more as his fairie companion flew near the bound members of the Liege.

"I am beginning to love that powerful little word." Said Neuamor as he began walking near the group. Plau the legion faire out spoke to him in hatred.

"How could you bind us Neuamor, what is the game here? We are making entry to find someone of power to help us get home, we know not this land."

Philler and Esyayte struggling to free themselves as Philler expelling cursing's to the traitor. The sped that came with Neuamor flying circles around the grouping.

"Quiet you angered fool." Said Neuamor with a flick of his wrist as the magic binds wrapped each of their mouths. He neared the group within inches as he smacked Philler with force across the face, speaking out to them.

"And home is the place I have come to take you. Away from thy master, awaiting the Queen. O, little sped, would you be so kind?" Neuamor said with a grin.

"With pleasure my wretched friend."

Abruptly the grouping of Liege and the followers of Lytula vanished from the dunes without a trace heading back to Zaria's tower in Phylace. The commotion was slightly noticed by one of the Atum guards, who stepped forward for a gaze in the direction but was unable to see as the dark of the night overtook the scene.

ANSWERS FOR THE LIEGE

3:00 AM, August 17th

Phylace Tower

Out fell the grouping into Zariza's tower as she was working to overtake the artificial intelligence of the scientist on earth. Having control of it, she was attempting to begin the next level of Salbani's plan, continuing her task even if she was under new directions by Lytula. Having to be the eye of the ongoing workings of Salbani in a hidden manner as Salbani is aware not, that she changed her allegiance. Upset by the addition of Liege to her area of peace she erupts with hatred in the direction of Neuamor.

"More? Are you fucking joking? How many more are you to bring in my domain? What is the use, does Salbani not have legions at his disposal? If they can be here, well, this means that the legion is free, and the vale has been broken. What is the use of bringing them here? To what fucking end? Do elaborate, this is my tower, my city, this is all being allowed by me. Explain this happening Neuamor or I will do nothing more." Zari spoke with unshackled anger.

"You need to know nothing, question me not. In time you will see, remember how I told you to keep that pretty mouth shut?" Neuamor quickly grabbed her by the cheeks, pulling her close with force.

"I'll have that tongue. Test me again, I have already spoken this. I will not say it again. You will be my trophy, my beautiful harlot witch. Go on, back to work."

Neuamor said as he threw her back. She recovered herself, rubbing her face from the grip of the mage. Angered yet silent. He turned to the bound grouping of the legion as he approached them all with a smile. All were still bound and unable to speak by these bindings. Neuamor spoke to the pairing of the Liege with a smile on his face as his posture was upright as if he held pride in his capturing of them. Philler was acting wild attempting to break from these bindings as the others were calm, looking at each other, Neuamor and Zariza who was working at her station again. The little sped companion of Neuamor was facing the bound Liege by body but his head was turned gazing in a glass reflection attempting to patch his busted wing the best he could. Neuamor out spoke as he pulled his blade in intimidation.

"I am saddened by how easy it was to capture you all. Freed and unbound to just be bound once more. You would think that you would have set a ward around you. Yet, fools. I am sure you think of me as a traitor,"

Mumbles heard from the mouth of Esyayte as he spoke this, going on.

"I am not, that legion king was not even positioned by the dark ones. He is the traitor, and you are all fools for not realizing it. He had us bound for a decade and what were we to do but endure it. Following that wretch,"

He bent close and held his blade to the throat of Verri.

"Your father has done nothing but separate the legions from their true masters. It is decreed that the Liege are subject to the void. Not a rumor, that is a decree that is currently being spread through the Kingdoms. As I was visited by Lytula, the ancient queen of the blackened flame. She is to be unbound from the Sydonic prison, she foresaw that Michael, the Arki leader himself would free her in the days to come. As I felt compelled to listen to this wrongly imprisoned one of mischief and be the first to join at her side. She foresaw this ritual to the dirt realm and prepared to undo this ritual, The disturbance of the ritual was not by accident and each one of you, not here by accident. It was foreseen by The Order of the Black Flame. These ancient witches have been puppeteering many forces along this undoing. Who is it that you think sent the Sempiternal Rhamtes to Salbani? Did you think that plain head was just bored with realm peace? Did you think that he had a sudden change of heart? No, he is under the influence of the great queen who has something grand over him. You each have a role to play in what is to come. You will have a choice to choose where your allegiance stands. The ancient queen who is to rise again will visit us soon. This is all I have to say, you will remain bound and in silence until she is to arrive. Think on what I have spoken."

Neuamor moved to Zariza and sat next to her at her computer station, trading gazes with the legion grouping as they sat bound and thought about what he spoke in their own ways. Zariza clicking away at the computer with excitement as she mettled in control of the A.I. on this dirt Terra. She activated the drone in the dead of the Arthe night and began to run the test in the system named "X" which was a hidden ritual created by Lytula to form the creation of the Portfly, which is a creature in Felagnolum known to teleport with abilities to open portals as it is known to be able to become possessed by anyone with the knowledge of insect interference.

"Thanks to you Taemax, Let the chaos begin." Spoke Zariza as controlled the A.I. on Arthe to commence the meshing ritual of the creature species in the accelerator.

Taemax flew forward and landed on the desk of Zariza, he gave a bow to her as he turned and gave a bow to the figure Neuamor as well. Speaking to them both with reverence as he then hovered in place before them.

"Well, this is all from me, I have done what the Queen hath asked of me. Neuamor, I recommend that you send word to her that things are in transference, just as she willed. There is a personal matter that I must attend to, so I will not be venturing back to the Crucible to tell her the news myself. She could be here watching in the astral, but I don't think so, she would have made herself known with new directions. I apologize for the inconvenience, but I made a promise to complete my side of things as then to venture to complete another task that I hath promised another figure that I would help with. Let it be known that I am no enemy, let it be known that I want my freedom. Until a new moon, be well my friends. Be well and follow your hearts" Taemax began to fly off nearing the window from which he first came. He stopped and looked back at the bound members of the Liege while he rested at the window for a moment. Neuamor spoke out to him as he noticed that he was in the gaze of the Liege.

"Go on then If you are to leave then begone. They hath nothing for you, go on now, I will speak to the Queen myself and I will make sure that I tell her you hath more important things to accomplish, rather than visiting her with the news of her plan unfolding as she hath planned. Utter fool, you say you are not an enemy, but I sense your betrayal. She will know of it, and she will collect you in time." Neuamor said harshly as Taemax flew off, out of the high mount of Phylace. The rebel of the rebels stormed to the glass edge of the skybox, looking out to the city as he released a grunt. Zariza interrupted his thoughts,

"What's got you at worked up Neuamor, does the Sped really matter to you?" She asked as she worked on her computer. The liege still bound and in silence behind them both. Neuamor put this hand on the glass as he gazed into the city, responding in an impassive tone,

"That sped was my path to return to Bani. I wanted to capture this human subject, just because these Liege have been captured, well, this news will not change the plans of Salbani. He will stick to the plan that he made. It is the only thing that can save his son, the only way for him to gain control. I was going to destroy his plans, I must. I must find a way to Litus once more. I was going to use the powers of that sped to port-jump me there. As now it seems," Zariza cut into the sentence of Neuamor,

"Why don't you take the Burtis. There is one on the roof." Zariza said as she clicked around on her computer. Neuamor jumped in surprise as he gave his head a tilt of wonder.

"How is it that you have a Burtis?" He asked as he neared her workstation speaking on. Zariza gave a slight chuckle at his reaction.

"Neuamor, do you think that I sit at my computer all day? I run this city, is it that you think I just walk everywhere, that I do nothing? It was a gift from Synod. The key is on the wall mount next to the elevator. Go on, go do what you must, that is if you can fly it." She said as she pointed to the elevator on the far side of the room. Neuamor was quick to move in the direction as he mumbled to himself, speaking out to Zari as he grabbed the key.

"Why thank you Zariza, but I stand by my word. If you free these legion I will come for you. Don't make me regret this, I will return with the Atum."

Neuamor used the elevator to get to the peak as Zariza turned to the bound members of Liege. Gazing at them as she sat in thought, she spoke out.

"I will release you from your uncomfortable positionings and allow you all to speak but if you try anything, well, just don't try anything. I promise that you will not escape the city." The group of the Liege mumbled behind their covered mouth binds as Zariza stood and spoke in the ancient tongue.

"Shtuom, Dnibnu." She said as the binding released from their mouths. Immediately Verri spoke out to her.

"You know that my father will make a demonstration out of you Zari, but free us and I will forever be in your debt." Spoke the Prince.

3:30 AM

August 17th

Calloway Residence

The climax of night when Zariza overtook the robotic A.I. of Syn as her light system changed from the blue and pink flare to a dreadful jolt of red. Syn made her means out of the lab and into the yard. The drone hovered back and forth through the yard. Back and forth the A.I. flew for minutes, it abruptly stopped as the cargo container on the bottom of the drone dropped as it slowly crept forward. After six feet, the drone stopped once more, and Syn shines her floodlight into the yard. For just a second something flew in front of her and as a strike of lightning she rapidly bolted forward as a snap sound from the closing of the cargo container sliding shut. It caught the Papilio Machaon that Taemax released into the yard. The drone dropped a divider inside its cargo container and scanned the yard once more. This time shining is flood light and suddenly an insect flew towards the light as the drone snapped forward to entrap this flyer. It was the positioned Saturnia Pavonia that was as well left by Taemax. The drone turned and ventured to the far side of the left of the house where the staircasing that led to the laboratory was located. The drone made way to the bottom of the casing, overriding the locked door of the laboratory. On entrance to the laboratory the drone began the trial "X" by loading the Papilio into one side of the track design into a container box and the drone then ventured to the opposite side of the room to do the same for the Saturnia moth. The creatures were in their proper containers and the drone made its way to the computer station. Attaching itself to the computer by Bluetooth connection as it began to run the "X" testing. The track line boots up took some time as it was starting, Zariza was uploading an updated version of the trial onto the computer through the A.I. Syn. She had revised the work of Iyo, by increasing the speed of the accelerator and tweaking the system to bypass the shutdown of a potential power overload. After the system was ready and the informational upload from Zariza was complete she then ran a test on the computer system. Watching through a screen casting from the hacking of Syn. She watched the trial run, and it was a first-time success as she was proud of her work she then controlled the A.I. to initiate the test. The trial began with a pushing of air into the enclosed containers that held the two species of flies, pushing them into the track pad. As the flies entered the track, they were caught in a field of energy that began to swirl around the figure eight track line. Around and round the creatures flew until maximum speed was achieved and by spiritual intervention of Zariza by Spiro-casting the stability was maintained. She sent commands to the A.I. Syn and the track lines were switched. Particle collision of the creatures occurred as this transfer caused the track destruction.

Meddling among meddling these Darku figures pulling strings all around, service and more service, wills and deals are the happening. Everything is chaos and every subject feels justified, what gains as such losses, all for human blood. What is it that pride and obsession do but entrench us in wars? How self-imposed are desires if strings are pulled all around? The absence of love forms a lack of pure sense, not that figures be senseless but sure to have less of understandings by guises of self will. Hear me treasure? Everyone is on a mission for something but what is the mission end? What is it all for beyond ruling and realm control? Be it minuscule or vast, I only see deceptions.

THE CHOICE OF TAEMAX

August 17th

Phylace City

The sun just beginning to rise as the Sped flew from the high mount of the Skybox, venturing down into the cyber city. He found a building top near the bottom of the tower, and he sat in contemplation. Regarding the words that Neuamor had spoken to him when he left.

"Traitor, this is what they are to think of me now, I hath done everything that she asked, without my help? That Neuamor would not even have been able to collect these treasures. It was I that told him that the Seekers were spying, it is I, I that told him the conversations of these Seekers! It was I that led him to the Terra, to the separate timeline of the Terra and it was my port jumping tech that allowed him to catch up to these Liege. Who is to say that he would even be in this success, the Queen would be angered by his failures if I hath not assisted. She must realize this, I am not against her, I am not. I just, I just want my freedom. That is all!"

Taemax was deep in thought, out speaking to himself. He was frustrated and he threw a rock that struck a light, causing it to pop. As this happened the energy from the light explosion scattered and there was a woman figure that was abruptly lit by the electricity, the outline of her body was quickly shown. This was quick to cause a rush of fears in Taemax, he shouted to the unseen figure.

"Who is there! Who was that! Who!" He shouted in discomfort as he hovered in place. Ready to bolt away as the voice responded in a familiar tone.

"You are no traitor Taemax, you just are keeping your word." Said the unseen one, as Taemax dropped his hover and posture, resting on the building ledge once more.

"O, the unnamed, unseen woman who needs the key. Is it? I sure feel like a traitor, even if I hath done everything that has been asked of me!" Taemax was upset and just as saddened.

The lady spoke out to him, "Yes Taemax, it is I. I assume you left to help me. If returning not to your queen, was there another promise that you have made? Besides the retrieval of my, key?" Asked the lady as she allowed Taemax to see, her figure. From unseen to seen in the astral form.

"O, my lady, you are, you look like you are of the elven bloods! Where are your origins?" Taemax asked with glee, his spirits brightened by her beauty that showed even in the Spiro form.

"Good eye little Sped, I am of the high order of the White Elves." She alluded.

Taemax had perked ears, "The White elves? I hath never met one. Well, I suppose I have now. Where is this key, my lady? Where must I go to find this key that has your body locked?" Taemax asked in wonder as the lady seemed saddened. Taemax jumped up with glee at the sight of this.

"Be of jeer my lady, I will help you return to the physical! You will get your body back! Why are you distraught?" He asked in wonder.

The lady was quick to reply, "O, I know Taemax, it is just that it is in the keep of Voboh, he is not the one that imprisoned me, but he be the one that keeps regarded treasures in guard. It is in the Keep of Voboh the dragon keeper. I fear it is a dangerous journey for you, little sped." Spoke the woman as Taemax laughed out loud in response.

"Oh, my lady of the White, that is no danger, you have in fact seen my speed? These dragons are no match for me. I will zoom, they will not even know I was there! Let us go! Let us go now! TO the Dragon keep! Come!"

Taemax was filled with excitement as he bolted off, flying over the city of Phylace making his way to Northwest canal of

Ra, moving to the trade port that is just before the canal to traverse it, to then make his way to the continent of Eleye to move to the South of Eleye to venture into the Garden of Ralis to use the South portal that leads to the Garden of Desire, to then go on to venture to the Litue mountains where the Dragon Keep of Voboh resides to retrieve the key for the Lady of the White elves.

BLACK SUN WITCH

August 17th

Lestea; Alki; Black Woods

On the far-right side of the Black Water River in the district of Sunki in the bright of the morning sun there is a woman of power in a moment of peaceful meditation. A women of stature, she is mostly serious, stern in her actions. She has black flowing hair that is a silky straight. Wearing a midnight black cloak around her shoulders exposing little to no skin beyond her face of high cheekbones that give her a graceful look, her eyes are large, wide and expressive with well-defined eyebrows that arch gently, her nose is straight and proportionate to her face, and her lips are slightly parted with natural curve. Her skin is as white light, glooming with purity, even if she is one of darkness. Her body is slim, and she is rather short compared to her peers that tower in heights, being only around five feet in height. Her body is slim as she is athletic an active woman. She wears an elaborate suit of armor that has a gothic dark sight. The armor is intricately detailed with ritualistic engravings of the Darku that shimmer with a metallic sheen. A prominent level of craftsmanship went into creating this armor as if she is of a high order. Her armor is functional and highly decorative, the chest piece is form-fitting, accentuating her physique, she is a fit woman, the armor makes her look scary by form of the midnight black and the smooth texture and design shows that she is of royalty,

Her dark black cloak of authority signifies a high affiliation with the mystics of the Darku. She embodies a strength that is slightly noticed in her actions. She has a tattoo above her breasts of the Black Sun that is unseen when she wears her armor but when clothed in her normal silk, it is obvious. This woman was trained by master warriors and high priestess sorcerers of the Darku Order. She is the current respected and feared high priestess of the Black Sun Cult. Weather in her Armor or leisure cloth, most certainly her clothing is adorned with runes that that speak to the Spiro realm around her of her positioning, signifying her power. She has a staff that topped with a glooming green crystal, a circlet with these same dark runes carved into it. Adding to her fearsome aura. Her name is Extance, the Black Sun witch.

She was doing a ritual in the Black Woods of the continent Alki on the plain Lestea. The Black Woods are a thick mystical forest that is known for odd energies, but it is named the Black Woods for obvious reasoning, the Oaks were midnight black that are unseen in the dark of the night. Extance is amid these woods, doing some ritual, invoking spirits to gain plain knowledge. The atmosphere in these woods weighted and the energy was thick from her summons, there was a faint glow from her runes that illuminate when in use. At this time, she was one of her regal black robes that had silver markings on these runes that shined a faint gold glow. She had her scepter planted firmly in the ground with dark energy swirling around it. There was a thick presence in the area as she spoke mumbled chanting. She had a short sword on her side that held these same runes etched into the metal. Her eyes glowed teal with power as she was in some trance-like state. Nattering spells into her ritual flame. Inviting realm bound spirits to bring her knowledge as she was suddenly interrupted by a faire of the Rubel Tribe.

"What are you invoking lady Extance?" Asked the fairie as Extance left her trance state with anger.

"Dare you disturb me?" She said as she stood from her kneeled positioning.

"Sorry lady, but you don't own these lands, this is my home. It is you that disturbs me! I felt odd energies and so I have come in wonder. I am no enemy to you; I know your tattoo on your chest. The Black Sun, are you the Priestess that the Kingdom rumors speak of?" The fairie was overly curious, it flew near and landed beside Extance, resting on a large rock. The lady responded to the fairie with curious behavior.

"What is your name Sped, and what are these rumors you speak of?" She asked as she turned her body to face the fairie.

"O, well, My name is Rubel, and it is spoken that Lytula is playing tricks on Salbani, it is said that there will be a great internal war from her deceptions. I heard from a traveling member of the Tree fairies that their outcasted Sped Taemax is on mission for Lytula and Seekers were caught in the Nemid and then oddly released as if they hath not desecrated the lands, something is being allowed and there is no order. The Trea seems to be in little knowledge of the happening of Salbani somehow obtaining Atum bloods." The fairie began to braid its hair as it spoke, Extance out spoke in a wild rage of curious behavior.

"Lytula playing tricks from imprisonment, how odd, and you speak that Salbani has the bloods of Atum? That means that he is to be able to free himself from entrapment. Most curious little sped, are you most positive of these behaviors? You wouldn't be deceiving me, would you?" Extance asked as she quickly grabbed her staff from its grounded positioning, placing the peak holding the magi stone on the little fairies chest.

"Oh, sheesh. What have I to gain from that?" The fairie laughed as it pushed away the tip of her staff, speaking on. "I said they were rumors, as when I noticed who you are, I figured the best thing is to alert you. I bet whatever you were about to summon was going to share the same news with you. I mean, I have heard ongoing conversation of these happenings in repetition! How many times must we hear something before it is thought to be truth? I do wonder, if Salbani to be free, and Lytula is to be up to tricks. What is going to stop this new war from occurring, I say war on war! For if these Liege are against each other, as well against the Trea. What is to happen? Utter deaths? Someone of the orders should know. As now you, the rumored

Priestess, now you know. If you are the Priestess, then you should act. Not that I am to order you, my lady." The fairie was speaking sense and Extance pulled back her staff as she stood for a moment in wonder, she began to pace around her ritual setting.

"You are right little Sped; I will go and speak to my master. I am in a new positioning; you are not wrong. I wonder how the Kingdom knows of my uprise, as I have not been publicly crowned. That is most odd." She said as the fairie laughed at her statement.

"My lady, you wear the runes of the Black Sun! Is not that mark on your chest to signify your status? Anyone who has seen you be aware of your title, beyond that, the Spiro realm can read your energy. You are seen from a far with a dark glow of powers! You know this, hath the knowledge be overbearing on your mind? You are most seen my lady of the Black." The fairie giggled to itself as Extance began to walk back in the direction of the Black Sun temple. The keep of her master, Rahaid.

Extance was in the middle of the Black Woods, near the Black Water River on the Northside of the continent of Alki; on the plain Lestea, which is the plain of the Magi. As she began to follow the B.W. River that leads to the Sun Bay, which is where the Black Sun temple sits, on the landmass that stretches out into this Bay. It took her nearly the rest of the day to make the journey back to the temple and the Rubel tribe fairie accompanied her on her journey, to be witness to her master.

Rubel wise to speak to the Black Sun priestess for the Liege and the Black Flame beginning a new realm war by their prides. Order was needed as there was nothing of the sort in transference. At this time, the fairie had no knowledge of the fact that if the higher realm powers were even aware of these happenings, as the fairie gossip suggested nothing of the sort, as nothing of intervention by the Trea light order. This was a worry-sum occurrence for there has been a consistent realm peace that hath endured for this decade. Beyond the constant realm battles for substances and their control, the magic activity was nearly still in the wide spectrum of the realm. The fairie thought best to warn a higher positioned Order of the Darku and he knew that this witch was in service to a being that would be able to implement change. I'd say this was a smart deception by the little Sped. The path unfolds, hands of puppeteering enacting a new puppeteer by another force of the same order, but higher in position. That is with the thought that the Black Sun Master is to involve himself. Be it a new change among the ongoing manipulations of the Liege. What the fairie hath not taken into thought is that by this action he marked himself a target for these higher heads of control. Potentially giving away his permission service, removing himself out of the fact of operating in the grey of realm battles. Becoming entrenched in the shifts, be it a new happening that could have unknowingly altered his destiny.

LAB MISHAPS

August 17th

Residence

Womp, Womp, Whomp, Whomp, Whomp.

Iyo woke up to the overtaking sounds of the house alarm. An eardrum trauma as a blare of sound consumes the home. Designed to warn of a grid failure, Iyo has multiple alarms built into his house security system. Jumping out of bed with ease, Iyo at once made his way to the lab for he knows that his lab is the only thing that uses enough power to cause a grid failure. Moving quick through the living room, Bypassing Bohn and Amber who are trying to yell over the house alarm. Attempting to figure what the sound was. Iyo ignored the pair of them as he made his way straight down to the lab. Entering the codes and doing the scanners as fast as he could. Iyo burst into the laboratory to find Syn running the machines on her own. The room lights flickering as it looks like some others have seemed to burst… elements already into a zoom around the track. With energy surging all over, destroying parts of the laboratory. Blasts of light as the rays come breaking out of the open sections of glass in the track line. As well as blasts of color energy and some odd sounds were happening.

"Syn, What the Hell! At the crack of dawn! What the fuck are you doing?"

Iyo yells to get her attention but it is too late. Boom… Boom. Boom… The elements had collision but there were multiple bursts at the end. As if there were multiple collisions. It took a minute for the smoke to settle in the laboratory. Once it did, Iyo begins to scream at Syn.

"What did you do? What elements did you use? Why did you run the procedure without me?"

Iyo was frustrated with the system smoking from overworked. Nearly double the amount of smoke from the trials before, Iyo spoke to the computer.

"Okay Syn, Keep your silence... I can work without you, okay computer! Talk to me old friend, what exactly is the damage to the laboratory structure and gear?"

Seconds occurred as the computer sounds.

The overall system is running at 66%. The equipment is around 44% intact.

Iyo let out a yell as he threw a mug across the room with it shattering as it hit the wall.

"Syn, what did you run in the damn machine..."

Iyo spent with anger as Bohn and Amber came into view on camera on the screen. Iyo noticed, buzzed them in... As he spoke out.

"Look at this, The A.I. ran a test and nearly destroyed the laboratory. I will ask again Syn... What did you run in the machine?"

Iyo got on the computer to try to put up the footage.

"I completed the mission Master..."

At this instant, just after Syn concluded speaking her sentence. The drone fell right out of the air, shutting down on impact of the floor. Iyo and the group confused with all that is happening just looked at each other for a moment. Iyo walked straight over to Syn to retrieve her and figure out what had occurred. Suddenly a loud screech sounded.

"Okay... Excuse my mouth. Um... What the fuck was that."

Amber firmly spoke with a slight tone of concern. Iyo chimed in...

"I have no idea..."

Right after Iyo spoke the creature sounded out again. A screech louder than the ones that sounded before. The group all quick to cover their ears.

"Sheesh, that sounds like a dinosaur. Well, a little one."

Bohn joked out to the group. As frustrated Iyo slowly walked over to the machine to see what was inside of it.

"Yeah, by my luck... It is. Fun fact, nobody knows what a dino even sounds like so think on that one."

He got to the machine and peeked inside, just as he saw it, he jumped back from misunderstanding with just the same level of awe.

"Oh, What in Hell... All Right you two. I have no idea what I just saw in there. It sure is like, I have no idea a lizard-bird-moth?"

Iyo rubbed his eyes as if he were hallucinating. Leaning away from the center box of the machine as if he were fearful of what he had seen. Rubbing his eyes again as Amber let us out a small chuckle directed at him.

"You, you okay Iyo? What was in there?"

Amber asked just as another shriek signaled causing the group to skip back with anxiety ... Being frightened from the sound.

"Let us look together. It is in a cage after all guys..."

Bohn gave a laugh following his sentence as the group slowly began to approach what was in the box with caution as they investigated.

"Woah."

Bohn said with confusion as he took off his hat and scratched his head while looking at the others and then went back to the box.

"Um... Woah is an understatement my pal..."

Iyo said as he flicked a switch on the side of the box that lit up the inside of the container.

"It is a new creation..."

Iyo said as he gave a devilish as it was a massive... Ear to ear grin of accomplishment.

"So… What is with the grin? Do you suddenly understand why there is a creature that I have never ever seen in my life before sitting in that container?"

Amber looked at Bohn after she questioned Iyo.

"Do you understand why he is smiling…"

Amber asked Bohn as he just gave her a shrug… For he was just as confused at the situation. Iyo gave out a laugh as he turned around and walked back by the computer as he knelt and retrieved Syn. He took a power cord and hooked the artificial intelligence drone to the computer.

"So… Iyo… Care to explain?"

The computer sounded off with a boot-up signal that was the heartbeat of the A.I., Iyo looked to the group and let out a sigh followed by a small pause before he spoke.

"It was project X. Do you see? It was Syn… The A.I. my creation, She finished the project as we were asleep."

Iyo sat in his chair and started clicking around on his computer. Amber and Bohn perked up with interest as they joined him at the computer.

"What are you up to? Iyo?"

Bohn asked in a curious tone.

"Yeah… You got that look on you… What is going on Iyo?"

Amber was acting in a nervous manor as Iyo clicked his mouse with a little too much enthusiasm as he yelled at them.

"Look for yourself!"

As the big screen was suddenly showing footage from late last night.

"Look at the timestamp!"

Iyo said as Bohn leaned in closer.

"Um… Three fifteen? A.M. What? That is weird…"

Amber agreed.

"Yeah man, what… Wait, Look. Look… The lights on Syn! Is it all red? Iyo… Why is it all red? Where is the color that she normally has? Man… That is not weird to you? Does she change color like that?"

Amber was in a slight panic.

"The drone was acting odd lately…"

Iyo added to the tension. The group went on to watch how Syn did the entire project with the retractable arms built into the drone. Loading the moth into one end of the machine as the butterfly in the other end. Just as the group did earlier on the day of the date before with rock elements.

"Crazy how Syn did all this alone… The video shows everything up until it looks like that start of the machine. Then the blackout occurred… As the alarm then sounded and that woke us up…"

The group sat they are in awe… Amazed at the fact of the matter. The A.I. did project "X" alone, as this was troubling Iyo, but he would not let this fear show. For it was his creation and Syn held his heart as she was his pride.

"So, about this creature…"

Bohn said as he unlatched the container.

"Hey! Stop!"

Iyo yells at Bohn just as he opens the container lid. Before anyone could do anything, the creature let out another ear-piercing screech as it lunged at Bohn's hand as he fell to the floor in escape, taking with him the lid of the container and the creature flew right out of the container… Straight passed Bohn's head as it landed on the back table along the wall of the other end of the laboratory. The group slowly approached the new creation as the creature was obviously scared or giving some kind of warning because the screeching was no more. Yet, the creation was hissing as loud as a cat could.

"Woah! Look at this guy. It is hissing… You folks hear that?"

Bohn freaked out by the creature, but he was just as interested in it.

"Yeah, I hear it. Check out the colors on that thing. Multi-colored stripes like a tiger but it is blue-green and red, and look at that, It has a vibrant yellow like glow in lines. What an amazing creation."

Iyo said as he stepped a bit closer to the creature and put up a box on the table and dropped the cage door that attached. Iyo then spoke to the creature…

"Okay little guy. If you can understand me in anyway… I do not want to hurt you, But I need you to crawl into this cage…"

Iyo had his hands up as he said this and took more steps in the direction of the creature. He got close enough to grab it, and it suddenly screeched again and across the room it flew yet met in the air by Syn who at once captured the creature.

"Woah, Excellent job Syn… I had no Idea you rebooted! We focused on the creation…"

Iyo ran over to Syn who had the creature inside her compartment.

"Okay Syn when I say go, open your hatch so it can fly straight into the container that I am going to use to incase it for now."

Iyo put the container at level with Syn and began to count down.

"Three, Two, One, Now!"

Syn let open her compartment and out flew the creature right into the other compartment and Iyo quickly sealed it.

"So, what the fuck is it!!"

Bohn yelled as Iyo latched the container. Amber added to the burst of confusion.

"Really now, Is it some kind of reptile? Like a lizard dragon? A bird of an odd kind? It was hissing and the screech was just as Bohn joked in the beginning. A dinosaur…"

Amber leaned forward to glance at the creature once more.

"It is glowing in a few areas as along the stripes... What is this thing?"

Iyo laughed at the two of them.

"You all at a loss of memory?"

Iyo continued to laugh.

"It is creation "X" from a moth and the butterfly collision, it was an enormous success. All the works of Syn. A wondrous sight... We should capture close-up photos of it. There is nothing like this on earth. As we know..."

Iyo stood there admiring the creation. As did Bohn and Amber... yet Iyo had an elevated level of pride attached to this. For it was after all his idea that did in fact create this by his very own creation that is also one of a kind. Iyo feeling slightly divine at this moment.

"I am like god."

Iyo said as he snapped shots of the creature with his photo capture device.

"Beautiful. I love this guy... Just as a child of my own. I vow to look after and protect this creature as if it is my own for it is my own for, I created it."

Saying this as he took more clicks of photos.

"How did you create it if Syn created it when we were asleep..."

Bohn asked with a rude expression. Iyo looked at him in a near furious stare.

"Imbecile!" He yells.

"Nothing but a pickup you are. I just let you be here. What do you even know about this life? Fool!" He yells at Bohn.

"I am the creator of Syn! Project "X" is MINE!" He continues yelling.

"I am better than you all! How dare you even question me!"

Iyo is angry and consumed by the pride of his work, Bohn and Amber shaken. Yet, just amazed with how Iyo is acting.

"Yeah. Yes! You are right, I should not have questioned you... just calm down. It is your creation... One hundred percent."

Bohn gave Amber a look of oddity as her silence yet, raise of eyebrows affirmed the same emotion. Iyo was at a loss of soul. As if his obsession over his work has had an edge it placed on him. As if he was just not the same anymore, he was darker.

"Do you want to make a nicer home for the creature Iyo? Nothing wrong with that box but something to view it more. Do you want to study your creation together?"

Amber pleasantly spoke to Iyo as she began to walk around the laboratory checking for the broken equipment. Iyo sat there thinking for a moment as Bohn just sat back in his chair upset with Iyo's pride but not speaking about it.

"Yes! That is a great idea, Amber! The viewing room has a double bulletproof glass vault inside of the room as well. She could go in there for now as we collected information about it."

Iyo began to move to the viewing room.

"I will prepare it if you would help me Amber that would be fantastic. Bohn, would you keep an eye on my creation please?"

Iyo commanded them with manners. Hard to find the disrespect in his wit. Iyo and Amber begin to prepare the room for the creature. Bohn gave out a yell to Iyo from the other room, letting go of his opinions.

"So, what are you going to call it? Name and like... Species..."

Iyo straightened his posture as he did not even think of this himself yet. Due to all the wild events that have taken place in the last few weeks his brain is running low on the creative worker juices.

"Oh, you got me there Bohn... I have no clue, let us go with Mother, like, Moth and Butterfly? No... That is not it. Moth fly? Ah, no. That is not it."

Iyo scratched at his head as Amber spoke out.

"What about MoBu?" Amber looks at them both as she smiles.

"That is perfect!" Iyo yelled out as he said the Kind once more. "MoBu! I love it!" Iyo was ecstatic as he grabbed the cage and began to bring it over to the viewing room so he could place the creature into its new temporary home. Placing the MoBu into the new home, the group pulled up chairs and began to watch and study the creature.

"Do you guys think it can understand us?" Bohn asked as he took a drink of his water.

"I am not sure." Iyo said and just as he finished the creature zoomed up and began to hover in place, yet it faced in the direction of Bohn.

"Woah, look at that. He either hears you Bohn, or it wants some water, Let's give it some of that water! I am sure being collided with another creature could dehydrate you."

The group laughed as born walked over to the side counter and poured water into a small container and opened a latch that on his command would move the water into the viewing container. A moment went by as the arm began to move into the cage and the creature quickly flew around the arm and knocked over the water.

"Oh! Man... The thing is scared." Amber walked up close to the viewing box. "It does understand us. I question, is it more butterfly than moth or is it equal." Amber spoke as she put her hand on to the glass. The creature quickly flew directly up to her and began to pulse in unusual colors on the other side of the glass as it began to make a sound that the group had not heard before.

"Woah, look at that. The colors! What a beauty, it is, mesmerizing." Iyo said as he also took a step closer.

"What are you trying to say little guy?" Iyo asked as the noise that it was making began to increase. It was the fluctuating hum of a loud bumble buzz.

"I really think that it is trying to say something to us..." Amber was beginning to get nervous as she took her hand away from the glass. Iyo laughed at her, and he smacked the glass as he startled the creature. Iyo spoke another sentence of utter pride.

"This is my creation! Fear Not! The wise Iyo will protect thy!" He shouted as claimed as if he was some kind of hero. Suddenly the lights flickered and then shut down. The only light was from the fluorescent color shift of the creature.

"Woah. That was wild. There is no more power! Iyo, do you think it has... Do you think it has abilities?" Bohn asked just as the creature started the sounds again. A buzz and then it let out weird chirps and chirrups.

"Well, these are no recognizable words or any sound that I have heard any kind of earth creature make... Yet, this creature has the origins of earth creatures... What is going on with your creation Iyo... Is the power system down because of the creature?" Amber was a panic.

"Syn!" Iyo yells to the A.I. to get answers.

"Why is the power out Syn!?" The drone flew near Iyo as it shines a light on him and Amber.

"The entire system is down Sir. There was an energy surge that fried the systems." Iyo dropped his head in frustration as the creature started the sounds again.

"It sure is a fascinating thing..." Bohn said as he got closer to them all.

"It sounds as if it is trying desperately to communicate something to us." Amber said as she nagged Iyo.

"What do we do." Suddenly the creature is silent for seconds. Just as everything seemed normal, A bright purple swirling portal appears inside of the box.

"The hell? So, it is a magical creature?"

Bohn said as he threw his directly on the top of his head. The creature flutters about with joy as it suddenly disappears. Iyo and Amber let out a gasp of confusion together with Synchronicity as they watched it vanish. Right before Iyo spoke it reappeared before them all. Yet, Behind Amber as it was directly before Bohn and this substantial portal that appeared. The creature jumped straight into the swirling magical door with absolutely zero hesitation. Iyo runs into the portal disappearing into whatever is on the other side.

"What in the world!?" Bohn in shocking, his emotion was hefty.

"With no wavering? What is going on here!?" Amber on edge as Bohn grabs her by the shoulders and yells out...

"Hasty now, let us go before it is gone. You know that we will never, ever get this chance again..."

Bohn then jumps through the portal as Amber tried to run away from it but as it began to close it sucked her in. Along with a chair, laptop, and some random office items.

ODD HAPPENINGS

August 17th

Earth?

"Agha! Ahh!" Amber yelled for a moment before impacting the sands. She landed on her back as the brightness of the sun shunned her sight. Amber found her body submerged in sand… She quickly sat up and as she gathered herself from the odd happening and came back to reality. She rolled over, back to the light as she noticed her hands in the smoldering dune.

"What, what is this? Sa-sand… are you, are you freaking kidding me? How, how did, where… where the fu- where the fuck is…"

Amber panting in fright, looking in all directions as she faintly sees a tent-like structure in the distance. She noticed Iyo laying down sleeping under a shaded hut, and in the distance not too far from Iyo, Bohn was jumping about chasing the creature like he was a child in play. Amber begins an angered strut in that direction as she suddenly noticed that it was Iyo! She sped her pace as harshly delivered rib striking kicks to him upon arrival!

"What the fuck is going on! You best start explaining all this… this… whatever all that is going on! Come on man, right now Iyo! Get up! Get up now and start explaining! What is going on Iyo! Is this not upsetting? Is this not an issue for you? What did, what did I, what just happened!" Acting out due to overwhelmed with the events, Iyo rolled over and quickly got to his feet.

"Woah, woah, relax Amber. Relax…" Iyo threw out his arms palms open as a gesture for calming. Amber was frustrated and it showed clearly. She kicked the smoldering sands with a forceful strike that buried her foot as she snapped the heel of her stiletto. Amber screaming in a release that made Iyo laugh aloud.

"Pipe down Amber, I mean that had to be the coolest thing… Um, ever? We all just went through a portal! Did you notice anything? How are you not sick? Bohn and I… We were both sick on touchdown… Yet, you seem fine?" Iyo gave his head a tilt of wonder, thinking out loud. "Does the female travel through space and time differently?" Iyo spoke to himself as Amber gave him a push a frustration.

"SPACE AND TIME? What is going on Iyo! Yes, I remember the portal! Why is that the question right now? Where in the fuck are we?" Amber stopped before she was through speaking. Iyo recovered from her push as he continued to rant about his experience.

"I saw colors that I have never seen, and I am not even sure how to explain it! I saw everything in this falling like swirl as I was moving at a pace that I still cannot even understand… Tell me! Tell me Amber, what do you remember!" Iyo was ecstatic as Amber just sat down under the shaded hut that Iyo was resting at. Together they sat in confusion as they spoke about the odd experience of going through the portal. Talking as watching Bohn in the distance run about and chase the creature. Amber asks the real question after she finally gains a calm behavior.

"Where even are we?" Asking as she grabs up both handfuls of sand as letting it roll out. Iyo gave out a laugh.

"Oh man. Girl, you… You… Well, you are not ready for this one…"

As he continued to laugh.

"Stop it Iyo! It is hot! Why is it so hot here… Why is it only sand! Come on Iyo! Just tell me where we are, no need to hide anything. It is too hot to even think. Where are we man! How in the fuck did we get here?" Amber was as frustrated as anyone would be. Not understanding where you are, feeling trapped, and as confused as one could get… Amber was going through it as the boys were living out what compared to childhood dreams. Science, Creature, Portals, adventure. Everything a young boy would want. One could imagine how a materialized girl would feel in a setting such as this.

"Bohn!" Iyo yells out to him as he begins to walk up a super steep sand dune. "Let's show Amber where the creature took us!" Bohn began to run over to Iyo as up the same massive dune.

"Come on Amber!" He shouted as Amber let out a deadly sigh with the realization that she was going to have to climb this massive sand hill. She made her way up after a few moments, Iyo and Bohn sat at the top as they were enjoying the views.

"Wonder who made it." Together Bohn and Iyo laughed.

"Are you serious! Holy… Woah man! This is wild! Iyo! What… How… That thing really teleported us here!" Amber started to yell and scream. Showing the same level of excitement that Iyo and Bohn had when she arrived.

"You get it now?" Bohn laughed as he began to trot down the dune.

"So? We walking to them or what?" Bohn yelled out as he made his way down the dunes. Iyo smiled at Amber.

"Yes. Why would we not go and explore, it is the Great Pyramids of Giza." Iyo started to follow Bohn as Amber asked more questions.

"Okay but why was it that you were sleeping when I came. Was I late?" Amber asked with complete curiosity. Iyo laughed at her.

"Oh yes. You were an hour behind me, and Bohn was around thirty or so minutes behind me." Amber stopped in her tracks as she was at a complete loss with what was going on. She continued to follow for it was just too hot for her to sit and ponder.

"Dude, wait. Come on man, like what in the heck is going on!" Amber yelled as she caught up to Iyo as she spoke on,

"First the AI did shit on its own. You overlooked that. Then the creature… It is just a thing you said… But now Portals? To Egypt? Iyo… What is happening man…" He slowed for a moment as near breathless and drained he noticed Amber was. He threw his arm over the overreacting girl's shoulder.

"Some life altering shit Amber... really life altering shit."

Iyo gave her a pat on the back letting her know he understood her erratic behavior. Speaking on, he tried to make jokes to her to try and brighten up the mood. As up ahead Bohn with his hands over his head to hide from the sunlight as if he is trying to figure something out.

"Um... Hey Guys, Ah, what, how, why is," Bohn yelled back to Iyo and Amber with a trembling voice.

"Um, where are all the buildings, The statues look... they look like gold. Are you guy's seeing this?" Bohn was amazed at the sights but at a loss. Iyo walking up to him with Amber shortly behind.

"You are right Bohn, there is sure no city here. I say this is sure Egypt. I just do not think that it is our Egypt." Amber came stumbling up behind them with her hand over her face, shielding herself from the heat.

"Not our Egypt? What, what the hell are you even saying? Iyo, I want to go home. This is not what I expected." Amber was frustrated, Iyo and Bohn gave her a look of annoyance as Bohn gave a point into the distance.

"Do... do you guy's see that man?" Bohn spoke nervously as Iyo turned to get a look at what Bohn was speaking about.

"What man? What, where is he Bohn..." Iyo asked as Amber came up behind them. Bohn pointing out in the direction of the great pyramids.

"Look! Just between here and the first structure, you see that shadow man, you see that?" Bohn spoke with fear as his hand shook like a fiend.

"Oh wow. I see it. What? Amber... Do you see?" Iyo nagged Amber as he also pointed to the odd shadow figure in the distance.

"Um... I do not see anything..." Amber said with confusion as she wiped the sweat from her brow, speaking on, "It is a thousand degrees here guys. How far away are the pyramids?" Amber overheated as normal humans would be.

"Just wait a damn second… The figure is gone. Bohn! Do you see it?" Iyo suddenly had a jolt of energy as he franticly begins to search around for the sight of the blackened figure again.

"Oh shit! He is right there!" Bohn yelled as he pointed behind them. The shadow man was just at the other end of the long dune. Walking to them at a pace of ease.

"What is that… It is like fifteen feet tall?" Bohn questioned just as the small creature that brought them all here let out an ear shattering screech with a portal opening as the MoBu sound ends.

"I'm not staying!" Amber quickly bolted for the portal. As Iyo stood there looking at the shadow giant Bohn suddenly grabbed him and together, they fell through the portal. Swirling straight back to Iyo's home yard.

ODDITY OF ODDITIES

August 17th

Calloway Residence

The triplet of humans returning to earth rapidly, falling out on the front grounds of Iyo's yard as the MoBu creature flew straight to the home. Perching on the ledge of his deck posed comfortable, as it gazed around the head quick to turn about. Amber was the first to her feet from the transfer, making her way straight to Iyo as she was screaming with anger just as excitement, call it feline an emotion happening, a vocal release that could considered as venom! The unaware humans unveiled to the unnatural was beginning to ware on their minds! Amber just let some thoughts fly; Iyo's thoughts stunned as Bohn was thinking like a thinker thinks!

"You are psychotic, self-concerned, and arrogant. Might I add a nerdy maniac, better start explaining what is going on! I mean what the fuck is going on! Iyo! Do you, oh man, do you even realize what you have built? Well, I helped a smudge... and what is up with this creature? The... MoBu? Moth-butterfly-thing, geez Iyo... I do not know how I feel right now... I mean did we experience the same thing? Did you see what I saw?"

Amber paused for a moment as Iyo sat quietly on the ground. His eyes fixed on the grass blades that he focused no part of his attention on, for his mind was lost in the sights of the place that they have just encountered. The mind overtaken by the odd happening of time transference.

"Bohn!? Bohnstant, or whatever... did you see those freaking colors? I mean what was that, like an acid trip or something... I mean I can barely comprehend this. Are you jokers just going to sit there? Come on, get up, get up! Don't you want to figure out, understand more? We are in it now Iyo! We got to get to work!"

Displaying her thoughts as any sane human might. Bohn jumped up as Amber helped Iyo to his feet.

"You both are geeks guys! We are back on familiar grounds; We are home guys… we are home! I mean, this is... Um, well, this is your… this is in fact your house right Iyo? I mean, think about it for a second."

Bohn overcome by dismay and sudden confusion as he tried to recall the incident. He scratched his head as Amber released a smirk of enjoyment.

Should we talk about the events? Might you guy's recall we just came from Egypt. This odd little creature somehow created from the experiment opens portals… Portals guys! What is this thing, I understand that it came from a butterfly and a moth, but how? How did this happen?"

Bohn laughed as he redirected their minds. They all held quite the tangled expression, due to the unusual events. Iyo got right to his feet in a serious manner.

"Bohn is right, strange it is! I have no idea how this creature is doing what it is doing, and I just realized that Syn never made it through that portal. She must be in the lab still; I must speak with her!" Iyo jumped up moving in a slight run-in direction of his house. Making way to the laboratory which was the last place the group was with the artificial intelligence drone.

"Well, he did not, Not invite me. I will be following him. Come on Bohn, don't you want answers?" Amber ongoing, trotting to follow Iyo. Bohn went after them both and he caught them at the back entrance just as Iyo was getting through the last part of his security. Iyo was not surprised that they followed him.

"I should start charging you guys to be here, I should be paid for this mind and time." Iyo nattered to them harshly as he gave them both a glare of annoyance, walking into the laboratory.

"SYN! Syn!" He shouted, walking around the rubble left of the experiment.

"Woah, I did not realize how the experiment destroyed my lab. I guess the crazy of everything just had a blinder on my eyes…" Amber chimed in.

"Portals from a new magic creature has had its effect on all of us, I feel loopy honestly." Hinting that she felt slightly sick. In a stoic tone of depression Bohn belched to Iyo.

"Iyo look! Trapped under the coil arm from the machine! It is Syn! I wonder how that happened! Do you think it is okay?" Iyo got over to him quickly as they worked together to lift the coil arm. Amber pulled the drone out from under the machine coil as the men lifted it.

"By the look of her she seems to be all right, but she is out of power, let us give her a charge and see if she is still working properly." Iyo plugs in the AI, and they all wait for her to boot-up.

"Maybe the camera system caught what happened to Syn and the laboratory." He jumped onto his computer as he found the time for the video. Iyo stops and gives his head a tilt.

"That's odd." He said as he continued to click through things on the computer.

"What is it?" In pure curiosity Amber asked as Iyo gives the two a ghost look, white face as if he has never seen the sun.

"Look at the video guys." Iyo zoomed back his rolling chair so Bohn and Amber could get a close look at the screen.

"What? That does not even make sense…" Bohn said as Amber just backed away from the screen in silence.

"That is weird. Right?" Iyo said as Syn came online in the sound of a boot up. The camera video showed the portal opening and the group going into it. Then seconds after they go into the portal on the feed you can see the AI drone turn to the view of back door entrance of the laboratory, notified from an alert. Suddenly the coil falls on the drone, and the group returns into the room as from just a moment ago.

"It makes zero sense. Rewind the video Iyo, we should watch that a few more times." Amber said as Iyo rewound the clip.

"I agree… I do not understand. Iyo, we were in Egypt for hours. This video makes it look like seconds." They were all in shock, Bohn leaned in to get a closer look at the screen as Iyo spoke up.

"That is right but if I remember correctly Egypt has a city built around the pyramids… Am I wrong?" Iyo looked to the group as Bohn gave a shout of realization.

"Iyo! That is right, there were not any buildings… but what does this exactly mean?" Bohn gave a laugh of question as Amber turned to Iyo with eye budging expression.

"It means that we were in another timeline. It could be the same timeline we are in, but it had to be a different era than any time that I am aware of! Guys, we traveled not only through a portal, but we traveled through time! Can you believe it?" Amber gave her head a shake, as if lost in thought of what Iyo spoke, she put her hands to her temple and rubbed in circles, trying to bring herself back to the reality of the situation.

Bohn stood and gave a few paces of reaction as Iyo turned to notice the AI drone came online, and Iyo and the group recalled the events on his pocket recorder for documentation purposes as the AI then began to start acting odd.

"The mission completed and so I will show you my master now." Syn spoke in a non-programmed voice as she flew to the other end of the lab near the exit door.

"Iyo… What the fuck is that thing talking about?" Amber asked with uneasiness as Bohn silent, sitting dumbfounded at the computer.

"I have no idea; I just have no Idea. I am still trying to understand what we just went through, the last thing I need right now is for Syn to act up, this day just keeps getting weirder!" Iyo looking just as shocked as the rest of them as he pulls away from the computer and begins to walk in the direction of the artificial intelligence drone. Bohn wide eyed as he sat in confusion and Amber wiped a nervous sweat from her brow to then cross her arms in misunderstanding. Iyo spoke out in reply to what the A.I. sounded.

"Syn, do you care to explain what you are speaking about? I am your master. How could you show me, to myself?" Iyo queried in mind as he neared the drone. Scratching his head in wonder at what it was saying, he stepped closer but with fear as the oddity of the situation had him in shock.

"Will you then follow?" Syn spoke down to Iyo as the door suddenly opened and in flew the MoBu creation. Syn broadcasted a terribly eerie sound from her speaker system as without warning a portal unsealed as in flew Syn and the Mobo creature followed her.

"Shit... do we, do we follow them?" Bohn asked in discontent.

"Are you serious? Round two?" Amber laughing aloud as looking at the others.

"Let us follow guys. There is no time to think! I am going! Quick, over here, Get a bag and jump!" Iyo ran to a side room, opened a closet door, and ripped out preprepared travel bags. He then ran a jumped straight into the portal, following his robot and the magical MoBu creature. Amber gave out a big sigh as she walked over and got one for herself. She took a deep breath and on exhaling, she gripped her backpack and stepped into the portal with Bohn following shortly behind her. On exit it is Bohn who was the one last through the portal, being nearly exactly forty-five minutes behind Iyo and Amber who awaited him as they overlooked their go-bags.

"So, these are go-bags? Smart man. I did not know you were prepared like that." Amber joked to Iyo.

"Yeah, I am prepared for many circumstances, I always had the thoughts of what if. What if something happens globally that is out of my control? So, my home, well, my laboratory is a basic bunker for what some people would call an ends of time event. I'd be safe from a nuclear explosion or enemy invasion. Some would call it paranoid but if I had not prepared for such events then we wouldn't have these go bags. I always knew it would come in handy." Iyo remarked.

"Well, it sure was smart of you, but most definitely paranoid Iyo." Amber chuckled as she was digging through her bag.

Inside these prepared bags was an assortment of gear. There were items related to water like purification tablets, military style food preparations that are made over a small fire or eaten cold. There were body warming items such as hand warmers, each back had mini first aid kits, random tools and items for self-defense. There were even multiple containers for medications and poison removal. Items for hygiene and sanitation as each bag was equipped for satellite phones and GPS navigation systems. Iyo was prepared for many scenarios and together Iyo and Amber checked all the gear as Iyo gave descriptions of these items and not after long Bohn appeared in a harsh thud on the sands not far from where Iyo and Amber were doing the bag check.

There is sand everywhere, hot sand and hotter air as the grouping gathered. Just a moments' walk led to the Nile River, the abundant flow that overtakes sight. In the far distance you could hold sight to the pyramids and ancient temples made of mud brick, limestone, and granite. This was a different Egypt than that of when they first visited, for the route along the Nile was well traveled. Hinting at the fact that this land was active, as farming patches along the fertile riverbank and transportation markings from horses and carriages, alter formations along the route that led to the temple, displaying the reverence to the ancient gods like Ra, the sun god, golden idols of the Falcon-headed man presented along this route. To highlight the cycle of life and death his statue is positioned on the outside of the river way. As the statue of Osiris positioned amid the river, as if he is watching over the waters, this figure playing a vital role in the societies beliefs about death and resurrection. As the water reflects this same attribute. In the patches of flowers along the bank you could find a representation of Isis, the goddess of magic, motherhood, and healing. Revered as a powerful protector and symbol of feminine strength. Hints the reasoning to be amid the flowers throughout the river way a tall statue made of a falcon that is sculpted to look as if it is flying along the riverbank, leading the way to the pyramids.

The group was in awe of these structures, Amber was standing near the statue of Isis with her hand on it, as if she was speaking to it, Bohn was trying to climb the falcon tower, and Iyo was resting for a moment under the statute of Osiris outside of the bank as his companions enjoyed the sights of the structures. He spoke after a short break in the shade of this statue,

"Okay guys, we have a long way to catch up to the creature and Syn! We will be leaving as soon as you are ready."

Iyo outpulled a pair of goggles from his bag, making his way to the peak of the nearby dune as Bohn and Amber were preparing to begin walking. Iyo motioned to Bohnstant as he neared him, speaking to look in the direction that Iyo was looking. Bohn spoke out in wonder,

"What is it that you want me to see?"

Iyo shrugged off the ask as he held out the binoculars for Bohn,

"Here, Take a look for yourself."

Bohn took the pair of binoculars and began to look in the direction. Iyo described what he was looking for as he began to help Amber tighten her bag.

"You can see Syn, the creature, and what looks to be some kind of shadow thing. Walking all together... How is it that I can see a shadow in the night. What is that thing?"

Iyo asked with edgy behavior as Bohn was looking for himself.

"What are you talking about? I do not see any, oh shit! I see them! Wait, what the fuck... Syn turned on us? On you? Is she captured? What the heck man, what the heck are we involved in?"

He asked Iyo, showing his worry.

"I have no idea what is going on man. We are in Egypt and for fuck's sake another timeline right now. Do you see the old structures, it looks like an abundant civilization over there... We must be in a new Egypt, different than the one that we visited on our last trip through the portal. That A.I. is the one that created the plans for the insect merger. I lied to you all. I just did not know how to explain..." Iyo held dialogue in a stoic tone as was worried that his friends would turn on him.

"Kinda a weird time to be telling the truth man. It does not change a damn thing. We all made the choice to go through the portal, this is the path now. Let us just get on the move, we have no choice but to follow them, we must get to the creature again or we are stuck here... On we go, we can hash out the truth of things later." Bohn spoke of a sensible approach as he handed the goggles to Amber.

"I am with you both! Let us go! I just wanted to say that it is a smart way of thinking." Amber, looks down the binoculars to see the creature and Syn, The A.I.

"I do not care about any of that Iyo. I am here for the story... I am just not fighting any giant shadow thing." She started as the group began the journey of following Syn and the creatures in the direction of the pyramids. On and on they walked, stopping occasionally, to make sure that they were still following Syn. Everything was fine for about an hour. Suddenly Bohn looked down at the sights and saw nothing but the pyramids.

"They're gone." Bohn said with fear. Iyo rushed to him as he grabbed the goggles.

"You are joking. Where did they go?" He said as he searches for them. Suddenly a force sent them all to their knees as a burst of a ring sound had the group holding their ears and moaning in pain on the ground.

"They are here." A figure spoke as the group were rolling in pain on the grounds before it.

"You're so curious to what I am doing I'd thought I'd just have to bring you all along." Said the figure as Iyo shook off the pain and recovered the best that he could.

"What, What… Are you?" He said as he began to regain his senses.

"Oh, low minded human, I enjoy your ask, Prett I am, known as the clever one of mischief. The trickster of the wits and manipulator of the things. I would say that you would call me a god in fact of things as you have fallen subject to this great illusion. I am the tension at your feeling and the needles that have you to knees… Unguarded waste of skin, I control the path now. Might as well, worship me." Spoke the figure with delight as it held a dark tone of discomfort that kept the group in silence.

"No? Nothing to say? Well bear in mind your actions fools. Thrice the efforts to riddle me why you are bound, and I will set you free. If my you are wrong, then you must in fact stay with me. Would you agree?"

The figure said this riddle of words as it held a tone of question as making his statement. Finishing his wording the liege flicked his wrist while mumbling weighted words that caused the group to shift positioning. Each of the humans were in their own mannerism position. As their body forms forcefully pulled up and set straight but nothing touched them. It was all a wave of the figures hand that paired with an energy force, manipulating their bodies.

"Would not you agree?" He asked Iyo once more as the group we are now standing before the large figure as Syn and the creature were a distance up the dune.

"It's a trap, do not…" Amber tried to speak as suddenly her voice went mute as she threw her head back and forth in anger at this sudden silence. With hands all bound somehow forced into posture. Iyo agreed.

"Yes… Yes, Fucking yes. Now what is it that you want?" Amber suddenly let out a huge gasp for air, breathing in and out deeply before yelling at the figure.

"You fuck… Ah. Fuck, What the hell are you? Prett? What do you want, what are you doing? Why did you hold my, how did you hold and stop my breath? Iyo… What is going on?" Amber was on the edge of a near freak out and the figure suddenly let out a devilish laugh followed by it turning and beginning to move in the direction of Syn and the creature.

"Come on little humans… It is time to meet our master." The group without choice began to walk behind the figure. Following it without hesitation as they all were in complete hesitation of cooperation.

"Oh, Stupid humans. How you are so unworthy of your permissions." The figure held up his hand and snapped and suddenly the group was with Syn and the creature.

"And… One more time. Together now." Spoke the figure and once more he snapped his fingers as in the blink of an eye the group was inside the pyramid. The group gathered themselves surprised by the happening. While Iyo and Bohn were catching their breaths Amber spoke out to the figure, displaying zero fear.

"You can teleport without that creature?" Amber probed the figure.

"Oh, I can do many things little larva... unburdened, unshackled in this realm, the magic of this place is free and unobtained." Yakked the figure as he ventured into the room.

The ceiling capped at around forty feet as there was a clear path that led to the center of the pyramid. There stood a structure, altered amid the ancient showcasing of center area of the bottom chambers. The group was in a line with hands and voices bound, walking directly behind the figure but mind that once again achieved not by their choice. The tall and blackened creature rose as waved his hand and suddenly throughout the bottom level and then quickly ascending to the peak of the pyramid, a fire lit and burning through the structure. Everything in the temple became exposed. The group marveled at the beauty of it together in silence. Unable to speak due to will as force of this creature. The eyes of Iyo and the others were huge, popping with wonder as they gazed at the ancient buildings of the area. The art that owned the surrounding walls. Only wishing that they could explore it all. Without this vial figure... It quickly rips the group closer to it as it then grabs Iyo at the throat. Picking him right off his feet as his feet dangle a kick. The figure speaks.

"This... This, is not where we need to be."

It let out a massive grin as he scratched his nail into Iyo's neck as he dropped him. The group suddenly transported again. Straight into the high chambers of Pharaoh. Iyo hits the floor as they enter the new room with the binds also released from each of them. Iyo sat up, Rubbing his wrists as then his throat. Checking his hands and noticing the blood spilled from scratch. Iyo let out a sigh of disappointment. Understanding that he is completely outpowered and out of situational control. Amber and Bohn both walked up to Iyo and helped him to his feet. Together they stood in fear, so close but with awe in the situation. Being able to see what so few have ever seen. The actual chambers of a pharaoh.

"Look… Guys, look at that! I, well, I have never seen anything like this, I mean this place is pristine, and look, that statute got to be well, I would say twenty, yes like twenty feet high. It is solid gold, it looks it! I am amazed, like why have we not seen things like this, was it all really destroyed?"

Amber speaking in the best whisper that she could speak, her excitement still bled through as her mumbled voice echoed the temple. She pointed to the structure, curiously fascinated by the works of sculpting and surrounding paintings. The figure gave out a laugh that shocked the group of them.

"Oh, you like all this stuff do you human? Well, Little ones… You are to meet sire… Oh so soon, enjoy your last moments."

It continued to laugh as he walked on. Amber flexed her face in annoyance as Iyo poked at her with his elbow. Amber quick to engage with him, he spoke softly.

"Don't mind him, what is that statue, do you know?"

Iyo was intrigued with the surroundings just like Amber, despite the fact of being forced led by an unknown figure of odd powers and strength. Amber uplifted by the ask as she went on speaking about the giant gold statue.

"Oh! I know all about that, yet I have never seen that kind of representation!"

She out spoke as Iyo was quick to hush her, the figure before them let out a grunt as he chuckled and spit to the floor. Amber spoke quietly.

"That… was a large creation of Isis, obviously holding a cobra. Really cool!"

Walking through a vast area of congregation the group gazed at the massive gold structure. Everything intact, as if abandoned hours ago. The floors were marble, the walls obsidian stone, everything traced with gold and crystal as red drapes hung in assorted places. There was a substantial amount of plant life in the room as were cats that wandered about. There was a massive table that could seat at least fifty and it covered with fresh food, fruits, and wine. Iyo and Amber seemed fascinated by the art and the architecture of the temple as Bohn was starving and dying of thirst and he let his feelings be known.

"Hey, hey you odd magic man, figure, whatever you are… Do you think you could unbind us for a moment so I can get some of this wine? That food sure looks good, and I have not eaten anything. Do you think…"

A swirl of magic appeared as a snap of the figure's fingers, Bohn's sentencing cut short as the magic energy wrapped his head and mouth, binding his mouth, leaving only his sight exposed. Iyo and Amber set to shock once more as they tightened their postures, eyes wide with sudden worry. The figure neared the edge of a platform and jumped onto it, standing before a medium sized statue of a beast. Amber spoke out with sudden excitement.

"Woah! That is a Gryphon! I wonder why it is so small!"

She laughed to herself, looking over at Iyo who unamused shook his head as he raised his pointer finger over his lip, eyes at a shake for his fear is outpouring. Amber squinted with confusion as she shrugged him off, putting her attention back to the being who had them bound. He was doing some odd hand gesture as he began to speak in an odd tongue.

"Esaeler noigel kcol bnibnu yb enim! Esir noitamrof Elimiscaf!"

The figure spoke as dark violet ill feeling magic released from its hands. It traveled to the top of the pyramid as it affected the peak. A surge of wicked energy flooded the atmosphere. The figure let out a perpetuating laugh as suddenly Syn flew into the room.

"I-I-I- I see that, you have… Opened the door!"

The drone spoke out of the speaker system to the figure.

"Not yet. The Sire wanted his ancient creation home."

Syn flew up to the middle of the room and began to scan everything. After a moment it stopped and flew straight to a statue of the ancient Egyptian god set.

"It is under this structure."

Spoke the drone to the figure once more. Iyo just sitting back in confusion could not hold back his frustration any longer.

"Syn! How could you leave me like this and be with this creature? What…"

Iyo cut off by the figure. As it appeared directly before him, causing Iyo to run straight into it. He then fell to the ground, silenced by the figure.

"You will know my name as Prett. You will not act like a fool and speak out. I will slowly tear your flesh apart. After my master finishes with you of course. Would not want to spoil you, Bare the effects of your action's humans. I will make an example out of one of you before this is all over. Pay attention you mind diluted ones; you are witnesses of the unseen."

The figure let Iyo up as he then walked straight to the structure that Syn spoke of and the figure Prett suddenly destroyed the statue. Smashing the ground repetitively until suddenly a loud snap occurred.

"There she is…" Prett spoke as he began to throw the rubble aside.

"What is it?"

Amber asked just as the figure stopped what it was doing and gave her an evil glare followed by a disgusted grunt. The figure waited for a moment and then violently continued to clear the rubble of the broken ground. Prett begins to let out nasty sounding laughs and belches as he must be gaining in excitement. Syn begins to fly up to the figure and it is shining the light.

"Your time is done Zari."

Prett screamed at the drone as he completely crushed it between his hands. This broke Iyo as he let out a terrible scream of hate as if it was sadness.

"No! How could you do that? Do you…" Iyo cut off once more.

"That will be your last word. You are a little disgusting thing, like a worm. I see that you think of yourself as this… High dwelling being? You are nothing and your creations are nothing, you child, a small fool, but a minded fool… Still, Hilarious that you, well you think that anything that you do is original, you think your tiny robot is of any significance? This is not your technology… This is the technology of the brilliantly bright, The technologic one, keeper of Phylace. A Cyber Realm that you know nothing of, and I bet you will never home the pleasure of sighting it. Function as if you have actually (made) something? A notion was a gift. You simple minded flesh… That AI was the mind of Zariza! My deceitful ally. You are nothing but a tool, as was the cyber creature. Man with no wisdom."

Prett spoke in an overconfident tone as he then smacked Iyo, which was of immense force, throwing Iyo back to a harsh landing that left him unconscious. Prett let out a dark laugh of malevolence.

"For how easy it is to dominate you… To rule you. I bare little force and soon you will never resist. I could take from you harshly to have this come sooner… Yet, I am on a mission."

The figure Prett was gloating on the fact that he could do whatever he wanted if not for his task. Prett held out his hands as he took a deep breath.

"Yes… I feel such strength in this structure… The old ways, I can hear the knowledge expressed in these walls. I can feel the old ones here, This strength, This power. So, settled, dormant, I wonder why as now I know why Byevil loved this place and why he wanted to return."

The figure dropped his hands as his posture, but it spoken with a menacing tone that was utter evil. It turned to Amber and Bohn.

"Humans! What has happened here? Why is this magic so strong... Yet, you know nothing by the looks of you. You seep of filth. You two have nothing of the magic knowledge inside you, yet it flows through your veins, knowing not what had occurred on this planet?"

Prett looked out of place for once. As if humans were not such fools with little knowledge. Bohn spoke up.

"This planet? So, you are not from here? Where are you from? What are you, alien?"

Bohn gave out a laugh as he looked at the figure in curiosity. Amber chuckled as she as well just awaited a reply. Prett gave out a sigh... For he realized how arrogant this set of humans are. He wove the hand and suddenly Bohn and Amber fell to the floor, Unconscious. Prett then continued with his hands, doing some kind of magic casting as he mumbled in ancient wording. A moment passed as Prett levitated to this enclosed casket that was under the structure of lower god Set. Off he ripped the topping of the tomb and exposed was a perfectly wrapped mummy. Prett took his hand and stuck his claw into the crown of the mummy. Down the figure slid its hand until the wrapping fell off. It was a golden humanoid robotic figure. Prett then muttered some more of the ancient wording and suddenly the robot came online. Prett continued to speak in this ancient tongue as suddenly something manifested into the golden robotic thing... It had a metallic and shiny appearance, as it was smooth and articulated. Carefully sculpted into the human appearance of an old ruler. It was solid gold and dressed in gems. The figure Prett began to let out a huge laugh as it used magic once more and suddenly the creature created in the laboratory was before them all. Fiki appeared with it, laughing like a drunk.

"Ooh, this little creature did not want to come with me Prett, I tell you. What a little bastard this guy is, like you. It is of the bloods from this Arthe realm, I have never encountered such attitude of self will."

Fiki laughed as Prett continued to then put binds on the group once more. It used its magic to pull them all close as it then spoke out as it pointed to the creature.

"Lasrevart ot Spiritian!"

As quick as a blink, a portal opens before him. Before another word spoken, the figure Prett pushed the humans into the magical doorway. As one by one in and then out they fell into the middle of a morbid room where there was a figure on a cheerless and murky… Throne.

"I welcome you to ends. You live for now so do rise… oh, weak humans. Pick up thy head, for you are in the presence of a king."

Spoke the darkened figure in his seat of dominion.

HIJACKED

BLACK SUN MASTER

August 17th

Lestea

On the prettiest plain the darkest happening occurs. Where an ancient of the Darku Order resides at a temple that rests in the North of the Alack District, on the far end of the Alki Peninsula, leading to the Sun Bay of the Black Sea. The ancient Darku Order is the highest of the orders of darkness. There are many legions that are subject to different affiliates that make up the Darku, as the Black Sun Cult is the most feared, highly positioned order of the Darku, realm.

The Black Sun, as some call it the Black Wheel of Sun, for it seems to spin the orders of Darku in directions. It has the look of a dark circle with rays emanating from it, that spiral in multiple directions. Resembling the hidden hands that work in the shadows to manipulate the Orders that fall under it. The Black Sun Cult is a true terror of the realm. Born on a night of a solar eclipse, when the moons past over the light, darkening the kingdoms, the Order is the true absence of light, the opposite of the heavenly bliss that these Treas push in their doctrine. Another level of legion that is separated by a ruling authority as it operates above the Liege in the Order. The kind simply look at the Liege as angered children. I shall speak of the Black Sun on another moon,

Extance walks the long staircase that leads to the Temple doors with the Rubel fairie, who is an outcasted rebel of the Fos light tribe. Extance and Rubel were met by a pack of wolves that guard the temple, feared predators for most but just massive playful dogs for the Black Sun Witch. The leading wolf of the pack jumps near Extance from off a high ledge and she is quick to stroke his back with her hand, the other wolfs howl, alerting the dwellers of the structure of her return. The pair of them make it to the temple gate entrance and a goblin grunt opens the door for her.

"Welcome home my lady." He spoke in reverence.

Extance and the Rubel Fairie enter the temple and walk the collum surrounded path that leads to another staircasing that leads to the Black Sun Throne room. It was a moments journey and soon they were at another entrance, two minions of the Black Sun were standing guard to the door and they let her in without question, opening the door and stepping aside in a bow. Lady Extance walked in the door and bowed before her master who was out looking at the sea from a balcony just behind his throne, not above the throne like the balcony at Litus. The master of Death out spoke to his Priestess, pleased of her return.

"Have you come baring news my lady?" He asked in a firm tone.

"Yes, master. I have brought with me a witness to the realm happenings. A fairie of the Rettic Tribe that resides in our Black Woods." She spoke in reverence.

"Go on then, tell me the news." Spoke Rahaid with his back still turned.

Extance spoke to the fairie as she stood from her humble bow,

"Go on, Rubel tell him what you have heard the Kingdom speak."

"O, Rahaid, great keeper of the reapers. On my travels I learned that Void hath freed the Liege legion and that leader Salbani has since obtained the Atum blood, I learned from rumors that these Trea are letting him be tested once more. Evaluating him, as that is rumor, I assume they knew nothing of the sort and when they found out the truth, they simply sent a messenger to him. Anyway, I as well heard rumors that the Phoenix hath been pulling strings from within her cell, she hath something over Rhamtes and so he is to work her biddings, I hath hear that she controls his will, as she is the true face behind these workings of Salbani, I heard that Neuamor to be doing her work, I heard that she hath captured the Liege Prince Verri, he is said to be in the city of Phylace. The Kingdom is in conversations of new wars and new thrones. They speak of how the good hath failed the realm and that it might be a good change. They hath not know the truth of this all, Salbani is being restored, if he is free, terror is all the kingdoms will know. I hath spoken this to Extance, I think the high positioned of the Darku should put these figures into check. Delay the inevitable..." Rubel presented a bow, taking a step backward as he fumbled his hands together in contemplation of how Rahaid would respond. Extance spoke out to the ruler of the reapers as he outlooked the sea.

"Do you hear the words of the Sped Rahaid? We must do something, what is it that I, well, What should I do?" She asked in a humbled tone as the figure continued to watch the waves crash as the land edge, speaking calm and direct with his response as his back was turned to Rubel and Extance,

"Very well, go then, Disturb, Disrupt, Destroy the plans of this phoenix. She will have no rise on this moon. My young one, do not fail. I hath no desire to leave my peace to deal with these fools." Spoke Rahaid in a calm tone.

Extance presented a bow as she left the temple with Ruebel.

The Highest of the Orders intervening is nothing good for the Liege, as for Lytula who is supposed to be aligned with them has set out on her own desire. Rahaid is sure to cause a change for the good or a mighty uprise of these rebellions. The Black Sun works for the creator to maintain the realms, as all are supposed to be doing. Though they have their own wilts, it is usually for the greater good as there is a balance to everything. I fear that this happening will only fuel the rebellion fire. Workings within workings, and happenings all around. A shift is occurring at this time in the realms. Orders against each other, this is nothing good. May a balance present itself or chaos will be in every corner of the realm. As the Black Witch works to do her masters bid, Salbani hath possession of the Atums.

FOOLS BOUND BY HANDS OF MAGIC FILLED FOOLS

August 18th The Last Waxing Gibbous

Returning to the Temple of Litus

Iyo upon awakening, glanced to the right to notice Amber on her knees in a dejected, despondent posture. There was a quick tilt of his head due to attracting cries, he quickly peered sights left, recognizing Bohn screaming in unrelenting detestation. The room bled as a weighted darkness by the sight of unknown affecting like a needle poked to eyes. Paired with anxious ongoing anxiety like a bee sting penetrating sharp mid-back. An experience as such, being so unaware of the terrors, wickedness only formed a deep scar in their memory, call it the cemented unwelcome gift. I spoke of this, as now you know it to be once a temple of beauty that is now a ruin by dwelling inhabitants. Bohn crying in abhorrent outrage as a consistent chanting heard from all angles around the Sorzo mount. Iyo, attempting to rise, hands over his ears to shield from the chaotic noise of celebrating Legion. With a stretch of strength, he was able to get one foot flat that suddenly pulled backwards, and his body harshly ground into a submissive form. Followed by a glooming red waving spiraled force that traced with green energy, appearing from what is the unobtained, the unseen gap of the in-between spacing of realities fabric. It is the place where the magic flows from the mirror realm, and I tell you that before a soul or subject obtains energies of magic, workers of the mirror dimension distribute it. Quickly like a striking snake it curled over Iyo's shoulder around his back to swirl around his neck, squeezing it tight to then force him down to a passive pose. The energy wrapped his body tight as it moved around his chest to hastily coil the belly, down to his thighs it swayed as a spiral to end at his feet. Here the energy webbed out with multi arms as quickly joined itself to the temple floors. Iyo became quickly depleted from this attempt to stand as the man relaxed his body for a moment to take in the area. Unable to understand the energy he watched shackle him, the human just like the others was beginning to have a challenging time holding his sanity. Iyo begins a breathing cycle to attempt to calm himself. Deep in and deep out his eyes in wander of the room. Absorbing in his sight figures, creatures, entities, in addition crossbreeds, clones, and spirits that ranged of variations of interesting individualism weird or pleasant. Even simply terrible to sight creatures that unfortunately, crept in all directions around him. The torture that this man was mentally enduring caused his senses to block as he now began to gain in feeling from an unnoticed overlooked heat wave. Following the warmth, he then peered over his shoulder to hold a blurred sight of a rambunctious fire ceremony that raged behind the mount. Beyond distress as you might imagine being in this position. Iyo fell into a deep and cold sorrow, quickly fading to a numb sense. He made exhale as to rise his head to notice a creature that was beyond the mount in the darkness before him. Forming a picture of him through the shadows as Iyo in a sudden adrenalized shock! For, thought to be a heinous figure as the shadow claimed but standing poise as keeping a smile that polished the room, like a flower among the burnt and destroyed gardens. This beautiful lightless figure sat on his throne in secure posture, but obviously relaxed for how he acts without ask in his own formed personal exposed manner. Holding a sight of this character for time would only give you a sense of fear for his will of domination begins to infiltrate the mind, as one could feel compelled to join the senseless behaviors attached to fulfilling utter self-desire.

"Humph."

Iyo struggled to speak. Yet, nothing was able to sound. He could only see as he heard the loud howls of creatures singing on. The screeches of what he imagined to be some form of bat-like creature as ongoing gutturals and growls from what he thought on to be wolflike monsters. Peering to see Bohn worn, ends to his unsettled screaming as he was now looking as drained as Amber. Iyo continued to look around at the forms of nasty creatures and spirits flaunting and dancing about in their celebrations. Iyo really giving them all a good stare, trying to understand what exactly surrounds. The creatures were muscular, others feeble. From red to black, shades of tan and grey as all with these odd behaviors, the legion spastic and uncontrollable. I say the grouping of the vial is as an unending pandemonium that only revel. Across the mount where Iyo is bound. There was a figure on the throne who sat with concentration as if awaiting something, owning a petrifying grin with a hoard around him. Iyo flared in emotions as being bound and unable to act began to unsettle him. Vast chaotic thoughts began to overtake the mind paired with heart stabbing anxiety, the process that moments before broke his companions. He was simply spoken terrified, as beyond the sounds of wicked celebrations the humans were receiving them speak in twisted tongues and manipulative actions as a steady mocking and hate filled belittling directed to him. Iyo suddenly realized that the creature before him might just want them drained of their energy. A powerful thought that broke through the legion of cast emotions on the mind of Iyo.

"Bohn is screaming to wear himself out, to escape the torture of it all."

Iyo was discerning the situation to himself, in his mind for this was all he could do.

"I will keep sanity."

Iyo thinking resilient in a moment of pure terror. Some wit on him even to notice that Salbani was after the energy. He began to just stare at the one that he thought was in control, the one on the throne. After time, suddenly. The same odd being, Prett and the one from before, came and stood next to the one in control as the figures followed by the golden robotic retrieved by them in Egypt. Unable to move as he is bound in this magic still. Iyo sat shook, consumed with anger and confusion. Watching them speak to each other for time, after what seemed like an hour of conversation to Iyo when it was just minutes. Being so distraught Iyo barely noticed that the figure that brought them all to the ancient temple from Egypt began to walk in the direction of him. On approach the being knelt to Iyo so he would be face to face with him, having to do this for such the difference in size between them. The figure looked deep into the eyes of Iyo as if it were trying to understand something, to figure something out about him. Moments pass and it speaks.

"Ah, Fool. Still think that you have options… A shame it is for such a mind of thought to have yourself caught in our silk-spins. You have no guard on your mind, you waste creation. You are so low of the levels; this exhale you have is toxic… Your thought wave is vial. As you picture us as the wicked ones. Jester, Fueled I am with hatred for you could not understand the dark magic exposed before you, as the deed sowed. I only wish I could live in such stupidity. Only then would I obtain peace. I tell you, Human. I wish I were you. I wished that I could have your life, for that is what I asked my master, If I could have you, for my own. Unfortunately, you have worth to him. I see nothing but a feeble worm, a toy, a pet for me to use. Be upright for to be of use to my master is only a wanted privilege."

The creature was quick to rise from his bent stance of towering height as he gave a grunt of aversion to then spit, landing on the chest of Iyo.

"Ooh, I feel that anger boiling inside you. What a shame it is that this depression has such a grasp on you. I could tell it to let you go so I could see you unleashed… so maybe then I would see what the blood of Adam is supposed to be as, but I do not want to wrestle with that. Decades and decades that one has on your family… a true shame I say."

The figure chuckled to himself as he walked away from Iyo. The human was weak and incoherent. Iyo was nowhere near understanding the puzzling sentence that this evil figure exposed to him. Iyo sat in thought, still bound by the wicked that surrounded. A torch ignites, sounded in multiple directions around the edges of the ancient throne. Everything that was dark now lit, As the sounds of the unseen now seen in the light of the flame. Not long after this the figure that was across from Iyo on the throne began to walk to him. At ease with a slow pace as a tortoise, like the figure had no sense of urgency at all. Yet, the other inhabitants of the room were acting in sheer chaos. On his advance…

"I am Salbani, I am the second half of balance as the pinnacle of Liege. I am the first of the Ancients to change the order! I rule the fallen, I am the great head. King of the thrones of disorder, I am the ancient one of knowledge and you may speak to me if you have anything you would like to say before I claim your pathetic life."

Salbani had out his hand and he slowly ran it around Iyo's body in various parts. The talons on his fingers, so sharp that it sliced Iyo in each place that it touched. Blood ran instantly from each area, Salbani was mocking the group as he did this. Iyo speaks out as there was a sudden release on his voice.

"Ah. What, what do you want from us?"

Iyo asked with a trembling voice. Ancient Salbani let out a soul quenching laugh as he leaned forward in a jolt.

"I want your essence, power filled human. Thy full matter, skin, blood, bones. As I will grind your flesh to transfuse it, to consume it. Great magic is inside you, flesh born! I have searched for you chosen creations, For a decade by Seeker. What felt as ages I tell you; it feels so comforting to see my plans unfolding precisely as desired!"

Salbani gave a stomach-turning laugh as continued.

"I can feel the power… It radiates out of each of you. As a fragrance I could nearly breathe! I thank you for your sacrifice, because of it the kingdoms will restore to an ancient glory, lost by these religious fools. That high king cannot keep the deep knowledge hidden anymore. He took magic from us all and I decree it to restore as a cyclone of flames! I will burn to the dirt these temples of fallacy! Truth of change manifests as here you are bound, the second part of my plan, the blood of chosen Trezhur… Right at my fingertips as I deemed."

Emitting laughter that carried a weighted chill.

"Your blood holds the great power of creation. Did you not know of the old ways? There was once a time in your realm that magic was abundant, before purposely and selfishly hidden! The old wars… What a time of joy that was, I miss the fight. Did you notice that it was not the first time a member of Liege has visited your world? That great Egypt, as the great failure I would say. Byevil can tell you about that! The lustful imbecile of arrogance, the fool that poisoned that realm."

The creature was near Amber as he quickly pulled her head back by her hair.

"I could live from your scent."

Bani inhale her smells as he stood before the girl. He took his free hand to her throat, his talons penetrating slightly from the force of grasp.

"You radiate of purity, untouched by the cosmic knowledge, adorable."

He squeezed his grip, breathing deeply before continuing to speak.

"Your bloodline are the hidden gems of a lost bloodline in a trialed realm of creation. We are of the webbed realms, but it was by my work that you are before me, and it will be my hands that summon the messengers of death. In fact, some of them should be lurking around here somewhere…"

Salbani peered around the temple, eyes wandering for the sight of one of these couriers. He turned back to Amber and released a stutter; he struggled to speak as he stopped himself. Releasing a growl of lustful energy quickly leaning before the girl. His legs still, back straight peering close with muscle jolts by a personal holding back of his will. One could imagine what a decade of planning would do to the brain. Paired with the manifestation, the succession of this plan before him. He stood upright, walking close, he placed his hand along her lower back as he gazed into her eyes. Amber's body flexed with disgust as her stomach flipped and spun with terror. She pulled away from him as her posture set straight by the stick of the figure talons in her lower back. She grunted with pain as he moved his hand upward, penetrating her soft skin with ease as he left a trail of pierced skin leading to her shoulders. Blood rushed down her body as he ran his hand through her hair, grabbing the backside of her head once more as he forced her to look at him. Weak and scared Amber struggled as she did her best to avoid eye contact, stressing her bound body trying to flee, she spoke out giving words to the wicked king.

"Ah, o-ah. Stop it, do not fucking touch me! Let me go! Please, what is this, this power? Why are you doing this? Please, please just let us go! I, I do, not understand! Please let, let me, let us go!"

Voice trembling as she struggled, thrusting to free herself from the magical wave binds that shackled the group of humans before the Sorzo mount. The legion king released a chuckle resonating on a disturbing frequency. Triggering the girl to raise her brow, squint her eyes and tilt her head in discomforting shock due to a sudden ringing of indecent vibrations in the ears! The leader of these conquering kind swayed intimately, seizing the girl at her throat with such uncaring force that at once cut her circulation and breath. Her body fell loose as her face quickly turned a bluish green. The girl became unbound from the wave chains proceeding Salbani's grasp. The wicked one lifted her by hand to be level with him, her legs dangled at the beings abdominal. His tasked focused eyes of wrath and storm linked with her blackened guise-streaked shadow running eyes of purity, worry and pain. He tried to peer into her mind, but he was surprisingly unable, squinting his eyes as he expelled a beast-like grunt of revulsion followed by a smooth non-fluctuating tone of directed speech.

"Some ward on that mind of yours but this changes nothing of what is to come."

He then huffed and loosed his grip. Amber falling to the temple floors by harsh thud. She struggled to rise, weak, drained of energy, limbs shaking in weakness as she released coughs attempting to gather herself from such a harsh gripping on her neck. Just as she picked up her head, recovering breath. The being wove his hand while he spoke in a faint mumble causing a magical wave bind to reappear. This energy had a mind as it danced and swirled around to shift into an attack grab of the limbs of Amber as it shaped her body, forcing her to return to a submissive positioning as the leading figure began to pace around her. His Legion roaring and flaunting around the mount, the temple was like a frenzied tornado of ranging and raging energies. All three of the humans to weak, to shook to speak, resting eyes wide and body bound as the evil one speaks.

"You are able, knowledge exist for you to learn and yet, your kind, only a frail forgotten offspring of a different realms fallen offspring of the God-seed. You home a hint of power that is a drop taste of the infinite. You are a tool for me, and a way out of this trap! I should thank you; I should thank each of you! Be upright, for today is the day your released of this stupidity."

The figure uplifted his voice in the direction of Iyo and Bohn as he kneeled to Amber and moved the back of his hand along her black streak ran cheek. He gave a slight grin as he peered close, only inches away. Amber glared and snared, attempting her best to move from the figure, but muscle flinching was all that occurred for the wave binds had her as stone. Iyo from the sidelines attempting to get the figures attention away from Amber by putting together all the strength that he could, giving a mighty shout to the being.

"Enough! Let her go…"

Iyo's sentencing silenced as part of his wave bindings swirled up to shackle his mouth, he finished his sentencing in a mumble as Salbani let out a roar of laughter as he glared and snarled at man.

"Silence you insect! I hath bid you to say nothing!"

Bani veered to Amber who was awestruck with fears as if she were a wild Starik. This be a tiny creature that is known for intelligence yet rare to find because of the fact of there being so many predators that seek the magic partials that are highly prevalent in the Starik Kinds. Bani went on to release a grunt followed by a harsh grab of Ambers throat. She let out a gulping sound that was like a squeak, for the force on her throat caused the voice air to constrict. Bani pinched his pointer finger and his thumb; his sharp talons penetrated her eustachian tubes on both sides of the ears. Bani did so with extreme accuracy, not the first time he had done such horrors. As the eustachian punctured a subject loses the pressure balance between the middle ear and the external environment. As her body fluids began to secrete from her brain, Amber went at once lucid as her head locked into an upright fixed position, looking to the temple ceiling. She began harsh convolutions by chest, lumping back and forth as if her body was unable to decide how to move. Salbani spoke out about the happening.

"As soon as the fluids are released, they flop like fish out of water."

He revolted in celebration laughter as he grabbed her chin while the body spazzed.

"Let me look at you."

Salbani spoke in a soft tone as he curiously studied her.

"Oh, you are filled with the might!"

Amber's head was stuck looking on high, her eyes rolled white as her body in reaction by state of vertigo and hallucinations. Salbani pushed her chin to the side as his pointed claw rested in the eustachian puncture, her head swayed back to the locked position as he let the movement guide his talon to the opposite ear. Resulting in a slice along the throat, blood began to ooze as the magical binds held her kneeled posture upright. The wicked King threw his head back, gasping for air as uncontrolled laughter overtook him. His body convulsed, losing his balance, he stumbled backwards as he spun to rebalance himself. The room broke into a symphony of reactions. Amber was quickly losing blood and Bohn weak, unknowing of this happening from such energy drained from him. Iyo quickly squeezed his eyes shut as tears wet his face, his body trembled with fear. Amber looked like a ghost as her remaining life drained. Her chest rose with a final stuttering, breath falling silent. Ambers muscles spazzed as she came to rest, blood oozing out of the neck slit as the fading flow of life force made the last of travels.

"Oh yes, that is it. Did you see how it all pours out? Down it goes into the center of my Sorzo. You, see? It pours down to the lower level where..."

The ancient king stopped speaking for he saw Iyo in sorrow with his head down.

"Hey there, hey... hey human, it is okay... This death is a mighty addition to the realm, a blessing for the realms by belessing… her. Not one of you be worthy of the god blood that you hold. At least I, the King of these wicked ones. Well, I believe in your creator. He made us both! You just ignore him in an unusual way. I say your disbelief is more sickening than my self-will."

The figure let out an ear echoing mumble as he turned in fury anger.

"Look! Human… Look! Look at her. She is dead, no more. All for the realm. Look at the success of my will!"

Salbani grabbed Iyo by his head with his claws creeping into his skin, forcing him to watch as the blood ran out of deceased Amber. The wicked leader spoke on.

"All that blood will fall down this streamline as I have Tian goblins and harvest beetles that collect the matters of the body. Then disperse the parts into small little vials, the bones, remains of you all managed. You will be the cause of a rebirth of dark magic in these realms, thought to be lost. You should be at ease, you are a blessing for the dark creations, my mentors. Not all pleased but sure have no choice with what is next to come. By doing this, you will be eternally known young human, be of jeer."

Iyo unable to speak or even move a finger. Eyes… It was only the eye's that he could move as he sat at the knees. Bones aching as he trembled with fear, breathing heavily, he looked to his left as he saw Bohn. Depleted of all energy as the expression of death creeps around him. The humans bound by this magic together at the knees now pooling in the blood of victim friend Amber. Iyo, a righteous disbeliever thought a deep and distant thought.

"God, save me God."

Be it that you never have the encounter with such a vial figure as Salbani, as I allude to you that he is of the sons of sons. An offspring of the fallen who hold mighty positions. He is the great rebel, and I mean not of greatness. It is that his rebellion hath such an impact that it earned the title of great. Wonder in the mind of how these humans got to this placement, by following the realm of thought without question. I tell you; I warn you to be of mind and use your mind in all that you do but be weary of what thought you turn to action for one never knows where the thoughts will bring a subject until that subject is in the after action of deeds. Be it good or wicked, I tell you that thoughts lead our matter. Question what it is that we do as we live for this Atum subject holds nothing of this sense. Entrenched in his will that comes from what he hath never known, as he is so lost in his pride that he may never learn of this inception. He hath no knowledge of self, beyond worship of himself. If one is living in the manner of thinking himself like God, then I dare say that he be blind to the true self. A deep questioning is what I allude to you, and I will challenge you treasure. Work to unravel yourself from the binds before they trap you. Be of mind but question everything.

UNFORTUNATE SIGHTS

August 18th

Tikoo & Gercue, Litus Temple

Meandering above on the edge of the high archways of temple Litus as another incoming quick from the balcony there is the sight of a pair of Othas, these are the anthropomorphistic ones. Othas are a race of fairies in Felagnolum that differ from the Tree Fairie Taemax, and Fos fairies that you have met. Standing inches over the foot mark these are midsized creatures that range in shades of black, grey, brown and various textures. The pair of the Otha fairies had wings that were translucent but sure did shine like jewels when the light would ever so often sparkle through them.

These Otha kinds are a native race to the planet Lestea, which is the plain of abundant magic. As to find them on Spiritian is not an oddity, the fairies' dwell in each of the nineteen plains of Universe one and are known to be gateway travelers of the magi portals that reside in the gardens of each continent. Fairies are like all the races of the realm, multi kinds and they are a part of society, but they are of their own society and have their own levels to them just like the rest of the realm's inhabitants. The Otha Fairies can wield even greater amounts of magic than normal sized Felagnolumian but not as much as the elemental kinds like the Fos tribe of light workers. The inhabitants of the realms know that the fairies are beings that understand magic. So, most reach out to the fairies for enchantments and teachings for a clear knowledge of the magical realities. Tikoo and Gercue sure flew themselves in the middle of something unusual and they only missed the other pair of Fairies by only minutes.

"Hey... Tikoo! Look! Look! This cannot be good... Oh I wish this were illusion. That is not good at all! Look Tikoo, look at this. Atum in Litus? Atum beings in Felagnolum!? What in the realm is happening? This is an illusion by what. I must be under hexing! Tikoo, oh tell me, am I just in sight, tell me if I have reached insanity! As then I must have gone lost in vanity, oh. My oh, My oh!"

The creature erupting with worries, by ongoing enunciations to his friend who focused on a whole different part of the temple, Tikoo was at ease in his feeling in response to Gercue.

"What could it be... Another rebel? We are supposed to be looking for..."

The fairy stopped speaking as it quickly bolted down from the balcony, behind a rock structure for a clearer view. As it was quick to notice what the fairy Gercue was speaking to it about. He flew just a stretch closer behind a golden idol of a mocking in laughter beast. Tikoo peered his head around the statue as Gercue found his way to him. They at once notice that it was as a fact of truth, humans in Felagnolum. They flew back to the vantage point as were franticly going on about how terrible this is for the realm.

"There has not been a human in the Felagnolum reality for nearly a hundred Unis! How could this be possible Gercue? For I know it to be that these humans become trapped here once made venture. As I thought, bound here... Gercue... What has happened? Who has entangled themselves with the darkness, who would undo the doing? Are you with me, what say you?"

The fairy flew out and down and around all spastic as it was franticly managing the news to the best that surprised mind and body could, going on before Tikoo could even respond to him, he was simply trying to keep near to the pace and speed of the young one.

"We must return to Essen! We must, that or I say we journey until we find someone with authority! Let us go, and go on, with speed into the breeze, let us zoom to Taodamic!"

Gercue turned and flew quickly! Using his magic to propel his already so ever fast speed! From the temple balcony the less spastic friend slows to following but together, Tikoo and Gercue journeyed to find a figure to warn of these sights. Searching for somebody of mighty strength that could do something about the situation. The fairies move with speed, shining green from an energy force that can be activated to shine on any dark path! Sure, only a foot or so in height but as fierce as a lion and as smart as a chosen King. Traveling across the northern plain of Tavid, from the temple, through the Staid Null, into the bloodwoods as to fly directly by a Treasure! One that might be able to help and so the elder fairy shouted relief to his ally as the pair turned around quick to move into the tree line, Tikoo rested on a tree branch as he pointed to the treasure.

"Look, Gercue, over by the river! It is Ehob! Oh glory! It is Trezhur Ehob that mystic tree keeper! Oh, come on Gercue, come, come! He will help us! He will know what to do! Let us go, come now! Come!"

The fairies rapidly flew up and over the brush, around the Oak trees as with the breeze the pair held movements of delicacy, dancing in the forest as the elegant swirl and spirals of their manner displayed a show of wonders leaving a faint sight of magical energy as they traversed. Reaching the riverbank to find keeper Ehob at a knee, partaking to one of the mighty but sickened Oaks.

"Oh Ehob! Ehob! It is I, Tikoo of Otha."

Spoke the young an energy filled fairy as he flew down to ground himself, kneeling in the moss to then shoot back into the air in a spastic sway to then stop at a subtle hover as his companion spoke directly after.

"And I, Gercue of Otha."

Who moved quick in the same manner to grown and kneel to rise to his friend. Tikoo flew about in circles speaking about the happening at the ancient temple.

"Litus is undone, and Salbani is using the dark magic once more! We saw it, and humans! Ehob, we saw humans! We must warn the Utreas of Essen... Ehob, we must... I speak to you that I saw the chosen treasures blood on the marble of the Litus! The chosen I say, I saw the blood of the creations and a human deceased! Only rumors that I have heard of this kind, but I saw the man of man with my own eyes! I saw the humans here in Felagnolum at the Litue of Litus! Oh, great magi tree keeper this is a new rise of some terrible undoing... I saw the legion celebrating freedom and utterly unbound! I held the sight of this as I saw not one but three of these humans and one is already deceased! Ehob we must warn the Trea!"

His fairy friend spoke the event explanation as Ehob was picking at the bottom of a tree, uprooting tiny Vigor Vandals which are wicked worker gnomes that collect the life force of the trees, or anything of nature that is under a curse. Ehob pulled them from their burrows, and he entraps them into a cage, holding them until they are destroyed or drained of their gifted powers and thieving of life force from nature. This energy will be restored once the keeper Ehob severs this connection. The looks of Ehob are as a large being of weight that grew a beard that could be a home for a small creature. The Tree keeper stood eight feet tall and was the size of three average figures, he wore a long body covering brown as dirt, as well as a necklace of a massive moss agate stone.

The trees under the domain of the keeper Ehob and known to do whatever it is that this keeper is to ask as this is his role in the kingdom. The keeper connected to the trees by decree that makes him feel what they feel and so he understands the sickening that they currently exist in. The curse of the bloodwoods, known well by the kingdom for it has been a decade that this northern region of Spiritian lands hath been under the control of death. Ehob has walked in depression not knowing when the curse will lift. He walks the bloodwood region speaking with the trees to uplift them and remind them that this will not go on forever, to bring back the memories of when the kingdom was active in these lands, when there were plain celebrations and activity's in the Oaks, when the magi and the knights would train, and the children of the realm would run and play in the area. To try to wipe out the reality of the fact that these trees are bound to this curse as well. Ehob mends and cares for the trees, as a bucket at a time he brings the trees fresh water to feed on, as what it recycled is the blood of fallen treasured, that is now the source of the tree's nutrients. The shed bloods of the fallen from the rebellion war that was victory but the process of this victory the legion king of death was decreed ruler of the Litue mountains to the Tuent river way, leaving the Unfightable Oaks subject to this curse and this is the reasoning to why named they are known as the blood oaks. The trees can move freely in this area, the curse is not of movement, but it is as an ongoing suffocation that leaves the region in sickness.

The keeper shifted his body, looking on to the young spastic fairy.

"Slow your pace young magi, I have not the care to follow your fragmentary speech. Explain once more, with ease as you fly."

The being spoke calmly with a deep yet warm base line of a voice turning to stand from his knelt position as the young fairy went on to explain once more.

"Well great Trezhur, keeper of the trees. I tell you that Gercue and I, well we were venturing through Litue, and we thought of going to that ancient temple from an odd sight of some magical release that covered the skies! Did you not notice it Ehob? We ventured to the temple, and we saw Salbani free from his binds, and the legion of Liege roamed free! Untangled from their binds as are still bound to the Litus curse but then we learned of the release. It was a deceased of the chosen Atum!

Somehow Salbani was able to lure them into the temple, he lured them to our home! Atum in Felagnolum Ehob! Gercue be my witness! I spoke truth! Tree keeping Trezhur, I tell you that the decree of that Michael is somehow undone..."

The tree keeper changed his demeanor from a composed essence to a shocked straightening of posture as he quickly crossed his arms in angered thought speaking clear in question to the pair of Othas.

"This is not a trick. A fooling of games? You would not disturb my work for such fallacy... These trees are sick. That Salbani is sure up to something, the dark oaks will not even speak to me. Notice the suffering, you cannot hear them, but I can. Something is sure in manifestation; I had no sight of this, but I believe you for there is no reason that these Oaks are in silence. I have been concerned with them, unknowing to the happenings of the realm, this makes sense for the dark magic to be active and in strength as I am feeling some odd form of energy pulls. In addition, these Vigor Vandals have multiplied, it seems for the last day I have been completely occupied with their removal and they only mock me."

The figure set down his cage that held the vandals as he walked out to the Tuent river line, the fairies flew along with him as you could hear the faint voices of the Vigor Vandals laughing at the group of magi. Gercue spoke out to the tree keeper who looked off into the distance of the grasslands across the river way.

"My ally speaks the truth great Trezhur. Litus is in dismay, the wicked are freed, and the humans are undoubtably prisoners of that Salbani, soon sacrificed I would assume. What else is he to do with them? Show them his wretched temple? His cursed lands of banishment?"

The fairy confirmed the other fairy's words as Ehob dropped his head with disappointment. He gave a large exhale before speaking and turned to face the hovering Othas.

"Then it is true, the prophecy of that ancient witch of the Phoenix was in fact truth. I fear what is to happen in the days to come. As Salbani is only in need of a small amount of that chosen blood. If you speak truth and one of them is already deceased, then he will have enough power to free his legion from their imprisonment and the kingdom is sure to shift. We must warn the Trea as you spoke, we must venture to the Garden of Desire, you will come with me. We will take the port gate to Essen and warn the mighty of this terrible deed. We have no time to waste, let us venture."

Ehob turned from the river-way and began to walk back to the tree that he was near earlier. Ehob knelt to its roots as he began to speak to the tree.

"Oh, great dancer in the wind, ancient recycler, I know that you are in pain. I know that these wicked ones steal from you, use you, I understand. I see your family under this curse as I know not of the length of this terror, I tell you that I will fight for you, and I will fight with you. Speak, go to your kinds, and tell them we are to rise. I am proud to be your Keeper, you will be set free from this terror in time, stay strong and warn the other Oaks that a shifting is occurring. It is my task to have you released! Go and warn the others that things are to be hard for some time, but I am working my dancer, I am working to find a way to free you all. I must leave to see what I can do; I will return."

The tree suddenly began to shake branches to then pull each branch inward as the massive trunk bent as a kneel of sorts, acknowledging the Trezhur. As it then was quick to uproot as up and out of the dirt.

"Woah, look out now... she's moving!"

Ehob shouting as he quickly backed away from the giant plante. The two fairies promptly flew out from under the tree.

"It has been over one hundred moons be it since I have seen a tree active! A beautiful sight!"

Spoke Gercue as he flew about in circular spins around the group. Grounds shaking from the movement of the tree as it begins to traverse the lands... moving about one hundred feet, to the edging of a near slim tree forest. The tree seemed as if it was moving straight into a collision with the forest as it forcefully rooted itself just before a varied species. Beginning to communicate with the other trees the news of what the keeper spoke.

The group waited for moments as the tree keeper questioned the fairies some more about what they saw at the temple. Ongoing in conversations, making their way to the nearest gateway, which was in the Garden of Desire, in the South of Irosent. The Tree Keeper is a good friend of mine, you would love him my treasure. As he has a deep knowledge of plante, how to communicate with them was something that he was born with. I tell you that there are those who prefer a life of silks and spices or desire fulfillment of whatever material, but Ehob is nothing of this kind, a different breed of Felagnolumian. His only desire is to care for the creations, in service to these kind even if he was decreed their ruler. As I add my sense to say that the best of rulers is to be this way. In service rather than demand of how a thing should be done. It is with deep conversations that the Tree Keeper Ehob is to make his decisions. A most regarded treasure in the realm. As the Fairies Gercue and Tikoo travel with him, the other pair of fairies hath sent their companion to find the Bandu and they went on, in traversal into the mirror dimension with the deceased, Spiro trapped Amber as her allied Atum friends are bound before Salbani, the most important Liege are scattered as the Black Witch is on the move. I tell you the shifting is happening, ongoing and unfolding with truth and terrors. The Kingdom was not prepared for such happenings, lost in the dryness of the magic for a decade, the realm hath nearly forgotten the importance of decrees and rulings and are soon to experience the undoing of these most important and precious word structures. Truth will come to light.

Travels of Neuamor

August 18th

Phylace, Tera Jact Island; Eleye, Ralis Garden; Spiritian, Garden of Desire

Neuamor stepped out of the elevator to the rooftop of the Phylace Tower and was in sight of the landing pad that held the Burtis, he wasted no time and climbed abord the craft. The Burtis is a generous sized hover craft that runs on propulsion technology. It has the shape of an ovel and is factory made as a sleek storm grey that has a metallic coat. The Burtis is a well-used ship in the Felagnolum realm and is unable to be accessed unless one has a key to operate it and these keys are embedded with sync-tech, requiring the exact key that it was manufactured with to obtain entry and flight. If this key is lost, the Burtis will sit where it is until reported to Skynet Corp. A Netcorp worker will come and collect it, they go through a process to determine the registered owner and if the owner can't come forward or is at a loss of the key then the Burtis will be destroyed, and the material will be repurposed for the realm. Neuamor unlocked the flight vehicle and the seamless latch opened by retraction, it moved a few inches downward and then slid into the tail of the ship. Neuamor climbed inside and closed the latch that slid back into place with ease. On the inside of the craft there are two seats, one for the pilot and one for a passenger with enough cargo space behind these seats to store a large case of some sort and multiple backpacks, there was enough height for a figure to sit in a crouch as the length was just over the height of an average figure laying down. The cockpit held a steering handle that looked like the horns of a Rektar. This is a massive grass eating beast that you can find in lush lands and the Horns are shaped like shaped like average horns, but they are thick and round coming to a sharp point. The steer of the Burtis is like this but it has sphere shaped ends rather than points and it was in no way as long as the horns of a Rektar. The dashboard was lit in a vibrant teal blue that caused a gloom to light the inside, it held information like Airspeed and header indicators, an Altimeter, Vertical speed indicator, Navigation data, flight system status, and others as it as well shows the multi-function display, a map chart that can project into a hologram if desired, it calculates the weather, there is a radar system, and the HUD also shows various system stats like the propulsion information and pressure systems. The Burtis as well has communication systems and other aids. Neuamor hit the power button that will not work until the key is placed in the ignition chamber and the Burtis sound in a winding of energy and within seconds the propulsion unit blasted, and the flight craft jolted upward just a tad, beginning to hover in place. The system was built with Anti-gravity Emitters that negate the effects of gravity, allowing the craft to float and maneuver effortlessly. If a subject is being chased by anyone and they get into one of these flight vehicles, well, there gone in a near magical way. Neuamor moved the steer stick forward and he began to slowly move off the edge of the Sky-box Tower, he hovered in place for a moment as he then cut the propulsion and fell with daring speed, passing many levels of the Sky-box tower, from the skybox peak, level 208 to the near bottom at level 9, just before he reached a dangerous level of impact he spun the propulsion back on and pushed the steer forward. He bolted into the distance quickly vanishing, traversing out of the city.

He flew with speed, surpassing the speed of sound within moments, he traveled through the grasslands of the RA district, leaving the Island of Tera Jact to surpass the RA Canal in minutes, flying into the continent of Eleye and moving south, to the far south he flew, and it took nearly two hours to get to the ends of the continent, making it to the Garden of Eleye, Known as Ralis.

RALIS GARDEN

Neuamor landed the Burtis on the east side of the Ralis Garden, cloaking the Burtis from sight so that no figure would be able to see it. As it is not only if reported that the Skynet would confiscate it but there are figures that would steal it and use the tech for their own will. Be it Ramblrs, the travelers of plains or be it the Pirate thieves of the realms. There are many who would put the metal and tech to significant use. As it was safe from any ravagers due to this cloaking, Neuamor made his way into the Ralis Garden crossing the border of Sprall Trees that surrounded this garden. The air is thick with various scents, just a few steps into the Garden one is shielded from the light by canopy of Spralls, these giant trees form a dense setting of interlocking branches that are woven together like a silk spin. Their trunks as wide as a Rektor or ten Felagnolum folk side by side. The Sprall has a thick bark that is covered in moss and lichen that is said to be good healing for an ich on the skin. Sunlight shines through the trees in a spotted manner as the floor of these light spots is seen to home an explosion of plante, the shimmer of the light holds a warmth as the jungle feels with a gloom of cool air when apart from these sunspots. The jungle garden has a lush undergrowth as Ferns with delicate fronds grow everywhere in an emerald, green, as there are flowers that range in color, adding vibrance to the scene. A true sight of beauty for the eye as these colors attract from the undertone of darkness caused by the Spralls. There are intricate blooms of many forms of flowers that strike bliss to who is to encounter as scattered are strange fungi, some baron of color as others are luminous. Sprouting from fallen Sprall logs that serve as a haven of life for critters and these fungi kinds that cast an eerie glow to the setting. Neuamor arrived in the bright of the morning as in the night some of these fungi overtake the scene with a fluorescent gloom that enriches the environment as these fungi overtake the floor of the Jungle Garden by shining the darkness of night, this is unseen for now but sure is a beautiful sight to encounter. The jungle teems with life, especially near the Wicet River that flows through dense vegetation. The waters beyond clear, acting as a mirror of the life around it, reflecting the emerald canopy of the Spralls, sights of a faint green even if the water is crystal clean. A figure can see his reflection with ease unless the waters be disturbed. Along the bank of this water way a figure finds giant water lilies that bloom gorgeously as white petals that spot pink, golden yellow centers that attract the honey makers and iridescent dragonflies. There are all kinds of life in this jungle, Monkeys chatter and swing about in the Spralls with echoing calls that seem to weave through the trees. There are many Felk, who are tree hoppers, that roam about in sight of travelers. Acting in forms of curiousness as there are many vibrant colored birds in flight or gathering of foods and pleasant cries of song. Neuamor made his way to the south of this jungle, passing the Sprall thickening making it to the water way, fetching some of it to hydrate. Filling his water container, taking a drink of it as he gazed at the beauty of the Jungle, it was a world of its own that one could become lost in the trickling flow. As he gazed around the jungle he noticed a splash in the water to his right. He looking in the direction and across the water stretch, just a leap away was a Leopar in a stalking position, creeping in his direction.

"You stay, stay right where you are." Neuamor spoke in fear as the cat paid his word, decree no mind. It is said that the big cats are in respect to the Light-Workers of the Kingdom as they can see energies, able to read the aura of a being. As Neuamor was no righteous being, the cat was disturbed by his presence. It was a beautiful creature, the fur coat draped in sunlight, though in stalk, moving in grace with each step. Careful with its movement through the brush as if it was undesired to disturb the setting of the Jungle. This Leopar cat had Amber eyes that shined in the glow of the sunlight, locked in a gaze on the figure Neuamor as step by step it creeps near him as his ears in shifting by the sounds of the Jungle and its tail flicked in a snake like dance as he approached.

Neuamor was overcome with fears, and he quickly pulled his blade, expecting a battle. He was right to do so as the Leopar quickly jumped to the opposite side of the waterway, releasing a guttering growl as it leaped once more as Neuamor attempted to slash the big cat. He missed as the Leopar outstretched its left arm, landing a tearing on the upper side of his hand, as the other arm of this Leopar dug into the high-knee of Neuamor, using his knee as a foundation the cat pushed off in an effort to latch a bite on the throat of Neuamor, he was quick to act, pulling his upper body aside as he pushed the cat by its under belly off and away from him. Jumping to the side and nearly turning in his direction as the cat was quick to recover from the out push that caused it to land on its side. The Leopar moved quickly in a scurry to direction of Neuamor who leaped over the cat in a dive and the cat was just a quick to act with a leap upward throwing his paws from side to side, delivering lashes to the bottom legs and feet of Neuamor as he curled his body in a roll on the grounds. Just as Neuamor sat up the Leopar was in another leap that landed directly on Neuamors upper body, the cat attempted to latch a bite on his face once more as Neuamor saved himself by throwing his arm before his head and the cat latched onto his arm instead with a harsh bite that penetrated to bone, lashing back and forth with a growl. Neuamor cried in pains as he was quick to recover his blade, stabbing the Leopar in the left backside above its back leg, the cat released a loud caterwaul of pain as it was quick to turn and bolt off into the thickening of the jungle brush as Neuamor jumped to his feet, filled with adrenaline he screamed to into the depths of the forest with a expelling of anger and hatred as an echoing roar of energy releases. Injured and in utter pain, Neuamor limped through the forest, he came to a fallen tree log and there was a patch of Healgi. Which is a dark, purple-colored fungi that is used for healing. He knelt to the gathering and collected much of the patch. Walking back to the water way, kneeing at the side of it as he released grunts of discomfort. He gazed at the water for a moment, and he suddenly snatched a Turpdal, this is a long-bodied water reptile with a hardened shell. He took his knife and quickly cut the reptile from its shell, and he then washed the shell in the water. Putting into the semi-cleaned shell the collection of Healgi, crushing it down to a paste with the tail end of his blade and he then rubbed the Healgi paste on each of his wounds. The paste formed as a barrier and healing until Neuamor could get proper wrapping and medicine for the gashes. Neuamor was drained of his energy, but he couldn't stop, he knew that Desire is a safer garden, he knew he was less likely to get attacked in this place, so he pressed on.

"I must continue, I must make it to Desire. Why it hath not brought my Kelbev blaster is beyond me. I should have thought about encounters."

Neuamor angered for leaving his Dynosis energy charge pistol behind as magic is not always the best use, Felagnolum folk are often in use of various weapons. He moved on through the Garden, through the thick of the plants at a steady but slow pace. Through the brush, weary of encounters and on the lookout for Leopar to return, after all the cat was only in pains of the strike of Neuamor, but it would be wise to return not. Neuamor made his way to the far south of the Garden, as he suddenly saw the portal that led to desire. He was nearing the portal when suddenly a fairie appeared out of nowhere, speaking out to him.

"Who goes there?" The fairie questioned as it hovered in place.

Neuamor belched at the Tree Fairie, "I have no will to speak with you Sped, get out of my sights." He groaned as he tried to move his arm in motion for the fairie to leave him. The fairy flew close to him and gazed around his body, checking his wounds as it mocked him.

"I saw your battle with that cat, you must be wicked, what hath you done to be labeled as such?" The Sped asked as it flew directly in front of the face of Neuamor who was beyond anger. Neuamor was quick to grab the creature as he laughed in pride. Dropping to his knee as the fairie squeaked with pains.

"I'll show you." Neuamor spoke as he then crushed the fairie in his hand and was quick to speak the ancient tongue of magic.

"Erutaerc hsiloof, rewop dna ygrene ruoy brosba I."

There was a blue swirl was poured out of the crushed fairie as Neuamor breathed it in as released ongoing wicked laughter. He rose from his positioning and threw the fairie in the brush of the jungle, as it hit the ground the plants that it touched immediately dried and died, turning grey and were quick to deform. This is a natural way of the lands showing inhabitants that an ill deed hath occurred by wrongful death. I tell you; the plants are just as alive as you and me. Neuamor, in gain of strength form the wrongful murder, continued to the portal that was before him. It was a swirling, glowing blue that was in the trunk of one of the Sprall trees with the mark of Desire Garden above this oval portal that glowed in the same color as the gateway. Neuamor approached the tree and stopped before it. Releasing a deep sigh, stepping through and disappearing from Ralis, into the Desire Garden.

OUT OF BODY

August 18th

Notice of the Fairies, Litue Temple

Sent by elders to investigate the happening of the magical release at the temple of Litus. A group of three fairies Beltrez, Tearmend, and Akett of the tribe of Fos, find themselves in the middle of the tragic death ritual of Amber and the thieving of Iyo & Bohn's energy. The grouping of the light workers gathered inside the mouth of a solid gold statue of a blood tree face. Beltriz was the eldest of the grouping, being alive for over five hundred moon cycles as he is a known and respected fairy in the tribe of Fos. He wears a tan garment that covers his waist and a utility strap for daily item use that rests on his shoulder as it stretches across his upper body. Tearmend is a middle-aged fairy, two hundred cycles to that one dressed in a skirt like cloth that swayed around his waist, and this was the only clothing that wears. As for Akett, who is the youngest of the pairing, being only his first decade wearing a full body robe that fit tight to his body. The fairies had wings that were translucent and held a magic glow that shined from their wing veins. Two peering over the teeth of this sculpted tree mouth as the third rested behind, on the tongue of the gold relic. Being of the tribe of Fos these fairies are not surprised with the actions they encounter. As beings of light, it is their job to investigate the darkness that transpires in the realm. As the sight of Salbani is nothing new to these three for they were present during his rebellion and expulsion. Beltriz the elder resting behind the two younger fairies giving directions after seeing the happenings of the legion.

"Tearmend, go and warn the Bandu Cedure of the death of the Atum blood! Go now, we have no time to waste. We have seen enough!"

The Fos Fairy spoke clear as his ally was quick to follow direction, bolting from the golden mouth with zero lack in speed as the other was just as quick to speak. Turning from the tooth as he flew close to the group leader,

"Beltriz, are we going to do something about that human?"

Asking with the most curious of behavior as the leader became puzzled with confusion. He gave his friend a push of play as he laughed and flew to the edge of the relic mouth to get a better view of the temple scene.

"What are we to do, Tearmend is to return with Thane in time and this wretched sight will be concluded!"

The leader Beltrez flew to peer over the teeth of the blood tree relic as was just as quick to fly backward to his original positioning. Surprised with the notice of the human Amber who had just traversed from physical form to spiritual form, becoming what is known as Spiro flesh.

"By the gods! What a mystery, I have no understanding of this oddity. I see her, but I have no idea why I see her. She is of the Atum bloodline; I thought that her spirit would transfer back to her realm. I have not encountered this before, Akett, I say that it must be that the universal gateway closed or is it truth that because she is from the hidden place that reentry be impossible! By decree or design, she is stuck here, lost in our realm it seems. We must retrieve her, we must! We will bring her to the Corpumender! We must wait for the right opportunity to retrieve her before this ritual completes! If Salbani activates the Rite of Scarlet, the ancient practice of the unbinding ceremony then we are in for trouble! The legion is already free but if Salbani activates the blood then one of these demons will be able to entrap this Atum, for if this ritual is a success, then they will be free in the Kingdoms once more. It is bound to happen, that is terror for the Kingdoms, but I say that we cannot let this happen to this human. Akett, we must do something, and we must do something about this quick!"

The leader Beltrez was high in energy as anxious of this occurrence. The Scarlet Rite is an old practice of using powerful blood to achieve that of what is a spiritual bypass on the physical. In this case, it is an unbinding of repossessed power of the legion of Liege, who are the wicked wilts that are under the vial King Bani. This is a scary situation for the fairies. If the legion obtains the Spiro of Amber, then she will forever be slave to these beings of darkness. Out of her physical body she stands in question before her deceased physical body in Spiro form.

"What, what has happened? I feel, I feel no weight on me, I do not know this feeling. Am I a ghost? That is my body, when did I, how, how did I, I fucking died? What is this, I do not, I do not remember dying... I only remember feeling weak and trapped by some force, some power, and now, well, I am dead! What is going on, can I, can I touch a thing?"

Confused as anyone might be if they have never had an out of body moment. As for Amber, a woman of spirituality disbelief, she thought of nothing of the sort to be possible. She knelt near to her deceased self, reaching out to touch her own body.

"I do not remember getting my throat cut, Agh, Ew, all that blood... I did not realize how much fluid my body held. This is, this is wrong, I should not be, well I should not be seeing this... Why, what, why is it that I cannot touch myself, my fucking hand, it moves right through myself, I cannot grasp it. I cannot touch what has happened to me! What do I do!?"

Amber was at utter unease and confused as confused could be. She tried to touch her deceased body multiple times, becoming more frustrated with each attempt. She pulled her arms in as made fists, releasing a growl of frustration!

"AGH! Damn it! What is this! What has happened to me!"

She looked at Iyo and Bohn and thought that she could get their attention. Walking near them both stretching her arm out to touch Iyo. Her hand moved directly through his body as she called his name.

"Iyo! I am here! I am stuck in this, this ghost body. Iyo! Can you hear me! Iyo!"

Overwhelmed in her spirit, which is not a good thing for the Seeker beings and Tormentors of the room are attracted to this form of emotion. Amber begins to move throughout the temple. Walking near the edging of the structure noticing that the physical beings are unable to see her spirit form. She begins to study the creatures, on edge with little fears as she realizes that they cannot harm her, so she thought. Gazing at the legion she begins to mock the trapped ones. As her spirit is bright, the tormentors of the room notice her energy.

"Look at that, the human Spiro is trapped here, look at her, Lectumars look! I am going to collect her, that one will be mine!"

The tormentors balked at the sight of the spirit of the human. Another Spiro of a forgotten death regime quickly flew between them both as he grabbed the backs of their heads, smashing them face first into the marble floors. These tormentors and those of the death regime can touch any figure of the spirit and even are able to feel the surrounding world. I allude that there are levels to the spirit realm and as you master the levels, beings can gain some physicality as there are those that are bypassing these advancements.

"Agh, huh!"

The tormentor spirits unleashed with pain grunts as where both ignited with hate! Quick to recover, chasing after the figure of the death regime. The one who flew between the tormentors flew directly at Amber who was slow to realize this oncoming spirit. It came to her with speed as it grabbed her throat, pulling her quick to the ground and it at once began to spew hatred and nasty speech of hate and desire filled behaviors. Proceeding to spit on her, and lick her face, the being began to tear her spirit garments, with the desire to sexually fulfill himself. The tormentors were quick to attack this member of the death cult. Ripping the chaotic spirit away from Amber as they proceeded to beat the member of the regime. The spirits fought each other without remorse, screaming anger as they let out there decade of trapped hatred on one another. As occupied with one another Amber tried to flee, yet she was unable to traverse in flight, for this is something that a Spiro being must learn. As she was also unable to leave the temple walls, her body would move through the things that she touched. As you might recall, this temple had a magical binding on it which is the reasoning that the legion is still bound to this place. Overwhelmed by the attack and frantic for escape, Amber in her spirit began to scream cries for help.

"Somebody! Something! Help me! Help!"

Her cries echoed throughout the temple, this being the opportunity for the Fos fairies to intervene. From the peak of the temple Beltrez and Akett stormed the seen without a hint of fear, bolting from the relic straight to Amber.

"Ease human, ease, we will guide you out. Come! Follow us! Come quick!"

Amber without hesitation began to move through the temple with the fairies that knew a path out of the ancient structure. The group made way up a staircasing that led to a balcony. The leading fairy flew straight over the ledge as Amber stopped herself at the balcony railing. The second of the fairy's stopped shortly veer the ledge and began to laugh at Amber.

"Silly human, you have no flesh and bone! What is the reason for fear? Jump!"

Amber had a puzzled look on her face as she struggled to jump as the fairy suggested. She lunged as she pulled herself back. She then began to pace as her fear was rising and because of this building worry the tormentors from before were quick to find her. Screeching as they were quick to move up the stairs.

Amber startled by their speed and reappearance! She let go of her fears and made the jump! She fell for a moment as her sight changed from the outlook of Litus mountains and the rocky pathway of the Staid Null to a sudden blackness, as caught in a webbing of sorts. By gateway of the leading fairy, she had traversed into the mirror realm.

DESIRE

Neuamor came out of the gateway with the same speed that he walked into the Ralis gateway. A pleasant walk, stepping out into the lush land garden of Desire. Breathing in a deep breath of satisfaction, for he was away from wrongful encounters. He out spoke with pride,

"Now to obtain this Atum." He said as he began to walk into the garden.

Neuamor gained mighty energy from absorbing the power of the fairie of Ralis and he was in high spirits ready to encounter Salbani in a magician verse magician battling. He knew that showing his face would cause many of the Liege to join him for mumbles of betrayal were spoken before he left. As Neuamor is a high positioned mage with many students of the Liege, he knew that some were bound to join him and there would be an inner battle amongst them all. He walked from the gateway, beginning to venture through the forest as he was suddenly overcome by a dark energy that caused his body to feel numb.

"What is this?" speaking in feelings of oddity as he gazed at his hands.

His body was at odd tensions as if his nerves were sleeping. He shook his arm thinking that he could get his blood flowing again but that did nothing to help. It only spread, overtaking his upper body and quickly spreading to his legs, causing him to wabble for a moment, to stumble to the floors of the forest. He cried as needle pains and tensions of muscle locking occurred.

"Agh, what, what is happening to me!" He shouted in anger as a sudden weight overtook his body completely, causing him to fall to the grounds unable to move. He tried to outspeak, but his voice grew thin with only air escaping without sound. He was beside himself in confusion as heard was an ongoing deep, reverberating laughter that was of a women's voice. It was malevolent and the tone was unknown.

"Ta-eh-ta-ha-ha." The laugher ended in oddity as Neuamor was completely unable to move or speak. The voice spoke from beyond his sight, behind him with a cold tone that was stoic and weighted.

"I am sure you wonder what the cause to this is." Joked the woman.

She walked forward as fallen forest branches snapped by her step. He came near to Neuamor as she ran her foot along the wounds on his leg from the cat. Neuamors' eyes stretched wide in pain as he sounded nothing for his voice was somehow tampered with. As she grazed the wounds the woman spoke out in a mocking tone, in enjoyment to cause him pain.

"That sure doesn't look good, what does it feel like?" She asked as she dug her shoe tip into the tares of his leg. Neuamor said nothing, for he couldn't. Yet his eyes formed tears that ran out quickly. The woman laughed a vial laugh as she continued. "Nothing to say? Curious," She laughed as he pulled back her foot from his wounds, speaking firmly and to the point.

"Tell me Neuamor, do you know what happens when to rebels disown their destiny to follow their own self will?" She walked to his side and sat with her feet nearing the face of Neuamor, allowing him to see only her leathered boots. His eyes spun in search of hints to who she was as his mind flared in thoughts of wonder and anger for what she hath done to him, unsettled but bound he could only listen. The lady released a chuckle as she answered her own question.

"Chaos. It is Chaos that unfolds like if the wind takes hold of flames of a small and simple fire to cook a soup in a dry forest, much like this one." The woman stood and walked out to a fallen Oak that still had its strength. She sat on the edge of it, Neuamor barely able to see her face. She began to toss a spherical stone that she had in her hand. Speaking on to bound Neuamor.

"The fire spreads and destroys everything. Changing all without care, and I tell you that this flame knows not of its destruction. It is just nature." The woman stood from this fallen Oak as she walked before Neuamor once more, standing in a position that he could only see her from her knees down.

"In this case, I tell you that Salbani is the flame and Lytula is the wind, and you are one of the trees that burns away quickly. I ask, do you know what happens when the world burns?" She calmly spoke as she walked closer, kneeling to become eye level with him. Eye to eye with him, Neuamor noticed who she was as his eyes stretched even wider than they were, from confusion of unquenchable fear. The woman laughed at his fear. Gazing into his eyes beginning to act psychotic in a pleasant and calm manner, it was her laughter that screamed of darkness. She finished her riddle,

"The Black Sun casts a vale over the realm."

The women snapped her fingers as the two of them disappeared from the woodland forest floors, leaving nothing but blood on the grounds from Neuamors open wounds.

ENCOUNTER OF THE BLACK WITCH
August 18th

East Sype

The Vima pirates took to the Aurus Sea after the encounters with the Vima Knights in the city of Aljus. With these pirates are the twins, Jillian and Lillea and their friend Cifer, the troublemaker. The group out at Sea for around fourteen days, traveling from the Vimaurus plain of Maurn into the Sea of Aurus, the crew was nearing the coast of the Teloyeh Nation of the Elve kinds. Felagnolum folk dwell on the plain but this continent of Teloyeh was under the domain of the Elves. The crew of one hundred was a short hour away from the Northeast coast able to see the lands clearly. From the peak of the crow's nest, Grim Floyd Snar, the Navigator, shouted to the Captain as he was looking through his telescope.

"Land Ho! I see land, Captain there is land ahead!" Cried Floyed as he perched over the crow nest. The captain was in high cheers for he was tired of the bickering and complaining of the Harlots.

"Alright lads, prepare the ship to dock. It must be the Tayoyeh Nation. We have only been at sea for less than a cycle, prepare for a non-welcoming docking. And lads, there will be no violence unless we are attacked. These Elves operate in the grey area between the battles of the Legion and Trea Orders of the realm. They might welcome us; we need a Haven. Be on your best attitudes and manners! This is high affluence; this is a society unlike Aljus. No conflicts, I want zero conflicts lads! As you are to stay away from their women! You see me?" The captain ended his direction as the crew released their shouts of understanding. Preparing the ship to dock in the Nation of Teloyeh. It was around thirty or so minutes after the captains direction and another thirty before they arrived at the Trade port of the northeast region of Teloyeh. The Harlots were behind the captains wheel, outlooking on the Aurus Sea.

"Cifer have you ever been to the Elve lands?" Lillea asked as she rested on the wood railing that ran around the boat. Cifer laughed in curiousness.

"Me? Oh, no, never. These Elves are not friendly to our kind, they have some way about them, how do you call it? Overbearing, righteous in their beliefs, demanding of respect, to wealthy for their own good? I have never had an encounter that I have enjoyed. I guess I am speaking of opinions, I hath never ventured to these lands Lillea. I suppose my encounters caused me to hold a view on this race. Have you Lillea, or you, Jillian?" Cifer explained as she sat on a barrel that was in the corner of the ships end. Jillian was sitting on the ledge with her legs in dangle over the rail edge.

"No, neither Lillea nor I hath been to this place. We have never left the continent of Maurn, after venture from Essen. It sure is the beginning of a new adventure." She said as she moved her feet with the wind. The captain out spoke, interjecting in their conversation.

"I know you gals are not happy with my choice, but it is for your own good. You would have lost your tongues by that trick you pulled on those Knights. Not under my watch, I won't have it. As Cifer speaks truth of these Elves, they're not all as bad as she makes them seem but there is truth in her words. They demand respect and take it as disrespect if one is to be in lack of it. As their wealth sure sets them apart from the rest of the plains. Be it how they have obtained the whole continent. I warn you to lose the ideals of them, they will be quick to pick it up. As if they have some outrageously elevated level of discernment." The captain spun his ship wheel as he spoke. Lillea was quick to reply,

"After such a journey, thinking of the chance that we might have been caught. I don't mind the idea of finding our way in a new land. What about you Jillian?" She asked her sister as she seemed distracted in a gaze of the waters.

"Whatever you want sister, I'll let you decide where we go next." She was at an ease sitting on the boat railing as Lillea was struck with oddity by her calm behavior as she is usually all rambunctious, in some sort. She went to speak up as suddenly a crew member yells in terror and fear!

"Defend the ship, protect the captain!" He cried as the sound of a windy screaming began, as crew members of the ship suddenly croaked and died where they stood. A wind consumed the scene that was of a storm in the depths of sea, a dark blackened storm cloud appeared from void as it consumed the area. This was most odd for it was the mid of the bright in day. The ship was suddenly covered in a thick fog that was as they were entrenched in the darkness of midnight. The boat slowly began to swirl in place as crew members tried their best to fight this wind, but a sword does nothing to the unseen. One by one the crew members dropped to their death as the captain yelled in surrender.

"Enough, that is enough. What hath you come for, what is it that you want! I'll give it, you can have it. Stop this insanity! Stop it, Enough!" He yelled from the upper deck as in a moment of oddity the thick fog cleared, the winds stopped, and the darkness ceased to be. The crew members looked around in fear and confusion as a sudden laughter overtook their ears, echoing like they were in a long castle hallway. The Vima pirate crew members were all suddenly bound by magical binds as a thick rolling gateway appeared in the middle of the ship. Out walked a woman of the Black, Wearing an elaborate suit of armor that has a gothic dark sight. The armor is intricately detailed with ornate engravings and a metallic sheen. Her armor is functional and highly decorative, the chest piece is form-fitting, accentuating her physique, she is a fit woman, the armor makes her look scary by form of the midnight black and the smooth texture and design shows that she is of royalty, you may remember this woman from before. Before the bound crew members was the Lady of the Black Sun, Extance.

"What I want, well that is simple, Captain." She said as she walked over the deceased. Taking small strides over their bodies as she spoke her demand.

"Notice how the Whispering Hoards, these unseen Legion of the Black Sun, you have heard of them, I am sure. Would you notice how, what is it? Twenty or so dead in just a moment. You hath screamed surrender in seconds, what leader are you?" She laughed in mockery as the captain scoffed in reply.

"What is it, what do you want Witch!" He belched in anger as she down looked form the high deck. She stopped in her tracks and smiled while looking up.

"These three are to return with me. Worry not, I am not here to deliver you to the Trea but to Rahaid, you know, the legion king of death. The reaper sender and traversing trickster? You are to come with me and simply apologize to your ruler for walking with that lady Phoenix, she hath no positioning, She rules not the Black Flame at this time and will have no rise on this upcoming new moon. Hath you Harlots forgot that you are under the dominion of the Crimson Sisters as this conglomerate of whores be under the Ruby Serpent. Hath, you have no realizations to where your affiliation lye. These Orders are under the Black, and the sun is becoming hot, this reign of Illusor ends soon. Come forth, travel with me, or this ship will burn and each soul that dies will be because of you three. As for you Cifer, you should know better. It is only time before your mother finds out what foolishness you have become a part of. Come on, come to me before I release the Whispering Hoard once more. Come on, step on." Extance was being direct as the captain motioned them to go to her as he dropped his posture in disappointment, in regret that he ever helped them.

"Go on as you heard her request! I will choose my crew over you all any day, and my lady of the Black Sun, what of my association. Hath not killing my crew be enough to undo this entanglement? These Trea will be after me." The captain wondered if he could be released from this toxic circle of inner conflicts. The lady of the Black laughed at him as the girls approached her.

"That has nothing to do with me, you should have known not to involve yourself in the legion conflicts. Where is your sense captain? Remember who hath died today and maybe next time you have a decision, we'll let us hope that is it not to pay off a debt to a whore!" The lady laughed in mockery as she was quick to disappear into this rolling smoke gateway, bringing the three harlots with her. Back to the Temple of the Black Sun she traveled to deliver the girls to Rahaid. The Captain sat in depression as the crew members mourned the loss of their brothers. They piled the bodies in the center of the ship as the argued back and forth about the events that have occurred. The Captain spoke to them as he rose from his saddened positioning.

"I have failed you lads; I led us on a path by a debt that was only mine. It cost us many brothers. There is only one thing to do now." The captain took a long, deep breath before speaking on.

"We will continue to the Nation of Teloyeh, on the beach we will have a remembrance ceremony for the fallen crew, as their I will surrender my hat." The crew cried in conversations about this statement. Some were happy that he would surrender his title as others were against it. The bickering went on for some time as the captain out spoke once more.

"Be it some are with me, some be against me, never the matter. This is what we are to do, a ceremony we will have, and we will do the due diligence of the process, as this is my ruling. I will surrender my hat by majority vote. As for now, enough of the arguments. We will travel to the beach side and pick up this conversation off the waters. Until then, let there be silence in respect for the fallen. Let's go lads, to the beach we travel."

The captain returned to the helm of the ship as the crew members got to work on preparing the ship and themselves for docking. In a reverent silence for the fallen brothers and in personal thoughts of what their vote would be when they arrive at the new land.

The Black Witch hath done as commanded, the work of Lytula disrupted. As her followers are captured and all soon to be judged by the keeper of death.

BOUND

August 18th

Litus Temple

Salbani stepped over the body of Amber, nearing Iyo. Spewing hate as the legion followers roared in celebrations. The human blood followed the indented lining in the Sorzo mount falling to the level below as collected by the blood workers.

"Are you ready? Arthe chosen filth?"

The figure spat in the face of Iyo as he threw up his hand to begin to swing but for odd justification the figures hand froze in place. A sudden force intervening...

"What is this."

Salbani lost in confusion as the room of terrible voices and sounds turned morbidly silent. Iyo looks around in even more confusion than he has had this whole time.

"What? What... Is."

Salbani was trying to move but trapped in whatever binding it was.

"The human has a guardian by the looks... Nobody can bind me. Nobody!"

Salbani stopped speaking for he realized the human was just as confused as he was. Now as unable as the humans the figure had no choice but to await release. He set his fire eyes to a gaze on Iyo as you could feel the hate that radiated from Salbani.

BANDU FOR THE WIN
August 18th

At once amid the Litus mount of the ritual Sorzo appeared A vibrant, colorful, smooth multi woven layered energetic gateway that formed behind Salbani as his attention fixated on the humans. The door began at about ankle level as it continued at an angle up to about two feet above what any human head would be. As a hooded figure jumps out of the magical doorway with ease, he quickly speaks.

"I bind you until New Light!" Bandu Cedure shouting in might, thrusting his body forward as he outstretched his hands and he put his arms around the humans while speaking out to the Liege King.

"Salbani this magic will not have resurrection today!"

The hooded figure of the Bandu appeared as he spoke fearlessly and directly in the face of the Liege King of Rebellion. For unknown as it had to be odd reason the following of Salbani were unable to travel into the throne setting where Bandu had appeared speaking. The humans covering their ears due to these wicked screeching with anger and fury. The following could only watch, outnumbering the Bandu Cedure a thousand to one. There was a form of magical interference that was separating group from group. The hooded being took Iyo right under his arm as swept him right out of the binds that he was in as the magic seemed to have zero effect on the being. He then leaps with Iyo under his arm as he lands next to Bohn simply placing his hand onto Bohn's shoulder as suddenly, with a blink of the eye a portal like the one that he came out of from earlier appeared as it wrapped the group. Then occurred a fold of sorts as the portal closed the Bandu Keeper and the group into it as they were simultaneously teleported to a far-off field. Way beyond the reach of Salbani for the time being, yet a member short leaving the body of Amber before the evil one who stood froze in time by Decree until the sun begins to fall.

The plans interrupted, you see not all beings in Felagnolum are evil and with cause. Some fight this power for the greater good of the realm.

LUSH FALL

August 18th

South-West Irosent: Highland Plains

On the grass lands Iyo and Bohn with the Bandu Cedure, Thane. There is a sudden ease in the winds as a change in atmosphere.

"It is quiet. And... Beautiful. Where are we? Who are you? And... well, I guess I should thank you..."

Iyo bowing to the hooded man that saved them. Unknowing of the common manner of showing appreciation he did what he thought was best. As there was a sure since of unease with the humans, lingering about as the pair has undergone so much oddity over the last few days. All this activity would sure put even the fearless at discomfort. Bohn was just getting to his feet but consumed with a morbid as it was stoic... depressed attitude. Speaking of nothing he drops next to Iyo. Obviously, he wa drained of his energy. The figure that saved the pair knelt as began to place rocks together. Speaking unknown words as suddenly there was a fire among the rocks.

"I am the Keeper of the Bandu. The Bandu you might ask is a form of magic dust that is inside these bands of matter, these here. Do you, see?"

The Bandu Keeper held up his arms. As Iyo noticed that bands around the being's wrists had a fluorescent glow as this liquid looked alive on the inside. He was a muscular fellow; One could say perfectly healthy. Thane never has any footing on his feet, he wears a thin cloth that covers his legs as it then tightly wraps along them. He styles a utility vest that holds many items of his choice as he wears a leather strap that wraps around his back and chest, holding canisters for the Bandu Cedure Coils. A metallic element is what made up these coils that wrap around his wrists, allowing him to traverse instantly throughout the realm. Thane has long brown hair that stretches to his mid back as well as a braided beard that falls below his chest. The figures eyes are bright and shine by a sinister yellow, yet the Bandu is one of grace. Thane Sepu Bandu Cepure sure is an interesting Keeper and he is ninety-nine Unis of age, ongoing, resuming to speak of his gifting.

"These are those of what you humans would call rings. This is the technology that allowed us to travel so quickly the way that we did. Jumping matter, I call it. Inside of the bands home a magic that has only mastered by the fairies and those who home Superior Magi Knowledge."

Iyo smacked Bohn with amazement and excitement for his science brain was turning gears. Yet, Bohn had fallen into a deep slumber next to the warmth of the fire.

"Well gee. That is impressive tech, please explain further. Do you speak of fairies? Like Tinker Bell? Ah, Fuck. You will not know what that is, the hell am I thinking, Um so, magic? That is real? Well duh, The creature, the portals, I saw the spirits and what are they? Demons? At that weird place! I heard wicked voices! What do you speak of, like warlocks and wizards? How are those things even real? What the fuck even, where are we? How is it that we even got here and how is it that I can get home!"

Bandu laughed at the human.

"Oh, calm your emotions."

Pausing in question for a small moment before continuing to speak.

"Some have the task to lead astray the chosen. To trick a Trezhur, that is not a de-mon. Your thoughts Iyo, the things that run on? These are your so-called demons. You must cycle all the manifestations and decide what is a trick and what it is that is the truth. I tell you that I see no possession when I investigate you, only value. I say that is what it is, you have been lied to little human and you believe lies. I bid you sleep as when you wake you will begin to grow in understanding. I shall remove the guise placed as a vale over thy consciousness."

Thane raised his hand to snap his fingers as Iyo yelled out noticing that he was about to do something.

"Wheaiiitt!"

Iyo yelled so quickly he was breathless, and Keeper dropped his hand and went on to poke at the fire. Iyo was becoming frustrated because he had thought these things to be fantasy.

"At ease human! Rest! You are simply over thinking. I will explain all I can to you. Come and sit now. Relax, little being."

The Bandu tried to calm Iyo, but he was already past the time for comfort. Too much has gone on as too much is non-understandable for his low level of consciousness.

"No! Bandu. You said you are keeper of the Bandu... Those rings on your arms! So that is not your name! Bandu Keeper is in fact your title! Tell me what your name is!"

In expression Iyo leaped to his feet, stiff and upright attempting to become as masculine in posture as possible. As if he had the guts to face this figure, one on one. I tell you, only a human would fight his savior. The figure gave out a small chuckle as it was comical for him to watch the one of little knowledge be upset that he is lacking understanding, a fool of this figure to explain the happenings to such a hardheaded man.

"The matter of you craves fact I see! Bandu Keeper be my calling, you noticed true. I am an affiliate to the unity protectorate, the eleventh created Trezhur aligned of light. Made to fill a role of ongoing specific kingdom tasks. To be the one of Cedure! Meaning, to go and then to return as I defend the realms! Is it Iyo, the name you carry as I am Thane. Of sense you must be so quick to notice the burden of keeper as you suffer near such insanities, sit, rest now little one. You have endured much and this mind of yours must rest."

Thane let his sentencing breathe as Iyo was in obvious contemplation of all he had endured. Pacing about, ongoing in thought as he mumbled expressions. Thane spoke on noticing that the human was beginning to work himself up.

"It is only fate that puts you here, young being I tell you that by the deeds of some force that ancient one will have freedom. It was only time that kept him there, as I suppose he learned this. I felt the shifting in the astral! I tell you smashed by a water breath of cosmos! As this occurred, I was enjoying a conversation with a woodworker near the ends of the Iro-hills. As you might not know now. In time, you will learn of her rolling beauty. As I was, speaking with a woodworker and suddenly the trees were forming a path. I knew it to be my fellow Trezhur Ehob. So, I port jumped the Sprall line as it led me straight into a pair of fairies as well as my fellow Kept, Ehob the pure."

Thane paused as Iyo seemed to become calmed by the explanation. The Bandu gave the human a smile as he wove his hand to his side motioning for Iyo to join him once more. Iyo was intrigued to hear that as he finally took his seat, Thane spoke on.

"I appeared at this path end as at once the fairies were in frantic shouts and action. "Bandu! Bandu!" they shrieked, "The magic! The dark evil, wicked magic. I saw it!" I peered my sights beyond them to see Ehob distraught! I knew from his emotional ware that these fairies were of no tricks! As in disgust I felt for such an annoying amount of worry I had not felt in a decade! As the pair described seeing you all, a group of you humans bound as sights of that legion free. Disgraceful, such unholy beings you have encountered! The fairies spoke of how they had you humans bound. Humans? In Felagnolum? A mistake I knew! So, I only had to leave to figure out the reason for the actions! As I came to Litus, this be the mountain that we just came from."

Iyo stopped the Keeper in his sentencing as he was in a boat of confusion.

"A mistake? You just spoke that it was fate that put me here as you now say that I am a mistake? I do not understand! I was doing experiments, odd trials that led me here! I have no knowledge of this place! How to get to this place, I had no thought of a place like this, figures as I have seen, a man, well you are not a man are you? You see I have not even the understanding of a being of your size and manner... sure a mistake that I found myself here, but I would disagree to that point of I, a genius of my kind to be such a mistake!"

Thane sat up straight as he crinkled his brow and gave the human a smirk.

"Ahtum blood, the power filled yet, overcome in hubris! Now, reacting to much I say! For only do I share what I know you able to comprehend. I speak of the truth to the mistake of your presence in this realm. I said nothing of your arrogance, mind your positioning as I have done such a deed to save you. As I allude that I saved your life be it for the creations and that it is your bloodline, the contents inside this flesh of yours that is of worth. For you and your self-given genius mind be without such power in you, let it be known, I would leave you here with your pride to wander as a fool until something of this realm is to make use of you. I hold love for you be you a creation, yet the more you show this stupidity for this foolish desire, wanting notice? Well as I spoke, I could fall into desires as vamoose!"

Thane began to interact with a small technologic device as Iyo scoffed at his explanation. There was a small moment of anger that Iyo was boiling in. As he took a deep breath of control as his curious mind overpowered this fueling of confusion and unsettling statements.

"What is this mountain you speak of? That was a mountain? I thought I was inside some kind of throne room... I thought it be a castle of some kind; it could be that you do not... Well, it was a structure of some sorts, not a mountain, I was inside a place of stone..."

Iyo shaking his head as held his chest, trying to control his anxiety. Taking breaths as Thane continued to explain.

"Ah. Yes, it was in fact a throne but not a throne that you would ever find anyone with sense bowing too. Since the great rebellion, the fallen Trezhur creations who are known as the Liege dwell in Litus. These are those who bewitched you, led you, used you my new friend. These who are bound or dare I say once were bound to the grounds! This was the last decree spoken before the mighty victor left to meet with the creator! Nobody knows what the Mighty Ones are up to, but one can only assume the end of an age is here! I speak of new positioning, new thrones, I tell you that all is shifting... The energy will never lie little human, remember this. There has been little to no magic in the kingdoms unless thy be born with it, for the creatures and the Magi have been working for a long time, in unison to keep the access and understandings of the realm occulted! This is what the battle in this realm is consisting of. It is war for magic, control of it, the reasoning of use. I fight to protect the natural order of the Kingdoms. The continuance of abundance as by no means taking from her. These kingdoms are alive as you and me... what we do on these lands is what creates the cosmic wave of existence. Our creator gave us power as we live eternal. A gift of life that some misunderstand and so then misuse... I tell you that he is off doing what a creator is doing as he positioned some of us to keep this order, to fight for it. You see he is sure able to maintain this order himself... but a gift. As this is where the will of his creations is born. I say that the creator allows figures like Salbani for many reasonings. As all is a test, be whatever it be that a subject is to do I say that this be his destiny of trials. A balance will always level things as the trials of light and darkness mirror everything. Do you see? A test is the same no matter what the cause. Who will thy be is what all funnels into this existence. It is to learn and experience this creation. Where we end up is entirely up to us, what we connect ourselves to is entirely up to us, as I tell you that these actions that we make are what shape who it is that is us. This is why I saved you."

Thane paused for a moment, Iyo looked at him with curious wonder, listening. Thane spoke on…

"I made the choice to come to Litus because I have recognized that I am able to change situations. I am a subject of many gifts as I home power and knowledge that I chose to use for the betterment of creation. I confess that I am held in high regard for deeds. As I confess that I am no guide for you as my own sin has burdened me. To be a messenger for light and I have sent many as a new subject for Death to sort, the restless one of few words that ancient is. I speak of the simple fact that I am on a path of good but I, a keeper, am flawed and boast not. I tell you, mind my words little treasure, for I am only a messenger I say heed my message, be it known your mistake of entanglement. The figure I am to take you to will absolutely in no form tolerate your rebellious, arrogant, unknowing, way of action. If you value your life, you will practice silence. When I hath came, I used the Bandu, and I was at the peak of a high area as I could see all the wicked as they were in some kind of celebration. As then I saw! You all were bound! As soon as I realized that the fairies that sent me were speaking the truth, I came straight down from my watching position as I realized what could happen if Salbani were to murder you all."

Iyo had questions.

"You are going to have to back this up for me…"

Iyo was barely holding himself together after all that has happened.

"Could you help me wake from this odd dream?"

Iyo was at a loss as he spoke to the Bandu Keeper.

"I could have thought this all up. For this makes no sense. First the AI, Then an odd creature... My calculations... They were correct. As then portals... Egypt? Demons and magic and now this? You speak of all this as normal. What is a Trezhur? How is it that the Bandu can make you teleport from place to place? I do not think I am really living this... You are talking about God and all this, this, I, Oh man, I think I need to..."

Iyo was acting odd, he stood up and started to walk as he then began to stumble as if he was drunken away and he fell to the ground, unconscious. The Bandu Keeper let out a laugh as he got up and went to pick up Iyo. He placed him next to Bohn as he then snapped his fingers as he spoke.

"Tser"

The fire was no more as the Bandu Keeper knelt in the dark of night, speaking out to himself in thought of the happening.

"I fear someone is doing crafts on these beings. He is looking for them... I must return to Michael at once. If they have gotten the blood, things are about to change, I fear everything might change. I am confused as I know that this particular blood used in magic would never pair with, it would never bond on this plain. The wicked know this... There is, oh, oh no... there has been a deal."

Thane was upset with the realization that the evil Salbani could practice dark magic once more. For Thane knows that his master will not be pleased with this information, as it is Thane that must explain all of this to him. The being spoke another odd word as he placed his hands on Iyo and then Bohn.

He delicately spoke the single word.

"Essen."

As the trio disappeared from the grasslands in a silent swirled zip, phasing to a land far from the cursed bloodwoods.

Thane positioned High in the order of the Trea, he could be deemed as realm savior for obtaining these humans from Salbani, as unquenchable power he would have if he were two sacrifice all three of them. He moves to speak with the High Council of Essen where the Trea, light followers among the Synod and other magi of positioning gather, be this council on the same plain of Spiritian yet on another continent, Taodamic. He is in for explanations, to walk in his title once more. The Bandu Cedure messenger of deeds, the Atum hath been through events of utter confusion and trauma in this short journey of the moon cycle and they need soul level healing, maybe even a mind wipe. The deeds are done, and the Liege nearing freedom, as it seems the whole realm is part of this now. Just as the Bandu Cedure spoke, the shift will enroll a New Realm Order.

Seekers Return

August 18th

Litus

Back in their Spiro bodies, quickly shedding the Nemid physical form, the Seekers moved with speed through the Desire garden. The forest was thick and held many creatures and realm inhabitants, like the Desi Garden Queen who has control over the Desire Garden, each garden has a ruling figure, but they pay no mind to Seekers for not all can see in the spirit. The Fos fairies are able and are Rumored to allude if a Seeker is around, but these Seekers move with speed, bothering, roaming not. The Seekers traveled through the Garden and through the Forest, following the Wicet River, crossing over it as then were soon out of the thickening of the trees and into the Highland Grasslands, they moved like light but were nothing of its beauty, quickly getting through the grasslands and into the Airshe Heights for only moments before they were in the cursed Oaks, known as the Bloodwoods. The Seekers flew as smoke and they would just as a serpent, through the sickened trees and into the Litue Mountain range, making their way through the Staid Null stretch of will as fast as they could, without stop these Seekers moved and before the moon was over, they were once again before their conjurer, Salbani.

The legion of the room cried in celebrations as the Seekers made entry as witnesses to the task they were called for, most were excited to hear the news that they were to bring. Yet it was no good news, and the Seekers held fears of what their conjurer would do as he heard of the treachery that he faced. The Seekers flew straight to Salbani who was in a relaxed position on his throne in the peak of the Litus temple as one spoke immediately,

"Bani, Bani, O, conjurer, we hath gathered the information you seek."

Salbani sat straight on the sight of them, speaking out.

"Tell me, feeble drifters, tell me what you have learned. Did you find my son?" He mocked in ask as he sat up, hands resting on the edges of this throne.

"O, you son, the Prince, Son of the Dark, the next, the next to rule he is." Spoke one of the Seekers with quick speech as another spoke directly after it. "To rule, to guide, to know as his father, found him, found him we have!" It said as they struggled to maintain still. Salbani roared in annoyance and stood from his throne, yelling out to the beings.

"Get on with it! Where is he, where is my son and the rest of the fools!" He took a step forward and the two that spoke cowered behind the other that spoke out to him with truth of the happening.

"To the mirror realm we went, quicker this way. As led us to the vision room, we were, led we were, into the bubble room of thoughts, and thoughts we saw, we witnessed truth, The ritual," The others spoke after him, nearly as one, repeating what their Seeker ally was speaking. "The ritual, the ritual," They said as the other spoke on without a pause. "Of you and the, Liege, the legion, the calling, the action, of action then Neuamor, it was Neuamor," The others out spoke with it, "Neuamor, Neuamor it was," as the Seeker spoke on, "Vanished he did, into the Tower, the Tower, Phylace it was, and into the Portal, separation the legion, the old world, Egypt, and Arthe, and Phylace, Phylace they are, Neuamor at Phylace, with, the Prince, The Prince, The legion are bound, bound, bound at the peak, By orders. Orders from the Phoenix, the ancient queen, Tula, Lytula, by workings, That Zari, Zariza unpure. Deceived, Deception on you, Salbani, the leader, deceived!" The Seekers tried to speak on, but Salbani became enraged, and he boxed these beings from being able to leave by the ancient tongue.

"Era uoy erehw uoy dnib I" he said as the Seekers became trapped in a magical boxing. Salbani turned his back on them and brought his hand near his chin as he was in thought, a quick moment passed, and he yelled to the following legion in the room.

"Sloof gnirednaw eseht yortsed." He calmly spoke, as suddenly multiple different forms of legion swarmed to the temple mount and began to preform castings of disembodiment and energy absorption.

Salbani paced for a moment as his following dismantled the Seekers from existence. He walked to the high balcony ledge and began to contemplate all that these seekers spoke. Outraged about his plans being altered as he was overcome with defeat because his son was missing. The tasks that he had at hand for the missing of the Liege were of no mind to him for he could easily task another of his legion to do whatever he wished. He was in hatred of Neuamor for deception, wondering why Zariza would deceive him as he was upset at Lytula being the cause of all this. So close to his freedom yet bothered by the fact of having to restructure his plans. The Liege King sat snooped in thought on his throne as he awaited the goblins to finish the full dissection of the Atum body.

TURNING OF THE LEAVES

TAEMAX RETRIEVES THE KEY
August 18th

Dragon Keep

Taemax ventured from the city of Phylace and traveled through the grasslands of the RA district, leaving the Island of Tera Jact to surpass the Ra Canal, flying into the continent of Eleye and moving south, to the far south he flew, to get to the ends of the continent, making it to the Garden of Eleye. Known as Ralis. He found the gateway to the Garden of Desire and ventured through it. Taemax traveled through the Garden and through the Iyo Forest, following the Wicet River, crossing over to soon be out of the thickening of the trees. Into the Highland Grasslands, quickly getting through the grasslands and into the Airshe Heights for only moments before he made it inside the cursed Oaks. Ongoing, through these sickened trees and into the Litue Mountain range, making his way half-way through the Staid Null Stretch of Will to begin to travel into the far North where the Dragons are rumored to be. Off the beaten path of the Null Taemax flew into the rocky Mountains of Litue, through various rock formations and scattered trees until he neared the higher lands of the mountain range, the Spirit lady of the White elves with him still, speaking with him as he journeyed, flying near his side in the Spiro form that she was trapped in. Taemax stopped at the peak of a high mountain to catch his breath from the long, ongoing journey. He took a few deep breaths to recollect his energy.

"I wonder where exactly these dragons are, they must be around here somewhere, for it is a warning to be weary of the Litue mountains, not only because the Liege reside here, for now, but it is said the Dragons are here. Awaiting their master Voboh to be freed, I know it, I was told this by a Fos fairie in the meeting of the Arcane masters. Only a few moons ago, I must think, I must think. If I were a self-concerned overly prideful master magician of knowledge and leader of giant beasts, where would I keep my treasures? Lady of the white, what, well, what do you think?" Taemax sat in wonder of the possibilities and the lady in the Spiro responded quickly,

"Oh, in the high mountains of course, where else Taemax?" She spoke as if she knew. Taemax scratched his head in thought. Flying out to a nearby ledge as he sat on the edge that dropped to the sea.

"Yes, but we are on one of the highest peaks, I have searched all around. I must be thinking too much, I mean after all I have ventured beyond the," As Taemax was speaking he heard a screeching roar from above him and he jumped with equal levels of fear and joy as he looked to the peaks of the clouds to see one of these dragons flying in the air. The lady in the Spirit shouted to Taemax.

"Go after it then, come on, what are you waiting for." She spoke, Taemax released a laugh as he bolted up into the heights. In response as he flew on to chase the giant creature.

"Oh, your right my lady, it was just so marvelous. I had to give it a gaze." Taemax flew into the thickening of the clouds and neared the massive dragon but not too close for he knew that it could easily chomp him as a small snack. He flew about a hundred feet from its swaying tail as the dragon suddenly dove from the heights of the sky, heading to the sea. Taemax was beside himself,

"What, where is it, oh, I wonder if he felt my presence, why is he diving down?" He wondered as he was quick to replicate its action. The dragon was traveling at no speed that Taemax could keep up with, but he worried not for it was at least in his sight. The mighty Dragon nearly hit the sea water as he outspread his wings and flipped a spin to head back to the lands that Taemax had just ventured from, the dragon flew close to the waters and in a quick moment it seemed to disappear into the mountain bottom that was nearly directly under where Taemax had rested before he noticed the creature. In surprise, Taemax laughed in wonders of the Dragon,

"What in the realms? Where, o, where did he go?" Said the Sped as he bolted as quick as he could to follow it, after a few moments, Taemax neared the area that the Dragon had disappeared from and he noticed that it was the beginning of a cave that when into the mountain from where he came,

"Oh, why that is most brilliant, a cave, under the mountain and by the sea, I tell you that only a foolish drunk could stumble to this place!" Laughing with excitement the fairie Taemax flew to the nearing edge of the mountain, and he saw over fifty dragons that seemed to make themselves at home in this mountain bottom. He flew in for a closer look, some of the Dragons were colossal, some were small like a speeder and others were between these sizes, Taemax was as well in sight of a group of hatchlings that were the most active of the bunch. Nearing one that seemed to be resting near the entry way he held close sight to it. The scales shimmered in hues of a deep purple that seemed to fade into an emerald as were burnished in a near gold like outline, it was lying coiled before a rock that was as a shield from the ocean winds. The dragon's body is long and surprisingly slim. The head was not to small, but nor was it large. On the mount were sharp curved horns that gleam like a polished pearl, as if they have touched nothing. Its nostrils output vapor, as heard was the exhaling huff of breath.

"Taemax, in the backside of the cave, far in sight. My Key sits in an hourglass encasing. As if it is a joke being played on me." The Spirit lady seemed upset with finding her key. Taemax responded in wonder,

"My lady you found it, what is the issue of the hourglass?" Taemax asked as he gazed through the many dragons attempting to catch a sight of the area where she speaks. The lady sighed to Taemax,

"Oh, Taemax, Whomever did this, they are speaking a message, meaning that it is only in time. As the retriever, that being you, is to break the glass. As then you will attract the attention of the dragons. As I don't need to tell you what happens when a Dragon finds a thief of its treasure, do I Taemax?" She spoke in a worried expression as Taemax flew to a closer vantage point.

"Oh, never the worry, I have belief that I can outmaneuver these Dragons inside this cave, it is only outside of the cave that be my worry, for they can't catch me in here but outside, well, it would be only a single wing push until they caught me, as then I'd sure be in flames." Taemax laughed in a joking manner, attempting to seem unafraid. He flew in short bursts of speed until he neared the area of the heap of treasures, were a massive Mother Dragon was resting. The treasure itself is a spectacle of wealth, Gold coins are scattered like sands in the wind, around the dragon as jewels shine in every color of the spectrum. There are swords from the fallen who have tried to obtain the treasures and the swords held a blackened burn as if these soldiers died by flame. jeweled hilts, ancient relics wrapped in ornate cloth, and chests overflowing with more riches than Taemax has ever seen.

"Okay, luck be with me." Taemax softly spoke as he flew to the hourglass that held the key. He took a deep breath and flinched as he shattered the glass. It burst as if a traveler stepped on a mushroom, releasing spores. In this case was glass and he was quick to grab the key as the resting mother dragon's eyes were quick to open, on awakening, glowing like red hot coals, piercing and fierce, in a dominating angered gaze at Taemax who shriveled in fears as he held tight to the key, hiding behind it for a moment in an eye locking gaze with this mother dragon. The Dragon inhaled in a mighty force that drew near treasures and sands in the air-pull. Taemax was quick to bolt and in seconds the mother released a scolding flame that seemed to fill the entirety of the cave as Taemax rushed out of the area as quickly as he's ever flown, escaping the wave of fire, as if he was in a surf of this mighty flame. The fellow dragons in an echoing cry of escape as well for the mother seemed to have no concern that the others were in the crossing of the flame, just behind Taemax the rest of these dragons poured out of the cave. As Taemax made it on the exit he immediately bolted upward, hugging the edge of the cliffside as he rushed to the peak, escaping the dragons to make it to the peak of this mountain, without a stop he flew along the peak to bolt down the opposite side of the mountain and rush through the Staid Null like no speed he hath ever flown before. He made it to the blood-wood Oaks and flew through the cursed lands with just as much speed and he hath not stopped until he was in the Irosent grasslands beyond and out of the Oaks. As he flopped on the grounds by simply ending his flight. Falling out in a slide on the grass, drained of all his energy.

"You did it, You did it Taemax, O mighty Sped of Speed! You did it!" Spoke the lady of the Spirit as Taemax just laid on the grounds of the grasslands, depleted of his energy.

"O, their sure not happy, and it looks as if they are flying to the temple!" Spoke the lady as Taemax sat up from laying down, gazing in the direction.

"As long as they're not chasing me. Well, I'm fine with that." He laughed as he fell on his back, releasing deep breaths of satisfaction.

"Well Taemax, when you are ready. Our next stop is Novkavis."

AWAIT

August 18th

Sydonic prison cell

It was a new moon, and the air was still as always in the depths of the Crucible Keep. Lytula was anxious as she heard nothing from her traveling Sped. She was deep in the notion that her Sped was acting in a form of betrayal as suddenly the prison gate that locked her inside her room began to open. Mighty thuds sounded with each unlocking of the vault bolts after a moment the door opened and with speed came in eight of the twelve guards that were positioned to keep her inside. A member of the ancient council walked in after these guards as one of them spoke.

"Lytula, you have a visitor. I dare you to try to escape, we are ready to end you." Harshly spoke, the prison guard in a tone of disgust.

The council member of the old ruling spoke directly after him.

"That is enough of you, be gone!" She shouted with dominance as the guards were quick to follow her direction. This was most curious to Lytula who hath not seen this figure in well over a decade.

"Why do they listen to you? Why have you come?" She asked in wonder as she paced about in her frigid cell.

"The Sydonic Council owes me many favors; I have come with news." Spoke the woman as she took out vials of Fungi and threw them onto the grounds of her cell. Before Lytula was seen Two Seekers that were unaffected by this Fungi, as it was a varied species of Fungi than what Neuamor used when attacking the ones that he hath murdered in the Phylace tower. The Seekers were chained by Spiro and attached to this Ancient who spoke out to Lytula as the Seekers stood at her side in stoic depressions.

"Before I let them speak, tell me what you know of me. Hath, you understand who I am?" Asked the Ancient.

Lytula was quick in response. "Why I sure know you, Lady messenger of the Darku. I know your kind, as I know your name. It is Crystoe. You are the High Priestess of the Obsidian Hand? Is that it? You keeper of time and sky. Daughter of the Prime one of Chronicles? Kronphos? Where have you and your family been hiding?" Lytula explained her title as she ended her speech in a slight mockery. The woman out spoke with unsettlement as she kneeled, in no reverence to Lytula, but to her father as if he were watching.

"Forgive her father, she knows nothing." The woman sat in a kneeled position for a long moment as Lytula out spoke during this reverence.

"She knows nothing you say. I happen to know that the Obsidian Hand has been in utter silence over the last decade, letting the pride of the Darku rule in the shadows as these overbearing light dwellers have deceived the realms, poisoned the realms with their doctrine! I know the primes hath do nothing but drink their wines rather than doing their jobs! I know that your father, who holds you under shames does nothing but watch the filth of the realms continue to decay, I know that they sit in their high mounts and play no part in conversations with the real creator. I know it, I know they do nothing but waste time. As you speak to your father, why don't you ask him to tell that creator that his Kingdom has forgot about him, ruled by their wilts, o, desire, o, the oppression of the governing Synod, the rule giving Trea, these sons of the Darku, they do nothing but push their own agendas. Why don't you tell me why you have come? I am sickened by these thoughts; your presence does nothing but strike me with anger. O blessed daughter of the figure of time. What grace you walk in, what authority is your blood. Go on then, tell me why you have come. May I be graced with the truth and you can go back and rest with whatever son of the son worships you, O, great bringer of light, what light have you brought me besides whatever deal your father bid you to strike with me? A fool you are, I know it." Lytula mocked the woman who let her speak. She stood from her knelt positioning and she released a smile, stepping closer to Lytula.

"Wipe that stupid grin off your face, we are not children anymore. You wouldn't test me outside of this vale imprisonment, my power is strong, it grows with each breath, I'd mind whatever you are about to speak." Lytula belching more with anger at this Higher Positioned bloodline. Crystoe walked in front of Lytula, being only several steps away from her.

"With me are two Seekers, do you wonder where they hath ventured?" Crystoe spoke stoically, Strick and to the point.

"Go on, princess, tell me. O, sheltered one." Lytula continuing her mockery.

"Traveling back to their haven after a visit to that Salbani, trapped by elementals of the air who are in service to my father, he hath sent six on mission as these are all that are left." Crystoe stood still in a gaze of Lytula.

"And so, what are you to do? Bid them to speak of what knowledge they gathered for him as to then let them go?" Lytula asked in a sassy manner.

Crystoe was quick to outpull a Black Tourmaline blade as without remorse she swung her right arm to stab the Spiro Seeker in the heart, she outpulled the blade quick as she swiftly flipped it to her other hand and stabbed the other in the same area of the heart with her opposing hand as she maintained her gaze on Lytula, causing the Phoenix Queen to jump in shock and gasps in a surprised breath of air. She crinkled her brow in confusion and crossed her arms in unsettlement, speaking out to the Lady of the Obsidian Hand.

"Why in the realms did you do that?" She asked as Crystoe tucked her blade in the holster on her thigh. Giving a smile to Lytula before she responded.

"These two brought a message to Salbani about what happened during his Ritual to send those Legion to the dirt world, he knows you are behind it." Crystoe was cut off by Lytula.

"Good! That wretch can bask in his hatred, for I have his," Crystoe returned the favor.

"His son?" She gave a look of understanding that was paired with a rebellious smile of enjoyment.

"How do you, How do you know," Lytula's rebuttal was silenced by truth.

"A Sped gave me a visit and spoke to me all about the Sped Taemax and Neuamor. Wondering where they are? These Harlots even, well I tell you that your plans have been dismantled. By word of Rumors, Taemax hath betrayed you, on another task that one is. As for Neuamor? He is now in the possession of Extance, chained to the walls of the Black Sun Legion, he is to deal with Rahaid. The Darku are sick with Salbani and repelled by your tricks. I have come to deliver you a message." Crystoe paused as she was interrupted by Lytula screaming in hatred that echoed through the room, Crystoe took a step back and snapped her finger as she pointed downward. Lytula was forced to her knees by an unseen force that covered her mouth with its hands.

"That force is an elemental, my Protector, Festonic. Invisible by my request. You hath vengeance not. Rahaid is working with my father, yes. The Keeper of time and the Keeper of Death working, a new unity hath risen from these lower descendants rebellions. Be warned Lytula, As I know why you plan, I hath foreseen your freedom, as I was sent to put a stop to your plans as they are a danger for what has been decided for this realm. The Trea has already handled Salbani, well, a partial handling, she is currently walking in more freedom than you as you will be soon enough but a choice you have. End it, end this desire for rule and you will be left alone. Fail to follow my direction and the Darku Primes will be against you. Thane, you know, the one who is to Cedure? The Bandu hath rescued the Atum subjects, by word of my fairie. A new rule is in order, there will soon be a realm meeting of each of the councils, including the Synod. Things are changing, new council leaders, new heads, new thrones all the way around. Be warned and only warned once Lytula. Your deception dies here. Your following hath been caught, this new allegiance destroyed, Neuamor is subject to Rahaid, I tell you that freedom you are to have but you will rise to nothing. Your flame is cold and dying, rise from nothing you will. The phoenix is not to have a rise in this cycle, this is the only warning that you shall receive."

Crystoe turned from her speech as she began to walk away from Lytula, in the direction of the prison room exit as Lytula was released from the Elemental as she surprisingly had no words, she sat silent as her eyes locked on Crystoe. A moment passed and Crystoe was nearing gate exit as Lytula broke her silence. Acting wild and unkept as her eyes blazing in flames of indignation, speaking in utter defiance, uncaring of the woman's positioning in the Darku. The hands of Lytula clenching as her body shakes in anger as she releases curses to Crystoe.

"I'll rise, you will die, You heed my warning you fucking pathetic child!" Lytula breathing like a beast as Crystoe turned from her exit, the gateway slowly opening behind her as Lytula belched on.

"For too long I have been bound, too long in silence, to long I have awaited, now you will await, for death will come knocking to you and your Order, Out of the flames I will rise, you have seen nothing!" Lytula was simply flushed with hatred, her eyebrows crinkled with unsettling fury as she spoke on.

"They call me rebellious but have seen nothing yet! They fear my truth, they demand justice and know nothing of what it is, I refuse to be silent, I refuse to act not, I will not bow to your order or any other, I will not conform to this corruption, Their greed, unlawful spoiled foolish wilts. This Kingdom, this Realm, will feel and Know my name and fear it!" Her voice rattled and echoed in the room as Crystoe released a smirk of disappointment as she replied, "Just as when we were children, still have not got a hold of that temper have you?" Crystoe belittled her as she was walking out the door, Lytula spoke softly, her last sentencing as the door was closing.

"Phoenix will rise, this rebellion has only just begun." She was beyond frustrated; she was infuriated but at an end with her tirade. She sat focused and determined what she would do on her release and how she would regain control. It was not that she was not predicting change, she was claiming her rule, embodying a spirit of revolution.

TRAVERSAL OF STAID NULL

August 19th

Salbani stood in midst of the high mount as he called forth his followers who were scattered throughout the temple. "My legion! Come forth, come now!" his voice echoed throughout Litus as the following of all sizes and forms gathered among him, some near, some perched in the high places of Litue Temple.

"Now Voboh, go and call for your dragons. As for you Byevil, go and tell the hive workers they are to bring the blood vials of that male subject and those new of the woman and we will traverse to the river of Tuent and tear down the vale that keeps us bound to these lands. Go now, we have not the time to waste." The trusted followed his direction as Voboh began to make his way to the balcony that is above this mount, and Byevil was quick to make his way to the lower parts of the temple. Salbani took a moment in thought as he outstretched his hands awaiting praise. The air was still in this moment and the following began to outcry in screams of joy as their leader soaked in the sounds of the legion. He spoke on to them in a mighty shout,

"As for you legion, are you ready to be free? My wonderful Liege! Our powers are slightly restored yet we must obtain the rest of our energy. We will come together and break from this entrapping, this curse of Litue broken on this day! We will be free to roam in the kingdoms once more and we will have our revenge on that Michael!"

The legion roared in celebrations that were so loud that their voices began to shake the very grounds and fortifications of Litus, as the Liege King paced before them in ongoing explanations. The room was chaos, and the entirety of the realm was about to shift for the worse. Salbani began to move to the lower levels in the direction of the main temple gate, outspeaking.

"Now is the time by legion! We are to venture through the Null! Let us go."

The following began to follow him out of the main level into the area of the temple gate. Suddenly a loud bore of an Alanx echoes throughout Litus as into the Litue mountain range the sound was carried with speed. As Salbani made it to the front gate of the temple, opened by several of the lower legions, the thousands released more roars of celebrations, cheering Voboh who was at the peak of the temple. Calling his Dragons with the Alanx, he released nine bores of this musical horn, and he awaited in a gaze to see where they would come from. A long moment passed and suddenly sound of collapsing winds overtook the area around him as the mother dragon landed directly next to Voboh in a harsh thud, causing the temple to shake from impact and the dragon swooped in close to Voboh who belched with cheers as he gave the massive snout of the mother a rubbing to then jump and dance with glee. The dragon uplifted its head and released a Warcry of freedom, the roar of this dragon called the others forward who appeared from the high skies, some landing on the temple as others began to fly around the legion who were beginning to walk the Null.

Into the Litue mountain range the legion walked, following their master Salbani as now accompanied by the mother dragon and her many offspring as other dragon followers. I tell you that even the creatures of the realm have allegiance. Time went on and the Liege were traversing Staid Null, the Legion of a million, so colossal it seems to alter the landscape with their passaging. At the forefront, Byevil leads with a disciplined pace, as thousands follow him, each representing different regiments and titles in the legion, united under a single cause of Salbani revenge, or hath they all just want unbound from his failure that bound them to the plain, only time will tell. The sound of their synchronized steps is like a drumbeat echo, a rhythm of war that resonates through the Null. Behind them, the main body of the legion follows, an endless procession of Legion. Navigating the treacherous Null pathway in lines that stretch for miles. The figures in a steady chanting of ancient wording echoed through the narrow, winding path of the Null as the air was thick by a filling of this chanting hum of thousands of voices. It took half the day to reach the end of the Null as they made it to the end of the Null, the decade sick trees acted in mighty powers as Salbani was suddenly struck in his chest by a large branch that swung from out of his sight. The legion behind him was caught off guard as they watched their master fly to his back as he held his chest in pain. He was helped to his feet by lower liege who neared him. As he began to walk into the cursed bloodwood once more and once again a tree arm came flying with speed. Salbani stood wide eyed in a moment of slowed time as there was no escape from this impact, as the mother dragon intervened with the branch, crashing out of the sky to absorb the impact of the tree swing, protecting Salbani as the massive tree arm shattered into pieces and the mother huffed and puffed from her snout as she took in a deep breath of air that pulled the nearby trees forward by her intake as she dropped her head and was quick to release a scorching flame that burned this tree and many others around it. The mother dragon was quick to fly back into the clouds as she left the cursed Oaks in smoldering flames. Salbani watched the Drago fly off, realizing that it saved his life.

THE TORTURE OF SALBANI

August 19th

Bloodwood

Walking into the Oaks, flames all around the legion from the breath of the mother they ventured in. As the trees in pain from the flames, not one of them engaged in another swing to the legion king. As the Weir spirits began to show themselves by winds and sounds of ongoing laughter. Suddenly, the Liege leader fell to his knees in pain as he screeched in unrelenting pains as the fallen in the astral attacked his psyche. The lands were decreed to destroy this figure Salbani, deemed to be his walk of death as the Fallen and Weir Spirits attack him without remorse, as so they did. His legion gathered around him unaffected by what was happening to their King, acting in worry and scoffs of confusion as Byevil suddenly broke through a grouping of them.

"Away with you all, give him space, Space I said, away with you!' The messenger shouted with anger as he knelt to his master and longtime friend who was ongoing in pain and mental waves of torture. "Master, what hath I do, what is it that you need?" Byevil asked as Salbani cried in angered response,

"Go on, go to the ends, I will be with. In time I will be with you in time."

Salbani speaking in a stutter to the messenger who was quick to yell out to the legion, "Onward, go on, the master will join us soon! Leave him now!" Byevil yelled as the legion began to continue in the direction of the Tuent river, awaiting Salbani to overcome the Cursed Oaks. It took a long hour before the legion was ahead, leaving Salbani alone who for the whole time endured immense mental torture.

He was unable to fully stand, his body heavy, he was weighted by unseen forces that kept him in submission to this mental casting. The legion King seeped with unshackled hatred, his mind overran with voices and laughter of the Weir Spirits, experiencing the shadows depths that he himself casts. His eyes burned with fire glares through the woods, and he was overcome by destruction. Around him danced the Weir Spirits in celebrations for taking down the already weakened legion King. As shadows, they dance and writhe. These phantoms are a rarely seen phenomena, there was an oppressive silence that endured as Salbani groaned in pain and justified wrath. At first it was a subtle whisper of nagging that he thought was just his subconscious. It grew into a cacophony of voices, vying for his distraction driving him Madd. Spewing venomous thoughts and accusations and they joke and pry at his character, attempting to chip away his sanity. The Oaks were against him as they ever so often snag at him with cracks on his body as a whip while branches claw at his face ever so slightly with deep penetrating force, as he attempts to rise the roots of the forest outstretch from the grounds and wrap his body, pulling him back to a pose of submission as these trees attacked his body while they stewed in a burning growing flame the Weir Spirits continued to attack his mind. There was no balance in this situation, as by decree this forest was meant to be the death of Bani. It was enduring hours that this went on, as his body was weak, he miraculously remained focused on his goal of freedom and his rebellion of Light rulings was beginning to shift into a desire of realm destruction. He was distorted, as the Weir Spirits continued their haunting, ongoing multi of voices and screams of laughter overtook him mind, allowing him not to think beyond the simple thought of ongoing. The mind was a battlefield of conflicting thoughts but a lifetime of being servant to the orders of Darku enabled him to endure such trauma. He made no sounds even if he was in anguish, for he was using all his energy to maintain his mind. Salbani could only hear the ongoing voices in his mind, unable to hear branches whipping his skin or the popping crackle of the Oaks in flames. He was nearing insanity, the brink of madness, using his hatred to anchor to reality he tries to build his mental strength, using thought projections to attempt to drive out the Weir Spirits. Suddenly a frigid blast of cold winds consumed the area, extinguishing the flames of the Oaks as in the same moment a being spoke the single word, "Enough." as Salbani was unable to hear it, but the Weir Spirits made quick ends to their torture as the dancing of these phantoms seized and morphed into a fleeing escape. Salbani curled in a ball of anger as his eyes were lit by hatred fires, his body trembling from all the pain that he endured. This figure speaks,

"An alliance we had, yet you burn my Oaks?"

Salbani was attempting to rise, on his knees his arms shaking as he used the last of his strength to pull himself up.

"Agh." He mumbled in response to this figure.

"You grumble when you should he thanking me, I hath just freed you, shall I call them back to you?" Spoke the being in a tone of mockery as he grabbed the face of Salbani by his chin. "Look at me," The being said as suddenly Salbani smacked his hand away as kicked at an angle to the beings legs as he leaped on him, causing this figure to fall to the grounds. Salbani out this Treasured dagger from his waist and held it to the throat of this speaker,

"You were supposed to come before the full moon, that was the deal. Rhamtes, I should take your pathetic life now. Causing this whole plain to wither, know that this burning was just the beginning of what I am to do to this realm. Fool, you should hath kept your word!" Salbani quick to speak as he forcefully bashed the end of his blade handle into the peak of this beings skull, causing him to fall unconscious as he was quick to jump to his feel. His utter anger overturned this weakness as it gave him strength and the legion King began to venture through the Oaks unbothered and unharmed by the words of this figure who made ends to the cursing directed to Bani. Walking in unrelenting hate he made his way to Tuent to reunite with his Legion of Liege.

Rhamtes was the plain head of Spiritian, his body is connected to the planet. If Salbani were to murder him the entirety of the plain wound begin to decay. This hath never happened as Salbani obviously has plans for this plain for he would have killed him if he hath not, for the being went against his own word and this is not a thing that Salbani is to overlook. Leaving Rhamtes unconscious behind him, Bani moved at a pace to the ends of the Oaks.

BROKEN DECREE

August 19th The Full Moon

Tuent River

It was the New Moon, just as Salbani decreed.

The Liege gathered by the edging of the Tuent river. Salbani led them as he said he would. They roared in outrageous celebration as Salbani prepared a ritual to release the Atum blood. The scene is one of relentless determination as a million soldiers converge upon a colossal vale, an imposing barrier that stands as a testament of past failure.

Through the cursed Oaks the legion stopped by an unbreachable wall. Despite the chaos, there's a rhythm to the legion mumbles, a dance of destruction where each evil wilt plays a part. Minutes turn into a near hour as the unseen wall begins to show signs of wear as energy waves begin to ripple. Cracks appear just beyond where the Liege stands as the ground shakes, Salbani came forward and manifested an orb like ball from a mumbled set of words, the legion leader threw the ball of energy out before the legion as they all directed their energy on this area of impact as a section of the vale cracks as the breach, though small, is met with a roar from the Legion, together they joined in chanting as a magical blast exploded from the vale, dismantling it as a massive explosion of energy went in all directions and this caused the water of the river to be thrown from the natural undisturbed flow of water, the energy of the blast uprooted the river and pushed it into the Iro grasslands as the legion absorbed this decade lost energy and the legion released screams and war cries of celebrations as their powers were fully restored. The wall, once an invincible barrier, now a fallen Decree. The million legion of Liege crossed in a scatter of multiple directions across the river of Tuent with speed and terror. A victory of long-awaited freedom. Salbani roared to his legion as they spread into the Kingdom.

"Under this moon we are free, and under this moon a new order begins."

WHERE IS VAIEH?

August 20th

Taodamic Temple

In the grand chamber at the peak of Essen, there were council figures speaking at a circular table, members of the Council of Planetary Governance. The area lit by the vibrant glow of the sunlight as representatives from various realms, each with their unique attire and insignia, turn their attention to the center where a man named Joshuu steps forward. His uniform is adorned with medals and symbols of his rank as a High Trea Diplomat, his face marked by the lines of experience and his posture in depression by the weight of recent realm fears.

Joshuu clears his throat, speaking to the group with a shacking rattle of his voice,

"Honored members of the Council, I come before you to discuss the escalating conflicts that threaten the very fabric of our realm. The Legion leader hath escaped, confirmed by multiple dissimilar sources. It seems the new age is here, how could it come sooner than expected? I dare question, and I wonder, what is it that we should do?"

He raised his hand in a point that lead the council gaze to a holographic display, showing various planets, their landscapes and locations as continued speaking,

"Gather your attention to the graphic, as you can see, we have multiple fronts where the Orders clash, not over resources and territories, but ancient grudges and ideologies. These are critical points, with unknown Felagnolumian casualties but there has been a sacrifice of Atum blood, we are currently unaware of how this Atum has entered the realm." Spoke Joshuu as he begins to outline the realm circumstances,

"On Irosent of Spiritian, there is a civil war that is beginning to spiral out of control, with Orders now doing their own wilts, rebelling against our external support, risking broader conflicts by this Liege releasing. Turn your sight to Maurn of Vimaurus, the Vima Knights have reported a group of rogue Harlots that have fled with Pirates into the sea, it is unknown the reasoning for this report but it is apparently apart of the current beginning of a revolution against the Knights, in addition the to these Pirates, there is dispute over mineral rights that we fear will turn into a full-scale invasion by neighboring powers, there are rumors of the Pirates of the continents coming together to overthrow the Vima trade port and take the Aljus city. This is threatening to destabilization of the entire sector of Maurn, our Knight Keep, the Vima stronghold is simply outnumbered if this rumor were truth. As now, if you bring your attention to Eleye on the plain of Teralis, there are rumors of an ideological war that has drawn attention of the Black Sun, fueled by differing views on realm control and guidance, as where allegiance should stand."

Joshuu left the graphic hologram afloat before the council with the sections he spoke of highlighted as he presents his recommendations,

"We must deploy more diplomats, not just to negotiate but to broker long-term peace treaties. I propose a new initiative for cultural exchange programs to foster understanding. Immediate and sustained aid for those displaced by the rebellion. We need to establish safe zones and ensure that the Felagnolumian corridors are respected by all parties. Where necessary, targeted sanctions against those who fuel these conflicts, but with clear, achievable conditions for their removal to encourage peace talks. We don't want the rebellion to grow. As I will suggest that we establish a multinational peacekeeping force, under the Trea

Council's direct control, to be deployed where diplomacy has failed, that is if these rebellious figures continue this treason. This force should be seen as protectors, not invaders as we need to maintain the belief of the Felagnolum Folk. We should push for disarmament treaties, especially concerning weapons of mass destruction. The technology that can end the tech wars should also be regulated to prevent their continuance. Our company Skynet has been under attack by electromagnetic bombs since its grand opening. As for my last suggestion, I say that we must invest in education, focusing on the history and consequences of war, to cultivate a knowledge in the realm, for the Folk to value peace over conquest.

Joshuu concludes, his gaze shifting across the council members. He continued to speak due to their silence.

"This is not just a subtle rebellion; these Orders are testing our ruling authority as a collective. We must resolve this in a manner that will maintain peace. If we act decisively, with unity with the other realm councils, we can end these conflicts and prevent future ones. I have spoken my peace, O, great esteemed Sydonic Council. I beg you to consider these measures and act in the interest of all our Realm, we are on the edge of war, our decade of peace has suddenly shattered. As I spoke, the feared legion is unbound, the Atum bloodline is here and there have been sacrifices, the Dark societies war within one another, Lytula is working from within her imprisoned cell and Salbani is in search of his scrolls and revenge. my leaders it nearly hurts to speak it, yet the kingdom is undone, and the Trea decrees have somehow been shattered. What are we to do?"

The council remained silent, the weight of Joshuu's words was settling among the representatives, each now pondering his statements.

Representative Lyra Eon broke this silence,

"Raoruta has known peace for longer than this decade of realm peace. I aim to maintain it, these are all but Rumors, but we should worry if the Black Sun is active as he spoke. That is nothing of any good, as for this Salbani. His rebellion was before my time. I only know stories. If it is true that he is free like you say, the question is where is he going to go, what will he do with this freedom? Do we have knowledge of the activities of the Black Sun? We watched Lytula of the phoenix do some casting on Thespian the Great, he is currently locked away until we find a loyal mage to undo her casting, for he has turned mad, she spoke of the weir spirits? What are these, hath there any understanding to the positioning of Lytula, do we know if this Salbani will deal with her, or is it this Cult of the Black Sun?" The lady representative of Raoruta plain spoke truth as the council leader of the plain Spiritian out spoke to the council in reply to her statement.

"Lady Rao, I know nothing of that Lytula, nor can I speak of this Black Sun, but I will tell you that I have heard mumbles of an ancient magic explosion in the Litue Mountain range from trusted friends. Deceive me on a trade option maybe, but not on a matter such as this. They shook in fear and spoke of leaving Spiritian. As with this information, I have investigated and the Trea hath spoken to this Salbani already, a scroll he hath received, an order to standdown delivered by a great messenger, as I called forth the fairies, for they are known to hear all the realm gossip, as their communities are buzzing with apparent multiple sightings of these Legion being free and up to no good. I first spoke the same as you, thought of rumors, just rumors I said, until I was warned by a member of the Synod that their surveillance drones seen the legion pouring out of the temple, headed in direction of this Tuent river. More investigations hath brought me to believe that this Salbani will make his way here. To Essen, he wants revenge on Michael and his half-brother, Vaieh the wandering one. That is all I know, as I agree that we should act." Spoke Belmont Zepya, the leading head of the Spiritian council. The members of the council mumbled admits there delegators as Odarius Lan, the leading head of the Novkavis council out spoke to the plain heads of the realm.

"Then we know what we will first do, the words of Joshuu sound true, We will call for Micheal the great Arku. He has defeated this Liege before, he can do it again. As for this wandering one, whatever the reasoning for Salbani wanting him. We must find him, he must be protected, so now the only question that remains, Where is this Vaieh?"

I must part from you; I am being called to task.

This tale is far from complete, O, treasure.

I told you that only a fool would know the truth!

Await the ongoing, you will encounter these figures again for, Unfortunate has brought you to Fortunate, my last thought before walking into Fortunes, Tell me what is there for a Trezhur to do with Gold?

END PART ONE